THE SCOTTISH BRIDE

Highland Secrets, Book 1

Susan King

ARE YOU SIGNED UP FOR DRAGONBLADE'S BLOG?

You'll get the latest news and information on exclusive giveaways, exclusive excerpts, coming releases, sales, free books, cover reveals and more.

Check out our complete list of authors, too!

No spam, no junk. That's a promise!

Sign Up Here

www.dragonbladepublishing.com

Dearest Reader;

Thank you for your support of a small press. At Dragonblade Publishing, we strive to bring you the highest quality Historical Romance from some of the best authors in the business. Without your support, there is no 'us', so we sincerely hope you adore these stories and find some new favorite authors along the way.

Happy Reading!

CEO, Dragonblade Publishing

Additional Dragonblade books by Author Susan King

Highland Secrets Series
The Scottish Bride (Book 1)

Celtic Hearts Series
The Hawk Laird (Book 1)
The Falcon Laird (Book 2)
The Swan Laird (Book 3)

To my own Sir David

Three lasses, three ladies, three brides all
Born and flowering in Kincraig's hall
One shall loose an arrow in the heart of greenside
One shall heal a king and woe betide
And one shall be the harper's bride . . .

—Prophecy of the Keiths of Kincraig

PROLOGUE

Veritas vincit (Truth conquers)
—Motto of Clan Keith

August 1306
Central Scotland

H AND OVER FIST, *she descended the rope, inching like a caterpillar on a branch. Cold wind whipped at her hair and cloak, chilled her hands where she gripped thick, rough hemp. Snowflakes fluttered over her cheeks and swirled away into darkness, down and down so far, she dared not glance there.*

Looking up, she saw the soaring wall of the castle tower and the parapet above it. From a tower window, the rope draped over the stone sill. Clinging below, she whispered a prayer. If they discovered her escape, one swift cut to the rope would send her to her death.

Hurry, she thought as she shimmied downward. The rope swayed in a burst of wind. Beyond, the dark forest, trees lacy with ice, spread away from the snow-covered castle hill. She descended, hand over hand, keeping the rope between her feet just as her brother had taught her when they were younger. Her skirts belled out in the breeze, the chill cutting through her. Down and down she went. Far over the mountains, the sky lightened toward dawn.

Pausing to catch her breath, she looked down.

The rope was too short. Swaying, she gazed at the ground, then heard footsteps crunch over snow. A man approached to stand just below her.

A knight, a stranger. Chain mail glinted beneath his dark surcoat. The soldiers had found her. Glancing up, she knew she might not make the hard climb back to the window; her limbs ached, trembled. Stranded, clinging to the rope, she looked down.

The knight lifted his arms and beckoned.

"To me." His voice, deep and quiet, resonated.

Light touched his face, gleamed over armor. The wind whipped through his dark hair. He was beautiful, strong. An archangel. Still, she could not trust him.

"Down to me!" he beckoned again.

Swaying on the rope, she watched him. Buttery light touched the treetops, the snow, the knight. Shouts sounded in the distance.

"Leap!" He raised his arms.

An arrow whizzed past. Another.

She let go of the rope and sank.

He caught her solidly, safe as a rooted tree. Looping her arms about his neck, pressed against cold mail and woolen tunic, she felt his arms strong about her. She looked up into eyes washed blue, like ice or moonlight.

He smiled. "Safe now."

"Am I? Who are you?"

"Later for that." With long strides, he carried her toward the dark woodland.

"What do you want?" She pushed at him in sudden panic.

"I came," he said, "for you."

Tamsin sat up in the darkness, clutching the bedcovers. *Just a dream.*

Alone in the bed, she remembered again how lonely she felt here, a Scotswoman in a Scottish castle garrisoned by the English. A widow, now. Some measure of security had existed when her husband had commanded Dalrinnie Castle, but his death seven months ago left her status here uncertain. Soon, she had heard, King Edward would decide what to do with the Dalrinnie widow.

The dream merely stemmed from her desperate hope for an escape, she told herself. Sometimes her dreams held elements of foretelling, and a few times she had experienced brief visions like waking dreams, that came true in small ways. She kept such things to herself at Dalrinnie. Only her family could fully understand the gift that appeared now and then in their lineage.

But this dream was not prophetic. Escaping down a rope, arrows all around, a mysterious knight helping her—unlikely! Nightmares came of devils lurking about, so her childhood nurse once said. The dream just echoed her fear of a precarious situation.

Oh, but the knight... She sighed. If only someone could help her. Though allowed to leave the castle, she was always under guard. Still, if King Edward decided to send her to a convent, that might be all the escape she needed.

Two years ago, Sir John Witton had married Lady Thomasina Keith for political advantage and bedded her twice. When no child resulted, he left his "Scottish bride," as he called her, to her household tasks and "pretty parchments"—the books she so treasured. Her husband was an English lord in command of a castle captured from the Scots—Tamsin had heard the previous baron of Dalrinnie was a Seton, though she knew nothing of that family—and while Witton had King Edward's support, he had few allies among Scottish lords. Though most Scottish knights and nobles pledged to serve the English king, her kinsmen among them, many did so unwillingly.

In his will and testament, Witton had left Dalrinnie and its estate to his Scottish bride, a surprising gesture. Yet it hardly mattered now. King Edward had sent word that he would determine the widow's future. Then he let her wait.

Burrowing under the blankets, thinking of the knight in the dream, she remembered that her Grandda Thomas told her to always heed her dreams. He spoke sincerely, for Thomas of Ercildoune had been a prophet, a poet, a counselor to lords and kings, and a kind great-grandfather.

I see the gift bright in thee, lass, he had told Tamsin once, tugging on her golden braid. *One day visions will fill thy head. What you will see is true. Remember that.*

Bewildered, she nodded. *Aye, Grandda.*

Though he was gone seven years now, his legend still grew. They said that as a young man, he had been taken by the Queen of Faery, returning after seven years with the gift of prophecy. True Thomas, harper and poet, could not lie, and his wisdom was widely respected. When he visited Kincraig to consult with her father, Sir Robert Keith, and other Scots nobles, he always found time for Tamsin and her siblings, Henry, Margaret, and Rowena, his granddaughter's children. The Keiths of Kincraig were family to him.

One evening, Thomas had leaned toward her older brother Henry and poked him hard in the chest. *Thee maun protect thy sisters, lad.*

Henry nodded. Certes, it would be his chivalric duty one day.

Nah, nah. Listen. Each lass has a gift. Thee maun keep watch over them.

Henry knew that one day he would make an oath as a knight to serve King Edward the First of England, pressed like other Scottish knights to place his fealty where it might not sit. Once he inherited his father's lands and title, he would be guardian to his sisters if they were still unwed. *My father will find good husbands for my sisters,* Henry answered.

Thomas snorted. *Our lassies need love matches, or none. You make sure of it. And thee, lad*—the old man poked him again—*seek what thy heart needs, too, and love and freedom will be yours.*

But that is what all Scots need, sir, and cannot find under English rule.

One day, Thomas gave each child a gift. He handed Tamsin a wooden box containing parchments with verses he had scribbled, and an inkpot made of crystal. *A queen gave this to me and now it is yours. You have the truthy tongue, lass. Use it wisely.* Then he whispered what she must do with his work someday.

After that day, she never saw him again. Rumor said True Thomas had disappeared into a magical hillside to join the faery queen. But his son, another Thomas, sent word that his father, nearly one hundred years old, had wandered into the hills one afternoon and died.

Sighing, Tamsin lay back against the pillows. Thomas had wanted his great-grandchildren to marry for love. But Papa had wanted protection for his daughters and alliances for the Keiths in the climate of the conflict between Scotland and England. So Tamsin had been yoked to an English lord, the only daughter to marry before illness took her mother and father both, leaving Henry, serving Edward, to sort things out.

Now she was no longer the Scottish bride—instead, she was the Scottish widow, trapped among the English. In these two years, she had learned to stifle her "truthy tongue"—her natural, sometimes lamentable honesty—in favor of silence when she could manage it. Besides that simple honesty, she also protected the touch of the Sight that she carried.

One day, a quick, alarming vision had flashed in her mind seemingly from nowhere, an image of her husband fatally wounded in a skirmish. She summoned the courage to warn him to be wary.

"Always have your men around you," she pleaded. "I have seen danger for you."

He had half-listened, then dismissed her with a harsh laugh. "Scottish nonsense," he had said. But she saw the fearful look in his eyes.

Now, wrapping her arms around her knees, she sighed. Eventually that day came for him. And for her, silence and a measure of boldness became her armor in this garrisoned castle.

I came for you, the knight in the dream had said. Fervently, she wished it could be so, that she could escape and yet be safe. But she must solve this dilemma on her own.

Henry, she thought suddenly. Of course! Her brother, riding for King Edward now, might not know her situation had become so dire. He might be able to gain audience with Edward to argue leniency for his sister so that Tamsin could be free to determine her own path in life.

Henry's last message, months ago, said he was leaving Edward's castle at Carlisle to visit English-held Scottish castles. If his orders did not change, he thought to come to Dalrinnie and then Kincraig by Yuletide.

But she had to find him soon or lose all.

CHAPTER ONE

September 1306
Lanercost Abbey, Northern England

"SO YOU REFUSE to speak," the old man rasped. Through flickering firelight, his rangy old bones draped in red wool, King Edward sat in a leather-slung chair and glared hard at the prisoner.

Sir William Seton, dispossessed baron of Dalrinnie Castle and environs in Scotland, stood silent, wrists and ankles wrapped in chains. Sweat trickled down his back and dampened his brow. The blazing hearth, together with the afternoon sunlight angling through arched stained-glass windows, made the room stifling. Motionless, without reply, he watched dust motes float in a wedge of light.

He had no reason to answer. It would not gain back his castle, held by the English now; it would not restore those he loved who had died; nor would it free him, a captured Scotsman, a knight, a rebel. Raising his head, he gazed at the king.

"Well, we will find another use for you." Edward leaned back in the carved chair, shivering even in the excessive warmth. Long bony fingers fussed at his elegant tunic; thin white hair, once blond, brushed rounded shoulders; his leonine head trembled. Stretching out long legs in woolen hose, the king, called Longshanks by some, was taller than most men, even hunched and aging. Yet the years that dulled him physically had only sharpened his wrath toward the Scots.

"Nothing to say? Though I wonder, Sir William," the king said, "if you might like to have the grant of Dalrinnie again." His eyes, hard dark blue, fixed on the prisoner.

Liam—the name he preferred in better circumstances—lifted his head and returned Edward's gaze directly. He knew better than to do that, but so be it. He was in the soup already, having resisted rough interrogation these several weeks of imprisonment. He had lost count of days and weeks. At least he stood in a warm sunlit room in Lanercost Abbey on a pretty September day instead of the damp, dark cell where he had been since early summer. There was that.

But he would not give up what he knew of Robert Bruce, lately King of Scots and now a renegade in the hills. Though he knew more than Edward could imagine, he would keep his silence. If he had to lie or cheat, bargain for his life, or worse, he meant to protect Bruce and the great cause.

He was surprised to be alive, considering Edward's vicious treatment of the Scots. He was even more surprised to be brought into the king's presence. But if this was his day to die, he would show Edward yet another Scot who would not yield.

The king shifted and snapped his fingers. A clerk emerged from a corner to hand him an uncurled parchment, which Edward studied.

"Sir William Seton, Baron Dalrinnie," he read aloud. The page appeared to be a roster of dissenters, Liam saw. The English diligently listed Scottish landholders, titles, and estates to exact punishment and sort traitors from loyalists.

Liam waited. The iron chains and manacles on his wrists and ankles pulled and chafed. The metallic odor was rank on his sweat-coated skin and he felt grimy and slick with filth. He had not had a wash or fresh clothing since the day Sir Malise Comyn, curse the fellow, had taken him down.

His hair was too long, unwashed brown-gilt waves gone blackish and stringy; his beard was thick and itchy, his hands dirty. Last night he had dreamed of a hot soapy bath and a tooth-scrubbing, followed by a meal of roast lamb and buttered bannocks washed down with wine of such clarity that he could almost taste each perfect Burgundian grape. He wanted to feel sunlight and rain, smell forest air; sleep in a soft bed with a woman in his arms, warm and curving and kind—

Judging by the king's expression, such comforts would only come with death.

"Dalrinnie in Selkirkshire, forfeited from you and granted to Sir John Witton. He was in our loyal service but is dead now. You could be just as dead soon." Edward glanced up. "How many times have you sworn your oath of fealty? Twice?"

He did not answer. Twice sworn, promised, and punished; lesson learned. Edward was a master of petty betrayal.

The old curse on Dalrinnie Castle had done its work again, Liam thought. The prophecy, though his family called it a curse, had been delivered by Thomas the Rhymer to Liam's great-grandfather, and had proven true for two generations. Now Witton, the English commander who had claimed Liam's forfeited property, had lost the castle simply by dying. A prize won, a prize lost.

Built by Setons, Dalrinnie would not stay with them until— what was it? Something about a harp. He almost laughed. In his youth, he had learned to play a harp, thinking to beat the curse. But whoever got hold of Dalrinnie next would lose it too.

He ought to feel bitter satisfaction. He only felt wooden and weighed down.

Dalrinnie, Dalrinnie, towers high and walls bold . . . How did the old Rhymer's verse go? His head was in a blur.

Still in a muddle, his mind wandered as he awaited the king's next move. Thinking of his harp, he was reminded of a story heard in his boyhood—the sad tale of the harper Tristan and Iseult, the king's wife. Here Liam stood, a harper, and King Edward was much like the story's King Mark—conniving in his power. A wounded king, sickly and cornered and cruel.

Things had not gone well for that tragic harper either, he thought then.

"Forest lords—is that what they call your sort?" Edward brought him back.

Liam glanced through a dark straggle of hair. "'Laird' in the Scots, Sire."

"Ah, your noble forest rebels. We will smoke them out like rats. Laird or lord, the Scots will suffer for being disloyal and obstinate. But you, sir, could be lord of your castle again, should you decide to be useful."

Liam closed his eyes, weary. Another promise, another betrayal? He was Scottish to his bones and blood, no matter what fealty he was forced to declare. Scottish knights who paid homage to Edward and England often had to look the other way or straddle both loyalties to survive and keep lands and privilege. Some followed their conscience and would defend the Scottish cause to their last breath. Liam was one of those.

He did not want to think about his home, yet mind and body were weary, and thoughts accosted him. He remembered betrayal, remembered walking out of the forest after weeks away to see charred walls silhouetted against the sky.

He had seen soldiers strolling the battlement, carpenters and masons shoring up rubble and making repairs. The attack had occurred while he had been away with William Wallace, a great soul damned for his courage. Those inside Dalrinnie had been killed or captured, and the nearby village of Heatherstane and the kirk had been ravaged too. His betrothed, Lady Beatrix, had been visiting the priest that day, making plans for their wedding. By the time Liam returned, she lay peaceful in the churchyard.

In the village square, he found his name on a parchment nailed to an oak: *outlaw, wolf's head, renegade, traitor.*

Cloaked against rain and recognition, he had melted into the forest, hunted and hiding with others, fighting where his sword was needed, sleeping where he found a spot. His anger had banked hot within him, leaving him only ash inside those years.

Offered king's peace—*come back, be forgiven, gain back your lands*—he took another oath of fealty to protect his kin and his lands. Yet Edward denied him title and estate again. So he slipped away once more. After Wallace was gone, Liam pledged to serve Robert Bruce, a warrior-lord of steadfast determination, a man with the skills and insight to save and rebuild Scotland someday.

Months ago, Bruce had made an ultimate and dangerous move, killing his rival, Sir John Comyn, for the throne, claiming it for himself. When he went on the run, Liam went with him.

Now he was captured. But just before that, he had fulfilled the new king's request to bring Bruce's tenants a certain message, and he had been able to send to Bruce the pledges gathered from those kindly folk. More support would follow, though Liam feared that his capture might prevent that from reaching King Robert.

Standing with the weight of chains on him, Liam would sooner give up his own life than betray Robert Bruce and his supporters to the bitter man who sat glaring at him.

"Seton," Edward said. "What do you know about the stabbing of John Comyn?"

So that preoccupied the old king. "Happened in a small kirk in Dumfries," Liam drawled. "Other than that, I know nothing of use. I have said this repeatedly."

"You were seen there, I hear."

"Only Bruce and Comyn were inside that church, so only Bruce knows what happened." He felt filthy, hungry, tired, resolute. What was Edward after here?

Edward turned a page. "We see you applied for a pardon and the return of your castle three years ago in exchange for entering the king's peace."

"But you did not honor your promise in return for my oath."

"You betrayed our trust." Edward shrugged. "Kin to Christopher Seton, aye?"

Sharp as a knife, the words cut. Liam drew a breath. "Aye." And proud to admit it.

"You do not want to suffer his fate," Edward murmured.

Liam did not answer. His cousin, taken in the same skirmish that had landed Liam in Carlisle's dungeon, had been cruelly executed. But Christopher had been married to Bruce's sister, Lady Christian, who was herself Edward's prisoner now. Liam was a compatriot, but not kin. So far, that had spared his life.

Just weeks ago, Bruce's women—his queen, his young daughter, two sisters and two cousins—had been captured in the Highlands, where Bruce had sent them in hopes of safety. Liam, Christopher, and others had ridden to their rescue to no avail. The women had been taken south. Now Bruce's queen and his daughter—not yet twelve—and a sister were in English convents; his other sister and a female cousin were confined in iron cages specially constructed for them at the king's order, displayed at Roxburgh and Berwick. Christopher Seton, as well as Bruce's brother Neil and other staunch followers, had been publicly and horribly executed. Liam and others had escaped.

Liam felt sick with rage over it. He looked away, nostrils flaring, fists clenched. Standing here wrapped in chains, he felt helpless. But nothing could be done for the dead, or the captured women either, no matter how much he wished he could help.

"Tell me, Seton," Edward went on, "would you like to regain your castle?"

Silent, Liam slid a flat stare toward him.

"If you want it, then find me the Rhymer's daughter."

That surprised him. "Rhymer's daughter?"

"Thomas the Rhymer. Surely you have heard of him."

"Dead years now. What of his daughter?"

"She has a book that belonged to her father and I want it. She is called Lady Thomasina Keith. Find her and get that book from her. She would be quite old by now. It should be easy enough."

Go after an old woman for a book? Edward was losing his mind, as had been rumored for years. "Perhaps if you ask nicely, she will send her wee book along."

"Insolence does not help you. Fetch the thing and bring it

here."

"Where would I find this old daughter?"

"Dalrinnie."

So Edward would send him back to his forfeited home to accost an old lady. "You are certain she has this thing?"

"You dare question this?" Edward growled. "Get the book. You might regain Dalrinnie if you come back into king's peace. We could use your knowledge. But there are conditions and consequences should you refuse."

He could guess the consequences. "What conditions?"

"God's wounds, he is as obstinate as the rest of his kind," Edward muttered. "Be glad you are still alive."

"I am."

Edward gestured, and a servant stepped forward to pour a cup of wine, dark red sparkling in the light. The king slurped as he studied parchments. He seemed to have forgotten the prisoner.

"Send a message to this fellow." Edward handed a page to the clerk. "Tell him I want his best hawk for my next hunt. They say his birds are the finest in Scotland. If he refuses, I will have them all."

"But Sire, the physician forbids you to ride or hunt."

"Get me the damned bird! I will hunt again when I feel better. See it done."

"Aye, sire. Also, the knights you summoned are waiting outside."

"Let them in."

Waiting, Liam shifted his weight to his right leg, easing the ache in his left knee; imprisonment had slowed his recovery after the attack that had nearly killed him.

A door opened at the periphery of his vision. Two knights entered, chain mail chinking, one in a red surcoat emblazoned with Edward's golden lions rampant. The other knight wore a bright blue surcoat embroidered with three golden sheaves. Liam knew that insignia too well.

Each man dropped to a knee, greeting the king, then stood as

Edward conferred quietly with them. Liam clenched his jaw and watched the knight in blue—Sir Malise Comyn, the one who had taken him down, causing him to stand in chains in this room.

Tall, blond, and handsome with a deceptively angelic face, Sir Malise was first cousin to Sir John Comyn, murdered claimant to the Scottish throne. Malise had given his fealty wholly to Edward, pandering for favor, Liam remembered. After his cousin Sir John's murder, Malise aligned himself further with Edward by demanding vengeance.

Liam knew Comyn's arrogance and his sword arm too well. The blow to his head from the flat of the man's sword had healed and his knee was healing too. Christopher and others were gone, deaths that should darken Malise's soul. Yet the man did not even glance at Liam now, as if none of it mattered.

"The lady of Dalrinnie?" Comyn said. "Sir John's widow. I know her. I can do this for you, Sire."

"Be quiet. Stand over there." The knights obeyed, stepping back. Despite age, Edward of England had a powerful presence, a calculating lawyer's mind, and a petty nature that had ripened to a dogged, relentless brutality toward the Scots.

Edward turned on Liam again. "Seton! Do you agree to find this lady and fetch what she possesses?"

"I am thinking about it." Liam shrugged.

"Ingrate," King Edward snarled. "I ought to marry you to this old crone. That would be an unpleasant punishment, I vow." He laughed, short and harsh.

"Sire. Your Grace. If I may," Malise Comyn said, "I know this lady, as I said. I will do this for you. You cannot trust that man." He jabbed a thumb toward Liam.

"I have not yet decided what you are to do, Sir Malise."

"I implore Your Grace—"

"Silence!" Edward held up a hand. "Seton! If you are a canny Scot, and I think you are, you will renew your loyalty to the Crown. Scotland is a losing cause. Fetch this woman's book and prove your worth again. Earn the right to command Dalrinnie."

Liam huffed. "A book in return for a castle?"

"Or you could be dispensed with, here and now."

Sir Malise shifted a gauntleted hand to his sword hilt. "Sire, let me help."

Skin prickling, senses on alert, Liam felt the trap closing. Too many Scots who were lured into king's peace seemed to provoke the king's ire immediately afterward.

"Sir William knows Selkirk and that damnable Ettrick Forest, full of rebels. That could be invaluable." The king peered at one of the parchment rolls on the table. "You have family in Dumfries and Selkirk?" He smiled. "A monk, an abbot, an abbess?"

Ah, there it was. Liam fisted a hand, iron chinking. His brother, his uncle, his sister—along with another brother and some cousins, all the kin he had left. "They are dedicated to the service of God and the Church. They pose no harm to anyone."

"Every Scot poses harm. You do know we recently captured Robert Bruce's kinswomen." When Liam did not answer, the king continued. "I ordered cages made for some of the Scottish ladies. One cage is still empty. The old lady of Dalrinnie would fit in it if she does not give up the thing I want."

Locking an elderly lady in a cage was not beyond this king. Liam waited.

"You know the region. And Bruce's plans. Get the book, bring that and news of Bruce with you, and you may enter our good graces again."

"I know nothing of Bruce's actions."

"But you can find out easily enough. Especially if a certain abbey and convent were to burn," he said, "with all inside."

"The Church might want an explanation from you," Liam said. "God, too."

"Sire, I beg you to listen," Comyn interrupted.

Edward rounded. "You were tasked with finding Bruce and made poor work of it. Someone else will have to do it now."

"But Sire, this man? I will bring you this book and Bruce too. I swear it."

"A book that could end this war is too valuable to entrust to you."

A book that once belonged to Thomas the Rhymer, end the war? Liam frowned. But it was the frustration on Comyn's handsome face that decided him.

So Edward wanted this book. If Liam could get his hands on it, he would take it straight to Robert Bruce.

"Sire, send me," Comyn was saying. "You cannot trust this outlaw. Even if you harmed his kinfolk, he would not—"

"Such eagerness is annoying. You stand to lose what favor you have."

"Your Grace, I will go to the lady of Dalrinnie—"

"Sire." Liam raised his voice. "I will do what you ask."

CHAPTER TWO

Lochmaben Castle, Scotland

"KEITH. SIR HENRY Keith," Tamsin repeated. Standing before the constable who sat at a table in the great hall, she folded her hands patiently, though she felt anything but. "I had word he might be here at Lochmaben Castle. Thank you for seeing us."

"Do you know him, Sir Constable?" asked her cousin, Lady Kirsten Douglas, standing beside her. Kirsty's bright smile melted most hearts yet did not seem to affect the constable. But Tamsin was grateful Kirsty had accompanied her here. Their other companion, an older lady, the sister of Dalrinnie's seneschal, rested in another room, exhausted by traveling, despite her insistence on coming along on what she called a foolish mission to find Tamsin's brother.

"We were hoping he would be here, sir. Pray tell us where he is," Tamsin added.

"Keith was here perhaps a fortnight ago." Sir Edmund Merton turned to the clerk beside him who sorted through loose pages and rolls of parchment. "Was that the one who brought a message from the king?"

"Young Scots knight?" The clerk unrolled a parchment. "Aye. Sir Henry Keith of Kincraig. Pledged to King Edward, rides as king's messenger. He brought a letter from Edward here two weeks ago."

"Where did he go when he left?" Tamsin felt disappointment draining her. She and her companions had ridden a half day's journey so that she could inquire about her brother here. Where could she go next?

"Your man is not here," Merton barked.

"Sir Henry is not my man. He is my brother and this is urgent."

"Everyone's business is urgent these days. Go home. It is not wise for Scotswomen to travel alone." His eyes skimmed down, then up. "That plaid cloak does you no favors here."

Instinctively lifting her chin at that and straightening her shoulders, Tamsin pushed back the heavy swing of her long blond braid. Anyone who knew the weft and warp of the tartan she wore might know her for a Keith of Kincraig. She wore it defiantly here, weary of living among English soldiers with all their disdain for the Scots, all their conniving and untruths. Merton seemed to be one of those.

"We have an escort from Dalrinnie Castle," her cousin Kirsty said. "They left on a brief errand but will return soon. An older lady is here as our chaperone."

"Who are you?" Merton gave Kirsty the same up-and-down look.

"Lady Kirsten Douglas of Thornhill." The girl lifted her chin.

"Douglas of Thornhill lets his daughter travel about as she pleases? Trouble will come of that," Merton muttered.

"Our lady chaperone is unwell," Tamsin said. "We would leave here as soon as we can," Tamsin said. Lady Edith had proven a poor traveler, prone to aches and complaints. Just now, she was resting in the small solar above the great hall. Tamsin hoped Sir David Campbell, Dalrinnie's seneschal and Edith's brother, would indeed return shortly so they could all leave Lochmaben, and she could continue her quest to locate Henry as he went from one place to the next for Edward.

The little bit of liberty she retained as lady of Dalrinnie would not last. Once she was outside the castle, she had considered fleeing for better freedom, but she could not endanger her companions. Besides, Sir Davey, for all his loyalty, would be obliged to find her. He and his escort had ridden out only briefly, promising to be back for the women soon. She could rely on their protection.

"Sir Constable," she pleaded, "please help me find my brother."

"As I said, he is not here. Clerk—look through the rolls. See if his name is listed elsewhere with a note of where he went. These ladies have time."

"Our escort is returning to fetch us. We are in a hurry," Tamsin said.

"I am not," Merton said, perusing a document. "So you can wait."

SMOOTH AS GLASS, the waters of the moat reflected sunset and the castle as merchants and servants went back and forth over the drawbridge. Liam Seton narrowed his eyes, leaning a shoulder against an oak, its leaves sheltering him from view. He studied the towers and walls, counted the visible guards, and judged the distance between gate and road to decide how best to get in and out quickly with his prize.

Round towers jutted above sandstone walls overlooking a slope down to the castle loch, with a long view eastward toward the River Annan. On the battlements, sentries—eight at least, helmets glinting in the setting sun—had a wide view of loch, forest, and river. Foursquare strong and well-situated, Lochmaben belonged to Robert Bruce, lately King of Scots—self-declared, so the English insisted. But Edward had wrested Lochmaben from the Scots to fortify it for English use. Robert Bruce, among other fierce intentions, meant to reclaim it along with other

Scottish castles.

Liam had come here for one reason only. Rumor said he might find his quarry here. Just days ago, he stood chained in King Edward's presence, ordered to find a book. He intended to fetch the thing—but had no intention of bringing it to Edward. He rather thought Bruce might like to have it.

But how the devil was he to snatch an old woman out of this castle, where he had learned she might be—and take her over the hills to find Bruce, wherever he was hiding?

The sun dipped as he waited under the oak. He shifted his weight to flex the knee that still ached somewhat, and he watched a few stragglers and carts crossing the drawbridge. Good. The portcullis was open but would likely close at dark.

Lifting the leather satchel at his feet, he slung it over his shoulder to balance its wedge shape. The strings inside chimed a bit. Tugging his hood down against a breeze and recognition, he walked toward the moat...

Then stopped short when a knight on a dappled charger cut diagonally across his path to block his way. "Halt, you," the man ordered.

His red surcoat embroidered with gold lions, worn over chain mail and a blue tunic, brightly marked him as one of Edward's knights. Though not all who rode in Edward's name wore the lion rampant, this fellow's surcoat announced his affiliation, even at a distance. But his wooden shield, painted dark blue with three gold shields, stated his family; and the cloth beneath his saddle was a swath of tartan wool crisscrossed in red, black, and gray.

Liam knew shield, tartan, and man. "You, sir, are in my way," he groused.

"Hey, harper," said his younger brother. "What is your business here?"

"Coming to Lochmaben in hopes of a welcome." He patted the sheathed harp.

"Not likely, if they discover the harper's true name." Sir Gilchrist Seton regarded him. "I will go with you if you like. They said the Keith lady arrived earlier today. Likely she is still inside."

"Simple enough to get in and out if the lady cooperates," Liam said. Gilchrist knew his mission; last night they had met with a cousin to briefly confer at an inn on the Dumfries road, and his kinsmen had offered to help. "You should go about your errand to follow De Valence's orders."

"Edward's general expects Finley and I to report which Scottish castles could be ripe for the plucking. Oddly like your work for Bruce. And it gives us the freedom to see to other matters."

"Indeed, it does. What is next on your list?"

"After Lochmaben, then Morton, Thornhill, Oliver Castle—"

"Ruined, that one. Burned nearly to glass, and Sir Simon Fraser of Oliver captured and torn to pieces in public." His stomach turned with grief and anger over the cruel death of yet another friend and compatriot. "The English can have the smoking walls. The place is useless. After that?"

His brother paused. "Dalrinnie."

"Taken four years back," Liam clipped out. "No need to go there."

"Edward has still not decided who will replace the commander who died months back. De Valence wants to know how to take Ettrick Forest from that angle to go after the rebels hiding there."

Liam felt a muscle jump in his cheek. "The English will try, but they cannot penetrate the great forest."

"Besides thinning it of timber, aye. Best get up there before they raise the drawbridge and close the gate. The guards will ask why a brawny Scot seeks entrance." He gestured toward Liam's plain brown tunic and trews, worn under a shabby leather hauberk studded with iron rings, old but protective. His hooded cloak of dark gray was lined with the same red-and-gray tartan Gilchrist carried. "Where is your knight's gear?"

"Stored away. I am just a harper looking for supper. And an old crone with a book," he muttered.

"Pray they do not ask for a tune, brother. Is that your harp, saved from the fire?"

"Aye. The miller at Heatherstane found it and held it for me."

"Good. Look there—they hung that evil thing recently." Gilchrist pointed.

Liam had seen it earlier: a lantern-shaped timber and iron structure lashed to the outer wall of a tower. "Mercifully empty," he growled. "Why is the cage there, if they have no captive? Bruce's women were captured in the Highlands three weeks ago."

"Some of the Scottish ladies are caged in such devices, but I have not heard of plans for a captive here. The cages are a taunt meant for Bruce, saying he cannot protect his women."

Deep as it shocked him, Liam could not take his gaze from the ugly thing. "And they call Edward a paragon of chivalry," he drawled. One of the captured women, a cousin of Bruce, was a friend, the very lady who had taught Liam to play the harp years before. He lacked her skill but did well enough, and he was even able to guise himself as a musician when needed. Like now.

"We can only pray Bruce's ladies remain safe until they can be rescued," Gilchrist said, "since King Edward refuses to negotiate their release. Edward intends to make examples of them. Beware, lad. It is a miracle you escaped his temper after you were captured."

"Edward is more interested in this mysterious book than he is in me. So I am pledged to serve again, under duress." He had not told Gilchrist of the threats to their kin or his need to protect them. Nor would his latest pledge change his innermost loyalty and dedication to the cause of Scotland and the Scots. Liam had found a stronger purpose after his lands had been forfeited. There was some benefit to outlawry.

"See you soon." Gilchrist lifted the reins to turn his charger. "If the guards ask, tell them I questioned you and found you harmless. Though you look a suspicious rascal to me. Go find the lady and bring her out."

Liam shifted the leather bag. "Old as she is, this may take

time."

"Be careful. Edward is furious, berating his commanders because Bruce has not been captured. He vows all will suffer if the Bruce is not taken soon."

"When I find this lady, I mean to bring her to Robert, not Edward. If Longshanks wants this book, Bruce will find it equally interesting. Perhaps it will help the cause."

"What is this book?"

Liam shrugged. "Some bit of prophecy, perhaps. Edward is growing old and weak. He may depend more on such things if his reason is failing."

"This old woman is the Rhymer's daughter? Any daughter of his would be long in the tooth by now. They do say Thomas the Rhymer was stolen away by the Queen of Faery," Gilchrist mused. "When he returned home, he had the gift of prophecy."

"Fireside tales." Liam had left belief in faery magic behind in childhood.

"If this crone is a seer like her kinsman, perhaps she knows when this accursed war will end. That would help us all. Well, try not to get caught up there."

"Good advice." Liam waved a hand and walked away.

Exaggerating his limp, he crossed the drawbridge behind a brewer's cart laden with barrels. As two sentries at the tower gate stopped the brewer, Liam hunched his shoulders to lessen his height and brawn, needing to look more a traveling musician than a Scots warrior.

He could be recognized, he knew. Though released by the king, he was not pardoned of other offenses. Sir William Seton was an outlaw due to his forfeiture, his actions, and the company he kept. While most would not know him on sight, word was out about a brawny Scot with Nordic-blue eyes. He tucked his hood over his brow.

One sentry held up a hand. "Your business?"

"I am Wat of Selkirk, sir, a harper, hoping to barter tunes for supper and a bed." Just a man, just a town.

"What did yon knight want with you?" The taller guard gestured toward the road.

"He questioned me and saw no harm in me trading music for supper."

The sentry scowled. "We do not need music here. Go away."

Liam pointed to the brewer's cart now rumbling into the bailey yard. "A garrison needs music on a night when there is fresh ale."

"Eh, true. We should let him in," the stocky guard said.

"Strapping lad like that should be fighting for the king," the other replied.

Liam gave a thin smile. "I did. And was sore wounded in Edward's service. My harp earns my way now."

"Go on, then. Find the constable of the castle. He will decide." The tall guard pointed. "But be out by midnight, even if you find a chit to share a blanket."

Liam chuckled. "Is there much chance of that?"

"There are few women here and none that would swive a harper," one guard chortled. "There are two fine Scottish ladies inside, but neither would look yer way."

"Three Scottish ladies, but one is an old bird," the shorter guard amended.

Old bird? Was she the one he sought? Liam waited.

"They should be thankful we did not toss them into the cage," the other griped.

Liam sucked in a breath. "Harsh punishment for a female."

"King orders it, we do it. Go inside!"

The bailey was a crowded and noisy yard where servants, soldiers, merchants, clerics, knights, and noblemen tended to errands or clustered in conversation. Seeing the brewer removing kegs from his cart, Liam lifted a hand as he walked past.

"A Scotsman?" the man asked low. "We watch out for one another, hey."

Liam nodded and headed for the stone keep that soared over the yard. He paused, anonymous amid the commotion, noticing sentries, doorways, pathways, barriers. The best chance of finding the Scotswomen here was in the keep, its main door accessible by an open timber staircase.

He headed for the steps.

CHAPTER THREE

T HE CONSTABLE LEANED toward the clerk. "How many are left to see? 'Tis late."

"Just one, sir, over there." The clerk pointed toward the doorway, where a man cloaked in gray stood beside a sentry.

Glancing there, Tamsin saw a tall, broad-shouldered man whose hood shadowed his features. Yet she felt his keen gaze as a shiver sank through her. Did she know him? Nay, she thought, turning back.

"Is that your servant?" Merton asked her.

"Nay—oh!" Tamsin felt Kirsty pinch her arm.

"Aye, our servant," Kirsty said. "Part of our escort come to take us home."

Tamsin looked at Kirsty in confusion. Her heart pounded. The smallest untruth could sometimes unnerve her, all part of the truth-telling urge she had inherited from Grandda Thomas. But Kirsty's quick thinking could help here.

Merton frowned, studying a parchment. "Dalrinnie is a contested area, being close to Ettrick Forest. Bruce's men have been sighted near there."

"We are not rebels if you imply that," Tamsin said.

"I said your man is not here," he barked. "We are done. Go."

"But if my brother is with King Edward, would he not be at Lanercost?"

"Your name again?"

"Lady Tamsin, wife to Sir John Witton of Dalrinnie." She omitted that he was dead, nor did the constable blink, perhaps unaware of Sir John's passing. Tamsin hoped he had not heard that she had inherited the estate, making her valuable as well as vulnerable.

"A risk to leave your stronghold and travel here, madam."

"Surely Sir John Witton's wife deserves your protection," Kirsty said.

Merton turned beefy red. "Henry Keith is not here, ladies. Go back to your castle and pray for safety."

Tamsin sighed. Where was Henry? He had joined King Edward's service to protect his family and his properties. But when Robert Bruce had killed Sir John Comyn to take the Scottish crown and Scotsmen began flocking to Bruce's side, Edward had raised the dragon banner—a declaration of 'no mercy' where Scotland was concerned. Henry's sympathies leaned toward Scotland, but now especially, he had to seem wholly loyal to Edward.

She, too, must appear loyal. The safety of her two sisters still residing at Castle Kincraig, now their brother's property, could depend on the behavior of the rest of the family. Glancing at Kirsty, she saw her dark-haired cousin's cheeks pinken with frustration and temper. Meekness was not in her nature, but Kirsty had good common sense and knew Tamsin must find Henry before she lost all.

"My brother is devoted to King Edward," Tamsin said. "The Keiths have always supported the Crown."

"Any Scot bears careful watching these days," Merton said.

Though she pressed her lips together, her reply slipped out. "Most Scottish knights honor their oaths of fealty to the king. Yet Edward does not honor his promises to them."

"You, lady, would do best to keep your pretty mouth shut." The constable's narrowed eyes and a lick of his lips expressed something darker than concern.

"It is the truth and you know it."

Kirsty took her arm. "My lady, our escort is here. We must go."

Hearing footsteps, Tamsin looked to her left. The cloaked man approached to stand beside her, the protesting sentry hurrying after him.

Despite his limp, the tall stranger had the determined stride of a warrior. Though a man in shabby gear was a common sight in downtrodden Scotland, Tamsin stared at this one. Handsome, strong, compelling—with a rather stunning masculine beauty. Distracted, she tilted her head, regarding him.

He nodded toward her but did not tug at his hood. He was no subordinate, she realized. Was he wearing a disguise? A Scottish spy? She frowned. If he was working for the Scots, she wanted to help him, trust him.

Merton ignored the man, reading a parchment page. "Lady, you will stay here until I am satisfied that you are who you claim to be."

"I am the lady of Dalrinnie and you have no reason to detain us."

"But you will stay until—what the devil do you want, man?" he snapped, addressing the stranger. "You were not invited forward."

"Sir, he insisted," the guard said.

"I did," the man said calmly. "I am here to escort the ladies to Dalrinnie—in the spirit of king's peace, of course."

Tamsin gaped. Had he heard them talking—or was he genuinely their escort, sent inside by Sir David Campbell, Dalrinnie's seneschal?

"Is that so, lady?" Merton asked.

Her mouth went dry. Even a small falsehood was a challenge. "I, ah—"

"Campbell sent me to accompany the ladies," the stranger said, as if he had read her thoughts—or had indeed been sent by Sir Davey. "If they stay to supper, I also hoped to offer my music then. I am a harper." He inclined his head with the offer.

His voice, deep and warm, sent an unexpected wash of comfort through her. Confused, she wondered what to do. She looked at Kirsty, who shrugged.

Merton laughed. "A minstrel, escorting ladies? Rude damn Scots."

"A harper is no minstrel. They are highly regarded in Scotland," Tamsin said. Indignant, she wanted to help. "My grandda was a harper and was very well-respected."

"Huh. Lady, do you know this man?" the constable demanded.

Tamsin looked at the man again. He dropped his hood back to reveal brown hair in long, untidy waves, a lean, square jaw dusted in dark whiskers, and remarkably blue eyes. Fatigue or concern crinkled his eyes and etched creases from arched nose to firm lips. Life had set fine tracks in a face both beautiful and hard, though his lips had a tender curve.

The harper gave her a wary glance. *Do not give me away*, it said.

She frowned. His satchel was harp-shaped, but he seemed like a warrior, brawny, with a reserved and powerful presence. She sensed something more. The voice, the eyes...

The knight in her dream. But that could not be.

"I—I know him. At Dalrinnie," she stammered, letting the dream justify her words. But her knees went weak, untruth and uncertainty—fear too—tilting her off balance. She put out a hand, and instantly his forearm was under hers, a hard and courteous brace. That was the gesture of a knight, not a harper.

She caught her breath and let go of his arm. Whoever he was, she felt strongly that he had secrets, yet she felt oddly safe beside him. She sensed worth, strength, innate integrity—and danger. The very air seemed to spark like fire around him.

Meeting the harper's glance, she looked away, then glanced back. Flickering glimpses, rippling excitement—she felt a strong physical attraction, but it was only foolish fancy. She was a lonely widow coming out of an empty marriage, facing many long years in a convent, a young woman with a yearning heart and an uncertain future.

Here and now, she must think only of her brother and their two sisters, and of her promise to her late great-grandfather. The wellbeing of her kin was as important to her as her own.

"You, musician," Merton was saying. "Play for your supper and leave after that. These ladies will not be going with you."

"Constable, would you treat a harper with discourtesy?" Tamsin asked. "As I said, here in Scotland, bards and harpers are respected and lauded. By tradition, they would be seated at the right hand of lords and kings."

"Which is why Scotland is failing in this war," Merton snapped. "At a king's right hand should be his general, not his musician. Sergeant—take these ladies to the solar. They can wait there until they dine with me at supper."

"You have no cause to hold us," Tamsin said.

"Scotswomen asking about King Edward is reason enough. You could be spies. This harper might be a spy too."

"If we were spies, we would have done what we came for and be gone already."

The harper laughed outright. Merton sent Tamsin a scathing look. "Take them away. Harper, you can find the steward below stairs."

Turning, Tamsin and Kirsty followed in the guard's wake. The harper came after, his limp rhythmic across the wooden floor. When the guard crossed the threshold first, the stranger reached above Tamsin's head to catch the door, letting Kirsty step out first.

Gliding beneath his outstretched arm, Tamsin felt her shoulder bump his chest, hard muscle through layered clothing. He smelled good—fresh air, leather, woodsmoke. Yearning plunged through her again. Why did the man affect her so? She glanced up.

"You are no harper, sir," she whispered. "What are you about?"

He smiled, a quirk of the lip, a sparkle in the blue, blue eyes, but did not reply. Tamsin walked past him, climbing the spiral stairs with Kirsty after the sentry.

Kirsty leaned to whisper. "Can we trust him? We cannot stay here, and—"

"And he is our only hope of escape," Tamsin agreed.

CHAPTER FOUR

I N TORCHLIGHT AND shadow, Liam sat on a leather stool in the great hall near the hearth's warmth. The notes of his harp were all but lost in the din. Plucking a final chord that went as unnoticed as his song, he set the harp on the low stool positioned in front of him, and when no one called for another tune, he took a moment to sip wine from a cup and survey the room.

The hall was a bustling, noisy, smoky place, the light of torches and candles flickering over faces he did not recognize. Garrison soldiers were seated at long trestle tables while servants carried platters of food around the room. Searching for old Lady Thomasina Keith, the woman the king had mentioned, he could not help but notice young Lady Tamsin again, seated not far away. For a moment he studied her delicate oval face, her hair like spun gold, her eyes the gray blue of a thundercloud.

She sat with her companion at a table with Merton, the women two beautiful butterflies; the blonde wore a blue-and-green plaid cloak and the white veil of a married woman half-covering a long golden braid that spilled over shoulder and breast to pool in her lap. The other wore a russet cloak and dark gown, her long dark hair loose and uncovered, apparently a young lady unmarried as yet. They leaned together, murmuring, glancing about, looking wary, though the dark-haired girl smiled, coaxing it from the other.

Bold to wear a Scots plaid amid English soldiers, Liam

thought in admiration. Lady Tamsin wore it proudly. She stood slender and straight, all grace and determination. She took a risk here, and he suspected she had the will and backbone for it. He had seen the snap of temper and intelligence in her eyes.

Then he noticed beside the dark-haired girl an older lady, bent and cloaked, head veiled, her mouth pursed like a beak. He could only hope this was Lady Thomasina.

He had heard enough earlier to glean that Lady Tamsin was sister to Sir Henry Keith, that Lady Kirsten was a cousin, that an older lady was with them. He knew too that they waited for Sir David Campbell, once his seneschal at Dalrinnie. So the man had stayed when the English took the place.

He frowned. Then Lady Tamsin must be the Scottish bride they said had come to Dalrinnie with Sir John Witton. He had heard the news; any mention of Dalrinnie whispered in alehouse or rumor had burned into his mind. But he felt bewildered. What tied Dalrinnie and these ladies to the old Rhymer's daughter?

No matter. He only meant to get that damned book and give it to Robert Bruce. The new King of Scots had known Thomas the Rhymer well, working with him for the Scottish cause. Bruce deserved to have that book far more than Edward did.

Missing a note, thinking about other things, he recovered and played on. He had to take the book to Bruce, perhaps take the lady to him as well. If she could help Scotland, and if all this could regain Dalrinnie Castle, then he would follow the old woman and this mad mission to hell and back if necessary.

For now, he must find a way to escort the ladies safely out of Lochmaben and convince the old one to give up her book. Then he would be on his way.

The women sat apart from Merton, the table strewn with plates and goblets, with platters piled with chicken, cheese, cakes, and more. The constable held out a cup for the ale a servant boy poured from a jug while the women picked at their food, speaking quietly. Lady Tamsin seemed tense, pale. No wonder. Merton's decision to keep them here was a subtle threat at a time when all Scotswomen were imperiled.

Liam meant to get them out of here. He had volunteered as their escort, and would take that responsibility to heart.

He sipped wine, watching the soldiers, noting the room. Best to spirit the women away tonight and help them find their Dalrinnie escort, he thought. Taking up the harp again, he began another tune, his fingers plucking chords as he sang, his voice carrying through the hall. No one paid him much mind, though he saw Lady Tamsin glance his way.

Ending the song, he noticed Lady Tamsin standing, walking toward him now. She had an uncommon beauty, simple, with a glow like a soft light within, and a tensile, shining strength. She took his breath away.

Stop, he told himself. Nothing, not even a beautiful girl, could take his mind from what he must do. He had walled off his heart to such.

He rang on the metal strings again to begin another song. A chunk of gravy-soaked bread landed at his feet, and someone laughed. Liam played on.

Yet when the young Keith woman came closer, almost standing beside him, he missed a note with a sour *plonk*. One of the strings had gone off-tune, its ivory peg loosening. The plonk became an annoying twang.

He did his best with the song, aware that she was just there, her cloak tossed back from her slender shoulders. She moved like a queen, yet she had a certain vulnerability, as if she was fearful, somehow.

What sank through him then, crown to foot, was a strong and surprising urge to protect her. All the Scotswomen here, but especially her. He frowned against it as his fingers stumbled once more on the strings, *plonk-twang*.

She stood but an arm's length away, listening, watching him. Her companions walked past, a sentry in their wake. The women were leaving. He should end the song and follow, or risk losing the old woman altogether.

As he rang off the harp, the weakened string spun off its peg, twirled out, and snapped the young woman's arm. Wincing, she rubbed her sleeve.

"My lady, I apologize." He gathered the string back. "Are you hurt?"

"I am fine." Her laugh was bell-like. "I forgive your harp."

"And the harper?"

"Oh, not he." She leaned toward him, her braid sweeping down, gold brushing his arm. Her silvery-blue eyes sparkled. "'Twas not the best of tunes, indeed."

"The truth pierces like an arrow." He set a hand to his chest in mock torment. "Though I admit, I am not the best of harpers."

"Then I wonder why you play. Or are you here for another reason?"

Her bluntness startled him. "For love of music, of course," he replied lightly, sliding the harp into its satchel.

The guard came forward. "Lady, you must come with us."

"I am speaking to the harper. Just a moment."

"I can see the lady to the solar," Liam said, buckling the leather cover.

"You are still playing for your supper, are you not?" the guard replied.

"I am done. A string broke, and I have no spare."

"Huh." The guard was uninterested. "Lady, you have only a moment." He walked away to wait with the two women by the door.

"A metal-strung harp has a heavenly sound," Lady Tamsin said. "I have heard most harpers use sheep gut, though some who use metal may have silver and gold in the strings."

"That is sometimes used for the two center strings. They ring the same note. We call them the Lovers." He glanced up and met her gaze.

"Are your strings lovers?"

For some reason, his heart surged. He looked away. "The strings of my *clàrsach* are humble brass wrapped with silver. They do well enough. I leave the lore and legend of it to harpers better than myself."

"My grandda was a harper. May I ask... Have you ever played at Castle Kincraig? You seem...familiar."

"I have not." But he knew the place. Standing, he settled the covered harp over his shoulder.

"Have you ever been to Dalrinnie Castle?"

She did not mince words, this one. He had not set foot in Dalrinnie's hall since before the place was stormed and overtaken by the English in his absence. "I have not entertained there, my lady."

"I only wondered where I might have seen you before. Well, perhaps it was just—never mind. Thank you for the music." She paused, then spoke again. "You said you were sent to escort us. Sir David Campbell sent you?"

"I just thought you were having some trouble, that is all. The others are waiting for you, my lady." He indicated Lady Kirsten, who approached with the older lady.

"Lady Tamsin, I told the guard we needed fresh air before we go upstairs. Would you like to go out with us?" The dark-haired girl's cheeks held a pink blush. She seemed anxious too, Liam thought.

"We cannot go out without the guard." The older woman sounded irritable.

"I would be pleased to escort you outside if you wish to go," Liam offered.

"The night air would be welcome," Lady Tamsin said. "If the harper would be so kind, we would not have to trouble the guard."

"This is inviting trouble," the old one said. The younger women did not answer.

"This way." Liam led them to the door of the hall and into the corridor. The guard was nowhere in sight, which gave him some ease, so he guided the women to the keep's outer door that opened on wooden steps descending to the bailey. As he went down, they followed, skirts whispering over the wooden platform and steps. The older lady groused under her breath, and Lady Kirsten shushed her.

The night air was chilly, the moonlight clouded over. In the yard, servants and sentries moved about, yet Liam saw no sign of the guard assigned to the women.

If he intended to spirit them away from here, he needed to act quickly. He looked about, seeing sentries on the battlements, soldiers milling in the yard, and the brewer loading empty kegs into his cart. None looked toward the small group by the steps.

The old lady fretted about the chill air and uneven steps as she came down. Liam turned and offered his arm. "Madam, if I may." He helped her down, and Lady Kirsten took the woman's arm. Turning to Lady Tamsin next, he offered his elbow.

"Hands off," the older lady barked. Liam tipped his head in apology.

"Master Harper." Lady Tamsin looked at him. "Are we safe out here?"

"Do not fret. I will watch after you."

"Sir." She set a hand on his arm. "I think you are here for another purpose. Whatever that may be, if you could help us leave this place, we would be in your debt."

"Do you want to leave now?" he whispered, bending closer to be heard.

"Very much." She looked at him, eyes so gray and limpid, they rivaled the moonlight. He saw earnest need there. "Please."

"What of your escort?"

"They should be here soon. I would prefer to wait outside the castle for them."

"Aye then." He touched her elbow lightly to move her ahead. The other women followed, the older one questioning, the younger, hushing.

The drawbridge was still open. That was luck indeed, for Lochmaben was surrounded by a moat, the open gate and drawbridge the only way out. Then he realized that the guards were waiting to let the brewer out before they shut the castle for the night.

That might be their chance.

"This way," he said, strolling casually toward the brewer. The women followed.

"Wat of Selkirk. Is that truly your name?" Lady Tamsin walked briskly beside him. He looked down and saw her regarding him curiously. "Why do you help us? What do you want?"

Again, he recognized that blunt manner, that quick perception. He found it intriguing, even charming. "I came here to look for someone and found you. But you can trust me, I swear."

"Where are we going?" the old woman demanded.

"Hush, my lady, please," the dark-haired girl said.

"He is helping us, dear," Lady Tamsin murmured.

"We do not need his help. He might be a spy."

"Not a spy, but a friend," Lady Tamsin said calmly.

"Hey! Harper—stop!" A guard hurried toward them, with another following.

Liam put out an arm to move Lady Tamsin firmly behind him with the others. He faced the guards. "The ladies wanted some air. The hall is crowded and smoky. I offered to escort them."

"Escort them back to the hall and be gone yourself," said the guard. Liam recognized him from the entrance gate earlier. "You were told to leave after supper. The ladies must return to the keep."

"Sir, we just came out to look at the moon," said Lady Kirsten.

"Which you have seen. Go back to the hall," the second guard ordered. "The harper must go out the gate."

"Let me see them to the keep." Without waiting, Liam ushered the women along. Then he glanced back to see that Lady Tamsin had stopped. She held a hand to her throat. "My lady, what is wrong?"

"Nothing," she said, her voice strained. Then, as if rousing from a dream, she gave her head a slight shake and hurried past him.

Men in a scuffle, blades shining in the moonlight. A man collapsing, his cloaked figure a dark sprawl on the ground. Harper-knight, the harper-knight—

Walking quickly, Tamsin put a hand to her head. The images that had just flashed through her mind—nightmarish and quick— were already gone. Her heart beat rapidly, her hands trembled. Just an instant, an unexpected vision—unwelcome, unsettling. She drew a breath against its effect, keeping it to herself. She had learned that lesson well in two years at Dalrinnie. Outside of her own family, visions were suspect and could condemn her as mad, or worse—even if they proved true, as some did.

But the harper had not fallen to the ground. He was here, safe and solid, striding beside her now. She drew a breath. Perhaps she should warn him of danger. Yet he would likely think it ridiculous—or lunatic.

"Is aught wrong, my lady?"

"Just... I feared the guards might stop you. Arrest you."

"For a moment, I feared the same." He chuckled so genuinely that she smiled. As she and the others followed the harper like ducklings, he led them across the yard.

"Where are we going now?" Lady Edith asked.

Another guard passed them, then stopped. "To the gate, harper," he said.

"I am escorting these ladies," he said. The guard shrugged, moved on.

The lady looked up. "Do you ever tell the truth, Master Harper?"

"Sometimes."

"Truth is always best, I think."

"Is it?" he murmured. "Sometimes life turns better on a falsehood than a truth, I have found. A small lie might help us see the light of a new day—and we can save friends from trouble. Truth, virtue though it be, can put us in the kettle."

She tilted her head. "Falsehoods help us survive and avoid disaster?"

He laughed. "That is not quite what I meant. Some events in my life have peeled away my ideals like an onion, my lady. Now I see the nature of truth as layered."

"Oh," she said, surprised, not having thought of it that way. "I suppose it is."

"Once," he went on, "I was an honorable fellow with noble aspirations. I defended what was right and spoke out in truth when others did not dare. Had I been more...nuanced, you see, a friend might yet be alive." His voice went graveled, fierce.

"I am sorry. I think you are an honorable fellow, Master Harper."

"Thank you," he said simply.

She craved suddenly to know more about him, to ask who he was, where he came from—but a commotion of shouts and hoofbeats sounded near the gate. She saw knights on horseback pounding across the drawbridge and into the courtyard, dismounting and calling out, urgent and impatient.

Even in darkness, she knew the lead knight. She caught her breath and stepped behind the harper, grateful for the shield as she watched Sir Malise Comyn dismount.

"Is aught the matter, Lady Tamsin?" The harper turned, drawing his hood deeper over his brow as he spoke, despite the shadows where they stood.

"I do not want that knight over there to see me. The one in the blue cloak."

"Aye, he is one to avoid."

"You know him?"

"A bit."

Sir Malise Comyn had worked often with her late husband as a Scots lord scheming with an English lord on behalf of Edward's invasion. Overhearing those discussions, Tamsin worried for her kin and all Scots, especially after Robert Bruce killed Sir John Comyn, a cousin of Sir Malise. Just last February inside a church, of all places, Bruce had stabbed his rival for the throne and then rode off to claim the Scottish throne and begin to build a resisting army. The chain of deeds last winter had given the rebellion new heart, even though their leader was now an outlawed king in the heather.

Scottish to her bones and unable to speak freely inside Dalrinnie's walls, Tamsin had seen events conspire from the perspective of an English garrison. She understood Sir Malise Comyn's fury and indignation as he called for revenge and gained King Edward's support. She saw the king promote him, grant him lands, feed his wrath, and order him to find Bruce at any cost. Sir John Witton and all Dalrinnie had been drawn into that vortex while she watched.

Oh aye, she knew Sir Malise. She knew he thought less about honor than advantage, less about revenge than royal favor. Less about others than himself.

If Sir Malise saw her here, he would press her about her purpose and perhaps her brother. That could lead to uncomfortable questions about Henry's loyalty. She stayed behind the harper, watching Comyn.

The harper noticed and took her arm. "Come with me."

"Where are we going?" Edith asked.

"Shh!" Kirsty said. "Just come with us, my lady."

"Hey! Harper!" The brewer called from his cart. "Do you need a ride? I am off home while the bridge is down."

The harper walked toward him. "Master Brewer, might you have room for more?"

The man leaned forward to talk quietly. "Scotswomen? Och, aye. Get in the back." He gestured, and the harper waved the ladies toward the cart.

"The man is a friend," he told them. "He will take you outside."

"In an ale cart?" Lady Edith asked indignantly. "We will wait for our escort."

"We cannot risk that, dear." Tamsin looked over her shoulder. Sir Malise and the others were talking, now gesturing toward the keep. Malise turned, glancing around the yard with interest. She touched the harper's arm. "Please, we must go!"

He did not question, only drew her toward the cart to boost her inside. His touch was warm and strong; somehow Tamsin felt the tingle of it along her spine.

Sitting in deep straw, she curled her legs under her cloak. Within moments, Kirsty sat down beside her, helped by the harper. Then he turned to Lady Edith.

"Allow me to help you, madam, so you can all leave."

Edith pursed her lips. "Very well. Only because the girls want to do this. And I do not like this place. Nor do I like that one over there." She pointed to Sir Malise.

"I agree, my lady." He helped her to clamber up to the bench beside the brewer.

"Ye're safe here, luv," the brewer told her. "I may need yer help if ye sit there. Just smile and wave at the gate. You could help save us all, my luv."

Edith raised her brows and began to speak. Tamsin held her breath, but the older lady nodded. "Whatever we must do to get away from that fellow." She looked again at Sir Malise.

The harper stood by the cart. "Keep quiet and out of sight. All will be well."

"Are you coming with us?" Tamsin asked.

"They expect me to leave alone, and they are unlikely to question the brewer. Duck under the straw." Tamsin and Kirsty complied, hefting straw and cloaks to cover themselves.

She heard him hit the side of the cart. "Go!"

CHAPTER FIVE

T HE CART RUMBLED ahead, slowing at the gate. Tamsin heard the brewer say goodnight and then heard Edith—Edith!—simper and laugh, letting the guard believe she was with the brewer, as his wife or his leman. The guard did not seem to care.

"She is enjoying this," Kirsty whispered.

"I am glad," Tamsin laughed faintly as the cart moved ahead, rattling over the drawbridge and then rolling out over the meadow path.

"Come out," the brewer said after a while. Pushing away the straw, Tamsin sat up, feeling a cool, damp breeze from the castle loch. All was bathed in moonlight.

Kirsty sat up too. "Where is the harper?"

Tamsin looked back. "There, coming down the hill toward us."

As the brewer drew the cart into a grove of trees, she saw the harper striding toward them without much of a limp. Was that false too? He came near, pointing in the distance. "Is that your escort there?"

Peering toward the far end of the meadow, Tamsin saw three riders coming at a good pace, bringing three riderless horses with them. She nodded. "That will be Sir David Campbell with Dalrinnie men."

"Then they will find you safe here." He stepped back, shifting the harp's bag.

"Must you leave?" She felt a sense of alarm, remembering the odd flash of vision that she had seen—the harper on the ground, injured or dead. She was tempted to pull on his cloak and urge him to come with them. "Wait here with us."

"I should not."

"Where will you go?"

"Wherever my music is needed," he said lightly.

"Come with us to Dalrinnie," she said impulsively.

"Not me. You will be safe with the escort. You and the lady widow."

"The who?" she asked.

"Your elderly friend. The widow of Dalrinnie. Lady Thomasina." The harper tilted his head toward Lady Edith.

"That is Lady Edith. She is not the widow of Dalrinnie," Kirsty said. "Why did you think so?"

"I was sent to find the widow, a Lady Thomasina of Dalrinnie. An elderly lady. I was told she might be found at Lochmaben this week. I have a message for her from King Edward."

"Elderly!" Kirsty half-laughed. "What would King Edward want with the lady of Dalrinnie?" She glanced at Tamsin.

Tamsin felt sick. King Edward! She had been wrong about the harper. So very wrong. He was no rebel helping Scotland's noble cause. He was looking for her, and he was dangerous to her. King Edward's message to her would either order her into a convent or an unwanted marriage—or an iron cage.

Her breath came quickly. She felt betrayed, began to panic. How foolish she had been to trust him. This man, this beautiful, devious harper, had charmed and cajoled her.

A small lie helps us see the light of a new day. She valued truth more than anything, and he had led her along to help the king claim her estate and ruin her life.

Fighting the compulsion to tell him what she thought, she sat silent. Staring.

"My lady?" He tipped his head as if puzzled by her sudden glare.

"Lady Edith is not the widow of Dalrinnie," she said, repeating what Kirsty said.

"Where is she? I can share this message only with her. If she is at Dalrinnie—then I will have to go there." He frowned.

She sensed he did not want to go there. Good, she thought. "Why do you think the lady is old?"

"The king called her the Rhymer's daughter. Thomas the Rhymer, if you have heard of him. If so, she must be very old."

Rhymer's daughter! That was the teasing name her family used for her because she had so admired her great-grandfather that she had wanted to be like him, a prophet, a person of wisdom. But if King Edward knew that name, it had only come from someone familiar with her family. Henry would not have discussed it—but her late husband had heard, and might have told someone.

Ah, she thought, Sir Malise. That must be it. And in trusting the harper, she had stepped into Edward's trap. He was looking for her, and the harper was his messenger.

She lifted her chin. Nothing for it but the truth. "I am Lady Thomasina Keith." She wanted him to hear the coldness in her voice.

His brows lifted. "You! That cannot be."

"It can. I am Thomasina. Tamsin," she said. "My family called me Rhymer's daughter as a teasing name. But very few know that." She narrowed her eyes. "And I am not old."

"I see that. I apologize, my lady." He looked bewildered, pushing a hand through his hair, hood falling back. "Then the message is for you. We must speak in private."

She looked at the approaching horses. Suddenly the urgency of that strange little vision returned. "Come with us to Dalrinnie. Explain yourself there," she said on impulse. "Get in the cart, Master Harper."

"Not now." He frowned, his eyelashes black crescents. "I will find you later."

Her head was all in a muddle. She could not trust him. She

did not know him. She was rightfully furious with him. Yet she feared for his safety and could not let him leave.

"You will be hurt, sir—do not go—you will be followed—"

But he stepped back. "I will bring you the message. Farewell, Lady Tamsin. Lady Kirsten. Lady Edith," he added.

He thanked the brewer, then went striding quickly over the meadow toward the road that skirted the loch, which would take him to the main road, north or south. Moonlight glittered over water, and soon the man was just a swiftly moving silhouette.

"Godspeed," Tamsin murmured. Fear spun within. She wanted to stop him, and yet she did not know what to think, what to feel.

"Look there." The brewer pointed behind them. "Riders coming from the castle."

Hearing hooves thudding over the meadow from another direction, Tamsin turned. Visible through the screen of trees, several riders were coming from Lochmaben Castle, riding fast, soon pulling up near the cart. She gasped as Sir Malise walked his mount forward.

"Lady Tamsin!" he called. "So it was you in the yard—I thought so! What are you doing at Lochmaben? Are you in need? Who is this fellow?" He gestured toward the brewer.

"Sir Malise," she said, "this is Master Brewer. He was kind enough to bring us here to wait for Sir David and the Dalrinnie escort. They are just coming there."

She pointed in that direction, wanting to deflect his attention away from the harper walking near the loch. She smiled, hands folded, fingers shaking.

"Sir David is coming? Good." Malise gathered the reins of his horse. "I am glad of the chance to see you, my lady. I want to be sure you are well. I know how difficult it may have been for you since your husband's passing."

"I am fine," she said, a bit surprised, yet touched by his chivalrous concern.

"I will come to Dalrinnie," he said. "I have a suggestion—to benefit you. Sir John was concerned about you. I will not forget it."

Startled, she nodded. "Thank you." She had no desire to see him again, but his mention of her late husband gave her pause. He could be sincere. She had seen that in him.

"Be safe, my lady. I have business at Lochmaben, but only came out now to stop that scoundrel yonder. We must hurry to catch him."

"Scoundrel?" she asked.

"The harper?" Kirsty asked then.

"No harper, that one. An outlaw. A wolf's-head I have been searching for. I recognized him in the castle yard. With me!" he shouted to his men, then turned with them to canter, then gallop, after the harper.

Ahead, the harper began to run, the slope taking him out of sight. Men and horses followed in hard, fast pursuit. Tamsin heard Malise shouting.

"An outlaw!" Kirsty said.

"But the harper had a message from King Edward. Malise must be wrong."

"It is a puzzle. What did Sir Malise mean when he spoke to you?"

"He seems interested in my welfare." She watched the riders thunder over the meadow.

"More than that," Kirsty said. "Look! They are nearing the harper!"

Tamsin leaned over the side of the cart, heart thumping as she peered through the darkness. The pursuing horses drove forward so swiftly that all she could discern were moving shapes, then the glint of metal in moonlight. She heard distant shouts and the clang of steel.

Angling across the meadow, the Dalrinnie escort came closer. Shadows were falling fast now, a dark veil swallowing horses, men, and the meadow in murky, inconstant moonlight. She could hardly see the cluster of men and horses on the rim of the slope in the eerie light.

"They have him," the brewer growled, standing up in the cart. "He is down. They are dragging him—"

"Oh, dear saints," Lady Edith said. "He was a lovely man, the harper."

Tamsin strained to see an agitated cluster of men and horses in a blur of darkness. This was not justice on Malise's part. This felt like treachery. The certainty made her breath come in gulps as she gripped the cart side.

"Nay," she whispered. "Stop—leave him be—"

"They are lifting a body," the brewer said from his higher perch.

Dear God. Tamsin put a hand to her throat.

"Jesu," the brewer said. "That lad was right enough, a good Scotsman. But Edward's men need no reason to take down a Scot. Looks like they killed him. A shame."

This was wrong. The Scot was Edward's messenger, one of them, not Malise's enemy. The harper had been sent to find her—which made her the cause of his death. Covering her face in her hands, she bent forward.

Now the Dalrinnie men arrived, horses thundering around the cart, riders pulling on reins. Sir David Campbell dismounted and came forward.

"My lady! How is it you are here? What was all that about?" He gestured widely.

"Oh, Sir Davey!" Tamsin felt close to tears. The seneschal offered a hand to help her climb down from the cart, then turned to help the others.

"Well, Davey," Lady Edith greeted her brother. "Finally, you are here! They just captured an outlaw. We thought him a fine Scotsman—but we were in terrible danger!"

"What happened?" Sir David looked toward the loch, but there was little to see.

"Sir Malise Comyn was here. He said the man was an outlaw," Tamsin said. "But he was a harper. He helped us. It is cruel, what they have done."

"A harper? Curious." Campbell took his sister's elbow and ushered the younger women ahead to help them mount the extra horses.

Dalrinnie's seneschal was a strong, steady fellow, fatherly and practical. He had been at Dalrinnie Castle before Sir John Witton, before Tamsin, and he had become one of the few people she trusted there.

"We were all but prisoners in that castle," Edith said. "I will say he helped us."

"This is Edward's business," Sir David said. "We cannot interfere. Likely we will never hear more about that fellow."

"Could he be alive? The brewer thought him killed," Tamsin said.

"He would be lucky to be dead if you ask me. Edward shows no mercy to Scots these days."

"Brutal attack. Fine young Scot," the brewer said.

Sir David took coins from his belt pouch and thanked the brewer, who touched his cap and urged his pony and cart over the meadow.

Soon, Tamsin rode among the others, her legs to the side, cloak tucked around her. Ahead, cool moonlight revealed horses and knights in the distance, vanishing southward. One horse carried a form slumped across the saddle.

Sir David slowed to ride beside her. "If Sir Malise went after the man like that, he must have been an outlaw."

"He mentioned having orders from King Edward. He was one of them."

"Many Scots act for both sides, my lady. Some do what Edward orders. Some, like Malise Comyn, try to gain privilege. Others are a thorn in the king's side. No matter what the harper told you, he may have been a thorn."

Tamsin nodded. She had caused his death. She shivered as chill air and guilt tore at her. Autumn was in the air, and her world was changing fast around her.

She had seen it before it happened. Men, darkness, the glint of steel—a man on the ground. The harper, dead. She had tried to warn him, but he had not heard.

With a shout, one of the Dalrinnie men rode toward them. "Sir! We found this." He held up a leather satchel. "It might be of value, but it is broken, by the sound of it." When he shook the bag, Tamsin heard wood rattling, heard a sad, sour chime.

"The harp!" she cried. "I want to keep it."

She had failed to save him. But she would not leave his harp behind.

CHAPTER SIX

E VENING DROPPED STEEL gray and quiet as Liam stood
watching Dalrinnie Castle through bare-branched trees
patterned against the sky. The woodland settled around him,
hushed and darkening. Beside him, a chestnut stallion nuzzled for
grasses in a thin layer of early snow. His sight-hound, tall and
alert, stood beside him, wiry coat the color of thunderclouds.

Home. He had come here as fast as he could, having slipped
free of that fool Malise Comyn. A few troublesome days, but easy
enough to get away. He was just deeply glad to be standing here
now, gazing up at his home.

Dalrinnie towered on a hilltop in blue dusk. The sentries
walking the parapet were unlikely to notice the knight standing
among the trees at the base of the long slope with its new coat of
snow. Dalrinnie's woodland was part of the outermost fringe of
the vast dense tracts of Ettrick Forest—The Forest, as it was
called—a massive canopied woodland of oak, birch, green gullies,
rushing streams, and endless paths that only some knew. The
English had never been able to penetrate it.

All was quiet now, but not an hour ago, dozens of English
troops arrived to be hallooed through the opening portcullis.
They were led by a temporary commander, so Gilchrist had
reported earlier that day. More would come soon to fill the
garrison.

He had escaped Comyn's capture by working his way free of

the ropes that bound him tossed over a horse's saddle. Dropping to the ground to roll away, he had run into the woodland and away. Now he flexed the shoulder that ached from the fall. No matter.

He had met with his brother Gilchrist and cousin Finley, knowing where to find them, and then made his way up the River Annan to the safety of the Ettrick Forest. There he met with friends, found the knight's gear he had packed away, and borrowed a horse. All the while, he had worked out a plan.

He would find Lady Tamsin—Lady Thomasina—at Dalrinnie and obtain that bothersome but important book. Then he would take the lady and her book and go in search of Robert Bruce's latest encampment. Let the renegade King of Scots decide what to do with the Rhymer's book and the wee Keith lady. Liam intended to return to the forest and the fold of loyal men, all of whom had broken their fealties to King Edward for the finest reasons—freedom and dignity and the right to defend their own.

His greatest risk in this, he realized, was not his life, but the lives of his kin who were dedicated to the Church. Edward knew about them. Liam had to reach them, warn them, and convince them to go elsewhere, for they would be as hunted as any outlaw once Edward learned what Liam had done.

Just yesterday, Gilchrist heard that King Edward had taken to his bed, ill again, unable to hold audience, accept fealties, or even issue orders. The king's illness could give Liam and then Bruce the time needed in this matter of the Rhymer's book.

"You could find the lady of Dalrinnie," Gilchrist had suggested, "get this book, and bring it to Edward as ordered. You will know what the book contains, and can take that knowledge to Bruce. That is worth something. And if Edward is pleased, you will be in command of Dalrinnie."

Liam shook his head. "I do not want Englishers in my castle."

"Then just be careful," his brother had cautioned.

Now Liam stood on his forested land, gazing at his castle, deciding what to do.

Here, in Dalrinnie's shadow, boots on Dalrinnie soil, he could think more clearly. Here, he asked himself if he could obey Edward and betray friends and kin, and knew he could not. But he knew how to proceed. It began with the lass and the book.

He only needed to get inside the gate and ask for the young widow. But fresh English troops had arrived. That was a problem.

Gazing at the castle now, the nearly forgotten verse came back to him. Thomas the Rhymer had uttered a prediction for Dalrinnie long before Liam's birth. His grandfather had heard it from the prophet's lips and had told his son, who repeated it to his sons, Liam being the eldest. He had struggled to remember it in Edward's hot and stuffy chamber. Now it came clear, still a puzzle.

Dalrinnie, Dalrinnie,
Towers high, walls bold
Knight nor baron can hold
Nor good fortune unfold
When Dalrinnie falls three times and more
No king can restore, nor harp sing its lore
And Scotland will burn—

He had always thought something was missing, but that was what was shared between generations. Part had proven true, so the Setons of Dalrinnie called it a curse rather than a prophecy. Knights nor barons could hold the castle, and it would fall three times and more. His grandfather had lost it; his father had regained it; then Liam had lost it. That was twice. Did Sir John Witton count as the third—or was defeat reserved only for Setons? He rather hoped Malise would be the fourth, he thought sourly.

He had learned the harp because of that verse, but he had lost the castle anyway. And now his very harp was gone. Sighing hard, he watched the tower on the hill.

Beside him, the dog made a low, gruff sound. Liam rested a

hand on the great gray head. "Hush, Roc, *mo charaid*. Soon we will go home." Home was a forest encampment; home was Dalrinnie. He meant both.

The castle was his boyhood home and his inheritance, and he wanted it back, wanted his kin and tenants safe, too. King Edward had no right to claim any Scottish fortress, yet he did so with abandon. Which meant Liam must proceed carefully.

Watching the castle walls, he thought about the young widow inside. In the forest, he had asked others what they knew of Witton's widow. She was quiet, they said. Small and veiled, sometimes seen riding to hawks and hounds with her husband; sometimes she visited the monastery at Holyoak to speak with the abbot and look at books. The lady was inordinately fond of books, they said.

Books. Curious, Liam thought. And she knew Holyoak. So did he.

They said, too, she was generous to the Church and good to her servants, a true lady in spirit and demeanor. But it was expected that soon Edward would send her to a convent and fully claim Dalrinnie for the English.

That meant Liam must act soon. Lady Tamsin had become not just the lady with the book. She was his best hope of seeing his plan through.

The dog woofed, and Liam heard the crackle of brush behind him. Turning, he saw Gilchrist and their cousin, Sir Finley Macnab, riding slowly along the forest path, Gilchrist in the king's red, Finley as well. Liam waited, stretching his left leg, easing the ache in his knee, an older injury. Leather creaked, chain mail rustled. He hated the red surcoats his brother and cousin wore, declaring them king's men despite their true affiliation. But the colors provided an advantage, including the convenience of authority.

Glancing again at the castle, he saw a light glimmer high in a tower window. He knew the location. The lord's bedchamber. A shadow moved past the window, fairy-like, graceful.

She was there, he thought. Lady Tamsin, all cream and golden and delicate. He felt sure of it somehow. For a moment, he thought of Beatrix, gentle, sweet, and gone. Loneliness swamped him for a moment. Life had wrenched his dreams away.

So be it. He had no time for happiness. He had bargained with the devil and must see it through.

As Gilchrist and Finley came toward him, he patted the dog's head. "So, Roc. We will come back here one day. But for now, the lads will take you to a safe haven, aye?"

His dog was more than dear to him, a valuable creature, and all he had left of the Dalrinnie he knew. The dog was power and calm, his friend. No one knew if all of his dogs had survived the fire that had brought the English in and sealed Liam out. That mystery had near broken his heart. But if Witton and his lady had hunted with large hounds, perhaps his dogs were alive and cared for. He had to trust that.

"Seen enough of your castle, then?" Gilchrist asked quietly.

"For now. Soon I will knock on the gate. Then I will see more of it, hey."

"Better you did that with a thousand Scots at your back," Finley said.

"And where are they?" Liam glanced around. The others chuckled. "I will get the book. You take the dog to Holyoak for safety. Then—" He paused. "I will do what I must."

"We have your back, lad," Finley said. "Always."

Liam nodded, throat tightening.

CHAPTER SEVEN

D RAWING UP THE hem of her gown, Tamsin hurried down the curving stone steps. There were riders at the gates. Stopping to glance out a narrow window in the turret stair, she saw a group of knights riding into the bailey just as dusk fell. She smoothed her gray gown and the gauzy linen veil that touched her shoulders above her long, thick braid. Patting her keys and embroidered pouch secured on her leather belt—visible reminders that she was lady of this castle—she headed for the great hall.

No one summoned her at the arrival, she realized, because she had naught to do with the garrison. She was just the Scottish widow who inconveniently owned the castle after her husband's death. But if these men brought orders from King Edward that would change her status, she had to find out.

Pausing at the last step under the flare of a bracketed torch, she heard men's voices in the great hall, heard the thud of boots over floorboards, the *chink* of armor, and calls for ale. Exhaling, anxious, she crossed the small antechamber toward the hall.

Suddenly, she recalled a scrap of a dream from days ago—a breathless sense of running, of darkness and rain. And a curious chanting, someone singing: *Married by All Souls Day, married by All Souls. . . lost and found, chased and bound, married by All Souls . . .*

But it made no sense. That date was weeks away, and she expected to be sent to a convent soon. It was not a truthy dream, she assured herself.

She hurried past a dark corner, an empty chair, past painful memories. In this small chamber, her husband had met with knights, merchants, priests, tenants, and others. On chilly evenings, Witton sat by the fire basket while Tamsin read aloud from an epic poem in French or some other text. She favored Arthurian tales like Galahad or Tristan and Iseult. Witton wanted treatises on hunting and weaponry.

Last March, after he had been wounded in a skirmish, his sickbed had been placed just there. She looked away. Her empty marriage had been an alliance for the Keiths. Now her father and Sir John were both gone, and she waited to learn her fate.

But she was still lady of this castle, and the men arriving this cold, gloomy night would soon know it. She pushed the door open, reminding herself to hold her tongue.

Two years at Dalrinnie had taught her to watch her habit of blunt speech that had so irritated her husband. She had learned, too, not to speak of dreams or visions. She could not prove their truth. Silence, hard-won, became a bastion of safety.

She walked boldly into the room to make her way through the crowd of men, knights in armor, others in surcoats and fur cloaks. Most ignored her as she passed; a few moved aside or nodded a greeting. Some were of Dalrinnie's garrison, others unfamiliar. To a man, they looked weary and concerned.

"I bring no request—this is a direct order from the king!" The shout came from the far end of the room.

She knew that nasal note of disdain. Sir Malise Comyn, tall, blond, handsome, and deceptively angelic, faced Sir David Campbell across a table strewn with flat and rolled parchments. With Sir Malise stood his brother-in-law, Sir Patrick Siward, lean and dark. Both men had visited Dalrinnie often to conspire with her husband on behalf of England.

Edging her way through the crowd, Tamsin moved past several tall knights who wore chain mail and hefty capes. They were absorbed in discussions, hardly noticing her. Torchlight glinted on steel, pooled on the floorboards, glittered in the ale poured into cups of pewter or shaped wood. She lifted her chin and came closer.

"Sir Malise, if you mean to take this castle—" Campbell began.

"Edward has put me in charge. Here is the writ." Malise Comyn handed a roll of parchment, ribbons dangling from a wax seal, to Campbell.

Her husband had once said that wherever Comyn went, conflict followed. If Malise had a king's writ for Dalrinnie, likely he had one for her, too. King Edward had made it clear she would not remain. A convent was tolerable; an unwelcome marriage, worse. Soon she would know.

"Royal orders," Comyn told David Campbell, his voice carrying over the din of voices. "You must comply. Do not expect Bruce to reclaim this place."

"Which king would a good Scot choose?" Campbell's question was bitter and bold. Tamsin had realized long ago that Dalrinnie's seneschal had reliable judgment and secret loyalties. She hoped he had not stepped too far just then.

"If you are revealed to be a traitor, Campbell," Comyn muttered, "it will go poorly for you."

Walking past the central iron fire basket, Tamsin felt the hot glow on her back. Firelight glinted over her golden braid and gleamed along the swords and helmets stacked along a nearby wall as custom required. A large dog resting near the fire basket stood and turned to lope behind her. The leggy hound, rangy but with natural dignity, nosed at Tamsin's hand.

"Good girl, Oonagh," she murmured, ruffling the great gray head.

"It may be impossible to find Bruce," Sir David said. "We have tried."

"King Edward is in a fury over it. Bruce must be caught. And I will not rest until my cousin's murder is avenged."

Campbell turned with a slight smile. "Ah, Lady Tamsin!"

"My lady." Patrick Siward nodded. He was swarthy in the low

light, shorter but brawnier than Comyn, a man she knew to be tough, taciturn, but often sensible.

"Sir Davey." She inclined her head. "Sir Patrick. And Sir Malise. Welcome."

"Lady," Comyn snapped. He turned to Campbell. "We know Bruce was moving freely through Selkirk and Galloway and has managed to take back Dalswinton Castle. We do not know where he may go next."

"He could be in the area, hiding in the forest or hills," Siward said.

"Clever and elusive," Sir David replied. "King in the heather, some call him now."

"Coward, I call him," Comyn said. "Murdering my cousin, Sir John Comyn of Badenoch, has increased the conflict, not solved it. We will stop Bruce. *I* will stop him."

Listening, Tamsin slid her fingers into the dog's collar. She had heard talk of Bruce among the garrison but had not heard of his latest movements. She frowned.

"Edward thrives on fury. It is in his nature," Sir David said. "And he will be furious so long as Bruce's men nip at English heels, ambush king's men, steal back Scottish castles, erode English hold where they can. But only Bruce's small circle knows where he is day to day. No military strategy will find him. You cannot outthink unpredictability."

"We will find him." Malise dropped one parchment and picked up another.

"Bruce is furious too, especially with the cruel treatment of his women weeks ago." Now Campbell glanced at Tamsin. "With pardon, my lady."

"I agree, Sir Davey. Edward's scheme of caging the ladies is heinous."

"They are not all shut in cages, you know." Malise sounded annoyed.

"In the king's mercy, some were sent to convents," Sir Patrick pointed out.

"King's mercy? We can hardly blame King Robert for his anger."

"King Robert, is it?" Comyn gave her a sharp glance.

"His title, sir, whether or not you think it deserved."

He tapped the page under his finger and turned to Campbell. "If Bruce is near here, I will find him. That is why the king put me in command of Dalrinnie."

"Your command?" Tamsin's heart sank.

"This castle is poorly protected." Comyn sifted among the parchments on the table. "Where are the castle orders? Ah." He opened a rolled page. "Here . . . 'Sir Malise Comyn is directed to provision Castle Dalrinnie with men and victuals and act with all expedition against the king's enemies and rebels.'" He gave her a smug smile.

"But Dalrinnie is mine, by my husband's will," she argued.

"No longer, madam."

"Lady Tamsin, it is late," Sir Patrick said. "Perhaps you should retire."

"Perhaps join my sister, Lady Edith, who may be anxious this evening." Sir David's expression was grim, his hair silvery in the candlelight. He looked weary.

"I will not be sent to bed like a child. I will wait to hear what pertains to me."

Comyn scowled. "Lady Tamsin, we are discussing important matters here."

Clutching the dog's collar as if she could absorb the animal's calm, Tamsin stifled her reply. She had heard that King Edward regarded Malise Comyn as strong, bold, and loyal. Her late husband said he had distinguished himself as a jousting champion in Edward's court, and his handsomeness made women swoon. Tamsin found him pretty, yet arrogant and knew that his potential came less from stellar character than from a compulsion to take advantage where he could.

"I will wait," she repeated.

"Fine. There is an order, but we will talk about it later,"

Comyn said.

"I expect to be sent to a convent. Just give me the news."

Malise huffed. "Why a convent?"

"A woman who takes the veil gives up the rights to her property."

"Priories are havens for widows, but Edward can still marry you off as he likes."

"A widow may choose her own. Though my brother may find me a good match."

"Henry Keith!" Malise crossed his arms. "Have you heard from him lately?"

"Not recently. He rides for King Edward and I pray daily for his safety."

"Pray hard, then. He was given a task that will put him in harm's way."

Alarmed, she narrowed her eyes. "Where is he?"

"Go to your chamber." His voice was flat, dismissive.

"Do you know, Sir Patrick?" She turned.

"I have not heard this news, my lady."

She folded her hands. "I want to know what concerns me and mine."

Malise ignored her. "Campbell, show me on the map where you and your men went searching for Bruce." He tapped a page spread on the table.

"Sir, 'tis courtesy to answer the lady," Sir David said.

"Since you will insist, come here." Malise took her arm in a firm grip. "We will talk now. Silence that hound, will you."

Tamsin hushed the growling dog, curling her fingers tighter around Oonagh's collar. As Malise pulled her toward a shadowy corner, the canny hound pressed between her and the knight.

Malise loomed over her. "Dalrinnie is mine now. You need to understand that."

"But my husband left the grant to me." Flexing her fingers in the dog's gray coat, she felt Oonagh lean into her, protective, trembling with stilled power.

"Would you question Edward of England?" He gave her a thin smile. "I was in a private audience at Lanercost while he decided the fate of Dalrinnie and its widow."

"I would think the king would prefer a more experienced commander here."

He bristled visibly. "This location is crucial, being so near Ettrick Forest. And I assisted your husband often in the effort here. He took me into his confidence. I came here often and did what I could to help."

She gave a bitter laugh. "He thought well of you. But when he lay dying, you rode off to the king carrying tales. Now you return as its commander. That seems deliberate."

"You wound me, madam. I took the news to the king in haste."

"You hurried so he would decide in your favor." Breathing fast, she felt sparks rise within. *Silence,* she told herself.

"I thought only to protect you. A lady alone needs a friend." He smiled again.

Once that charming smile would have fooled her. Now, she felt wary. "I am protected enough."

"Sir David? Your absent brother? I doubt it."

"Tell me the king's decision."

"Very well. I am directed to strengthen this castle—and marry the widow."

"Marry?" Her stomach knotted. The dog growled, bumped against her.

"I have the king's writ and seal upon it." He waved the rolled document still in his hand, ribbons fluttering from its glossy wax seal.

"Show me." He unrolled it quickly and closed it again, but she glimpsed her name, his, and the king's signature. A messy document, she saw, with blots and words crossed out or scraped away. "That looks written in haste."

"In times of war, decisions are made quickly."

"And if I refuse the order?"

"You cannot. As a widow, the king is your guardian and protector."

"I am Scottish. We do not recognize Edward as king."

"Is that a clever argument—or an admission of treason?" He took her arm again. Oonagh ruffed at him, but Tamsin soothed her with her free hand.

"Not treason. Truth."

"Marriage will benefit you. Your property is in my keeping now. You will stay in your home. Any woman wants that. But this must be done quickly." He waved the parchment.

"Banns take weeks," she protested. The blood pounded in her brain. *Married by All Souls, lost ... bound ...* She did not want that to become true.

"An exception has been made because Edward believes John Witton's widow is old and will not last long. He seemed to enjoy yoking me to a crone." He grinned. "I did not tell him that widow is young and lovely, with more to offer than property." His fingers caressed her upper arm and grazed down the side of her breast. She angled away. The dog growled again.

"Hush, Oonagh." She wanted to order the dog to pounce instead. Oonagh was a gentle creature, but on hind legs she stood taller than most men, and her powerful jaws could take down a wolf.

Heeding the dog's warning, Malise let go. "I will have Dalrinnie. And you. Trust that. I care for you, my dear. I always have, ever since you were Witton's young bride."

He said it so gently that Tamsin wanted to believe him—but she knew he could turn this way or that as it suited him. And just now, she was uncertain, fearful. After all, this offer was just another form of imprisonment.

Yet this marriage would allow her to stay at Dalrinnie, where she had a home apart from the garrison, had run a household, had found peace to work on her manuscript pages—the jumble of writings, poems, prophecies, and scraps of thought that old Thomas had entrusted to her, which she was slowly, carefully, copying over in neat pages. Because of her work, she was almost tempted to relent and stay. The alternative was a convent, and though she could write there, the rest of that life was not genuinely to her liking.

Malise sensed her moment of faltering, for he pushed the dog aside to take Tamsin's waist and pull her toward him. Oonagh tried to nudge between them as Tamsin pushed against his hard chest. He pulled her so close that she felt his need for her, a heavy pulse between them. Oonagh barked, gruff and low.

"Call off that hound before I have it killed for disobedience."

That ended any thought of relenting. "Leave my dog be," she snapped. "Oonagh, sit, girl! And sir, get your hands off me. You frighten me. Repulse me. And I will not marry you," she said, quiet and fierce.

"You do have a sharp tongue. Sir John once said his wee Scottish bride looked like a saint and was as biddable as a little demon. He was right."

"He said that?" Unaccountably, she felt hurt.

"But I like a spirited woman. You will not bore me." Malise glanced down at her breasts, pressed against him in the forced embrace. "We will get on well. You will have a virile husband who can put sons in your womb. The old man never did that for you."

She pushed in his arms. "No local priest would perform a marriage that I refuse."

"Then I will find one who will, and we will do this tomorrow."

"Let go!" Beside her, Oonagh made a threatening sound at the base of her throat. He let go suddenly. Tamsin stepped back, the dog buttressing her again.

"Listen well," Malise said. "I wonder what your kinsman, that old soothsayer, would tell you now. Will your brother survive? Are your sisters safe? Who will you marry? Sir John spoke of your kinsman. He said you are very like him. Prophecies, he said. Visions. Interesting."

Tamsin masked her surprise and a trickle of fear. "I do not know what you mean."

"Rhymer's daughter. That is what John said your family calls you. Is there a reason for that, other than kinship?"

She stood silent, heart pounding.

"So you do not admit to a gift of prophecy? Your husband said you have the tendency. He was not keen on it. But I rather think the king would be interested to know you are very much like your great-grandsire. He likes—to know the future."

"I cannot do that." *Not that I understand myself. Certainly not on command.*

"The king would be pleased. But he thinks you are an old woman." He laughed. "When he finds out—well, you can win his favor."

"I do not want his favor." She smoothed over her arms where he had gripped her.

"And if he wants me to marry you, he will be disappointed."

"Not just that. He wants the Rhymer's book."

She looked up, stilled, her heart pounding. "Book?"

"Your husband said you possess a certain book. Edward wants it."

Inwardly she reeled, grateful that Oonagh buttressed her. "Which book is that? I have many."

"Sir John said you have a book of the Rhymer's prophecies. Edward wants it. In return, you will have his thanks."

"He cannot order me to give up my books."

"But I can. A husband has the right to his wife's possessions."

"Sir John misunderstood what I have. Just a few of Thomas's songs and poems. Only a bard would be interested in those." Her mind raced. Something told her not to reveal that what she had was a collection of Thomas the Rhymer's prophecies, written on scraps of parchment and cloth over the many years of his life.

What had Sir John truly known of her work? He rarely asked what she worked on with her pages and inks. She thought he understood only that she wrote about her great-grandfather. He had called her a little monk and left her to it.

The harper, she thought suddenly. The man who had died—he had wanted something too, had a message for her. Did it also have to do with the Rhymer's work? Her heart pounded. She had given old Thomas her solemn promise to care for his work, to prepare clean pages, to protect his legacy. His family's legacy. Edward of England had no right to that. Only Thomas's kinfolk had the right.

"Give me the pages of the Rhymer's prophecies." Malise moved toward her.

"I do not have them," she blurted. "I gave them to a bookseller for the pages to be trimmed and bound." That was true. She had given the bookman a sheaf of pages to preserve for her family. Only for them.

"Where is this fellow?"

"I—I think he has a shop in Edinburgh," she said, flustered. "Selkirk too. He promised to deliver the book when the work was done."

"You lie," he ground out.

"I never lie." She stared, direct and defiant. She had said too much, she realized. But the Rhymer's blood flowed in her veins. Truth ran through her very being.

"A bookseller who also binds books should be easy enough to find in those towns. If I cannot get the pages, I shall bring *you* to Edward to prophesy for him."

She drew a shaky breath. "A lot of trouble for a few songs. We are done here. Good night, sir." She began to move away, the dog with her. Malise grabbed her arm again, and Oonagh gave a throaty woof.

"Listen to me," Malise said. "We will marry, or I will burn Dalrinnie to the ground. We will marry, or I will see the Keiths destroyed." His eyes went cold. His grip tightened. "You will tell the king what he wants to know—the defeat of Scotland. And, devil take it, I will have that book of you soon."

"Let go." She wrenched away, surprised he allowed it.

"Sir Malise." Siward approached. Tamsin looked up in relief. "Sir, we would ask for your opinion on this map." He glanced at Tamsin. "My lady?"

Campbell was just behind him. "My lady, you look pale. You should rest."

"Aye. Thank you. Good night," she said in haste, turning away. The dog followed.

"Sir Malise," Campbell said behind her. "The lady seems upset."

"The king's orders surprised her. But his decision is in her best interest."

CHAPTER EIGHT

"H E GAVE ME time to think," Tamsin told Lady Edith, "so I think I will leave now."

"This is madness," Lady Edith answered.

Grabbing a linen shift from inside a wooden chest, Tamsin tossed it to the growing pile of things she intended to take with her. "It is best."

Picking up the shift, Edith folded it. "You are making a mess and talking nonsense."

"I am perfectly calm." Tamsin balled up a pair of long, cream-colored woolen hose to add them to the rest. "I know what I need to do."

"Walk out the gate bold as brass with a satchel on your shoulder?" Edith pointed to the leather bag on the floor. "You would be stopped as soon as you are seen."

"Then I must not be seen." She threw a pair of leather slippers after the hose. "Not the gate. The window. With that." She pointed to the pile of bed linens coiled on the floor. In the middle of the night, while Lady Edith snored on a little cot in the corner, Tamsin had knotted together every bedsheet and linen towel she could find.

"Where would you go, even if you could get away? Lady Kirsty is at Thornhill now, but they say it may be taken by English soon. Her father would take you in."

"Sir Malise would send men there, knowing they are my

cousins." She sat back on her heels. "Edith, please, you must not tell anyone what I am doing."

Lady Edith sputtered. "I promised you I would not, even if it is lunacy."

"I am grateful. But I do not want you to be in trouble, so you must know very little." Last evening, she had told Lady Edith some of what had happened in the hall, enough to vent her anger and fear. It had been good to talk to the older woman about it.

"Shall I say I woke up to find the bed linens hanging out the window?"

"If you must. Sir Davey will make sure you are free of blame. I shall go to Kincraig to find my sisters," she continued. "I am determined."

"You are mad, is what you are." Lady Edith picked up the shoes and other things and shoved them into the satchel.

"I wish I had found my brother," Tamsin said, rummaging in the chest. "But they may have news of him at Kincraig. He intended to go there, at least by year's end."

"Stay here and we can send word to Kincraig once more. You have not heard back from them, last you sent word."

That was true. She only hoped her sisters were still there and that the place had not been affected by English takeover. "But if I stay here, I will be dragged to the church steps and married tomorrow. There is no time."

Edith sighed. "Aye then. What about the monastery at Holyoak? You have friends there. They would give you sanctuary until you come to your senses. The abbot is a kindly man. And that nice young monk let you use their library when we visited."

Tempted by the idea, she shook her head. "Sir Malise knows I have visited Holyoak. He might look for me there."

"Then go to Thornhill, to Kirsty and her father. It is closer than Kincraig. That is, if you can get even out of the castle with all these soldiers here. And do not ask my brother for help. Davey Campbell should not suffer for your foolishness." Even trying to be supportive, Edith had an edge.

A little thread of fear grew. Ignoring its pull, Tamsin glanced toward the window shuttered against the night air. A gap in the wooden panels showed darkness lifting toward dawn. She had only slept a little, restless all night thinking about the demands and the threats made by Malise and the king as well.

Leaving Dalrinnie seemed the only way to escape imminent marriage. Striving to be calm, Tamsin lifted a gown of dark gray wool from the wooden chest. The hem was embroidered with laurel sprigs, traditionally regarded as lucky by the Keiths, who displayed laurel on shields, garments, doorways, and in brooches for good fortune. The gown was comfortable and warm, and she needed some luck and fortitude.

"I will wear this." Stripping off her plain gown, she dropped the soft gray wool over her shift, belting it.

"Stay here. We will send a message to Baron Thornhill," Edith tried again. "Someone will come."

"I would be married by the time word reaches him." Closing the chest, Tamsin went to a small table, where she had collected some things to bring with her. She sorted through the items—a few small books, a leather pouch containing quills and lampblack for ink. Lastly, the beautifully polished wooden box that Thomas had given her, along with a packet of folded parchments wrapped in leather. "I must find my family. But first I must see the bookman in Selkirk before Comyn goes there. Malise wants what I gave the bookseller, you see."

"The one who came to Holyoak when you brought your pages there? What does Sir Malise want with those old scraps of writing you copied? Such a lot of work you did, and for what?" Edith shook her head. "It makes no sense to me."

"I did the work for my family. And I love doing it." She slid the books into a woolen sack.

"You could go to a convent. Lincluden is not far from Thornhill. That is, if you survive this mad scheme to leave here."

"I will. Edith—I want you to do something for me."

"I am doing enough," Lady Edith complained. "What else?"

"Oonagh. Tell Sir Davey—privately, please—that he must put her somewhere safe, and ask him to take care of her. She will miss me, and I do not want Sir Malise to catch sight of her. Please do that. I will worry so."

"Oh, fine. She is a good hound. I will tell Davey. Why are you taking more books? This is all madness! Here, you will need good shoes." Edith crammed slippers in with the books as she spoke.

Tamsin knew it was a mad scheme. Silent, she took up her blue and green plaid cloak and drew it over her shoulders, fastening it with the heavy silver and amber pin that had belonged to her mother. The pattern of dark colors would blend in the forest on her way to Selkirk, where she now realized she must go.

She would have to travel cautiously, even hide at times. Rebels lived in the forestland that covered the hills. If she encountered them, she could only pray they would aid a Scottish lady escaping the English.

Picking up a little book of hours, its boards wrapped in red leather, she handed it to Edith. "This too. And this." She took up a book of remedies that sat on a table.

"You and your books," Edith said, stuffing them in the sturdy bag of boiled wool. "This is too heavy for you to carry."

"I will be fine." She latched the buckle on the leather bag.

"Sir Malise will have an apoplexy when he finds you gone."

"Which is why I must leave while the castle is asleep."

"What if you meet outlaws?"

"I will pray they are friendly."

"You have an answer for everything. But this is a foolish thing you are doing."

"It may be. But I have to try." She rummaged in a small enameled box on a table, taking from it some coins, a jeweled pin, and two gold rings, which she dropped into the embroidered purse on her belt. She would need to pay her way here and there.

Her heart pounded. Truly, she was terrified. But she had no choice.

"Edward of England will be furious." Lady Edith gave it a final try.

"He has worse troubles than a young woman running from a marriage."

"He could take out his anger on your brother. And your sisters."

Her hands stilled on the pouch. Fear rose again, but she shook her head. "Henry is in the king's good graces. He has some privilege now. I did not agree with his choice to ride for Edward, but he was wise to seek protection there."

"Perhaps, but where is he when you need him?"

Malise had hinted that Henry was in danger. Hands shaking, Tamsin opened another box tucked on a shelf and took out a slim leather sheath with a small ivory-handled dagger within. The engraved steel blade gleamed in the candlelight.

"*Veritas vincit*," she read. "Truth conquers. The ancient motto of the Keith clan."

"Being truthful is not always helpful to you Keiths," Edith muttered.

"Aye well." Tamsin looked toward the window, where light infused the darkness. "I must go before dawn breaks."

She embraced Edith, who clung to her. "At least try the door. If you can go that way, you will not risk a broken neck. Silly lass."

"Very well." Shouldering the leather satchel and the heavy woolen bag, she went to the door, eased it open, then closed it quickly.

"There is a guard outside," she whispered. "Sleeping by the steps. Malise must have sent him. I must go out the window. Please, Edith, help me."

She went to the window, pulling open the shutter to a fresh blast of cold air. "I knotted one end of the linens to the stone pillar. Help me test it."

Together they tugged on the fabric. "It will hold," Edith declared. "But it is a far drop to the ground."

"Henry taught me to climb ropes when we were children. It

was a game we played. Our mother hated it," she added, kneeling on the seat beneath the window that was set with thick glass above and shutters below. She opened the shutters farther and leaned to look out.

Her cloak blew back and her hair lifted in loose tendrils. The tower was a dizzying height, and she saw that the ground was still coated with a light snowfall from two days earlier. Snow in October was unusual, and the grass would be slippery.

Something tapped at her memory and fled.

"Wait," Edith said. "We will go to market and you could slip away then."

"I tell you, I will be married before then if Comyn has his way. Nor would he let me go anywhere without a close escort." Again, something flitted through her mind, just beyond her racing thoughts and rising panic.

This was lunacy. She gazed out over a canopy of dark treetops. Dawn was just a slight lifting of gray, the crescent moon still high. The castle perched on a slope that descended toward forestland that spread thick, dense, and dark for miles. She could hide there and travel for quite a distance on her way to Selkirk.

She knew of a tavern along the road where she could go directly, perhaps hire a horse, even a cart and driver. But she had to go. The alternative was unthinkable.

With Edith's help, she hauled the makeshift rope of silken and linen sheets and blankets to the window. "It seems sturdy," she said, tugging again.

"Madness," Edith said.

"I cannot carry these down with me." Tamsin picked up the leather satchel and dropped it out the window, hearing the thud as it hit the ground. Next she sent the heavy woolen bag, praying her books and pages would not be damaged. Taking off her cloak, she sent it spinning downward. "Now I have to go. My things are down there."

"You will freeze to death. You will break your neck. You are deranged."

"I am desperate. I love you, Edith," she said impulsively. "Farewell. I will see you soon, I swear it. Soon we will be safe. All of us." Somehow, she thought.

Drawing a breath against fear, she sought the boldness she needed for this. Dalrinnie was no longer her home and haven. She would find her siblings and find the Rhymer's bound book, and keep it safe from Edward.

Setting her hands on the cold stone frame, wind nipping her cheeks, she boosted herself up to the sill, blew out a breath, and slid one leg out the window to find the makeshift rope with her foot. Straddling the sill, feeling the strength of the cold breeze now, she grabbed the linen draped over the stone framing and stretched her other foot downward to find the fat knot. Her gown billowed around her legs, and in an oddly ordinary thought, she was glad to have worn woolen hose.

Hands gripping thick fabric, she slowly, cautiously sought the next knot as her skirts blew in the breeze. Down and down she went, knot to knot, swinging on the rumpled line like a clapper in a bell.

One of her boots loosened and fell. Cold wrapped her foot, but her step was sure on the rope. Pausing, she glanced down.

Then she remembered the dream. The knight. Herself on the rope. It was true. Some of it, at least. The rest was foolish, she thought. No one was there to catch her.

She went slowly, carefully. The wind batted her about like a willow wand as she inched downward.

CHAPTER NINE

S OMETHING MOVED HIGH on the castle wall. A bird? A shadow? Liam peered through the screen of autumn-bare trees and walked toward the edge of the forest. Dawn was coming in gray and dim, promising a cold day with rain, even snow. He had come back to this place in darkness, planning to hail the castle once the portcullis opened. Gilchrist and Finley were to meet him here but had not yet arrived. They would find his horse tied to a tree, nosing about to breakfast on grasses.

His nail-soled boots crunched on the frosted, fallen leaves as he walked. He patted Roc's head as the dog moved quietly beside him. A scatter of birds left the trees as he made his way toward the steep hill that supported the massive fortress.

Roc gave a low, breathy woof, and froze, watching through the trees. Something had his attention. Liam looked, hardly believing his eyes.

A fat rope had been slung out a high window, and someone clung to it, moving down. With a surprised huff, Liam walked closer, blinking in surprise.

A girl, climbing down a rope of linens. Liam's heart lurched in fear for her. She was slight, determined, and could fall to her death at any moment. Slowly he began to ascend the slope, not wanting to be seen, not wanting to startle her.

Reaching the ridge, he saw a litter of things on the ground—bags, a cloak, a small boot. Pausing there, he looked up. The wind pushed the girl's rope and belled his cloak. She must be desperate to do this.

Well, no lass would break her neck on his watch, he thought. "Roc, stay," he murmured. Boots crunching over snow, he walked to stand just beneath her, looking up. The rope dangled out a familiar window. The master's chamber. He narrowed his eyes.

Jesu, he thought. It could not be. Yet, seeing the young woman's pale braid furl outward, seeing her lithe form, her determination, he knew she was Lady Tamsin.

He had come here to find her, and here she was, swinging not twenty feet above his head. Divine timing for both, should the lass fall. He waited.

She paused to look down. The rope spun a little. Her feet had come to rest on the last knot. There was still a good height between that knot and the ground. Liam sighed and lifted his arms.

"Down to me." He spoke calmly, wanting to reassure rather than startle.

Swaying, she gazed down at him. Light spread across the sky, glossed the snow, kissed her gray gown and her long blond plait. Liam beckoned. "Come down."

"I cannot." She looked up, then down. "I will fall."

"I will catch you." He opened his gloved hands.

"You will summon the guards."

"You are safe. I give you my word." Even hushed, his voice sounded too loud.

She swayed. "Who are you?"

"Jump." He beckoned. "Do not fear."

"If I was fearful, I would not be on this rope."

"True." He widened his arms. "Jump!"

She let go.

Liam sank to his knees as the girl filled his arms, her weight less burden than the force of her fall. Swathed in skirts, she was trim and light. Gasping, she clung to him, head on his shoulder.

Bracing a hand on the ground, he rose to his feet holding her.

"There," he said, as relieved as she must be. "There."

She pushed away, found her feet, stepped back. "Thank you, sir. I am fine." Turning to pick up her scattered things, she stumbled and fell to a knee.

Liam grabbed her arm. "Go easy."

"I must hurry." She glanced up at the castle walls. "They will come after me."

"No one has seen you, I think. Come with me." He gestured down the slope toward the forest.

She stepped back. "Who are you? Why are you here?"

He knew her. But then he realized that she did not recognize the harper, seeing a knight in chain mail, a stranger, a threat. But there was no time to explain. Silently he picked up her things— two bags, a cloak, a narrow boot.

Draping the cloak over her shivering shoulders, he braced her arm while she hopped to pull and lace the boot. Then he tossed the bags on his shoulder—one had real weight to it—and led her down the slope.

"Careful, the hill is icy." He took her arm, balancing her baggage on one shoulder. Roc, pacing and eager, ran toward them and went straight to the girl rather than Liam.

Astonished, he watched his dog nudge her as if greeting a friend. If he rose on his hind legs, he might knock her over. Liam steadied her.

"Roc, down! Good lad." He reached out to pat the dog as she did, their hands meeting, his gloved, hers pink and raw from climbing in the cold. "I apologize," Liam said. "He would pull you over just to show he is glad to meet you."

"He is friendly," she said. Roc licked her hand and woofed in delight. "Perhaps he smells my dog on me and my clothing. He is very like my dog," she added, reaching out to pat him.

"He is not usually this friendly with a stranger, so it may be that he has the scent of your hound. You must tell me about yours," he added. The mention of a dog inside Dalrinnie caught his keen attention. "Down, Roc. This way, my lady."

"My lady? Do you know me?"

He was glad for the shadow of his coif and hood. "Would a serving maid slide out a window on silken sheets? Or wear a fine embroidered gown? Good Lord," he said, shouldering her bags. "What is in this thing? Rocks? No, not you, Roc," he added as the dog woofed. "I am talking to Lady Tamsin."

She stopped short. "You do know me. But I do not know you."

"This is Dalrinnie, is it not? And you, its lady? You are in a hurry and in some sort of trouble, I would guess. We had best not linger where we might be seen. Questions later. This way." He led her deeper into the woodland.

"Why should I go with you?"

"Shall I drop your things here?" He stopped.

"Perhaps, since I do not know you or where we might be going." She drew up the hood of her plaid cloak, shivering a little.

"Given the manner of your exit, someone will be looking for you. It seems to me you need help. So I am helping you."

With an impatient sigh, she stomped ahead, passing him, her boots crunching snow and bracken. In her haste, she stumbled over a tree root and fell to her hands and knees. Helping her up, Liam set an arm around her shoulders to guide her. For a moment, she set an arm about his waist as if to help him too. That gesture of trust surprised him.

"You are limping. Did I hurt you when I fell on you? I am sorry."

"Old injury."

"Truly I am indebted to you, sirrah. I do not mean to be ungrateful. But have we met? You seem familiar." She tilted her head, looking up at him. He tugged at the hood of his gray cloak and half turned away.

"I am a knight in the king's service."

She gasped. "King Edward? But—you do not wear the kit of an English soldier."

"Later for that. Trust me or not." Again, he took her arm.

He had to think. Providence had dropped Lady Tamsin, as if from heaven, literally into his lap. He had come here to find the widow and the book, finding that Sir Malise Comyn had arrived at Dalrinnie before him. Though he might have saved the lass, she had saved him from knocking at the gate, and receiving a possible knock to the head for it.

Why would she take that desperate route? Was the infamous book in her bag, or did Malise Comyn have it by now? The man had practically begged Edward to let him obtain it, though Edward—out of spite, perhaps—gave the task to a rebel.

First, get the lass to safety. Then sort this out.

Ahead, he heard a quiet hoot among the trees. Gilchrist stepped into sight, and the lady pulled back.

"They found me," she gasped.

"Easy. He is not with the Dalrinnie garrison." The lad's accursed red-and-gold surcoat had alarmed her.

"Liam, we must go. Is she coming with us?" Gilchrist, who had likely seen Tamsin's escape, acted as if a lass dangling on a rope and falling into his brother's arms was nothing unusual.

"Nay," she said.

"Aye," Liam said at the same time.

"Will you seek entrance to the castle?" Gilchrist asked.

"It is not necessary now." The lady was in his keeping, and he would prefer not to bang on Dalrinnie's gates without an army at his back.

"Who are you?" The girl looked from one to the other. "Have we met? You both look familiar. What do you want at Dalrinnie?"

"We are not Comyn's men if that worries you," Liam said.

Her cloud-colored eyes narrowed. "How did you know Comyn is there?"

"They made quite a clamor riding in. Hard to miss. I came here—" He stopped. "I came here for you, lass."

"For me?" She stared up at him. Her cheeks, pink with cold, went pale.

"But you seem eager to escape, so we will do that." He took her elbow. Without protest, she came along beside him.

Ahead, Gilchrist cleared the way with long steps, crushing bracken and slipping between trees until they reached a small clearing where Finley waited by the horses. The dog bounded ahead and turned to wait for the others.

"By the saints, what a brave thing, lass! Are ye hurt?" Finley asked. "What bad thing would make a wee girl jump out a window like that?"

"I did not jump. I climbed down."

"Is she coming with us, then?" Finley asked his cousins.

"I would advise it, but we should ask the lady," Liam said.

"I can go along by myself now. Thank you. I thought to head to the high road, where there is a tavern. I can hire a horse or a cart there."

"Hire us," Finley said. "We will take you where you need to go."

"We are not mercenaries. Where do you want to go?" Liam asked.

"I must find—a friend in Selkirk who can help me."

"The lass can ride with me." Gilchrist set foot to stirrup to remount. "We should go now. Someone will discover she is missing soon." He beckoned toward her.

Cradling his hands for her foot, Liam boosted her to his brother's horse. She settled on the blanket behind the saddle, legs to one side, used to riding as any lady would. Liam set his hands at her waist briefly to ensure she was stable, sensing her slim, firm body beneath her cloak and gown. Then he stepped back.

Gripping Gilchrist's belt, she looked down at Liam. "Thank you."

He nodded and crossed to his horse, lashing her bags to his saddle, then setting foot to iron stirrup to launch into his seat. "What makes these sacks so heavy? Did you take the iron candlesticks when you left?"

"Books," she answered.

"Books! A curious thing to take in a hurry."

"I like books."

"Do you now?" he murmured.

"Please," she said suddenly, "I do not want to go back to the castle."

"If we intended that, you would be back inside the gates already," Liam said.

"I want to trust you, even though you are English soldiers, but—"

"Scottish knights all," Gilchrist assured her, "and we know how to treat a lass."

"Scottish knights ride for England, too," she said.

No one answered as they set out. It was an uncomfortable truth, Liam thought, riding ahead. Saving the girl from a disastrous fall was excitement enough, but important questions remained. Her books, heavy on his saddle, weighed on his mind.

Finley moved ahead then to lead the group along a narrow well-trodden path that wound toward the high road. Roc, the hound, trotted along beside them, then ahead, pausing now and again to nose around, investigate, and catch up.

Finley turned. "Lady, was it Sir Malise or his men after you?"

"You know Sir Malise?"

"Aye, we all do. If you need to get away from him, we are glad to help."

Liam glanced at her. "The lady must have had good reason to pitch out a tower window on the laundry."

"I did. Besides, my door was guarded so it was the only way out."

"Guarded on Comyn's order?"

She nodded. Yet another reason to throttle the man, Liam thought.

He saw that her head was bare, her blond braid unkempt, a creamy ribbon unraveling along its length. So she did not wear the linen coif she wore at Lochmaben. That told him she had been in a rush to escape.

"You claim to be Scots, not Comyn's men, yet two of you wear Edward's colors." Her arms were snug around Gilchrist's waist, bunching his red surcoat with its golden lions. Finley wore the same. She looked at Liam. "But not you."

"I dislike wearing Edward's brand on my back." On his mail sleeve, he wore the Seton badge, three red crescents on yellow. The painted shield suspended from his saddle bore the second part of the arms, golden shields on dark blue. He would not wear Edward's lions willingly. In the forest days ago, he had reclaimed his old dark blue surcoat and chain mail; his studded boots were worn but sturdy, and his gray cloak was lined with tartan cloth woven by his mother. Though he had lost Dalrinnie, his loyalty to the Seton name endured.

"Under oath to Edward, like most," Gilchrist said, "but not assigned to Comyn or any castle hereabouts. We ride free for now. And that one does as he pleases."

"I do not know your names." She looked at Liam again. "And you, sir, I would swear upon the Virgin that I know you, though I cannot think where."

"We may have met." He would keep his old mail coif up and pray for shadows until he could explain all. "Lads, I should introduce Lady Thomasina Keith of Dalrinnie Castle." His kinsmen would know what it took for him to say it.

"My lady. I am Sir Gilchrist Seton. That one is my brother, Sir William Seton. And this brawny lad is our cousin, Sir Finley Macnab."

"Seton?" She paused. "I know that from somewhere—well, it is good to meet you. And Sir William, thank you for saving my life."

"You would have been fine had the rope been long enough." Liam gave her a fleeting smile. "Once we reach the tavern, where will you go?"

"I must travel east to Selkirk, then northeast to find my kin."

"A long way for a lady alone. Selkirk is a long way through the heart of the forest."

"We are heading that way," Gilchrist said. "Liam?"

"Aye. You have business in Selkirk, my lady, and friends there?"

"I do. Could you take me through the forest to Selkirk? I would be grateful. I could offer payment."

"We are not mercenaries," Liam said again.

Her smile was shy, prim. Whatever she was about in Selkirk, she would not share it. If she had friends there, he wanted to be sure of it and not leave her on her own. As before, a powerful need to protect her—though he knew little of her—rushed through him.

"We can take you there. Better than danger finding you," he said.

"It is just an errand in Selkirk. A merchant. Then I must be on my way again."

"A lady escaping from a tower needs to buy something pretty," Finley said.

"Not that," she said. "I have all I need."

"Books, perhaps," Liam ventured. "You like them."

She flashed a look at him, her gray eyes intelligent, stubborn, and surprised. Yet she smiled, impish and perfect. The lady had secrets, he thought. And a hidden strength to her, as if her fragile golden beauty hid the heart of a lion, even a dragon.

Thomas the Rhymer's kinswoman fascinated him. And from what King Edward had said, that mysterious book held something important. He frowned.

"Before we head toward Selkirk," he said, "we have an errand at Holyoak Abbey near St. Mary's Loch."

"I know that abbey. I have been there."

Now that was interesting too. Even more, he wanted to know why she fled Dalrinnie and what she needed in Selkirk. "My lady—"

"Lads," Finley said, holding up a hand for quiet. "Listen."

Liam tilted his head, then heard the blast of a horn cutting through the gloom of the cold early dawn. Another blast. He swore under his breath. "They are alerted now."

"Where might they look for you, my lady?" Gilchrist asked.

"Kincraig or Thornhill, I think, where I have kin."

"Those are north and west. We will go east toward the forest," Liam said.

"Are you rebels, you three?" she asked suddenly.

Silence. Then Finley chuckled. "Decked in Edward's gear?"

"If you were King Edward's men," she continued, "perhaps you would know where to find Sir Henry Keith. My brother."

"We know the man," Gilchrist said, "but we do not know where he might be now."

"Sir Malise said he was sent on an errand for King Edward. A dangerous errand."

"We know nothing of that. Sorry." Gilchrist shrugged.

"If we cannot find him, perhaps I should go to Lanercost and ask to see King Edward myself. I have questions for him."

Liam sent her a quick scowl. "That is an odd plan, lady."

"No odder than a knight watching my castle before dawn."

"Or a lass making her way down the bedsheets," he drawled. "We were traveling this way to take the hound to a friend. But we spied a kitten up a tree."

"Is the kitten saved now—or is she caught by wolves?"

"Trust us, or do not. Either way, you are safe," he assured her.

"Sir," she said after a moment, "why take your hound to a monastery?"

"I am away for long weeks and do not have the household I once had. Roc stays at Holyoak with other hounds in the monks' care."

"The hounds of Holyoak?" She stared at him. "I have seen them there. My husband admired them too. I visited there sometimes to see the books," she offered. "Abbot Murdoch permitted me to read in their library. He is a kind man."

"He is," Liam said. "He cares for books and hounds and looks after souls as well."

"Do the monks train the dogs for hunting? My husband thought so."

"If a lord asks it, aye. I trained Roc myself, in the days before... Well, we—my kin—once bred and raised gaze hounds, but no longer. Times have changed." His father, another Baron William, and Sir David Campbell, too, had taught Liam and his brothers to work with the once-famed hounds of Dalrinnie.

"Were you hunting with Roc this morning? 'Twas early and cold for it."

"I might have, but Roc spotted a lovely creature in distress, so—" He shrugged.

"He is a fine hound. Wolfhound, they call the breed? But such a dog is not—"

"Not for the likes of me, a mere knight?" He was not just that, but no need to say so. He merely lifted a brow and her cheeks went high pink. "Wolfhounds are prized and allowed only for earls and dukes and kings? Those are English rules," he said. "In Scotland, fine dogs belong with fine masters, no matter who they are."

"He seems an excellent dog, with a worthy master. I do not hunt. I enjoy the outing and the chase, but not the taking down. My father cared deeply for his hounds and his hawks. And my husband had a pair of very fine dogs at Dalrinnie."

He exchanged glances with Gilchrist at that. The hounds of Dalrinnie belonged to the Setons. Liam wanted to know more—how many remained there, what was their health, did Sir Davey watch over them still.

"You have hounds like Roc at Dalrinnie?" He dared ask only that.

"Just one now. Oonagh, she is called. She is like Roc, tall and gray and gentle."

Oonagh. His heart bounded. He had raised her from a pup. "Is she safe there with you gone?" He had to ask.

"I would not leave her to Sir Malise, I will tell you that," she said briskly. "I asked a friend to watch after her."

"Good. They are handsome and dignified and aye, gentle, these dogs. As loyal a friend as one could have," he said. "Sight hounds, they call them, or gaze hounds, for their long sharp vision out in the field. Your husband had others?"

"Another, an older male. He died last summer. They do not live many years."

Colla. A brindled hound raised at Dalrinnie—perhaps the father of Oonagh's puppies. "True. Eight years is a good long life for a gaze hound."

"A pity. They are majestic guardians. Oonagh makes it her work to watch over me. I worry she will fret when she cannot find me at Dalrinnie. But the seneschal will watch after her."

"I am glad." He truly was.

"Oh! There is the horn again! Are they coming this way?" She turned.

Liam glanced back, seeing nothing much. "It sounds distant. They may have headed in another direction. But we may have a parcel of trouble if we linger. Come on."

After a while, they reached the wider road as the clouds brightened, still silvery and cold. Finley, slowing to come even with them, smiled.

"Look at us, three fine knights, a bonny lass, and a handsome wolfhound. Though it be autumn, we look like a May Day party. All we need is ribbons, bells—and a harper," he added with a wink at Liam, who gave him a glower in return.

"No harper here," Gilchrist drawled, as Finley laughed.

Riding behind the others, Liam shook his head. He was used to Finley teasing him about the Irish harp he played. Sadly, he had lost that handsome instrument the night Comyn had taken him down. Escaping, he had gone back to find it, but it was lost. He flexed his fingers as if to touch its strings.

"Lady, no ribbons or bells, no harp in your satchels?" Finley was in good spirits.

"The lady has books," Liam said. Finley made a wry face and Gil laughed, but Liam still frowned. He needed to know if she brought with her the volume he sought. Eyeing the woolen bag slung from his saddle pommel, he gave it a poke. Aye, books.

Rescuing the lady might prove lucky after all, a welcome spark of hope in this grim travesty thrust upon him by King Edward.

"Harp!" She turned to look at him. "You are the harper!"

CHAPTER TEN

"STOP," TAMSIN SAID, tapping Sir Gilchrist's shoulder. "Please, stop."

"But lady, we could be pursued," he answered.

"Just for a moment. I must talk to the harp—to Sir William." She glanced at that knight, her heart pounding and temper rising.

"Liam?" Gilchrist Seton looked back at his brother.

Sir William—not Wat of Selkirk, and not dead in the least—reined in his horse, as did Gilchrist and Finley. Dismounting, Liam Seton came toward her to lift her down. His hands were sure at her waist. She slid to the ground, boots to earth, and stared at him.

"You are not dead!"

"Should I be? Come here," he barked, taking her hand to lead her to the side of the road, while the others waited. Finley tossed a stick for the wolfhound to fetch. The dog watched it go with disdain.

Sir William turned to Tamsin. "What do you mean, 'not dead'?"

"What do you mean by posing as a knight? Or were you posing as a harper?"

"Both."

"I am confused—Sir Knight, Master Harper. Which is true?"

"Both," he said. "So you thought me dead? You seem angry to find otherwise."

"Nay!" She glared at him, then sighed, and shook her head. "Nay. I am just surprised. Relieved. We saw them attack you that night. Master Brewer, all of us, believed you were killed." Tears stung as she looked at him, searching his face, his eyes, blue as a patch of winter sky, his expression grave as he listened. "But you are alive, thank the saints."

"I do thank them," he murmured. "And I am sorry you saw the ambush, my lady."

"But what happened after? How is it you are here, a king's knight instead of a harper? I do not understand." She shook her head, strands of her night braid slipping loose. She pushed them back.

"I was injured, I admit. But I managed to get away and find friends. I recovered."

"Good. But if you are a knight, why did you act the harper at Lochmaben?"

"I enjoy the harp." He glanced at his waiting kinsmen. "Lady, we must ride."

"I thought you dead, and I was heartbroken. I thought I caused your death."

"You had naught to do with what happened to me that night."

"But I did. You came to Lochmaben to find me."

"Did I?" His eyes narrowed. She saw that his irises were ice blue, dark-lashed, startling and beautiful. How had she not recognized him earlier? But in the mail coif, in surcoat and chain mail, in shadows, he looked different. And she had been distracted, fleeing Dalrinnie.

"Liam," Sir Finley called. Sir William held up a hand to quiet him.

"You said you were looking for the lady of Dalrinnie that night," she went on.

"I was."

"You said you had a message for me. But you called yourself Wat of Selkirk. And now you are William Seton—" She gasped as a memory flashed, surfaced.

Seton—the name of the lord of Dalrinnie before her husband took it. She had forgotten that entirely until now. She knew little about the previous family, and yet—he had come to Dalrinnie. Was he one of those Setons? And she had seen him in a dream that came about, at least in part. A ripple went through her, an awareness of something more afoot.

"Whoever you are," she continued, "you were looking for me. Lady Thomasina, you said. That is me. So aye, it is because of me that Sir Malise went after you."

"Listen to me. I will explain, but not here. We must go. Now what?" He tipped his head, those eyes seeing beyond her silence, her thoughts. "There is something more."

He had a way of echoing her very thoughts. But he was right, they had to move ahead. She would have to save her questions. "I am just glad you are well, Sir Harper."

"So am I." He led her back to the others. "The lady will ride with me now," he said. As he mounted his horse and reached down for her, Gilchrist boosted her up to sit sideways behind him.

"Wait. I can ride astride," she said. "Without the proper saddle, riding pillion is more comfortable." She swung a leg nimbly over the horse's back, tucked her skirts and spread her plaid cloak. Then she grasped Sir William's wide leather belt.

They took the wide cobbled road heading south and eastward. After a while, Tamsin hugged her arms around William Seton's waist and leaned against him. She felt secure there. Grateful that luck and the angels were with her in the form of three knights willing to help, and a lovely hound who reminded her of gentle Oonagh.

Now she realized why Sir William had looked so familiar. He was the harper. Yet Sir Gilchrist looked oddly familiar too, though she could not place him. Perhaps it was a resemblance to his brother, the one dark, the other fair. For now, with the earlier sense of threat fading, she felt only relief.

Glancing at William Seton's profile, she saw him frown, somber and thoughtful. Was he annoyed by the obligation and delay of helping her? Or did something else, private and deep, trouble him?

As a Seton, what was his connection to Dalrinnie? And more importantly, what was the king's message that he had carried weeks ago, as the harper? He had not said.

And which was true—king's knight, harper, outlaw—or all of those?

Well, he was not a very good harper, she recalled, and there must be more to his story than he had let on so far. How odd that he had come to Dalrinnie just as Malise Comyn had arrived with the king's demands. Did William Seton bear the same message?

She could not sort it all out. Resting her forehead on his cloaked back, weary, fraught, she closed her eyes.

"Lady." He looked back. "We are six leagues away from Holyoak, where my kinsmen and I must stop. Can you ride that far?" The morning light made his blue eyes striking when she craned to meet his gaze. Her heart surged.

"I am fine," she said.

She watched him further, curious. Though he seemed only a few years older than her, perhaps thirty, concern had hardened his handsome features, etching fine lines at the corners of his eyes and mouth. His jaw was covered in a scruff of dark beard, but the full curve of his lips gave a hint of tenderness. He had dropped back the chain mail coif to reveal thick, glossy waves of brown hair streaked with gold. Earlier, had she seen him without the coif, seen those ice-blue eyes under dark brows, she would have known the harper straightaway.

Despite the perpetual scowl he had today, she thought, he had a singular and tough beauty. Riding through gray mist, he seemed the soul of strength and humility, a warrior-angel. She wanted, needed, to trust him, yet inching toward it, held back.

"Thank you," she said. "I do not wish to be any trouble."

"You are no trouble. Clearly you wanted to leave Dalrinnie."

She hesitated. "Sir Malise asked something of me that I would not do."

"Did he," he drawled. "I will speak to him about it if you like."

She nearly laughed. "I will leave that to you."

The hound ran past them, then turned to wait for the riders. Gilchrist surged ahead, Roc chasing alongside, while Finley dropped back to speak with William.

"Gilchrist is going ahead to make sure the way is clear," Finley said. "Where will you go after Selkirk, my lady? It is hardly safe for you to travel on your own."

"Kincraig, my family's castle. Though I ought to go to Thornhill to fetch my cousin. She could travel with me." She glanced at William Seton. The harper would remember Lady Kirsten Douglas, but he gave no sign.

Finley shook his head. "There is danger in traveling, especially for a woman, especially to those areas. The English are planning to take castles like Thornhill and Kincraig, if they can. Surely you heard of it at Dalrinnie."

She felt a frisson of alarm. "I heard nothing. Will my cousin be safe there?"

"Baron Thornhill sympathizes with Edward, which may count in their favor. Taking a castle down is not an easy thing to manage and may not happen quickly."

"They may have more news of English movements at Holyoak," William said.

Sir Gilchrist rode back. "All clear. Mist all about, and sleet beginning. Sheep on the hillsides, and the road empty north and south. This poor weather will keep others off the roads, but we should hasten for shelter. I do not like the look of those clouds, Liam."

"Holyoak is a fair distance yet. Those clouds threaten rain, perhaps even snow in this damp cold," his brother replied. "We can stop at the inn ahead for the lady's sake and rest the horses before we go to the abbey. This weather is unusual for October and should not last."

As they spoke, rain began to fall in tiny, icy pellets. Tamsin shivered in the bitter wind. "Are we safe on the high road?"

"For now," Gilchrist said. "English troops come up by road and water. But we will keep careful watch. Edward may send more men to Dalrinnie."

Sir William glanced at her. "Did you hear aught of plans at Dalrinnie?"

"They were looking at maps and talking of Bruce. But I do not know their plans, other than they intend to find Robert Bruce however they can. Could Sir Malise find us out here, do you think?"

"All too possible. I imagine there is quite a stir at Dalrinnie over your absence."

"Should I ask sanctuary at Holyoak? You are a worthy escort, but he could—"

"Bad as that, to need sanctuary?" He glanced back.

"He will be in a temper over this," she admitted.

"A monastery cannot house a woman alone for long except in the hospital there. They would send you to a convent, likely Lincluden Priory. For now, know that Dalrinnie's Scottish bride is safe with us, aye?"

That was what Sir John had called her. "Scottish widow."

"Just so. Why is Comyn so determined to find you? Did you steal plate or goods? Done murder or harm?" His lips quirked.

"Much of the plate and goods are mine. He wants me back for other reasons."

"There are easier exits than the tower. I wonder you did not take the tunnel that leads outside the walls."

Tamsin stared. "Tunnel?"

"From the tower to the postern gate. Surely you knew."

She shook her head. "I did not. How do you know of it?"

"A guess. Many older castles of that type have just such an escape in case of attack. How long have you been at Dalrinnie?"

"Over two years. But I never heard of a tunnel. My husband

never mentioned it."

"Perhaps he never knew. He was not the original owner."

"I heard little of that one. Only that he was away from Dalrinnie when it was taken." He went silent and she felt a strange tension rolling from him that began to build in her. He guided the horse, then spoke over his shoulder.

"That makes the taking of a castle easier when the owner is gone."

She would venture it. "Seton. That was the name of the previous lord. Your kin?"

"There are many Setons around, some in this region." He looked up at the gray and drizzling sky. "With luck, the weather will not worsen."

He seemed distracted beyond the moment. Something burdened him, a weight upon his heart. She desperately wanted to ask but could only wish him peace with it.

"You know more about me than I know about you, I think," she said.

"That may be."

They all rode in silence now, the weather worsening. Each step of the horses' hooves was wary and the men watched the icing grass, the hills, and the sky where the very clouds seemed to freeze. Drawing her hood higher against the cold rain, Tamsin huddled against the knight's shielding back, so tired she nearly dozed.

"Weary, Lady Tamsin? Rest if you can. Soon we will stop."

LIAM STRETCHED HIS legs before the fire, sighing as warmth radiated through the damp leather of his boots. Lifting a wooden cup, he took another sip of heather ale, recognizing its subtle flavor as a brew made by the monks of Holyoak. The abbey provided its excellent ale to local inns, religious houses, and a few local nobles, though they declined to sell to English garrisons. He smiled a little, remembering that.

Icy rain pattered against the window shutters and the oiled parchment stretched across casements that made the interior cozy but dim. Best stay inside for now, he thought; they would reach the abbey before dark if weather permitted. He closed his eyes, savoring the warmth and peace here. They were the only guests for now, the innkeeper and his wife moving quietly between kitchen and main room. Relaxed yet aware, Liam listened for horses in the yard, hearing only wind and sleet.

Lady Tamsin sat beside him, her slim fingers crumbling a bit of bannock. She sipped hot broth from the cup Dame Brown, the wife, had provided. Seated nearby, Gilchrist and Finley chatted with the innkeeper's wife as she set down another plate of oatcakes, hot from the griddle, a pot of butter, and a jug of ale.

He watched Tamsin Keith. She had a quiet strength and did not complain, though the day had been arduous for her. He had scant patience for fuss and weakness, and she showed none of that. He sensed she was resilient and astute, her fragility only on the surface. She was determined and was hiding something. He would wager good coin it had to do with that bothersome book.

"All is well?" he asked.

"The warmth and hot meal are welcome, I vow. Can we stay long?" A plaintive note in her voice told him how tired she was.

"For a bit. Dalrinnie is well behind us, and anyone following should be well behind us too, in this icy rain." But patrols rode out in any weather, he knew. Glancing out the window, he noted the long empty curve of the road, cloaked in mist.

Yet an uneasy feeling lingered.

Roc nosed out from under the table, and the lady slipped him a tidbit, then patted his head. He noticed the girl shivering in her gray gown, still damp, her plaid cloak drying by the fireside with the knights' cloaks.

As Dame Brown moved toward him to refill his cup, he smiled at her. "Holyoak's ale," he said. "I know the taste."

"And fine stuff it is, sir. It is good to have customers here in such weather. We have had no one here today until you lot. Are you heading north?"

"On our way to Holyoak Abbey, as it happens."

"Ah, good folk, the monks, generous with their prayers and their gardens, and they even keep a small hospital. Are ye ill, sir, or your lady? No? That's fine, then. They raise fine dogs there, like your own. They even have a room filled with books, I hear, which some ride far to see."

"So I hear," Liam said, with a glance for Lady Tamsin, who was buttering an oatcake. "I will give them your compliments on the ale, good Dame."

The woman nodded, then peered at him. "Do I know you, sir?"

Liam wished he had kept his cloak's hood up. "I have been here now and then."

"Perhaps a customer, aye. But you look very much like the—"

"And you may have seen my brothers in the area," he said, as Lady Tamsin sent him a curious glance. "The oatcakes were excellent. If you have something more, we would be hungry enough."

"I have a good barley soup in the kettle and will bring that for you." She beamed. "I know! You remind me of the lord what was at Dalrinnie years back. He was older but had grown sons—och, but the English took the place, did they not, and an Englisher came instead. He died as well, I heard. My lady, will you have more broth?"

"Thank you, Dame, perhaps soup," she said, turning a curious gaze on Liam.

"Hot soup will take the chill away." The wife hurried away.

Liam blew out a breath. Soon Lady Tamsin would either guess or discover his past and his ties to Dalrinnie. He was in no hurry to hasten that revelation.

"After we eat," Gilchrist said, "we should leave for the abbey."

"Aye," Liam agreed, as Dame Brown returned with a tray holding wooden bowls slopping over with steaming soup, which they quickly discovered was hearty with shredded meat, barley, and vegetables.

"I am sorry to have disturbed your plans," Tamsin said.

"The weather did that more than you," he said. "We are glad to help. We will get you safely where Comyn cannot reach you, and then be on our way." Liam tilted his ale cup, dark liquid and slight foam remaining. In part, he would welcome a chance to confront Comyn over his treatment of the lady. She would have been safe, with no need to escape, if Setons had been at Dalrinnie still.

He would have treated the lady respectfully and tenderly, as she deserved. The more time he spent with her, the more he felt awed by her intellect, her fortitude, her courage. Still, he felt distracted by her beauty, by her sweet curves and warmth, by the intangible allure he sensed when he looked at her. He was thankful to find her—

Stop, he told himself. He broke an oatcake, dragged it through soft butter and took a bite. If anything, he must find out what she knew of books. That was all.

He watched as she slipped a scrap of meat to the dog under the table again. "You like dogs," he said. "And books, I think. There are excellent books on raising hounds that might interest you."

"My father had such books, but nothing on dogs. He did have an excellent book on falconry, however. *De Arte Venandi cum Avibus*. I read that."

"I too read it years back. I found the Latin slow going."

"I managed it, though my French is better for reading, and I have a little Greek and Hebrew as well. I copied parts of the falconry volume as a gift for my father when I was a girl. I have a good hand for writing," she added, seeming shy about it.

"You had an exceptional education."

"My siblings and I were taught together by a priest at Kincraig. You have brothers," she said. "Sisters too?"

"Two brothers, one sister. She was educated with us and often outpaced us, to our great humiliation. One of my uncles is a priest and he was our tutor in those days. He was a tireless taskmaster, and we had him for confession as well."

She laughed softly. He liked the sound. The urge to tell her more about his family, about himself, swamped him for a moment. But that would be unwise.

"You are so fond of books that you brought a parcel of them away with you." He indicated her bag on the floor with the other things. "Do you have a favorite?"

Frowning, her lush lips pinched thin, she seemed to consider it. "I am partial to histories," she said. "And tales of Arthur and his knights and so on. I rather like the tale of Tristan and Iseult. Do you know it?"

"Oh, aye. The harper and the king's woman, runaway lovers fleeing evil to be together—a good story. I am fond of poetry and verses too. Songs and such."

"I sometimes write verses. But not very good ones."

"Did you bring those with you too?"

Her glance seemed cautious. "I have a little book of hours for prayers and a few others that I could not leave behind. I do not know if I can ever return to Dalrinnie."

"I would take you there if I could," he said impulsively. "Home to your books." Unlike him. A step too far into pretty chivalry. His nature was reserved, an observer, even a grouser. He did not easily dole out charm and compliments, though he managed the pretense while in the guise of the harper.

Lady Tamsin was having a strange effect on him. He wanted to please her, to see her smile. He had not felt that way about a girl since adolescence. Even Beatrix, his father's choice for him, sweet as she was, had not stirred him as deeply as this woman seemed to do.

"We share a love of books, sirrah." Her smile was quick and warm, like a sunbeam through a cloud.

"We do." They shared a love of Dalrinnie too, he realized. He smiled as well, which he did not do often these days. Then he caught himself. He was sinking fast. Best haul himself free. "Pardon me if I seemed to pry. We are strangers traveling together along a cold mile. Our paths may never cross again."

She frowned as if distressed and glanced away. "True."

Strangers. Liam felt a hard tug inside when he said it. He barely knew her, but she did not seem like a stranger. He felt comfortable in her company. Alive and strong, keenly interested in her thoughts, her life—

But she was not a lady to court. She was the means to get what he wanted. What he needed.

He sat back to put a little distance between them. She distracted him, with her silvery irises and rosy curved lips. The tousle of her fine-spun hair.

And he was increasingly aware that she roused in him an urge that was very physical, yet beyond it too. He needed to protect her, to know her, to be with her. That was dangerous. Soon he would have to betray her over that damnable book and the home she seemed to love. Best to remain aloof.

"Our paths may never cross again," she repeated. "But I am grateful."

"Just so." He looked away. She could capture him like a fish in a net. But he knew better than to let that happen.

He glanced out the window. Dalrinnie was well in the distance, yet no matter how far away, his castle pulled at his heart. And no matter what it took, or who claimed it now, he would regain his home.

As much as he disliked the idea, there was one way to do that.

Get the book from her, Edward had said. *It does not matter how 'tis done.*

CHAPTER ELEVEN

GILCHRIST AND FINLEY played dice while Liam closed his eyes
and began to doze. Beside him, Lady Tamsin laid her head
on her folded arms and rested too. After a while, he opened his
eyes, feeling lulled and enchanted, as if the Queen of Faery, as in
the old ballads, sat with him. He absorbed warmth from the
hearth, listened to the crackle of flames and sleet pelting the
windows, and lost his sense of urgency. Tamsin raised her head,
spoke to the dog in a soft voice. Gentleness emanated from her
like a glow.

It felt like love, he thought, just to watch her. She had talked
of what she loved, books and reading, dogs and Dalrinnie, yet
never mentioned her famed great-grandfather. The thought was a
dash of cold water to his spirit. Some matters needed his
attention, and he felt lulled, too relaxed.

He sat up, looked around, heard the rain against the parch-
ment-covered windows—and then Roc lurched to his feet with a
low ruff.

A torrent of noise erupted outside. Hoofbeats. Liam stood,
and at Lady Tamsin's quick anxious look, set a hand on her
shoulder.

"Let me see," he said, and went to a window. A commotion
of riders and horses hurtled into the yard—three, four, now five,
the inn's young groom running to assist.

King's men, certainly. Malise's men, likely. He turned as

Gilchrist joined him at the window. "Comyn?"

"Perhaps. We should leave. But if they recognize the lass, we cannot risk a chase in these conditions."

"Finley and I could go another way to distract them."

"For now, we watch. Here they come." He stepped back, looking around, judging how quickly he could whisk the lady outside and onto his horse. He went back to the table, pausing to speak to the innkeeper's wife.

"Dame, if you please," he said, "do not let these men know we are traveling to Holyoak. I must protect my lady. You understand." Reaching into the pouch at his belt, he produced a few silver groats. "For our meal—and your kindness."

"Generous, sir. I dinna want trouble here, especially for your lady wife."

Wife. He let that go with a smile and headed back, pausing to pluck up Tamsin's dry cloak along with his own, glancing to be sure her satchels were within easy reach. Their swords were by the door, daggers sheathed in belts, all at the ready. Good.

Tamsin Keith gave him a concerned frown as he sat again. "Soldiers?"

He nodded. The door burst open then and several men crowded inside, sweeping in a draft of cold, wet air. Liam drank from his ale cup, watching, wary. The men stomped sleet on the floorboards, shook rain from cloaks, and dropped their hoods.

Three wore red surcoats, two dark tunics, all were in mail. They removed their swords to prop them by the door, too near the swords Liam and the others had left there. Seeing the weapons, the men glanced around, then nodded toward Liam and his kinsmen.

The innkeeper's wife came forward to seat them at a table near the window, bringing ale and remarking on the weather.

Liam caught Finley's somber glance, Gilchrist's too as they sat and picked up the dice again. Lady Tamsin watched, eyes gray as storm clouds. Liam draped her warmed cloak over her shoulders and closed her brooch deftly. She lifted her chin to allow it, eyes questioning.

"Should we leave?" she whispered.

"Perhaps," he murmured. "Follow my lead. All will be well."
He touched her arm, lightly and away.

The innkeeper grabbed his cloak from a wall peg and went
outside to help the stable boy with the horses while Dame Brown
brought soup bowls and oatcakes to the new guests. She chuckled
as the knights groused about being seated away from the warm
hearth on such a day.

"We have other guests driven in by the weather," she said.
When one man asked a question, tipping his head toward Liam
and the rest, she nodded. "Och, aye," she said. "A lord and his
lady wife, traveling with their escort. I think they are new
married. So nice to provide a hot meal for a happy couple on such
a dreary day."

Tamsin's eyebrows shot high. Finley huffed a laugh and lifted
his ale cup.

"My lord, my lady, congratulations." He saluted and drank.

"But—" Tamsin protested.

"Hush, this may be just what we need," Liam whispered.

As the soldiers ate, they kept looking toward the other table.
Liam angled to shield the girl from sight and leaned toward her to
speak low.

"Draw up your hood against the cold. There." He tugged the
hood over her tousled golden hair, making the gesture intimate
and familiar. He disliked the way the soldiers' gazes roamed over
her. He needed to show them his firm role.

"I am too warm." She started to push the hood down.

"You do not want to be seen, lass." He pulled it back in place.
"Look carefully, now, and tell me if you know them."

She glanced there. "I have not seen them. But they could be
Comyn's men."

"They asked the dame about us, so they may be searching for
a young lady." Setting a hand on her shoulder, he murmured in
her ear. "Pardon, my lady, but for now, they must see that we are

not strangers."

"But we are."

"Honesty seems to be one of your virtues," he said with a soft laugh, "but just now, call me friend enough, aye?"

"Friend enough," she whispered.

"We know each other well, you see. We—love each other," he said low.

"But—"

"Love, aye, because I do not like the look of that lot." From the corner of his eye, Liam saw them cram bannocks into their mouths, swallow ale, wipe their chins—harmless enough. But one or two pointed toward Tamsin, muttering to their companions.

His skin prickled in alarm. "Gilchrist, Finley. We should leave."

"Take the lady to Holyoak," Gilchrist suggested, "while we take the hound by another route to the abbey."

"Wait a bit on the sleet. My lady," he added, "the dame gave me a thought. We will pretend to be husband and wife, aye?"

"But we are not." A flush crept over her pale cheeks.

"If those are Comyn's men, they are looking for one woman, not a married woman with an escort."

"That may be, but I do not like to lie."

"Then say naught and I will lie for both of us."

"The harper is good at that."

"I owe you more than one apology, I see. But for now, let us have a ruse of marriage. Think of it as your shield and protection." Seeing her pink cheeks and her frown, he realized the pretense troubled her. Regret tugged at him.

"Well, if they misunderstand who we are, we can do nothing about that."

"Now you have the knack of it." He smiled, then brushed back a tendril of her hair.

She sighed. "Very well. Pray do not say my name, in case they know it."

"I shall call you … Margaret. It suits you."

"My sister's name, but she prefers Meg. Oh! Did you hear that?" Liam frowned, listening.

"Castle Kincraig," one of the men was saying. "The chit has kin there and may head that way."

"The lass could be anywhere." The guard poked the man beside him and indicated Liam and the others. "She looks like the one we seek."

"Could be, but the dame said she's that one's wife."

Tamsin gasped, lowered her head.

"Hush." Liam closed his fingers over her hand, her fingers slim and fragile under his. She did not protest.

He knew he must make the message clear for the guards across the room. Lifting Tamsin's hand to his lips, he kissed her fingers. She caught her breath as he rubbed his thumb over her knuckles. One of the soldiers rose to approach them.

"My lady, I am going to kiss you now," Liam murmured as the man approached. "Aye so?" He tipped her chin up with his free hand.

Eyes wide, she nodded. Liam bent to gently touch his lips to hers. Though he meant it to appear casual, the kiss ran hard through him.

"Oh aye," she breathed against his mouth.

That nearly undid him. The marriage ruse was meant to protect her, but suddenly he was the one in jeopardy, for she kissed him in return, her little sigh soft against his lips. He thought the floor might give way beneath him, felt the fire's heat blaze to consuming intensity—or was that within him? He feared he might seize her in his arms as his body craved. Opening his hands, he let go, then drew back and pulled in a breath.

Looking up, he saw his brother and cousin gaping at him.

Tamsin touched his cheek and looked at him in wonder for an instant. By the saints, the girl had been married, yet looked at him as if she had never been kissed before. And he had not only stepped over a boundary, he had dropped into an abyss. His heart pounded. His body felt on fire.

If he did not put a cool distance between him and the lady now, he would be lost. Taking her hand from his cheek, he pressed her fingers to the table, his hand over hers.

"My love," he said audibly, his voice not sounding quite his own.

"Love," she breathed, staring at him.

This was not good, Liam thought. She was too trusting, this lass. He could not bear to fool her—or leave her.

The guard stood over them now, glowering. "In the name of the king, I demand that you identify yourselves. What is your business here? And who is this lady?"

⟫⟫✖⟪⟪

AT THE BARKED question, Tamsin caught her breath. Sir William's hand tightened over hers, strong and warm. She turned her fingers within the cage of his, seeking reassurance. Her head still spun from the surprising kiss, the unexpected power of it, the way her knees dissolved and her heart quickened.

She was thankful her hood shielded her from clear view. Liam Seton, his hand still over hers, looked up. "We are king's men, sir," he told the soldier, "as are you."

"Under whose command?"

"King's direct orders," Gilchrist replied. "And you?"

"We ride for Sir Malise Comyn of Dalrinnie."

Tamsin felt her breath go ragged. Holding her hand, Liam Seton gave it a subtle, reassuring squeeze. She let a breath out.

"Kinsman to the murdered Comyn?" Finley asked.

"You know my lord commander?"

"We know he faithfully serves Edward," Finley drawled.

"Aye, as do we. What are your orders?"

"Private, sir, direct from the king," Liam Seton answered. "I cannot share them. But I will say I am taking my bride to her family estate in the Borders. These men escort us. The king's men. Like you."

Tamsin pressed her lips together to keep from speaking truths that bubbled up. *I am running from Malise Comyn, I do not know what orders this man has from the king, he is not my husband...* She looked away.

"Just wed, so the good dame says. A newly married couple does not usually merit a king's escort."

"I serve as his messenger."

The man grunted. "I am Sir John Parsley," he said. "You have not given your name, however. My commander will require the names of anyone we meet this day."

Her so-called husband leaned toward the man. "My lady's family is well known and close to the king. He would be annoyed if we were compromised or delayed on our journey. He has a chivalrous regard for ladies, as you know, and we are expected soon."

"Ladies, aye. But he takes a dim view of Scotswomen," the man countered, sliding another glance toward Tamsin.

She felt Seton's hand tighten on hers. Feeling ill at Parsley's implication, she wanted to run as fast as she could from this place.

Finley lifted his cup in salute. "Many good Scots are loyal to the king, sir. Your commander among them, I vow."

"Of course." Parsley addressed Liam again. "What brings you north? 'Tis a long way from Carlisle and Lanercost, if you came north with king's orders."

"A royal errand can take a messenger far," he answered. "For now, we are waiting out the weather, just as you are." Tamsin saw a muscle jump in his lean cheek.

"Bad enough to drive even rats indoors," Finley said.

The soldier placed a hand on the dagger at his belt. "Best prove you bear orders from the king, sir."

Slowly, William Seton reached inside his blue surcoat to pull out a folded packet that Tamsin had not seen before. Crinkled ribbons dangled from the royal seal of England. Tipping it to show the soldier the seal, he did not hand it over.

The man grunted. "Well then."

Tamsin frowned, remembering that the harper—his other self—had come to Lochmaben with a message for her from the king. Was that the order? If so, why had he not given it to her? Sir Malise had had a similar document.

She eyed him, awash in uncertainty again.

"Enough? Then let us finish our meal in peace and we will continue our journey," said her false groom, her false knight.

"Understand me, sir. Many Scots cannot be trusted. We are on constant alert against rebels. They could be anyone." He looked at each of them in turn. "Anyone."

"Oh, we know," Gilchrist said. "We have been hunting for Bruce and his parcel of rogues for months."

"Ah." Parsley took a step back. "Well then. I still need your names."

"Seton," her pretend husband said. "Sir William Seton and his wife with a king's escort. Be sure to tell that to Malise Comyn."

Tamsin took a quick breath. John Parsley might not recognize his meaning, but Comyn would know it as a gauntlet thrown down. A dare.

"Seton?" The man frowned.

"Sir William Seton of Ettrick Forest. Tell your commander I will see him soon."

Tamsin frowned. The vast forest that stretched from the Border area well into central Scotland belonged to no single estate or man. Under a single sheriff—King Edward's man, Aymer de Valence, Lord Pembroke, whom she hoped never to meet—the massive forest tract covered dozens of miles in all directions. Its canopies, clearings, and gullies sheltered outlaws who had, so far, proved near impossible to find. And Seton said he was from that tract. Sir Malise would likely be furious.

"Very well." Parsley had little reaction. Did he not know of the great forest? Perhaps he was new to his duty in Scotland, she thought.

"My only concern now is my wife's comfort and wellbeing. You understand."

My wife. False though it be, the statement rang true somehow, bringing her a sense of comfort and purpose. She let out a breath, unaware she had been holding it.

"I just wondered what brings you lot out on such a day," Parsley said.

"Now you know. And you? On patrol?"

"Sir Malise sent us in search of his betrothed. Fool woman ran off after a squabble, and he wants her back, see. It is a miserable day to be riding after a woman in a snit of temper."

"Indeed, it is. A woman in a temper is a formidable thing." He wove his fingers with Tamsin's, pressed tight.

"They say this missing lady is small and fair. Like your lady."

"We will watch for her as we travel."

"Dear sirrah. Take me home, do," Tamsin said then. Her heart pounded. Liam's eyes caught hers, a flicker of amusement in the blue.

"My heart is my lady's." He stood, bringing her to her feet. "I know how tired you must be after our long journey."

"So weary." That was true. She had hardly slept the previous night and the day so far had been vexing. Glad for the brace of his hand, she moved away, aware of the guard's scrutiny.

Liam Seton stooped to pick up her satchels, slinging them over his shoulder while his brother and cousin preceded them outside to see to the horses. When he took her elbow to guide her to the door, she lifted her chin as they passed the soldiers.

"Aye, very like her," Parsley told his companions. "I would swear it. But she is that one's wife. And he is mad for his lady, that is easy to see. Edward's messenger, so he says."

Mad for his lady? She glanced at Liam, who took his sword from its place against the door, sheathed it, then took her arm again. He smiled down at her and opened the door. She went still, seeing his tender expression, his brow lifted in question, noting the light in his eyes. Mad for her. For an instant, she felt warmth rush through her. The knight from the dream stood before her. She wanted that man, wanted that dream, that true companion.

The kiss that she could still feel on her lips had not been false. She was sure of that somehow—it had taken him by surprise just as it had taken her. That smile, the look in his eyes just now— those were genuine too. She did not want to think he could be anything other than what she saw in this moment.

"Give me that adoring smile again," he said. "They are watching us."

The words felt as cold to her as the rain whipping through the door. Sending him a scowl he surely deserved, she stepped past him.

CHAPTER TWELVE

BREATHING IN THE damp, chilly air, Tamsin rode astride behind Liam, gripping his belt, gown tucked, cloak billowing. She leaned against his back as he set a good pace across rolling moorland under gray skies.

He said little, now again reaching behind to brace her with a steady hand as if he wanted to know she was secure. Looking around, she did not see Sir Gilchrist or Sir Finley. They had vanished over a hill a while ago, taking another route with Roc. Hoping none of them would be pursued, she kept glancing back anxiously.

The monastery was not far now, she knew, for she had traveled this way more than once with a Dalrinnie escort to visit Holyoak. The abbot kindly allowed her to study the books in their small library. Her sister Rowena had gone there occasionally too, assisting in the hospice located there. In that small Benedictine abbey, Tamsin would feel among friends. It would feel like a temporary sanctuary.

Yet, given the strict rules and integrity of the order, the abbot might insist she return to Dalrinnie or stay in a convent. She sighed, suddenly uncertain, still hoping she could count on them as friends when she needed help.

"Is something wrong, my lady?" Liam Seton's voice had a warm resonance that she instinctively trusted. Yet she felt uncertain about him as well.

"Just tired. Are you sure we were not followed by that patrol?"

"They may return to Dalrinnie to report to Comyn. But we are in luck. The rain is lifting and the ice melting." He urged the stallion to a canter.

She clung to his belt, noticing the muscled power of his long legs and the sure guidance he gave the horse. But she also felt urgency thrumming in him like a brooding storm. He seemed driven, determined; she sensed it in his wary glance, in his long silences as they rode. No longer her supposed husband, he was her grim and dutiful escort with a mission to accomplish and little to say.

Drawing her cloak closer, she watched the horizon for the familiar profile of Holyoak Abbey, with its wooden palisade walls and fieldstone bell tower, the whole set on the rise of a hill near a long curving loch. The waters that filled that blue crescent flowed eastward as the Yarrow Water. Beyond lay Ettrick Forest, and on the far side of that vast green sward lay Selkirk, where she must accomplish her mission.

But suddenly she wanted to disappear, never arrive at the monastery, never see Comyn again, never follow King Edward's orders to surrender the Rhymer's work. She closed her eyes, fighting tears, fatigue, frustration.

Seton glanced back as if he sensed that change in her. "Aye?"

"Aye, well enough." She was tempted to tell him her thoughts, craving the tenderness he had shown at the inn. Tears pulled and she dashed them away. She could not submit to some sentimental need to trust a harper, an outlaw, a sometime knight. God only knew what he wanted, for the man did not share his thoughts readily.

She needed desperately to trust someone, and she felt so keenly drawn to this man now that she only felt more frustration. Suddenly she wished he would keep riding fast and far to disappear over the next hill and the next, taking her with him, never stopping until they reached some distant hideaway. If only she could be with him, with his gruff kindness, even his secrets, they could discover trust, freedom, truth between them. Foolish as it seemed, she felt it could be so.

But she was only indulging a dream. He was not the knight of dreams, but a man with secrets. She was on her own and must sort this out for herself, even amid uncertainty.

Then she heard the bell. The sound rang through the air, rich and true, faint with distance. A chill wind streamed past, lifting her braid like a banner. She tucked it away.

"Holyoak's bell," she said, as it rang out again, three more times. "I thought it was telling the hour, but they are still ringing it."

"It is not a call to prayers. They are sounding it against the weather."

"The weather?"

"That old bell is said to improve the weather when rung. It is inscribed for it."

"Inscribed?" She leaned to look up at him. He slowed the horse, varying the pace, adjusting the reins.

"*Ego sum qui dissipo tonitrua,*" he quoted. "'I am the one who dispels the thunder.'"

"Truly! Does it work?"

He laughed. "Do you hear thunder? Nay? Then it works."

She laughed too. "You know this abbey well, I think."

"Aye." He went silent again.

At last she saw the foggy outline of the stone bell tower and timber walls, fronted by the crown of a massive tree. Holyoak was named for the ancient giant oak that stood like a sentry outside the gates. Now, its wide canopy was golden with autumn.

"Just ahead now. Faring well, my lady?" He slowed the horse's pace.

"Fine," she said, even as the sleet renewed, pattering mercilessly on her head.

"Aye so?" He glanced back.

"This is the most miserable journey I have ever endured," she blurted.

"Now she speaks truth," he said, and laughed.

Reaching the entrance, Liam dismounted, lifting his arms to help her down. His hands were firm at her waist as he set her on the ground, holding her for a moment when she faltered, her knees trembling with fatigue, toes near frozen in her boots. Then he went to the gate, pulling a rope that clanged a small bell on the other side and would summon a porter.

Soon the wooden doors opened and two monks in black hooded robes stood there, gesturing them inside. "Welcome," said the younger one. "We expected you, Sir Liam!"

Expected him? Puzzled, Tamsin looked from one man to the next.

"Brother Allan, greetings. So my brother and cousin arrived safely?"

"Aye, sir, with Roc." Brother Allan and the older monk turned to Tamsin, smiling.

"Lady Thomasina Keith," Liam said, "Brother Allan and Brother Claude." He took her elbow as they walked into the yard, muddy with rain.

"We are acquainted. Lady Tamsin, welcome," Brother Allan said. The older monk murmured a welcome in French.

"Thank you. *Merci*," she said to one and the other; she remembered seeing both on previous visits. Brother Allan closed the gate as Liam guided her into the center of the small courtyard, usually neat, but muddied and dreary this cold day.

She glanced around, recognizing the rectory, the chapter house and abbot's house, the large stone chapel with its main entrance outside the palisade, the hospital building at the far end, with an outside entrance as well, along with various other structures that made Holyoak a busy abbey despite its modest size.

Once a haven for her, today it seemed fraught with risk, for she did not know if she would be welcome, considering her situation. There was one monk here, however, who would be a staunch friend, she was sure. She glanced around for him.

"Brother Gideon will be here soon and will be pleased to see you," Brother Allan said. "Sir Gilchrist said the lady will need to rest, and the small guest house is ready. This way, my lady. Such dreadful weather! Do watch your step." The young monk began to lead her across the muddy courtyard.

"Wait," Liam said. "Here is Brother Gideon."

He knew him too? She turned, seeing Sir Gilchrist with a tall monk in a plain black robe who walked with a noticeable limp. He lifted a hand in greeting, the corner of his smile puckered on the left by a deep scar that curved from cheek to chin.

"Lady Tamsin—Liam!" Gideon said. Tamsin saw Liam stride toward the monk, grinning.

"Gideon!" he called, and the two embraced, standing in cold mud and icy drizzle beside Gilchrist Finley came running too, and now all four—knights and monk—were thumping shoulders, laughing, talking.

Tamsin watched in surprise, seeing how well they knew each other, what affection they shared. Smiling faintly, she waited.

On previous visits, Brother Gideon had escorted her to the abbey's library, staying for conversations about the books and texts. He had shared a little about what had brought him to Holyoak, and she had told him a bit about her life as well. He was warm and amiable, frank about the injuries that had landed him in the hospital here, and honest about his decision to become a novitiate, possibly a monk, one day. The avowal process was slow, giving the novice time to think about the ramifications of devoting their lives to God's work. For now, he was moving toward that, acting as a scholar-clerk and working with the abbey's book collection.

And she had been delighted to learn that Brother Gideon had met her sister Lady Rowena when she had visited the abbey hospital. Typical of her sister's curiosity and intelligence, Rowena had been eager to learn healing techniques from the monks who treated and supervised there and to share what she knew.

Tamsin loved Holyoak not just for its books or the connection with her sister, but for her friendship with Brother Gideon. He was knowledgeable, insightful, humorous, and kind, and in his company, she always felt valued as a scholar, a friend, an equal of sorts.

Waiting as the men spoke, she realized then why she had thought William—and Gilchrist, too—so oddly familiar. It was not just meeting the harper before, but more than that.

These men were kinsmen, she saw now. They had to be. They shared similar features, shared smiles, striking blue eyes, handsome faces, and tall, lean physiques. While Liam was dark, Gilchrist and Gideon were blond, though Gideon's hair was precisely shaved. They matched in many ways. Even their voices were similar, velvety dark in deep tones.

But what surprised her most was that Gilchrist and Gideon were identical. Twins, surely. No wonder she had thought her impromptu escort looked familiar. Finley, their cousin, was a sturdy and handsome man too, with brown hair and brown eyes. He was not as tall as his Seton cousins, with a brawny form and a dimpled and irresistible smile.

"You are brothers," she said then. "All three of you." They turned and smiled.

"Aye," Liam said. "And Finley, our cousin, was raised with us like a brother." He clapped that lad on the shoulder.

Gideon gave her a broad smile. "Lady Tamsin! Pardon me for not welcoming you yet. My kinsmen distracted me." Laughing, he rested a hand on Gilchrist's shoulder. She saw again how very alike they were.

"You know Lady Tamsin, then," Liam said.

"Oh aye," Gideon replied. "A great patron of books and a gracious lady. Welcome back to Holyoak, my lady. We heard of your dilemma today. I am sorry."

"Thank you, Brother Gideon. I am grateful for any help you can extend to me here. I hope Abbot Murdoch will allow me to stay for a little while."

"We will bring it to his attention. He is resting just now. But let us offer you shelter and refreshment. Brother Allan, will you see the lady to—where is the lad?" He looked around.

"Running after the hounds," Gilchrist said, pointing to the other end of the yard, where Allan chased Roc and two other tall, gangly hounds.

"I will show her to the cottage." Liam shouldered the two satchels that he had removed from his horse's saddle.

"Good. I will see when Abbot Murdoch is free to visit with you. He has stayed in his quarters today. Old aches brought on by cold and rain," Gideon explained. "Lady Tamsin, the guest house is ready for travelers who might need it for a night or two. Although—" He glanced at the others. "We send ladies on to a sister priory if they need a longer stay. There are not many convents in Scotland, to be sure, but we will send word ahead to see if Dame Agatha can take you in at Lincluden."

"We would like to stay for a day or two," Liam said. "The lady is set on traveling on to Selkirk."

"Selkirk? Is it so? Well," Gideon said, "we will set pallets for you lads by the hearth in the rectory."

"Thank you." Liam glanced at Gilchrist. "We have other matters to tend to and would not stay for long, I think."

Tamsin listened, smiling, still marveling at the similarities between the men. Suddenly, oddly, they all seemed dear to her, as if she had always known them. Yet they were still strangers. Perhaps her relief and gratitude made them feel like kin and friends.

"My lady." Liam turned. "Let us get you out of this rain." She nodded, aware of her fatigue. He gestured across the bailey toward a small stone cottage with a steep thatched roof, tucked against the back of the palisade.

"You must be hungry, all of you," Gideon said. "Brother Robert, our cook, has a venison stew simmering, a good meal against the chill. You are welcome to share what we have. The abbot will be eager to see you as well. He keeps to his quarters often these days, but he will want to see his kinsmen."

"Kinsmen?" Tamsin blinked. "Are you related to the abbot also?"

"He is our uncle," Gilchrist said.

"Oh! He is a lovely man. I hope he is well."

"Well enough," Gideon said. "I will tell him you are here."

"This way, my lady." Liam gestured for her to come with him across the yard, just as a renewal of icy rain began. He set a hand to her elbow as they rushed along. Behind them, the others ran for cover also.

Liam led her to a covered wooden colonnade that extended from the rectory to the side of the chapel. Sleet drummed on the wooden slats overhead.

"We can wait here." He paused with her there. "Awful weather. I am sorry. It has only made this long day even worse for you."

"A day of challenges, to be sure." She gave a low laugh at the truth of it. "From the moment I went out the tower window, I have done things I might never have thought of doing before. Meeting you and the others, going with you, being hunted, finding that you are—" She stopped, nearly saying "the knight."

"Finding me?"

"The harper," she went on. "And then riding through an ice storm in October—it has been a day of one revelation after another."

"Discovering that you had courage and stamina—was that a revelation to you also? I saw it in you, even if you did not." He spoke gently, reaching out to brush rain from her hood. "What more revelations will this day hold for you, hey?"

"I found I could pretend to be other than I am. Your wife," she explained.

"Was it so difficult?" His smile was a wry twist.

"Aye. It is hard for me to say a falsehood. My grandda called it a truthy tongue, always saying what you think, what you know is true. But it can be a sort of curse." She gave a flat little laugh.

He watched her, the rain shadowing his face. "Rhymer's daughter," he murmured. "If that did not come easy, then well done to you."

"Truly, it was nice, pretending to be your wife. But I prefer truth."

"I have to agree. But listen now." He leaned down. "They believed it, and we needed it in the moment. So was it a mere lie, or a necessary one?"

She nodded thoughtfully. "You said once that truths can be more harmful than falsehoods. Yet Grandda said I must always be truthful. He could never speak falsely."

"And you took it to heart. You are the least false person I know. Every bit of you." Rain slipped through the planks above. He brushed drops off her shoulder. "But playing with truth can be protective. And what is most true is that you cannot go back to Dalrinnie as long as Comyn is there."

She nodded. "Abbot Murdoch may tell me to go back there. He may feel obligated to support the king as well as the Church."

"We will know what he thinks soon enough." Liam's height and solidity blocked the wind, his presence a shelter, his calmness a rock on what had been a chaotic day. "And before I leave here, my lady, I want to be sure that you will be safe."

"Leave? Must you go?" she asked quickly.

"I have some obligations. I promised to see you through the forest to Selkirk, and I will," he added. "But Sir Malise will not give up easily, so it may be better for you to stay in a convent for a while before you visit your friends or your kin."

"I need to go there as soon as I can, and then find my family. If you must leave, I can find another way." But the thought of him leaving felt wrong somehow. Dangerous. A thought nudged at her, as if she had forgotten something important.

"Scotswomen are not safe these days, and that is true. Wait for me to return, Tamsin," he said, using her name intimately. "Can you do that? Have patience with me?"

She nodded. "I am so tired," she said, as it washed over her.

"Can we talk later?" Her head felt muzzy, dizzy for a moment, and paused.

"Tamsin?"

She shook her head. "I—I was surprised to learn that Gideon is your brother. He never mentioned brothers, but then he would not." She stretched for something to say, to cover up the odd fatigue coming over her. "He and Gilchrist look like twins."

"Aye. Younger than me by two years."

"And kin to the abbot as well? No wonder you know this place."

"Murdoch is my father's brother. My father is gone seven years now," he added. "Gideon came to Holyoak's hospital three years ago, sorely wounded. He found peace here, and needed it after—well..." He gave a thin smile. "You look tired. Let me take you to the cottage." He gestured toward the little building. "I will ride out with the others soon, but just for a little while. We want to be sure no one followed us here."

"Do not leave," she burst out, grabbing his arm, chain mail hard and cold. His hand slid to hers, fingers cool but enveloping. Fear went through her. She might never see him again, and knew so little of him, with no time to learn more. Something was about to change. Something felt wrong—

"Tamsin?" He gripped her hand.

"Do not ride out now." Her heart pounded. She felt fear, fatigue, and yearning all at once. Her head spun, the strain of the day hitting her like a tidal wave. That was all. She shook her head.

"Lady, what is it?"

"I need to rest. Will I see you before you go?" She should thank him for his help, just that. But she felt off. Her fingers found his skin in the gap under the chain mail. He felt warm, real, honest to his bones.

He watched her. "Tell me what is wrong."

Then the world spun. She stepped back, stumbling. He caught her arm, drew her close. Sleet tapped the wooden canopy overhead; rain blurred the yard. When the words tumbled out, she could not stop them.

"Fire," she whispered. "The yard—the walls—"

"Fire? It is raining like the very devil."

The bailey was awash in sleet and mud, the buildings a dull blur of stone and wood and thatch. Candlelight glimmered in the arched windows of the chapel.

Yet even as she saw the rainy yard, she saw flames dancing high, hot, and yellow across her innermost vision, like a waking dream.

"Fire," she repeated. "I see this place all aflame." She passed a shaking hand over her eyes, trying to wipe away the images.

"Jesu! You are shivering, lass." He pulled her close, his body blocking the wind, his arms around her now. She trembled, head to foot.

"Fire in the oak, at fair Holyoak," she whispered. "Torches at the gate and the tolling of the bell. Gate—watch the gate."

"The monks are cautious of fire, like anyone with house and hearth."

"Beware the gate. The broken gate." Her voice grew hoarse.

"What the devil," he murmured. "You said you were tired. Is it fever? I never should have made you ride so far in this cold and wet." He rubbed her shoulder, pulled her in, his arm around her.

The words roiled through her. "Fire at the oak, at fair Holyoak, men with torches and the ringing of the bell—" She could not look away from the vision inside her head, could not stop the message that poured through her.

"Jesu," he growled, then swept her into his arms. The swift motion halted the cascade of words in her head. She rocked in his arms as he strode through a whipping curtain of rain to the cottage step and booted the door open.

CHAPTER THIRTEEN

H E STOOD READY to catch her, hold her, whatever she needed. Pale and shaking, the lass sat on the narrow cot now, looking spent. She pushed back the hood of her sodden cloak. Her tousled braid loosened into ripples of wet gold. Lifting her hands, she covered her eyes.

"Lady?" Concern sagged his shoulders, his spirit. "Tamsin?"

When she looked at him, her eyes were bright, luminous. "Oh," she said, as if in a half-daze. "This is a nice cottage."

"It is." He felt relief at the ordinary remark. But what had just happened? He waited, glancing around the small guest house with its simple bed, straw mattress, woolen blanket, and thin pillow. By the window stood a small table, a bench. One shelf held a cup, a jug, a candle, and a wooden cross hung on the wall beside the small curtained window. Flames flickered in the small stone hearth in a corner, blessedly warm. Tamsin stood and crossed the room to warm her hands at the hot glow.

"Better?" he asked.

She nodded. "I am sorry. Thank you."

He drew a calming breath. "I will fetch your things." He stepped out in the rain to grab the satchels he had dropped, bringing them inside.

She looked up. "That was—that has not happened for a while. A truthy spell, my family calls it."

"Some might call it the Sight. Though the fatigue of the day would explain it too." He frowned. "You should rest. I will go."

"Stay," she said quickly, putting out a hand. "Please stay. If you can."

In answer, he went to her side, wanting to be there if she faltered, and put out his hands to the fire. As warmth eased the dampness he felt, he nudged his arm and shoulder against her, a buttress if need be.

"I am not sure what I said," she murmured.

"Something about fire."

"It must have seemed very odd to you."

"No matter. I just want to know you are fine now."

"I am." Long golden strands, wet and curling, curtained her face.

"You need rest and food. A bit of watered wine, or perhaps a stronger spirit. I can fetch something from the rectory. You say this has happened before?"

"Aye. Not often." She sighed. "My family has seen this in me. Grandda did the same, but he spoke with authority, with power, you see. He had the ear of kings and earls and great men. What comes over me is small by comparison. Few know about it. Grandda once told me that someday I would see things that are true, and not to fear that power. Still, you must think me foolish. Weak."

"I do not. A gift like yours," he said, "may start quietly and grow. If the visions prove true, word spreads. Leaders listen. My cousin is a soothsayer. Lady Isobel Seton."

She gasped. "Of Aberlady? I have heard the name. She speaks to earls and suchlike. I could never do that."

"You could and you may someday, if you are like your great-grandfather. And I think you are," he murmured. "When visions come to Isobel, she pays them heed and gives warning. She married a friend. One day—I could bring you to meet her," he offered. Would there be that day, when he could do such a favor for this lass? He frowned. It might mean a future with her beyond this moment, beyond his sorry promise to a ruthless king.

"I would like that." She ran fingers through her hair. "I am so tired."

"Indeed. This might help." Grabbing the crockery jug from the shelf, he opened it, sniffed. As he thought, it was Holyoak's own *uisge beatha*, a strong drink made from barley. A little might help bring the lady around, for she seemed dazed still. He poured a dram into a wooden cup and handed it to her.

She drank, then coughed. "Please—do not tell anyone what happened."

"You can trust me."

She looked at him over the cup. "I want to. But I wonder."

"My lady." Liam took her by the shoulders. "Whatever I do elsewhere, you can trust me." He emphasized the words.

"I am grateful to you, but I am cautious. You are a puzzle to me, sir."

"And you," he said, "bewilder me." *And enchant me,* he thought, *spin me round so I do not know what to think.* He rubbed her shoulders, down her arms and up. She felt good under his hands. Warm, no longer shivering. She did not pull away, though they stood so close. "Sit," he told her, leading her to the cot.

Seated, she sipped the drink again, then blinked. "Perhaps I would be better off in a convent. If I was a nun, or even an anchorite or a hermit in the forest, people would just think me mad and leave me to my books and my—verses."

"You do not belong in a convent. So the episodes of yours prove true?"

She rubbed her arm, shivered a little. "Sometimes, aye. I saw my first husband wounded and dead on a field. But I was wrong. He was wounded, aye. But it was weeks before he died. The wound festered despite all we did. My sister came to Dalrinnie to help," she added. "She has the greater gift, I think. Healing. But even she could not change his fate."

"Death is death," he said. "I am sorry. Your sister—did she come here to Holyoak? Gideon spoke highly of her."

"She did. I miss her. I wonder what both my sisters would say of the kerfuffle I have made for myself. Well," she said, shrugging. "Soon you will be free of me and my troubles—and my fits of truth, whatever they may be."

"I am in no rush to be free of you. This day has not brought good fortune to Lady Tamsin. She needs a friend. I will stay."

She smiled faintly. "I do want to trust you. I do."

"And still do not?" He lifted a brow.

"Dare not." She looked up. "The harper said he had a message for me from the king. But he vanished, then returned as a knight, who has not yet told me the message. Is it the same one I heard from Malise? Tell me. Here I am." She sounded bitter, weary.

"Here you are." He wondered how best to proceed. "I assumed, as Edward did, that the Rhymer's daughter was an elderly lady, only to discover the great-granddaughter was the one I need." *Need* suddenly seemed the right word.

"I suppose I am like Thomas in some ways."

"Far bonnier. I am told you have a book that belonged to the Rhymer. I am to take it from you."

"That book again! Sir Malise wants it too. He showed me a writ and demanded the book. When I refused, he threatened to drag me to the king to recite from memory whatever Thomas wrote. He threatened other things as well." She shrugged again. "So I went out the window."

"Well done. He had an order?" He frowned, remembering the day Edward forced the task on him while Malise insisted he would find the lady instead.

"I saw it. Is your writ the same?"

"Similar, I imagine. I must ask—do you have this thing Edward wants?"

"Tell me why he wants it." Cup in hand, she drank again, her eyes watering for a moment. It was strong stuff, Liam thought. And she was a slight thing.

"Easy, if you are not used to it. As for the book—he said something about it being the key to Scotland. A book of prophecies, from what I understand."

"All neatly put together?" She shook her head. "The key to defeating Scotland? I would not give it to Edward even if I had it. What will the king do if I do not comply?"

"He is Edward of England. What do you think?"

"I think he will force me to his will if he can find a way. But he has already taken Dalrinnie from me. I thought he would banish me to a convent, but he ordered Malise to—" She pushed her hair back, looked away.

"Take the book? What more?"

"The king ordered Malise to marry the widow. Me."

"Marry!" The blow felt almost physical. He went silent, grim. "Though Edward may have thought it a pretty joke on Malise."

"I beg your pardon!"

"I did not mean... Edward thinks you are an ancient crone, you see. Malise knows better but would agree to anything that brings him advantage. Still, I wonder about his orders," he murmured. "How they differ from mine."

"Does everyone know the king's plans for the lady except the lady herself?" she blurted. "Were you told to toss me in a convent if I do not cooperate? Or also told to marry me? Is this some contest for Edward's favor, with me in the middle?"

"I just want this book and have done with it. Edward did say he ought to marry me to the old crone. It was a cruel jest—marrying me to an old woman. Not you," he explained in haste as she gaped at him. "So he made Malise the butt of his joke. Still, it is a surprising order."

She huffed. "'Tis not uncommon for a widow to marry again, you know."

"True. By law, a widow is free to choose. So, why would Edward tell Malise to marry you, unless—ah, Dalrinnie. Did Sir John Witton leave his property to you?"

"He did. Malise knows that marrying me would give him Dalrinnie."

"Under English law, aye. Scots law grants women more rights

with property. But your husband's will might not be valid in Scotland. Either way, it is complicated."

"Either way, I had to escape. He meant to send for a priest immediately."

"I see. But Edward has yet to appoint a permanent commander there, and I wonder why he would choose Comyn. Edward told me—" Liam stopped.

"You seem to know a good deal about this, Sir Harper."

"I was part of a conversation in the king's presence." He was not ready to reveal the truth of the situation, but some would do.

"So the harper is a king's man after all."

The answer was complicated. He moved on. "You saw these orders?"

"A roll of parchment with the king's seal and signature. I saw Dalrinnie mentioned, and saw my name, Malise's too. Parts were scrubbed, as when a knife is used to scrape ink away for a correction. It did look hastily made."

"Edward keeps his clerks busy and changes his mind often. There are errors and scrapings on many documents. Did you notice aught else?"

"Malise waved other pages about, maps too, while speaking with Sir Davey, my seneschal at Dalrinnie. You may know that Edward expects Malise to capture Robert Bruce and base the effort at Dalrinnie, since it sits close to Ettrick Forest. They think Bruce's men—perhaps Bruce as well—might be found there."

"Sir Malise could not manage to capture Bruce before. I doubt he could do it now. Besides, it is difficult—even impossible—to find anyone in the depths of the forest."

"You know the forest well?"

He shrugged. "I have spent time there."

"Harper, knight, king's man—rebel too. One of those who rocks back and forth, as many must do. My father, my brother, many good men I have known. You as well?"

He gave a solemn nod. "With good reason. What else did Malise tell you?"

"He warned me of repercussions if I refused."

"He made threats?"

"A cage. I knew what he meant."

He sucked in a breath. "Do not worry. An empty threat." Reassuring her, he wanted to believe it too.

"But should I trust you instead of him, Master Harper? I gave you my faith at Lochmaben, and today. But you too want something from me." He saw a steel glint in her gray eyes. "This supposed book."

"Supposed?"

"I do not own a book of prophecies by Thomas. So there." She yawned.

"But you do have a book of his." Seeing her yawn again, he shook his head. "Later for that. You should rest."

She looked weary. It troubled him to see it. But he had been glad to see her spirit and spark return when she spoke of Malise and doubted the harper.

He took the cup from her—she had emptied the thing, he saw—and stood over her. He knew he hovered, but he needed to just then, to be sure she was fine.

"I do not need a nursemaid, sir. Still, thank you."

"Someone should watch over you for a bit. You have no woman with you, and the monks would be uncomfortable with it. So you have me."

She shoved her hair over her shoulders in a flow of gold. It was long and heavy, trailing to her hips, and he wanted to sink his fingers into that gossamer stuff.

"Sit down. Please," she added. "You are so tall, standing there like that. It hurts my neck to converse with you. That is, if we must keep talking about who has the Rhymer's book. Which I do not," she added.

"You do have a truthy way about you, lady."

"And I see that you are tired, too. Sit." She patted the blanket.

He sat beside her, causing the bed to sink so that she tipped against him. "The Sight tells you I am tired?" He laughed.

"No one needs a seer for that. You have dark circles under your eyes and you look—stormy. Shadows here," she said, touching his cheek. "Creases here." She stroked his brow. "I know I just bring worry to you, and I am sorry. Truly." She leaned in.

"I should have given you food instead of Holyoak's *uisge beatha*," he mused.

"Did you know your eyes turn dull blue when you are tired? Like bluestone."

"I did not know that." How would he?

"I like them best when they are bright as patches of blue sky. Though I like them all the time. I have not seen eyes quite like yours. It is as if your very soul is right there." She tapped his cheek below one eye. "Just there, watching me."

He shook his head, bemused, bewildered. "You, lady, when you are tired, chatter like a magpie. And your eyes sparkle like crystal—though sometimes they look like thunder. Or is it the drink doing that?"

"Not the drink. You know I liked it," she said, "when we—oh, I should not say."

When they had kissed? The thought flashed through his mind. "I liked it too. Perhaps you should try to sleep."

She sighed and leaned toward him. "I had a thought."

"Now what? You are full of thoughts. I cannot keep pace."

"In a few days, Samhain will be upon us. The eve of All Souls Day," she said.

He lifted a brow in quick comprehension. "A time when strange things may occur. And something strange . . . just happened to you. The vision?"

She nodded. "A time when the veil between this world and the Otherworld goes so fine and thin that one may be visited by spirits. Or have visions."

"Just so." What might seem mad suddenly did not.

"Perhaps that happened to me today. Each day closer to Samhain, we are closer to the veil, and I saw something out of the ordinary. Enchantment in the air, you see."

"I see," he murmured. Sitting beside her, feeling her warmth, her arm and shoulder pressed against him, her golden hair spilling over his arm, he felt entranced. Spellbound.

"And then," she said, "you kissed me."

His heart pounded. "I did."

"It felt like magic."

"Did it," he said, his voice gruff, low. He leaned in, his breath meeting hers. This time when his lips touched hers, it was for her alone, with no pretense about it. Her mouth softened under his, and her gentle sound of need surged through him.

She slipped her arms around his neck, and he turned to pull her close, enveloping her, the next kiss deeper, each one renewing with a power, a hunger, that was the very soul of enchantment—unexpected, irresistible, inexorable, dreamlike.

Then he pulled back, stunned in the moment, not sure what had come over him—or her. She was gossamer indeed, this girl. "We should not—"

She spoke in the same moment. "You must think me—so lonely. All turned about."

He soothed his hand over her hair. "I think you are tired. And lovely," he murmured. "I am the one all turned about."

"Samhain is a magical time, I swear to you. Watch what happens in the next weeks. I feel it already."

"I suppose that could explain—is that a knock at the door?" He rose from the cot, and in two long strides, crossed the small room to pull the iron latch. Seeing Brother Allan, he stepped back to allow the monk to enter.

"Pardon me, pardon please," Allan said. He looked from the knight to the lady, and must have sensed something, for a fiery blush spread from his neck to the roots of his red-gold tonsure. "I brought soup for the lady. And ale. And sir, your kinsmen want me to tell you that they are in the rectory and waiting for you to join them for a meal. Gilchrist message is 'where in hell are you?' Forgive me, I would not have said that myself, but he told me to say so."

"Thank you," Liam said, smothering a laugh. "Food is just the thing for the lady, I am thinking. Lady Tamsin," he added in farewell, as she went pink from her graceful neck to the pale curls spiraling along her brow.

"Sir William," she managed, as he closed the door behind him.

WIPING THE EMPTY bowl with a cloth, stacking it with the spoon and cup on the tray, Tamsin heard a quick knock on the door. Hoping that might be Liam returning, she opened the door quickly. Allan her his widest smile.

"I came to collect the dishes, if I may?"

"Of course. Come in." She stepped aside.

He set down a jug and a small packet wrapped in cloth. "Oatcakes, fresh from the griddle, in case you need something more. And watered heather ale. It is mild, good before sleeping. Is there aught else I can bring you, my lady?"

"I have all I need, I believe. Thank you."

"Brother Gideon says in a few days, he may be able to take you to Selkirk."

"That is good of him." Just Gideon? While she would be glad of his company, she felt a quick sting of disappointment that Liam Seton was not mentioned. Perhaps he had changed his mind about going with her. Perhaps she had misjudged his interest earlier. Even so, if she did end up in a convent, she would treasure those kisses, always. "But I will not inconvenience anyone. Perhaps I can make my way there if I could borrow a horse and cart."

"The abbot would not allow it, my lady. He insists you stay for a few days and leave only with an escort. Until then, he has instructed that no one be admitted at the gate unless we know them as friends. He is concerned for your welfare."

"And I am grateful, and I hope I can thank him in person soon." Dare she tell the abbot about her vision and reveal that protected part of her life? He might simply think her mad and dismiss it. Besides, she remembered little of what came to her, as often happened. Something about fire. Perhaps she should take it to Gideon, her trusted friend, although she had never mentioned her ability to him either.

As much as she cherished truth, she hesitated to share what came through her. But now William Seton had witnessed it. Would he tell his kinsmen? She frowned.

"My lady?" Allan brought her back. "The abbot wants to see you, but he has not been well and is taking his time."

"Of course. So Abbot Murdoch is kin to Brother Gideon and the rest?"

"Their uncle, aye. A sister is abbess at Lincluden. Another uncle, a Macnab like Finley—their mother's family—is a priest who follows the old Scottish church, as some do. Father Fergus has a wife and a large family and tends a parish in the remote hills."

"Truly! I thought the old ways of the Scottish Church were all but gone."

"Some still keep it, and some Scottish bishops turn a blind eye to country priests practicing the old ways, because they serve the people in the hills well, celebrating the sacraments and teaching them the lessons of the Church. Abbot Murdoch began as a priest of the old ways, then joined the Benedictines. He has been abbot here for years."

"How long have you been here, Allan? I have seen you about, though we never had a chance to talk."

"Since I was eleven, madam. I will be a full monk someday." He beamed.

"Brother Gideon will soon become one too, I imagine. I never knew he had brothers, though we chatted often." She smiled. "Will you have an oatcake? There are too many here for me." The lad, tall and rangy, looked like he had a good appetite.

"Thank you, if you do not mind, my lady." He accepted one and took a great bite. "So good," he mumbled. "Brother Richard is an excellent cook. Aye, having his uncle here was a help to Gideon," he said, chewing. "When he first came here, he was sorely wounded in the head and leg. They sent me running for cloths, hot water, and spirits that day and I was glad to help. He stayed, and felt drawn to the peace of our brotherhood and the good work we do here."

"To be so wounded, how awful. Was Brother Gideon a knight like his brothers? Forgive me," she said, realizing she was peppering him with questions. "I am curious about the Setons. They have been kind to me."

Allan crunched, swallowed. "Aye, he was a knight, one of the Setons of Dalrinnie."

Wrapping the oatcakes, she paused. "Setons of Dalrinnie?"

"Surely you heard of them, being lady there. And the Setons are your friends."

"I knew that Setons held Dalrinnie, but there are many of that name in the area." And William—Liam—had dismissed her questioning earlier. Was his connection to Dalrinnie closer than he would admit?

"True, there are many Setons in Selkirkshire. Abbot Murdoch is a Seton as well. But forgive me, my lady, I should not speak of matters that do not concern me. I would not want to have to confess that to our abbot." He took up the tray. "Do you need aught else? Blankets? Candles? We keep good beeswax candles here for guests, on the shelf there. Tallow smokes so."

"Thank you. Oh, one request. Could I visit the library and perhaps use a desk in the scriptorium? I have done so before."

"I am sure it is fine, but I will ask Brother Gideon." He gave an awkward bow and closed the door.

The Setons of Dalrinnie! She spread a hand over her chest and took a breath. Were Sir William Seton and his brothers the Setons of Dalrinnie? If so, he wanted more than the Rhymer's book—he wanted the castle too. Nor had he mentioned this to her. Was that dishonest, or deeply reserved? She shook her head, confused.

Then her temper, often quick, rose like steam. If he wanted

book and castle both, he could just return to Edward empty-handed. He could fight Malise Comyn for them and leave her out of it. She did not care. She would not comply with any of this.

But she did care, far too much already. Sinking to the bed, she put her head in her hands. He had kissed her—she had kissed *him*. And he had seen a vision come over her when she was not even sure what she had said. Would he report that to Edward too?

The reminder of the Setons of Dalrinnie turned her dilemma on its axis. Not knowing what William Seton wanted, she dared not trust him now.

Perhaps the Dalrinnie widow seemed ripe for the picking, between Edward's demand of the book and the temptation of Dalrinnie Castle. She had been lonely and vulnerable, wanting to believe in William Seton as the strong, kind, beautiful knight from her dream. She had made a fool of herself.

But she was certain his kindness was genuine, and those kisses were not false. Not at all. She felt it in the very core of her being. Yet he had not shared the truth with her when he could have. If he was a Seton of Dalrinnie, he could claim all from her.

Pressing a trembling hand to her head, she knew she must reach Selkirk soon and retrieve Thomas's writings. Only her kin should have them.

As for William the harper-knight, she must be cautious. He might be more of a threat than she realized.

CHAPTER FOURTEEN

"**S**HE LEFT DALRINNIE in secret? Well done!" Gideon sat with Liam and Gilchrist in the refectory as they lingered over the meal Brother Richard had prepared. "For so quiet and scholarly a lass, Lady Tamsin can be stubborn."

"So I am learning." Liam took a mouthful of the hearty soup. A glance toward the window showed the rain continuing. "Finley has been gone for a while."

"He will take time on patrol to be sure we were not followed," Gilchrist said. "I will take the next turn round."

"Then I will follow after dark," Liam said. "We mean to keep watch, Gideon, in case they ride near the abbey."

"I can come out with you as well," Gideon offered. "Our reverend uncle will allow that in this situation, I think. Lady Tamsin was right to leave Dalrinnie," he went on. "And what a blessing it was to see you lads at the gate with her. We had word of troops heading to Dalrinnie. And I am so thankful that Edward saw fit to liberate you, Liam."

"Just for this odd mission." Liam had explained the king's orders, though he held back some of what he knew.

"I had hoped that someday Edward might restore the castle and appoint you commander."

"I have not behaved well enough," Liam drawled. "He dangled that plum and I had to sign fealty again, but we all know how far his promises go."

"Your authority there would serve us well for other reasons," Gideon said. "I do not admire Comyn, and will say no more on that matter."

"Still working toward forgiveness?" his twin asked.

"Toward peace, at least. This place has a humbling effect on a man. Even me." Gideon shrugged a shoulder. "Working with sacred texts and in the hospital helps remind me life should hold more than revenge."

Liam understood Gideon's deep hatred of Comyn. They all shared it, not just because Sir Malise had captured Liam with Sir Christopher Seton—but because years earlier, he had treated their sister Agatha cruelly. "You have done well at Holyoak, brother. Some would nurse grievance to flame and then burn all in the name of revenge."

"You have been doing that for all of us," Gideon returned.

"I did try to master the temptation," Liam said with chagrin. "But I may incur the king's wrath again over that damnable book, or in stealing a commander's bride—we could all be accused of that. Gideon may have found peace in a penance of prayer, but such does not suit me," he told his brothers.

"Hold on to your anger if it helps Scotland find a resolution to this accursed war. If the day ever comes to forgive, you will know it."

"You do sound like a priest," Liam groused.

"A monk. But I have not yet decided."

"If you feel ready to return, then come with us," Gilchrist said. "We could use you. Our king could use you."

With a soft laugh, Gideon reached for an oatcake and broke it apart. "Our uncle wants to see you. He has news from Ettrick Forest, I think. A messenger came yesterday, but he did not share news with me. He is resting now but says he will see you tonight or in the morning."

"Whatever he needs. Gideon, what do you know of Lady Tamsin?" Liam asked.

"She visited a few times to study books in our library. I have been working as the library-keeper—our uncle entrusted me with the key to the chained volumes. I showed Lady Tamsin our collection, and we talked of texts and books. We are somewhat friends, though I have not seen her since her husband's death last winter."

"She seems a proper lady," Gilchrist said. "Educated, intelligent, courteous."

"Very much. I have never heard her speak ill of anyone, even the English or her English husband. Though she never said it directly, I gather she is loyal to Scotland and Bruce. But aye, a perfect lady born and bred, even if she did go out a window like a thief in the night."

Liam huffed at that, remembering the sight of the lady scrambling down a rope. She had fallen into his arms, then traveled with strangers without complaint. She had even allowed him to kiss her when it would save them all in the moment. He caught his breath at the memory of that and private kisses later, born of something more than lust, a feeling he dared not define.

"She is an interesting lady," he said simply. "How is it she married an English lord? The Keiths of Kincraig have always been loyal Scots."

"Her brother chose to ride for Edward and keeps to it," Gilchrist said.

"I suspect he means to protect his estate and his sisters," Liam said.

"I gather Lady Tamsin's father thought the marriage would protect her and add an ally for his family. She had no say in it," Gideon explained. "She said little of it, though she mentioned that her husband called her his Scottish bride."

"Scotland is full of Scottish brides," Gilchrist said.

"It was not said kindly," Gideon replied. "A Scottish lady in an occupied Scottish castle—she felt distressed. Trapped. It is why she enjoyed coming here to spend time in our library and our scriptorium. She worked on her pages too. She writes a pretty hand, you see," he explained. "And writes verse."

"Did she work on her great-grandfather's parchments?"

"She did."

"Then perhaps she does have this thing that Edward wants."

"Only she can tell you that."

"Therein lies the challenge," Liam murmured.

"Is she drawn to the religious life, to come here often?" Gilchrist asked.

"She is more interested in our library than our piety," Gideon said. "And interested in the work in our hospital as well. Her sister visited Holyoak too, you see. She is a healer of some repute in Kincraig, as I understand. Out of charity, Lady Rowena brings her remedies to monasteries with hospitals. I met her when I was a patient here before Lady Tamsin ever visited. Both ladies," Gideon added, "are beyond reproach. Their younger sister as well, I would guess."

"Lady Margaret," Liam supplied.

"Aye. Each one would be a marriage prize, though only Lady Tamsin's match had been decided before her father's death. One sister had been betrothed, but I believe the fellow died in battle. Sir Henry has the responsibility of finding matches for his sisters now, but he is away. Their marriages must wait."

"Hopefully they are safe there. Kincraig is remote enough to be a lesser target," Gilchrist said. "I believe their uncle is Sir Robert Keith, Marischal of Scotland. Being the Rhymer's great-granddaughters recommends them as well. Aye, Liam?"

Silent, he nodded. That the Keith sisters were valuable prizes would not escape the attention of King Edward—or Malise Comyn either. But with Sir Henry Keith away, he hoped Lady Tamsin's sisters were adequately shielded from a world in turmoil and suitors seeking advantage.

He clenched a fist, feeling again an urge to shield Tamsin from Malise Comyn and any who might tally her worth, or her sisters' worth, on their fingers instead of in their hearts. He was sure Henry Keith would feel the same way.

"Lady Tamsin praised her husband for sparing men to escort

her to Holyoak to visit. Some husbands would have thought their lady's interest in scholarly things to be unimportant."

"He encouraged her interest?" Liam asked.

"Tolerated it, at least. She convinced him to show generosity to Holyoak. He sent coins in her name on high holy days. He honored her."

"Good." Liam was glad to know that the man had respected her. Not that it should matter to him, he reminded himself.

"She was a good wife. When he was sore wounded last February, she sent to us for help. I went there with another monk." Gideon shook his head. "There was little we could do. A vicious wound in an aging man—he lacked the strength. She was left a young widow dependent on the king's whim."

"He has decided to marry her off," Liam said. "Malise has the order."

"No wonder she went out the tower," Gideon said. "She would do well in a convent if it came to that. She has a scholarly inclination. I vow she can write text as beautifully as any monk or nun."

"This love of books is why she insists on going to Selkirk," Liam said. "Friends there, she says." Once she went there, he might never see her again. What then of her, and his growing need to be sure she was safe? What of the grandfather's mysterious book and the king's interest in it?

He swallowed his ale quickly, the taste of the abbey's heather ale light and earthy. Though he had been to Holyoak often enough, he had never seen Lady Tamsin there. Nor had Gideon mentioned her—perhaps because she was the lady of Dalrinnie.

"What do you know of the books the lady owns?" he asked Gideon. "Is there anything of particular value?"

"All books are valuable, especially with the English burning our castles and libraries and carting away chests full of documents to destroy them or haul them south for Edward. I know Lady Tamsin treasures a beautiful wee book of hours and some others. She kindly promised to donate some books to our library when

Abbot Murdoch nearly begged her, hearing what she has."

"Did she ever mention a book written by Thomas the Rhymer?" Liam persisted.

"She spoke of his poetry. But a book? Not that I recall. Although—" He paused, shook his head.

"How did Edward find out about Thomas's book, I wonder?" Gilchrist asked.

"Wait." Gideon sat forward. "The day her husband died, I was at Dalrinnie. Sir Malise was there too. I avoided the man. But when it was clear Sir John was dying, I heard Malise tell Lady Tamsin that he would inform the king. He left without waiting for the man to die. He seemed eager."

"He wanted to be the first to tell Edward that Dalrinnie would need a new commander," Gilchrist said.

"Likely so. Perhaps Witton mentioned the book to Malise. They met often, I think, working together for Edward. I know Malise spoke privately with him while the man was ill. If Witton was concerned about his wife's welfare after his death, he might have told Malise she had something valuable, hoping to protect her. He trusted Comyn."

"Malise may have told Edward about the book," Liam said, "but then he let Edward believe the Rhymer's daughter was an old woman."

"He wanted the lady for himself," Gilchrist said. "If Edward knew her real worth, he might have made another decision."

"The lady and her wee book won me my freedom, and I am thankful for that," Liam said. "If she needs help now, I am her man. What now, lads?"

"Liam could take the lady to Selkirk," Gilchrist said. "See what her business is there and if it has to do with any of this."

"It may," Gideon said. "She knows a bookseller in Selkirk."

"Oh?" Liam looked at him quickly.

"He is a bookbinder as well. He came here months ago to see the abbot and mentioned that the lady gave him some pages. But I do not know what they were."

"Curious," Liam said. "I will take her to Selkirk and see what her errand is."

"You can get the book from her there. Steal it if you must," Gideon remarked.

"That does not sound like a priest," his twin said.

"Monk," Gideon corrected.

LATER, RIDING OUT of the gate in gathering darkness to begin his turn on patrol, Liam lifted a hand in farewell as Gideon stood back from the gate, black hood pulled high, face pale and drawn. Liam felt keenly that his brother wanted to go with his kinsmen, though he only watched them leave.

Glancing over his shoulder, Liam glimpsed the thatched cottage at the far end of the walled enclosure, where candlelight flickered in the window. He felt a subtle tug within, like a taut line stretching between him and the lady inside. Though he had met her weeks ago and again today, they had endured travel, hardship, risks—and impulsive kisses that had taken him by storm. His heart felt like a stiff and hesitating wheel creaking into motion.

Heaven had not favored him much since the day his castle had been taken, the day he had turned away in the rain to vanish into the forest. Hope and contentment vanished, too, when he became a hunted man. In his dedication to the Scottish cause, he had shut away the remnants of his dreams.

Seeing that small light in the window, he felt a glimmer of hope, not just this new chance to reclaim his property, but a sense within as if a locked door had opened a crack.

Leaving the gate and palisade behind, he thought of Lady Tamsin's odd episode, a vision, she had called it, of fire at the abbey. Such things happened too easily with hearths and candle flames a common necessity, but the monks were cautious. Yet she had mentioned men at the gate, as if in attack. Puzzling though they were, her words stayed on his mind.

Heading over empty moorland in misted moonlight, he saw no one about. Peace ruled, at least for now.

CHAPTER FIFTEEN

L IGHT STREAMED THROUGH the glass window above, falling over the page where Tamsin sat at a writing table in Holyoak's narrow scriptorium off the abbey's small library. The rain ended but the gloom lingered, and even in daylight she needed golden candlelight spilling over the parchment. She tipped her head, hearing the bells ring. Noon already!

Last night, exhausted, she had slept deeply, emerging from her cottage at mid-morning when Brother Allan brought bacon and more watered ale, and proudly produced the key to the library lent him by Gideon. He unlocked the chain holding a shelf of books and left her there to read part of the French romance epic *Huon de Bordeaux,* after which she worked on her pages.

Opening the little box that Thomas had given her, the box she treasured, she brought out the little crystal ink pot that he had once said was a gift from the Queen of Faery. She had believed it as a child; now she guessed it might have been made by a glassmaker, perhaps even in faraway Venice. Glass crafted there was said to be near magical in its beauty. She would allow herself that much fancy. Smiling, she worked a little wax plug free and swirled the bottle. The bit of ink inside was still good, a bit thick. Picking up a small cup of water, she let a few drops drip from her finger, then stirred the ink with a little stick, items easily available in this small but well-organized scriptorium.

The ink was a thick black-brown mixture made from oak

galls, iron crystals, and precious gum Arabic, which she had prepared herself. Those materials she had been forced to leave behind at Dalrinnie. She sighed, thinking of her little writing desk there, the perfect light, the quiet in that sunny upper room.

Then she took out a sheet of parchment, rolled and wrapped in a protective leather sleeve. She had last worked on the page at Dalrinnie. That seemed a long time ago, somehow—so much had happened since. Spooling it open, she weighed its corners with stones and smoothed it to begin the work.

The page was faintly lined and partially covered in her own handscript. She had been copying over more of Thomas's verses, and would use a little of her time here to add more to the neat page. The words she meticulously wrote were copied from Thomas's jumble of scraps, dozens of small bits of parchment, folded and creased, some of them with worried edges, letters faded and worn, not always legible. She rummaged in the box again to bring out a flat packet, opening it carefully to take out a curled scrap.

She strained to read it in candlelight. *On the morrow, before noon, shall blow the greatest wind that ever was heard before in all Scotland,* this one began.

Tamsin had copied this text earlier. The prophecy referred to the death of King Alexander years before—the fatal accident that had deprived Scotland of a king and had led to King Edward's fiery determination to dominate Scotland in lieu of a strong Scottish monarch.

Thomas had made many prophecies, some so obscure they made little sense. Line by line, page by page, she created multiple copies of his writings, multiple sets of the same pages, knowing how important it was to have more than one copy. He had entrusted the work to her and she would honor it.

Over a few years, she had created seven copies of pages she compiled from his own words, the brief and longer writings he had given her. Some she understood easily; some notes were barely legible and she had to guess. His handscript was spiky, hurried, often illegible. But she had come to realize that her life's work was to preserve what he had done. Just now, much of the work was locked in a chest at Dalrinnie.

Malise Comyn sat on a treasure trove of Thomas's writings and did not know it. And he must never find out, she told herself.

She would never give up those prophecies. No one knew for certain they existed but Tamsin. She had waited years—would wait longer—to reveal them.

The book that had gone to the bookseller, the book bound and finished with covers, was different. She had copied those pages too—a long epic poem that Thomas had written, an opus that seemed dear to his heart, for it was unlike his ballads or his prophetic verses. The story was a version of the ancient tale of two lovers, Tristan and Iseult, destined by their stars to find each other. But Iseult was married against her will to King Mark, who relentlessly pursued the lovers. The poem was beautifully told, the story poignant, heart-rending, and tragic. But it was not prophesy.

She had made a copy for her family and had given it to the Selkirk bookbinder to make something very special of it. Yet if King Edward got hold of the book, he would find only a love story that could crack even his old, barren heart. Each time Tamsin read the story, she wept for the lovers who ran from a bitter, angry king toward a tragic destiny. She had yearned for their happiness.

For an hour and more, she worked, copying scraps of verses and predictions that were familiar, for she had read them often in her great-grandfather's spiky handscript. Finally, she copied a line she had never quite understood. It was scrawled on a torn piece that did not seem part of his other writings. But it was lovely, and she was glad to include it.

Until luck returns...lady of gold...takes a harp...to hold...

A lady taking up a harp, her music bringing luck to someone. Whatever it meant, she loved the thought of a lady harper. Perhaps someday Liam Seton would show her how to play the harp strings—*stop that*, she told herself sternly. Likely the line was a scrap of a ballad; as a harper, Thomas had written many songs.

From a dish on the desk, she took a little pinch of sand and blew it gently over the letters to dry them. Setting Thomas's pages away, she decided to compose a quick letter to Henry on the chance that she could reach him by sending a messenger to Carlisle. Perhaps the abbot could help with that.

Though she had hoped to be off to Selkirk that day, she was grateful for the respite and time to work in the scriptorium. Nor could she overlook the good fortune that had brought her to Holyoak—a heaven-sent troupe of handsome warrior angels. She smiled at the thought.

Selkirk could wait a little longer. She could only hope Comyn would not find the bookbinder first. But if he found the pages hidden at Dalrinnie—all would be lost.

Sighing, she dipped a newly sharpened quill tip into the ink-pot set in the desk. Brother Allan had produced a pot of fresh charcoal black ink. Though ink made from charcoal paste was thin and faded quickly, it was suitable for letter-writing.

In the silence, her pen scritch-scratched over the parchment sheet again. The letter might not reach Henry, but she had to try.

. . . *I left Dalrinnie in the company of friends,* she wrote. *They say castles like Thornhill and Kincraig may be threatened, and I worry for our sisters and cousin. I will do my best to go to our sisters and to find you also. Send news of your wellbeing and where you are located, written in a note by your hand, to Holyoak by Saint Mary's Loch. The monks will hold the letter for me. I have an errand in Selkirk but hope to receive your reply—*

With luck, Gideon could find a messenger to take the note southward, but she knew a reply might be a miracle. Shaping one letter, then another, making a word, a sentence, a page, she knew she must take her work, and each day, a step at a time.

Inside, her stomach fluttered. A feeling of being hunted, lost, had troubled her. Yet Liam Seton, surprisingly, had influenced that dread—she felt better, somehow, near him, and could not say why.

Truly he was in her thoughts too often; ice-blue eyes that saw into her soul even in ordinary moments; the deep, creamy voice that poured through her body; the height and strength of him, the sureness and presence. She felt drawn to him.

But she shook her head against it. Her concern must be her siblings and her promise to protect the Rhymer's legacy.

She blew sand over the damp ink and folded the letter, then took brown wax from her writing box to melt it in the candle flame and seal the letter. With a small oval brass seal, minutely engraved with the laurel branch of the Keiths and etched with her initials, T and K, she pressed it and set the letter aside.

Taking one more sheet of parchment torn from a larger piece, she smoothed it and began. That page was already prepared, too, ruled with faint lines to guide new text, with a block of space reserved for the rubric, a large initial to be added with fine red scrollwork. Perhaps she could ask for a little vermilion ink to make the initials herself.

For now, she wanted to record what she could remember of the words that had come to her in the rain the day before. At first it seemed a blur. Then it came back.

Fire in the oak, in fair Holyoak, men at the gates and the tolling of the bell . . .

She gasped as awareness dawned. Fire in the abbey and men attacking the gates could not be ignored. Somehow, she had to warn the monks.

THEY RODE FOR hours patrolling the hills and the high road, seeing only sheep and goats on hills coated in thick mist, a shepherd with a dog, a farmer driving an ox cart filled with hay. Once, Liam and the others followed the sound of a loud, drunken song to discover an old man guiding a pony cart stacked with ale kegs, an oil lamp swinging from the bench like a star in the foggy firmament. Gilchrist waved him onward, advising him to head home and be quiet.

"Och, aye," the man said. "Soldiers about. Back that way."

Riding in the direction the man indicated, Liam and his brother and cousin traveled as day sank toward dusk. The rain was done but fog sat cupped between slopes near the crescent-shaped loch that hugged a stretch of the Yarrow Water. That route would lead back to the abbey, where the drunken man had insisted soldiers might be found.

Soon a cluster of knights crested the rim of a hill, helmets gleaming dull in the dim light. Two wore red-and-gold tunics and three held lion-emblazoned red shields like strokes of flame in the haze. Liam and his kinsmen cut across the moorland as the leader cantered toward them and raised a gauntleted hand. He was a swarthy man, bearded black, eyes dark, face framed by his chain mail coif.

Gilchrist lifted a hand in greeting. "Sir! What brings you this way?"

The man walked his horse closer. "I am Sir Patrick Siward, come out of Dalrinnie Castle. We are looking for a lady who left the custody of the commander of Dalrinnie. She may be in danger. You are king's men?"

"Aye, ordered to escort this fellow here." Gilchrist gestured toward Liam. "After that we may ride to Dalrinnie. Orders from De Valence."

"Aye then. Comyn would welcome more men at Dalrinnie should you go there. We saw you riding toward the abbey." Siward gestured toward Holyoak in the far distance beyond the loch. "Do you have business with the monks?"

"Not your concern, sir," Finley said.

"Some might disagree." He rested a hand on his dagger hilt. "What is your business there?"

"The abbot is my kinsman," Liam answered.

"And who are you?"

"Sir William Seton, acting as a royal messenger." He had been directed to take a book from the lady, after all. "We stopped at the abbey. My wife was weary and in need of rest." These knights were not the men who had gone to the tavern, but either way, his deliberate message—*my wife*—would reach Comyn. Either Sir Malise would look elsewhere or act on impulse and go after Liam, not Tamsin. He intended to be ready.

"We heard that king's men were escorting a married pair. But we are looking for a lady who ran away from Dalrinnie. She took something of Comyn's with her."

"She is a thief?" Gilchrist asked.

"She is the commander's betrothed. What she stole belongs to him, but he is more concerned about her safety."

Finley stepped his horse forward. "Who is this lady? What did she steal?"

"Lady Thomasina. Small, fair, if you should see her." Siward shrugged. "Whatever she took and whyever she fled, Comyn is in a fit over it. He thinks she may have gone to the abbey to beg sanctuary."

"No thieving runaway brides at the abbey," Gilchrist said. "You rode all day with no luck? Will you head back to Dalrinnie now?"

"Soon. Two or three patrols are looking. We will find her."

"Your commander sounds a taskmaster," Liam said.

"A lord and knight just doing what his king requires of him."

"A woman alone would be foolish to travel through this area. There are outlaws in the hills and the forest," Liam said.

"Outlaws? Say what you know." He kept a hand on the hilt. The soldiers on the ridge were well armed, Liam noted. He crossed his hands on the saddle pommel, silent, watchful.

"What we all know, sir. The forest is overrun with dangerous rebels," Gilchrist said. "None of us are keen to go there. Would you?"

"Not by choice," the man growled. "Very well. Since you know naught, we will move on. But you say you have king's orders? Who is the message meant for?"

"A private matter, confidential to the king." Liam reached into his surcoat to withdraw the king's order, letting the royal seal and ribbons flap before he put it back.

"Fine. Go on. Though we may stop at Holyoak in case the lady is there."

"Only one woman is there. And she is mine," Liam said. "Look elsewhere for your runaway. Most likely she headed north, not south, to avoid the king's troops."

"Possibly. Good night, sir." Siward gave a curt nod and turned to ride toward the men who waited on the misted ridge.

Liam turned to his kinsmen. "Get back to the abbey and secure the gates. I will watch to be sure they are gone." He rode slowly toward the hill as Comyn's men moved down the opposite slope. Waiting in shadows, he watched them depart.

Seeing the gathering clouds darken with more rain, he could not shake a growing sense of unease as he turned toward the abbey. Again he thought of Lady Tamsin's vision. He would be wise to heed it.

SHIVERING DESPITE HER cloak, Tamsin knelt on the stone floor of the chapel, hands pressed in prayer. A thin draft whispered past. Not long ago, hearing the vesper bells while in the library, she had seen a line of monks departing the chapel after their prayers. Troubled by the unknowns ahead of her—and still haunted by sultry kisses whose comfort she craved but was reluctant to admit—she walked to the empty chapel hoping for elusive serenity. Overhead, the sky was dusky and dreary. She glanced around, realizing she had not seen Liam Seton all day.

Whispering her prayers now, trying to focus, her thoughts veered again toward the man who stirred such longing and confusion in her. If Liam was following Edward's orders, she must be cautious.

Yet where he was concerned, she could not trust herself to tell good intent from bad, truth from lies, a genuine kiss from a false one. She sighed.

Behind her, the chapel door creaked open and shut and a dark hooded figure moved through candlelight. Brother Gideon knelt on the straw-scattered stone floor, crossed himself, and bent his head to his hands.

Tamsin turned away, running her fingers over the smooth paternoster beads in her hands. The wood and ivory prayer strand that she kept in the small pouch at her belt had belonged to her mother, its beads blessedly familiar as she soothed over them in silent plea. *Help me know when to speak and when to keep silent,* she prayed. *Help me to protect the Rhymer's work and find my sisters and brother.*

And please, she added fervently, *help me to forget William Seton. And if I cannot, help me to understand who he is—and why he is so much on my mind.*

Standing, she turned to go, passing the monk wrapped in his prayers. Dabbing her fingers in the shallow basin of holy water, she reached for the iron door latch.

"Allow me," Gideon murmured just behind her as he pulled the door open to allow her to precede him into the iron-gray twilight.

Drawing her cloak close, Tamsin paused. "Brother Gideon, please, a favor." Just that, though she wanted to ask about the Setons of Dalrinnie. More, she wanted desperately to confide her vision and warn him.

"What can I do for you?" A tall shadow under the black hood, he reminded her of his older brother again in appearance, and in that air of deep reserve that spoke of secrets, patience, and the habit of listening to troubles without sharing his own.

She reached into the pocket of her cloak for the folded letter. "I want this to reach my brother, Sir Henry Keith of Kincraig. But I am not sure where he is."

Gideon took the letter. "We can find a messenger for you. Where was he last?"

"Perhaps in Lanercost Abbey, where they say Edward is recovering from illness."

"Messengers come here regularly for Abbot Murdoch, and one may be here in the next few days. If your brother is there with the king, a messenger can try to find him."

"Thank you. And—if you please, I need to travel to Selkirk soon. Could I borrow a horse or cart in the morning?"

He shook his head. "That is unwise for a lady alone, and well you know it. The abbot would not approve it. I believe my brother intends to take you, but if he cannot, I could do so. Let us wait." Cool gray light edged his features as he looked down at her.

Nodding, disappointed, she took a chance. She trusted Gideon, who had been her friend for over two years. "Do you remember that I met a bookseller here at the abbey?"

"The fellow in Selkirk? Ah," he breathed. "You gave him a sheaf of parchments. Those were the Rhymer's pages, and not your own writings?"

"Aye." She wondered if his brother had told him what the king wanted. "That is why I need to get there. I need to get away from—your brother."

"He is no threat to you. We all want you to be safe. I know about Sir Malise and the book. And the marriage, my lady."

She nodded. "So he told you. I am sorry to bring my troubles here."

"My lady," he murmured, "we are invested in the troubles here at Holyoak."

"Do you mean the hospital?" She glanced toward the darkened building with the separate entrance, a separate world, in its way.

"More than that. We find ways here to—aid the cause, as it were. Keep that to yourself. As for my kinsmen, I swear upon the Rood, you can trust all of us."

"You are a friend. But your brother William has orders from the king concerning me."

"Liam is not one to blindly follow orders. If he pursues Edward's wishes, he has reasons of his own. Liam can help you best, I think."

"He confuses me, Gideon. Harper, outlaw, knight—loyal or

disloyal?"

"He does what is necessary. As do we all." His thin smile held a touch of sadness, making her wonder if Gideon had done something that had hurt his soul. "Liam has your welfare in mind. Very much so, I think."

"I want to trust him, but—I need to know what is true and what is not."

"Truth means much to my brother."

"When he pretends to be one thing, then another?"

"Honesty is the best road to take with him. You know that better than most, I think, forthright as you are. For now, the monks are gathering in the rectory, and I must join them. I will ask Brother Allan to be sure to bring your supper."

"Aye, but—I have not seen your brothers or your cousin all day. I wondered if I had been left on my own without notice."

"They would never do that. They are riding patrol, making sure all is well, and will return soon. The abbot wants to speak with them before the hour of compline, when we practice silence at Holyoak."

"Ah. Of course. I will be quiet then, too. What if they meet trouble out there? There are only the three." Comyn's men might be looking for her and could accost Liam and the others. She frowned, distressed.

"If they are not back by midnight, I will ride out myself to look for them."

"You care about your kinsmen very much."

"I do." He bowed his head a little and turned.

"Gideon," she said. He turned back with a questioning look. "Sometimes," she said tentatively, "sometimes I have—a sense of foreboding. I know things—that have come to be."

He tipped his head. "The Sight? I cannot say it surprises me."

She wondered if Liam Seton had said something. "You know?"

"You are True Thomas's kin." He smiled, patient and kind, and waited.

"I—had a sort of dream," she said, hesitant to admit to a vision here in this holy place. "That the abbey was attacked. That it was on fire."

Gideon studied her, thoughtful. "Tamsin, my friend," he said quietly, "thank you for telling me. I will make sure we are careful. Does Liam know?"

How curious he would ask. She nodded silently.

"Then he will be watching too. He thinks much of you." He nodded, turned toward the rectory.

A little sob filled her throat at his words. *Thinks much of you.* In better circumstances, she would cherish such words and feel hopeful. Walking back to the cottage, she glanced at the gate, sealed against the outside world. She felt the chill kiss of a breeze and the call of night birds, but heard no thud of horse hooves, no men's voices. Liam Seton and his kinsmen rode out because she was inside Holyoak. They willingly put themselves at risk because of her—and to protect their own.

Inside the cottage, she lit a candle against the gloom and went to the window. Dread turned inside her. She desperately wanted to see Liam ride through the gate, whole and hearty, with his kinsmen.

But she must leave Holyoak soon. Her presence here brought danger to those she cared about.

CHAPTER SIXTEEN

"THE FELLOWS LEFT? You followed them?" Abbot Murdoch asked Liam, who stood nearest him, while Gideon, Gilchrist, and Finley waited nearby. The fire in the stone hearth, bright and crackling, warmed the room nicely against fog and chill. The abbot reached down to soothe a hand over the ears of the tall gray dog beside his chair.

For a moment, Liam was reminded of the overheated room and his uncomfortable audience with King Edward. Weeks later, he would not have imagined himself here but was glad for it. "The men rode north," he replied. "I waited to be sure."

"Good. I am sorry to have missed you yesterday. It was a bad day for the aching joints, I fear," Murdoch went on. Liam suspected there was more to it than that; his uncle looked pale and drawn, and Gideon had said he was weak. He was glad, though, to see that Roc was with Murdoch, settled and attentive.

"I had a letter recently and needed to see you—and God sent you here to me." He smiled and shifted in his leather-slung chair draped with a woolen blanket.

"I am sorry I could not come sooner, Uncle," Liam said.

"We knew you had been taken—Gilchrist brought the news, and later told us you had been liberated. It is good to see you, lad. And the Lord brought you to our gate with Lady Thomasina. Let me come back to her. First, I received a message."

He reached toward the table with a trembling hand, and Liam

picked up the letter he indicated. Its broken red seal showed the tiny design of an equestrian knight encircled with castle and crown. Robert Bruce.

"In Robert's own hand, and bears his signature," his uncle explained, opening the creased page. "He mentions the English plan to evaluate castles ready for the plucking. He knows Gilchrist and Finley are tasked with that." He looked up. "And he mentions the royal ladies captured last month."

"Is there news of their release?" Gilchrist asked.

"Nothing yet. It may take years to negotiate their freedom."

"Last I saw Bruce in September," Liam said, "Edward refused to let the women go under any conditions. We all know that may not change until old Edward dies, stubborn as he is, and Prince Edward comes to the throne."

"The son can be as stubborn and cruel toward Scotland as his father," Finley said.

"But not as interested in pursuing the Scottish wars. That is his father's obsession," Liam said. "The old king is not well. I saw that for myself. The prince may abandon the assault on Scotland once he becomes king, especially if it proves difficult. And we are determined to make it so."

"Bruce says here," the abbot continued, "that Edward's treatment of the royal captives means danger for all Scotswomen. 'Those who may come under scrutiny or danger for their royal kinship or noble rank should be taken to places of safety,' he writes here. He wants them protected."

"Does he name certain women?" Liam asked.

"A few, including Lady Thomasina Keith, but he does not know she is safe here with us. He also mentions her sisters at Kincraig, and his daughter Elizabeth, called Lilias—one of his natural offspring. And he names Lady Kirsten Douglas at Thornhill too. Her uncle is one of Bruce's closest allies, so she could attract Edward's wrath. Bruce expresses concern for these women should the English attempt to take those castles."

"Aye so," Liam said. "I met Lady Kirsten at Lochmaben with

Lady Tamsin, and I know her father. We should remove both from Thornhill in case the English arrive."

"I will tell the king so in my reply, though it must wait upon a messenger who can reach him. Bruce also writes that he entrusted you, William, with another task, but must ask for this additional service as well. He trusts you. All of you," the abbot told them.

Liam nodded. "Before Edward had hold of me, I was seeing to tenants and rent-rolls on Bruce's properties, while also gathering support for him. Once we have seen Lady Tamsin and the others to safety, I mean to return to the work. We will bring Douglas of Thornhill out as well, though he may be loath to leave his castle."

"Some say he is loyal to Edward," Gilchrist said.

"No longer," Liam said. "He has been of great assistance in the rent-rolls."

"If he will come out of there, then you must help him as well."

"Tomorrow we head to Thornhill, aye?" Liam looked at Gilchrist and Finley, who nodded agreement. He noticed that Gideon began to answer, yet stopped.

"As for Lady Thomasina," the abbot said, "let her remain here until you return."

"Both ladies could go to Lincluden for an extended stay," Gilchrist suggested. "We could send word to Agatha to expect them."

"True, but it could bring a risk to Agatha if Malise pursues Lady Tamsin there."

"Malise," Gideon said, "must never be allowed near Agatha again."

"If we bring both ladies to the forest, they can disappear there," Finley said.

"If you think best," the abbot replied. "I have been giving the matter of your Lady Thomasina some thought, Liam."

She was not his lady, Liam began to say, but let it go. In some ways he had begun to feel that she was. "She is adamant that she find her friend in Selkirk. If left on her own while we are gone, she could be a runaway colt."

"Gideon will watch over her while you are gone." The abbot rubbed the dog's head for a moment. "I may have a solution for her unusual situation, but I want to talk with the girl first." He looked up. "The hour of compline is near, when we go silent until dawn. But this cannot wait. Bring her to me, Gideon. Liam, remain here."

Beckoning for Gilchrist and Finley to follow, Gideon left. Liam turned to his uncle. "Sir, what solution is that?"

"When Malise threatened the lass, you interfered by helping her. I am thinking you could interfere further."

"How?"

"Marry the girl." His uncle scratched the dog's ears, while Roc looked blissful.

"Marry!" The word jolted him to the heart. Even as he began to protest, a thought struck him. Married, Tamsin would be free of Comyn's plans; married, Liam might gain Dalrinnie through her. And married, she would be his, in his arms. He pulled in a breath.

"Do this," his uncle said, "and end the chase."

"The lady would never agree, sir. She does not trust me. Once she learns that Dalrinnie was mine, she will loathe me. I would seem no different than Comyn."

"A husband who would keep her safe amid this madness would solve her troubles. You will do that. Malise will not. And you could do with a wife."

Liam sighed, unsure of that. "At the least, she would not be forced to marry Comyn. It would be to her benefit."

"And yours. Do you agree out of chivalry, or because you see a good match, as I do?" His uncle regarded him. "Or is it vengeance against Malise?"

"All of that, sir," he admitted.

"Ah, here she is," the abbot said, looking up. "Thank you,

Gideon. You may go."

THE ABBOT STOOD out of courtesy, but Tamsin lifted a hand to dissuade him, seeing how weak the old man seemed, thinner and more feeble than when she saw him last. Beside him, Liam steadied his uncle's arm to help him sit again. Even Roc loped to his feet as if to help.

"Lady Thomasina, it is good to see you. I trust you have rested well while here."

"Aye, Reverend Father. Thank you for your hospitality and sanctuary. It was much needed, I am sorry to say." She avoided Liam's glance, unsure what to think, how she felt—or how he felt about her after their encounter in the cottage, visions, and kisses, and then her uncertainty about his motives. "Thank you for seeing me."

"Of course. My nephews told me why they brought you here. I understand your difficulty and I would like to help. Liam, some heather ale for the lady and yourself. And I would not mind some too."

As Liam obliged, pouring ale from a jug into small wooden cups, Tamsin glanced around the abbot's house. She had never been inside despite meeting him on earlier visits. The house had a humble simplicity, with whitewashed stone walls and a raftered, thatched roof overhead. But it was larger than her cottage, with a spacious, plainly furnished room where they gathered now, and a second chamber beyond a curtained door. Glancing around, she saw a few small windows studded with leaded circles of thick glass, shedding cool light on a few chairs, a bench, table, shelves—and books.

Volumes were stacked beside the abbot's chair and on a shelf; some were piled on the table, along with loose parchments, inkpots, quills, and a reading stand. The room was not entirely tidy, and Tamsin smiled to see the cozy environment of a man who loved books and learning and comfort. She liked him even more seeing the comfortable jumble of his home. It spoke to her of the man.

"Sit down, Lady Thomasina," the abbot said. Liam handed her a cup of ale and then opened a wooden folding stool for her. Rather than sit, he returned to his uncle's side and caught her eye. His quick frown seemed threaded with tension, his eyes a cloudy gray blue. His mood was somber, she realized, wondering what was behind it.

"I wanted to see both of you. I have prayed over your situation, my lady, and I have some thoughts. At first it seemed best to send you to Lincluden, but my nephews insist you will be safer in the forest for now."

"I appreciate it, Reverend Father. Though I must go to Selkirk to attend to a matter, and then go on to Kincraig, where my family lives. The route might go through the forest, but I did not think to stay."

"We can discuss that. You were a brave lass to do what you did."

"Brave or foolish, I am not certain which."

"I believe heaven guided you here. I have prayed on your dilemma, and a suggestion has come to me that might help."

"Aye?" Grateful for his attention but puzzled, she glanced at Liam. He stood with arms crossed, head tilted, subdued and expectant. She felt sure something had been decided before she arrived.

"I am acquainted with Sir Malise Comyn," the abbot was saying, "and I know what it is to deal with King Edward. Neither will rest until they get their way. But you cannot continue to keep just a few steps ahead of this. Comyn is intent on finding you. Would you like my advice?"

"Of course, sir," Tamsin said. Liam was silent.

"You must make sure that Sir Malise does not get what he wants. He will damage and destroy whatever he gains."

"He wants what belonged to the Rhymer," she said. "And he wants Dalrinnie."

"And you," the abbot said.

"So it seems. But I do not know what to do." She avoided Liam's steady gaze.

"Then it is time for honest talk. Will your errand in Selkirk help the situation?"

"It may. I must—I would find the bookseller there. He has the pages."

"The Rhymer's book?" Liam asked abruptly. "You never said."

"I did not tell you because you want this thing of me too."

"What is this book?" the abbot asked. "Tell us. We are not a threat, my dear."

She sighed, then relented. "My great-grandfather wrote of many things in a poor hand on scraps of paper. He gave them to me to copy out. He said they were very important to him. So when Brother Gideon talked of the bookseller and binder in Selkirk, I knew he could prepare the pages I copied into a book. My husband knew of it. I brought the pages to the bookbinder when he was here at Holyoak. But I do not know why anyone should want it but my kinfolk," she added fervently.

"Is the book safe in this man's keeping?" Liam sounded gruff.

"It should be. But I want to fetch it before Comyn can find it."

"And so you should." She had not expected so calm a response from him. She frowned, seeing again that something distracted him. She could sense his feelings somehow, like clear warm waves of awareness, as if they were wrapped with her own. Wanting to ask what bothered him, she could not.

Seton of Dalrinnie. Resentment returned like a slamming door. She looked away. She had said too much, feeling as protective of Thomas's writings now as the day he had entrusted his bookish little granddaughter with his work.

The abbot sipped his ale. "So you need to get the bound book. Then what?"

"I would take it to my sisters at Kincraig," she said. "I cannot return to Dalrinnie, for King Edward gave Comyn the keeping of it. But I refused to marry Sir Malise, so he cannot claim my right to the castle or any of my property."

"Therein lies the problem and the solution both, I believe."

"I do not understand. If I take to a convent, I would give up my claim to earthly possessions and properties."

"And Dalrinnie and your property, including that book, would be like leather balls, rolling free," the abbot said. "Edward would pounce."

"The king could assert that your properties reverted to him, as can happen when unmarried or widowed women enter the sisterhood," Liam added. "That is English law, not Scots or Irish, as is honored here. The king would claim the Rhymer's work that way. So a convent is not the answer."

"I see," she said. "I promised Grandda that I would protect his legacy. If entering a convent would undo that, then I cannot."

"Lady Thomasina," the abbot said, "I met Thomas the Rhymer years ago. An impressive fellow. And he might say that the most important thing to protect in this predicament is you, my lady. You are his legacy, you and your kin, even more so than his writings."

"My sisters and brother and I? That may be so."

"It is so," Liam's murmured.

The abbot smiled. "There is one course of action that will ensure what you need."

Seeing the quick sparkle in the old monk's dark-circled eyes, she had a sudden clear thought that made her gasp. "You think I should marry another?"

He smiled. "Thomas's lass indeed. Yes, I think you should marry...Sir William."

"Marry you?" She looked at Liam, bewildered.

His gaze was a steady blue clarity. "It is up to the lady."

"This is the most direct way to stop Sir Malise, I think," said Abbot Murdoch.

"If I agree, if we did—" She breathed in, out, vying for purchase as if she climbed a height. "The king could order our arrest. Or our deaths, both of us."

"Edward is predictable in his anger," the abbot agreed. "But I recommend this."

"What of you?" She turned to Liam, her heart a drum, beating out hopes, fears.

"If you marry someone now, it would deter Comyn." He spoke calmly, without emotion, yet his eyes were keenly blue, a sea-depth she could not quite read. Then he shrugged. "Or he might find a way around it."

"He would make me a widow and have done with it. That is what he would do."

"My dear, it could work. What do you say?" the abbot asked.

"Not marriage." She blurted out what came next. "Betrothal. A man cannot marry another man's betrothed."

"He can," Liam said. "But it might be enough."

"The banns of betrothal, once posted, are not easily dissolved," she argued.

"Banns are posted for at least a fortnight, giving others time to protest."

"But it would provide time that you may need," the abbot interrupted.

"Wait." Tamsin felt unable to meet Liam's gaze just then. "If I marry—Sir William, then he could claim what I own. The Rhymer's work. Dalrinnie."

The men exchanged glances, and Liam shook his head slightly. While Tamsin waited in silence, the fire crackled and the dog woofed in his sleep.

"I do not follow English law," Liam said at last. "Your things are your own."

"What do you say, my dear?" the abbot asked. "You could say vows tonight or in the morning. If not marriage, betrothal vows if you choose. But this should not wait. Liam leaves early tomorrow."

"You are leaving?" She felt as if the floor wavered under her.

"An assignment from the king," he said quietly.

She stood. "I must think."

Turning, she opened the door to step out into the evening light, and ran.

CHAPTER SEVENTEEN

HEARING THE STEADY peal of the compline bells as he walked toward the cottage tucked at the far corner of the palisaded walls, Liam passed a line of monks streaming out of the chapter house toward the rectory. Holyoak housed thirty monks in all, and he saw his brother among them now. Liam had just left Gilchrist and Finley in the rectory after a late bite of supper and an explanation of the abbot's suggestion; Gideon, hearing the plan as well, had left to escort their uncle to the chapel too. The older man suffered with trembles and weakness, yet did not complain. The work, he said, was good for him.

Liam felt impatient with the time spent here. Overfull with peace, prayers, and discussion, he ached to move, ride, do what needed done. He had promises to meet, help to give some, others to hold to account. Above all, he wanted what was not easily obtained—peace for all. For Scotland. For Dalrinnie. For Tamsin Keith.

Even more, he wanted her. The ache had a deeper layer, an urge to be with this woman, hold her, be the man for her needs, the heart for her heart. Wanting it so fiercely—and recognizing his greater need—was unlike him. He had locked up such feelings long ago. Somehow the lass found a key.

Days ago, he would never have anticipated this turn in his thinking. She had caught his attention keenly enough, a beauty, a puzzle. But this revelation had come suddenly. She was more than a golden lure. She was a golden strike of lightning in his life, undoing, remaking.

Compline silence or none, he had to see her before this night was out. Betrothal, marriage, or parting forever—whatever happened, he owed her some truth.

At the cottage door, he knocked. Waited. Knocked again. Finally, the door cracked a handspan and she peered up at him. Candlelight haloed her hair and its fat lovely braiding, with no veil to dull its soft gleam.

"May I come in?"

"It is late. We must be silent," she murmured.

"They can be silent. We must talk. Let me in." He flattened a hand on the door. "Please."

She stepped back, and he entered. The room was nearly dark but for a pool of light on the table, spilled by the honeyed flame of a fat beeswax candle.

In the sweet-scented light, he saw that she had been working on a parchment page spread out on the tabletop beside a small inkpot and quill.

"Lady, my apologies for the late hour. Would you prefer to walk outside while we talk?"

"It is chilly outside, and private in here. We will not be overheard."

"Do you plan to shout?"

"I might." She turned away. "Sit down. I am heating water in the hob—I wanted a hot drink to help me sleep. My sister used to prepare it for me with lavender, chamomile, dried cherries, and I believe she adds all-heal too. Will you have some?"

It did not sound very appealing. "I do not need a sleep potion."

"Not a potion. An herbal infusion that can be taken cool or warm. It relaxes me when I cannot sleep or feel a bit hither and thither. Rowena gave me a packet of the herbs that I keep with me. Do try some. It is nicer than ale or wine at night."

"I will try some." He wanted to keep on a good foot with her.

"Lady Rowena is the sister who makes herbal remedies? Gideon mentioned meeting her in the hospital here. It is a small place, if you have not visited it before," he added. "Eight beds or so, treating mostly injuries or aged persons. Gideon was there for a bit when he was injured."

"So he said. Aye, Rowena is a healer with a knowledge of herbs and such. But much of what she does is common sense, she says." Tamsin smiled. "She is modest about her ability, I think. Do sit."

"And you have another sister? Is she a healer too?" The simple wooden chair by the table looked too small for him. He chose to sit on the narrow cot instead. Straw rustled and the mattress sank on the rope supports, causing his hips to go down and his knees to come up. He stretched out his legs.

"My sister Meg?" She laughed as she stirred the little iron kettle. "She wanted to play with Henry more than with Rowena and me. She raced him, sparred with wooden swords, even bested him at archery. He was quite put out about that. She bested us at embroidery, too, did Meg. I was all thumbs, only caring about my books and drawings. Meg is a delight. I miss them both." She sighed, and taking two wooden cups, she scooped the steaming infusion into them, handing him one. Then she sat on the little chair facing him.

"But you are not here to talk about our siblings," she said.

"I am not." He sipped the drink. Tart yet mildly sweet, with an earthy undertaste, it reminded him of the hot infusions with honey, herbs, and fruit that his mother had made for her children when they were ill. A warm feeling came over him, remembering that. Tamsin sat watching him.

"What are you thinking about?" she asked.

"My mother, and the remedies she gave us when we were small." He sipped. "Now then. I know what my uncle suggested came as a surprise, even a shock, to you."

"Somewhat. You seem to favor it."

He held up a hand. "Only because it will ease your dilemma."

"Is that all? Or do you think—what many men might think about taking a bride?"

"And what," he murmured, "is that?" As if to spite his studied control, his body surged at the very thought. Oh aye. But he could ignore the pulse of heat running through his body. It was more important to be honest and find solid ground with the lady now. Somewhere along the way he had lost her, and he was not certain why.

"What does a husband expect?" She shrugged. "A wife to do his bidding in the home and elsewhere, a wife who gives up all she owns to his coffers and his inventory. A wife to cater to him in bed. And how is all this to her benefit?"

"You do not mince words."

"I have been married before."

"Not to me," he pointed out.

"You have not been a husband. Or have you?" she added. "I do not even know. I know so little about you."

"I was betrothed," he answered. "She died. The English." Nostrils flaring, he sipped the bland stuff again. No need to tell that tale now. There would be time later.

"Oh," she breathed, setting a hand high over her heart. "I am sorry."

He stared at his hands. "I would never expect my wife to do all my bidding in the home—or elsewhere." He shifted, the rope-slung bed creaking beneath him.

"If we married, we might not even have a home. Or a bed of our own."

"And would we share the bed if we did?"

Pink bloomed in her translucent skin. "We would be married."

The pulse bounded through him again. "You said betrothal would be enough for you. What do you want?"

"I want—" She drew a breath. "I want something true. I want caring that is honest, not delivered from a treatise on chivalry."

"I have not done that."

"I did not think so, but now I wonder at your reasons for agreeing to this."

"That morning at Dalrinnie," he said, "I would not have abandoned you there. I could not leave the kitten in the tree. I think you know that. I cannot abandon you now, in the middle of this dilemma."

"Then I need the truth from you now, because it seems to me all you want is this book—and now, the castle you could gain through me. In that way, you are no different than Sir Malise. Though I began to hope you were."

Frowning at that, he raised the wooden cup and swallowed the rest of the lukewarm herb water, wishing for something stronger. "I am nothing like Malise."

"But you came looking for me at Lochmaben before he ever did. You wanted something. And then I find out Edward sent you for a book that I do not even have!"

"But you will get it in Selkirk, which I did not fully realize until this evening. You have been secretive about this book."

"With reason. Those parchments," she said, "are just verses that he wrote that I put together for binding. There is no book by his own hand. And those pages will not save Scotland, I assure you."

"Edward seems to expect some collection of predictions."

"It is not that." She drank from her cup and set it on the table.

"Not prophecies? Nothing to save Scotland, or give England the advantage?"

"What would do that? He wrote an epic poem." She sounded defiant. "That is all."

"Then if Edward is wrong, then all this fuss is for naught."

"Who dares tell him? Take me to Selkirk and I will get the bound pages and show you how wrong it is. And I will go to Kincraig and you need not worry about me again. So we need not marry or betroth," she said, "or try to please your king."

"You," he said, "are the most stubborn woman I have ever known."

"Then I wonder how many you know, sir, for we are all stubborn and strong by nature. So many men prefer women to be meek that I sometimes wonder if we did not learn, as a breed of womanhood, to curve to a whim that Nature never intended for us. Birth, healing, making a home, feeding and caring for others—these take strength, body and soul. We are not biddable."

"I know. My mother was strong, my older sister as well."

"You have not said much of your sister."

"Dame Agatha," he said.

"Oh! The abbess at Lincluden?"

"The youngest they have ever had—a smart, spirited, beautiful lady. But she has her cross to bear, as they say. That life seems to suit her. You are thoughtful as well as stubborn," he added, glancing up. "I will say that."

"I am only stubborn when I must defend myself."

"Which you do well. And you seem to distrust me, no matter what I do."

"Because you are a threat to me. More than you know."

"You may be the greater threat to me," he murmured. "But I owe you the truth."

"You do—Sir Harper Knight, who does for one king and runs with the rebels of another. Among your many guises, which is the real man?"

He shifted on the uncomfortable bed, a leg stretched out, a knee bent tight, and set the cup on the floor. Leaning forward, fingers steepled, he looked up at her.

"I am," he said, "a knight who pledged to Edward and was betrayed. I am a baron who lost lands to confiscation, lost a near-wife, lost a castle to fire, and friends to bad deaths." He paused, throat tight, truth beating its way out.

"And a harper? Is that true?" She spoke softly.

"A harper, aye, who follows Bruce by choice." He looked up. "I am the forfeited laird of Dalrinnie."

"You." She stared at him. The candle flame flickered, snapped. Outside, wind whipped past the window and creaked against the door. "You were at Dalrinnie before I came there, then," she said, more quietly than he expected. Deserved. "Four years ago?"

"Three." He waited. Had she thrown something at him, cursed him, he would have deserved it. Her pondering calm surprised him. He almost preferred a kettle or cup aimed at his head. He had betrayed her by withholding the truth she valued above all.

"I was outlawed. Gilchrist was riding for Edward by then, Gideon too. I did not adhere—I ran with William Wallace, believing in his conviction, his bare honesty and fearlessness. I was away when they came to Dalrinnie. They burned the place to send most out, though it killed others. Including my betrothed, Lady Beatrix," he said. "The magistrate's daughter. He was not inclined to help an outlawed baron when I needed it."

"They took all from you."

"But for a brace of hounds that Sir David Campbell managed to remove, bringing them to Holyoak, to the care of my uncle. Gideon came later," he added.

"The castle hounds," she said faintly. "Oonagh. Roc."

"Sir David kept two in the castle and brought the rest here. He is a good friend, or rather, he was. I do not know his stance these days toward the Setons."

"He has been a friend to me."

"I am glad of that."

"So," she said, "do you think by marrying me you will regain Dalrinnie?"

Though he dreaded that, it begged to be asked. "I mean to take it back somehow. I am determined. But not through you. That is not my intention."

"What do you want?"

"Just now?" He looked at her. "Your safety. Your respect."

She took in a quick breath. "Thank you for speaking truly."

"Now you, my lady. Will you betroth, then? I will not force you to it."

"Betrothal," she said. "It can be dissolved, if we want later."

"Dissolved. Aye." His heart dropped a little. "So we are agreed?"

"Aye so. Should we take this to the abbot now? He wanted to know."

He hesitated. "These are the silent hours at Holyoak. And he needs his rest."

"But you are leaving in the morning. An errand for the king." She frowned.

"The King of Scots," he clarified.

He loved her quick smile. "I am glad to hear that."

"As long as we are being truthful—I am thinking it is best to take that troublesome book of yours to Robert Bruce. Not Edward."

"Not Edward." Her quick understanding brightened her eyes to silver. "I see. I want to hear more about that."

"You will. For now—"

"It is late. I know. But—I am relieved."

Relief washed through him. "We could take our news to the abbot in the morning," he suggested.

Tamsin began to answer but yawned, a sweet stretch of her mouth and throat, quite like a kitten after all. "When the bells ring for prime? Is that too early? When do you plan to leave?"

"A little after that." Tempted to tell her that Bruce wanted her cousin brought to safety, he held back. Enough for now, he thought, as she yawned again. "Your sister's infusion is taking hold, I see."

"It is. But I am glad—to know more about you." She cupped another yawn.

He held out a hand. "Come here."

CHAPTER EIGHTEEN

W HEN HE REACHED out, she felt no hesitation, moving toward him readily. He was so broad shouldered and tall, seated at the lower end of the bed, that she stumbled, stepping over his large booted foot, though he pulled back. Grasping her hand, he guided her down. "Sit, do. Yet another trying day for Lady Tamsin, I suspect."

"And for Sir William."

"Och, the lad is fine, do not think about it. You should rest."

"Despite lavender and all-heal, I am a bit dithery still. I do not think I can rest."

"So much truth, hey. You need time to think. Lie down and relax. I will sit here, away from you. See," he said, holding up his hands. "A courteous harper-knight will not advance upon his betrothed unless invited."

"Is that chivalric code?"

"We will make it so. Settle there now." She stretched on her side, facing out, laying her head on the thin pillow and tucking her knees under her gray skirts. He leaned back, pressed his shoulders to the wall. "Close your eyes, lass. Rest."

"But we have more that must be said—" She yawned again.

"Later." He patted her booted foot beside his hip. "I will keep my distance."

"Unless you are invited," she said, and her foot in its simple boot wiggled a bit against his thigh.

"Well," he said, "sleep. We can sort it all out, now we know what to do."

She half-closed her eyes. "When I was betrothed before, there was a wee ceremony. A solemn promise, a vow to keep and honor, and the priest was careful to phrase it all for the future. Fixing it in the present would make a marriage."

"I did the same with—my betrothed, years back."

That marriage had never come about for him, she realized. "We were wed a few weeks later, but the keeping and honoring was scant at best. Ignoring was more the nature of my marriage." An offering of sorts, letting him know she had not felt happy or cared for in those years, when she did not want to say it aloud.

"I see." He rested his hand on her boot, a finger warm on her ankle. She let it stay. "I do not think I could ever ignore you in my household."

"I would make sure of it. But we are only betrothed. No promise beyond the moment. No—"

"No future. No agreement. I know," he said. "Rest. Hush."

"Could we betroth for a month, do you think? A few months?"

"Magpie," he said softly, "rest, you."

"A year and a day?"

"That is more for a handfast, and different altogether."

"Ah, a handfast is a sort of marriage." She closed her eyes gently. His hand warmed her ankle just where the air felt cool, and she sighed into the pillow. "A betrothal that is consummated can become a handfasting or a marriage."

"A handfasting can also be agreed from the start for a year and a day." His fingers felt hotter now through the thin wool of her hose. "If there is a child, the agreement converts to marriage. Without a child, at the end of the year and day, the couple can agree to make it permanent, or dissolve it."

"Aye, dissolved," she repeated sleepily.

"But a year and a day with you—now that would be a lovely thing," he murmured, his thumb tracing the bone and curve of her ankle.

"Wherever would we live for a year and a day?"

"In the woodland. Deep in the forest, in the green and the lush, in the quiet, with the larks and the deer, ferns and fronds and great tall trees. There we would be."

"That would be lovely, aye. Away from all," she whispered.

"Not found unless we wanted to be," he agreed, fingers soothing. She shivered. "Do you not want to be found?"

"Sometimes. Would you bring your harp?" she asked after a moment.

"Too noisy. Besides, I lost my harp."

"I have it. Sir Davey's men found it. It is broken, but I kept it. At Dalrinnie."

"Did you! Now I have another reason to claim my castle."

"More than me?"

He laughed. "Hush and rest."

She sighed, quieted, then closed her eyes. Just for a moment, she told herself.

Then he began to sing, the sound of his voice low, creamy deep, yet with a graveled edge that sent delicious shivers through her.

Hey oh, hey oh,
My darling, my fair one, my soul and my delight,
My darling, my dear one, my candle at night
Hey, my treasure, oh my treasure . . .

His voice thrummed through her like honeyed fire. "You sing beautifully."

"Did you forget? I am not just a knight." He smiled, teasing and gentle.

"I did not forget. When I heard you sing in Lochmaben's hall, I thought you good, but it was noisy there, and I did not hear how true your voice is. What is the song? It is lovely."

"An old lullaby my mother used to sing. Old as the Highlands, she said it was."

"I thought you were just a poor harper and carper, as my grandda would say."

"It is a good guise, to be a middling harper no one notices."

"I noticed you. Will you sing again?"

He drew breath.

Flower of hawthorn, branch of oak,
My silk and my satin, my silver and gold,
Swan on the river, wee fairy woman,
Hey, my treasure . . .

The mellow sound warmed through her like a dram of *uisge beatha*. She stirred. "Do you play the harp half as well as you sing?"

"I hope better than you heard at Lochmaben, when a string broke."

"I want to hear you play again. You do a grand thing with a simple song."

"My lass," he murmured, "you have no idea what grand things I can do."

She answered with a soft giggle, too sleepy to keep her eyes open. Snuggling down, she kicked off one boot, then the other, vying for comfort. His fingers tugged to help, and then his hand rubbed her stockinged ankle again, rounded her foot, her toes. When it slid beneath the hem of her skirt, the center of her body throbbed suddenly and she caught her breath. His fingers stilled, the weight of his hand warm and sure, blending into her as if he belonged.

He sang again, low and deep, the sound thrumming through her, and she slept.

THE BELL WOKE her, chiming deep. She opened her eyes a little, seeing it was still dark. Lying on her side, she realized that a blanket was pulled over her, and the bed felt soft, comfortable and warm. She felt more relaxed than she had in a long while.

Listening to the steady clang of the bell, she counted. Lauds—the middle of the night, not morning. No need to rise. Rolling a little, she started to feel a warm body behind her. Liam! She put out a hand, found his side, his thigh, his woolen tunic. He lay above the blanket that wrapped her. She turned her head.

He was deep asleep, breath slow over her cheek. A nuance of moonlight through the window revealed his face. Not wanting to stir and wake him, she lay watching.

How was he here? She recalled lying on her side while he sang soft and low; then she had dozed. He must have fallen asleep too, seated on the bed with his shoulders against the wall, then had stretched out beside her, perhaps too tired to realize it.

She should have been alarmed to find him, might have leaped away, but she pressed close, comfortable in the warmth and quiet as his breath stirred her hair, as his hand slid, heavy with sleep, to rest at her waist.

Somehow, despite all that had happened between them—truth and falsity, doubts and fears—she felt perfect ease, as if he belonged beside her, in her bed.

Married by October—suddenly the phrase came back to her. Because she thought it meant Malise, the premonition had frightened her. But perhaps all along that promise, brought by the Sight, had meant Liam.

She studied his face, its planes and shadows balanced in beauty, dark brows, long-lidded eyes, tender mouth, the bristles of dark beard, a sweep of dark shining hair—and felt a sense of the true man. Suddenly she did not doubt that she could trust him, knew she had been foolish to resist him. The thought of a betrothal felt good and right now.

All will be well, he had assured her once. She wanted to believe it—believe in him.

Lifting a hand, she brushed back the dark hair that waved over his brow, let her fingers curve along his cheekbone, trace over the dark bristles along his jaw, textured like warm dark sand.

Trust and truth were hers now, she thought. With him.

Stretching a little in the dark, she kissed his jaw, feeling the slight prickle against her lips, her breath mingling with his. Then she shifted and turned to snuggle her back against him, closing her eyes, flowing toward sleep again.

Then she felt him move, his fingers sliding to cup her shoulder. Felt his lips in her hair, pressing gently at her temple. She turned a little, her shoulder beneath his cupping hand, and his fingers spread over her throat, along her jaw, tilting her toward him. He kissed her, tentatively at first, his lips seeking, questioning, a movement almost drunken with sleep. She smiled against him, answering with a tilt of her head to welcome his mouth fully over hers.

Heartbeat quickening, body surging, she spun in his arms, drinking in the next kiss and the ones that followed. The silence felt seductive, almost holy in this sanctuary of peace and safety. Betrothal or none, vows or none, she felt nothing amiss. All was well. Whatever she had doubted faded in an instant under his lips, his touch; whatever loneliness she had felt melted in the warm circle of his arms like ice on a hearth.

As his hands roamed downward, his touch rounding, discovering, she arched against him, letting him know silently that here in the cocoon between them, she wanted this. Her heartbeat quickened with desire, with hope. His hand slid over her breasts, over wool and linen, while her body tingled beneath, aching. When his fingers rounded over her hip, she rucked up her skirts, wanting—without thought, without judging if this should happen—to feel his fingers on her skin, sighing, pressing toward him.

She could feel him against her now, hard where she was soft, muscled where she curved, the fit natural, the heat of his body, through the wool of their garments, driving her to seek more. Darkness, silence, touch and kiss and caress, all of it at once surged through her, delicious, mysterious, alluring.

Looping her arms around his neck, she shifted, wanting him

to cover her if he wanted it too, if he was ready—wanting to let him know, without a word, that she wanted this too, more desperately with each kiss. Each heated, tender exploration of his fingers as they slipped upward, finding her breast and bringing it to pearling, sent a spike of desire through her. She gasped, a vibrant sound in the room's thick silence. They were sealed in privacy here by stone walls, thatched roof, a warm and intimate space for secrets, for the passionate affinity growing between them. As he traced fingertips down and then over her abdomen, her body fluttered, desire rising. His hands soothed over, down, upward and under her clothing, his fingers heated and rich with sensation. She leaped a little with his touch, curving against him, shifting to allow. Then, opened, aching, she pulled him toward her. His lips were on her cheek, on her throat, kisses tracing there, his breath as ragged as hers now.

"Are you sure?" The barest whisper, a deep and mellow thrum. "My lass, sure?"

Her lips muffled his words. "Now, love," she breathed, knowing the word was true, and she surged to meet him, accept his solidity, his thrust and his spirit with all that bloomed and burst within her. His hands buttressed her, carried her onward, his body rocking hers, breaths hard and fast and rising, a soft cry streaming from her, echoing his deep groan, his voice beautiful, soul beautiful rising through her—

Finally, there was a kiss and a separating, cooler air, and she missed him, wanted more. His arms came around her as he pulled her close.

"Jesu," he said, "dear lass, what have I done?"

"What have *we* done," she said.

"I am sorry"—he pressed his cheek to her head—I was half asleep, or would have stopped myself. I thought it was a dream. Beautiful dream. Forgive me."

"Do not." She pressed fingers to his lips. "I wanted this too, so—"

Bong. The bell startled her like thunder. *Bonnnng.*

"The prime bell. Dawn already." He shoved a hand through his hair. Then he drew her to him and kissed her, the motion loosening what was left of the plaiting in her hair, soft gold spilling over her, over him. He sat up.

"Now we have something else to sort out between us, lass."

"Aye, but what we did, sirrah, was neither harmful nor wrong. Though—did we make a promise of marriage when we talked last night? I was so tired, I am not all that sure. It may be binding, that agreement."

"We agreed to betroth, and that is binding in some circumstances." He tilted a brow. "Like this circumstance. At least in Scotland it is binding. What would you like to do about that?"

As she began to answer, the bells pealed again. Liam combed her hair back with his fingers, waiting for quiet. Shivers went through her, and she drew a breath.

"If we promised to marry, we—confirmed that promise just now."

"And that, my lass, is binding. Consummation is regarded as marriage by Church and Scots law both—providing they learn of it." He stroked her hair. "So it seems we have just married ourselves by law and Church, following our agreement to betroth."

"You know a good deal about Scots law."

"Before the troubles, I studied it." He lifted a shoulder. "My uncle asked if I wanted to go for the clergy, but I am not suited to that life. Though I did think to become a scholar at one point. I was young," he added with a half-laugh.

"You!" She felt unaccountably delighted. "Wearing a robe and cap, a scholar! Harper knight, I did not see that in you. Horse and harp suit you best."

"And sword. I realized it soon enough. What do you want to do, Tamsin?" His voice went low and somber.

"Well." Bringing her thumb to her lips, she pondered. "We could tell your uncle we agreed to handfast. A year and a day."

"You resist marriage. Why?"

She was silent, savoring the stillness, his closeness in the rumpled narrow bed. She did not want to disturb this island of peace. But he had been honest with her, and she must be the same with him.

"When I was married before," she said, "I did not catch, you see, when we . . . So my husband left me alone and went back to his mistress. He gave her a little house in the village outside Dalrinnie."

"Heatherstane? I know it."

"She was English, and he had been with her for years, even with his first wife. He was much older than I, you see. And though he had no children with her or others—or me—he said that he was without an heir because of his cheap Scottish bride."

"He was a fool."

"I did not mind being left alone in that way, with him. I looked after the household, did as a wife was expected otherwise. And he left me to myself."

"Some wives would count that a fortunate arrangement."

"I did. But I learned to dislike marriage. I was so lonely. I thought that would be my fate. But—he died."

"Were you ever mistreated, living in a garrison?"

"Ignored," she said. "Isolated. I wanted to be with my family at Kincraig. With my books, my work. With my sisters. We had such joyful times, we three, and Henry too, and I missed them so. I still do. And I wanted to complete the work I had promised my great-grandfather I would do."

"I promise you will not be lonely. I swear it."

"I think I have been wrong about you," she whispered after a moment.

"Not entirely." He gave a wry huff. "But if we—married, you would be a helpmeet, not a servant to run the household, or the bookish wee scribe in the corner, or the Scottish bride, disdained in an enemy compound. Never that."

He did not say she would be loved, nor did she expect that of him. Unsure herself what this was, she felt swept along when she needed time to think.

"You tried to tell me before, I think. I did not listen. I am listening now."

"Then listen well," he said. "You can trust this. Me." He tapped his chest.

Her throat tightened, and for a moment, she could not speak.

"Madam, the bells. We must see the abbot. What is your decision?"

She looked into his eyes, the blue of the sea, of a summer sky, the ice blue of some Viking ancestor who gave him height and strength and that commanding bright gaze. "Handfasting. Until next October, a year from tomorrow, if we fix the vows today. That should satisfy whatever Sir Malise might bring against it. Almost anything," she murmured, knowing full well the danger left unsaid.

"If that is what you want, that is what we will do. Tamsin, I did not mean to—"

"Hush you." The bells clamored again.

"I must hurry. The lads want to ride out this morning." Sliding away, he stood, straightening his tunic and trews. "First, you and I must see my uncle. Ah, here are my boots." Pulling them on, he held out a hand to her.

She stood. "Go ahead. I must change my gown and braid my hair for our handfasting."

"Lass," he said, "you could not look lovelier."

CHAPTER NINETEEN

"**N**OW HOLD OUT your hands—aye, one atop the other," the abbot directed.

With their simple promises said, Liam took a breath and faced Tamsin, gently stacking her hands with his. "The woman's right hand cups under the man's hand to pledge support. The man's left hand cups over hers to pledge protection," his uncle explained. "Now let this cloth bind you."

He held up a long, narrow woolen cloth, a blue and green tartan weave, handsome and strong. Looping it around their hands, he circled once, twice, thrice, then tied the long ends together in three loose knots. "A knot for her love, a knot for his, a third knot for joined love of children and others. These knots," he continued, "bind William and Thomasina together by the power of their vows."

The abbot hovered a hand above theirs. "What was two is now one, in love, loyalty, forgiveness, and devotion always, in all ways. God above and below, God before and behind, bless this union."

Liam drew a breath—this was happening so fast. Leaning forward, he kissed Tamsin lightly, and she returned it. Her gaze on his was dove gray, satiny and deep, and he smiled. He would never let her down. Never.

"Now pull apart slowly. The knots will keep." Abbot Murdoch handed the knotted fabric to Tamsin. "Handfasted, as you wished."

"For a year and a day," she said.

"For as long as you both want. I will post the banns of marriage on the door of our chapel here, and in the next village, so it will be seen."

"It must be seen," Liam said. Word must spread to Dalrinnie's gates, he thought. Clasping Tamsin's hand, he looked toward his brothers and cousin, who stood watching, smiling, Roc between them. Dawn broke pink and gold beyond the window of the abbot's house, and the fire in the hearth snapped and brightened. In that instant, he felt good. Hopeful. But he could not stay. "My lady, I must ride out soon."

"Where? You have not said."

"Come here," Liam drew her a little away from the others. When he and Tamsin had visited his uncle just after the prime bells with their decision, the abbot had been ready. In a whirlwind, it seemed, they were handfasted. He suspected his reverend uncle purposely gave them no time to think.

He led her to a corner near the hearth while his kinsmen poured out morning ale, laughing and celebrating. They had all wanted this, Liam realized, smiling a little. Well, it was done.

Now for the honesty he had just pledged to her. "We are ordered to Thornhill to bring your cousin and her father out and take them to refuge."

"On whose order?" she asked quickly. Uncertainty flickered in her eyes.

"Bruce," he murmured. "He sent the message to my uncle and named my kinsmen and I to the task."

Relief and understanding dawned in her gray eyes. "So that is the way of it for you and yours."

"It is." He gave it the space of a heartbeat, two, as she took it in. Then she nodded, and a little smile crossed her lips. "Thornhill could be lost if the English go up that way," he continued. "Sir Hugh Douglas may see it through, but Bruce wants Lady Kirsten removed. He wants other noblewomen of Scotland closely guarded too, including you and your sisters. As for you," he said, setting a hand upon the wall as he leaned toward her, "I ask that you wait here until I return."

"Where would I go?" she asked, but her lips quirked—luscious in firelight and so delicious in memory that his body responded, subtle and quick. Her gaze flew to his lips as if she, too, felt it, and she blushed.

Liam took her hand again. "I know you want to go to Selkirk. And I fear you will not wait for me, but try to go on your own despite the danger."

"That was my plan before I met you. We have been here too long." She bristled. "In a handfasting, there is no promise to obey."

"Nor do I ever expect it. But wait for me, do," he said, thumb caressing her hand.

She gasped set her free hand to her heart. "Liam, what if—some ill befalls you? How would I know?"

"You of all people would know, I think." Leaning down, he murmured in her ear, "I will come back and sing to you. Promise me you will wait, lass."

"I want to wait and yet need to go. I feel as if you have put a glamourie over me with your voice. Your touch." Her eyes sparkled, lips quirked.

"You are the one put a glamourie over me, love, kin of the Rhymer as you are. I only ask that you wait a few days, aye?"

"I must reach the bookseller soon." He heard the pleading in her voice. "Malise knows the book may be there. Not many in this region do that sort of work, so he could find the man before I do."

He sighed. "If I am not back in three days, I will ask Gideon to take you."

"Hurry, do. I need to hear your voice again," she whispered.

He began to hum then, a half-forgotten melody that came to him suddenly, and then sang softly. "A lady brisk and bold came riding o'er the ferny brae—"

Her skirt was of the grass-green silk, her mantel of the velvet fine,
And in every tress of her horse's mane hung fifty silver bells and
nine—

"That song!" Tamsin squeezed his hand. "Where did you learn it?"

"Ah, her truthy tongue. Not 'Oh, sir, what a gifted bard you are,' but 'where did you learn that song?'" He chuckled.

"Your voice is like wine and honey, truly. But where did you hear the song?"

"When I was a boy. I do not remember the whole of it, just a few lines. It came to me now. It reminds me of you."

"It tells the tale of Thomas and the faery queen. Did you know?"

He tipped his head. "I heard it in my household when I was young. But stories of your Thomas are all about. My own grandfather met him, I understand."

"Ah. Many did, it is so." The dog trotted toward them then and they both rubbed him affectionately, hands together, even as Liam frowned. He had meant to soothe her in his leaving, but she seemed unsettled by the reminder of her great-grandfather.

"My kinsmen are waiting and we have yet to put on our mail and gear. Even with Gideon's help that will take time. I must go."

"Hurry back. And tell Gideon to be ready if you are delayed."

"So heartfelt, bride," he drawled, kissing her cheek.

"Come back to me," she whispered, finding his lips.

THORNHILL WAS A stout castle cresting a long slope overlooking rumpled autumn-gold hills. Liam and the others had ridden the better part of a cool and sunny day, and now the sun was sinking beyond the hills as they arrived. Hailing the gate, they waited, horses nuzzling grass, until a guard opened the studded door in the portcullis.

"Sir William Seton," Liam explained. "With Sir Gilchrist Seton and Sir Finley Macnab. We have a message for Sir Hugh

Douglas. He knows my name."

"Your companions wear English colors but you do not. What is your purpose?"

"We bring an important message for Sir Hugh. We will wait," Liam repeated.

Within minutes, the double doors opened and the guard waved them through. As a groom took the horses, the sentry led them up stone steps to the keep's entrance and through to the great hall. There, the setting sun poured rose gold over wooden floors and walls hung with bright shields and embroidered banners.

Sir Hugh, portly and gray, rose from his seat at a table spread with parchments. Three dogs rose with him to run toward the newcomers, barking and jumping.

"Down! Down, I say! They are glad to see someone new, I tell you," Sir Hugh said. Two were long-legged rough-coated hounds that Liam knew—he had given that brace of dogs to Sir Hugh a few years earlier. The third, a small dark terrier, leaped about in a happy blur. Liam and his companions bent to have hands sniffed and pats welcomed.

"There, now go, get!" Sir Hugh told his dogs. "Well met, Sir William! I did not think to meet you again in this earthly life, sir." He clapped Liam on the shoulder. "The last I heard, you were not in good straits."

"All is well now, sir." Liam introduced his brother and cousin. "We are here on Bruce's orders. My kinsmen may wear Edward's gear, but they can be trusted."

"I see. What is the message? First, let me offer you wine and some supper. Arthur!" he called, as a lad came running from a far corner; directed to bring servings of that evening's stew for the guests, he hurried off. Sir Hugh poured wine into silver goblets, handing them about. "Good stuff," he said, "stolen from one of Edward's baggage trains, months back. We took wheat, too, for bread. I tire of oats," he muttered. "But wheat hardly grows in these rocky hills. Bread, though—ah! Worth stealing the grain."

He patted his belly, laughed. "Sit down."

As they drank, Liam explained their mission, while Hugh Douglas listened, frowning, tossing out a brusque question now and then. "My daughter," he repeated, rubbing his jaw. "Aye, she is here. Arthur!" he bellowed, as the lad entered with a tray holding bowls and bread. "Tell Lady Kirsten I wish to see her. Now," he added, as the lad scurried off as if the very hounds were after him. Instead, the dogs lazily watched the lad go back and forth, then settled to nap.

"We will see what the lass will do. She makes up her own mind, does my Kirsty."

"She has little choice, sir," Liam said. "Bruce feels there is a serious threat to Thornhill, and any Scotswoman with a tie to him or his is under threat too."

"Just as well she leaves here. Where will you take her?"

"To the safety of Ettrick Forest for now. We will send word."

Moments later, Lady Kirsten entered the room, the same slim dark-haired girl that Liam remembered, with a winsome smile and lilt in her step. Yet her brow puckered as she gave her father a puzzled look, seeing knights with him. As Sir Hugh introduced the men, she looked at Liam more than once, her frown deepening.

"Sir, I believe I know you. Were you at Lochmaben in September?"

He gave her a wry smile. "I was, my lady."

"Master Harper?" She put a hand to her chest. "We thought you had died!"

"As did Lady Tamsin when I saw her again."

"Have you seen her recently? We heard that more soldiers entered Dalrinnie."

"They have, under Sir Malise Comyn. But she is safe in Holyoak Abbey now."

"Sir William was sent here by King Robert," her father explained. "He and his kinsmen have been ordered to fetch you."

Though she startled at the news, Lady Kirsten listened calmly while her father and Liam explained. "These knights are here to keep you safe, my dear," her father said as she began to protest. "I want you to go with them."

"Papa, I cannot leave you and ride off with men I hardly know, even though I have met Sir William," she added.

"My dear, you must go with them. Listen to your father."

"But Papa, in September Sir William was carrying a message for Lady Tamsin—from King Edward, not King Robert."

Sir Hugh turned. "Is it so?"

"It was necessary at the time, sir. But Lady Tamsin has been removed from Dalrinnie and is in no danger now under our watch." He glanced at the others.

"I see. Then we want the same for my daughter."

"Papa, you must come too. You cannot stay here if Thornhill might be taken."

"It is my place to be here, and your duty to leave if King Robert orders it. I agree that our noblewomen must be protected after the fate of Bruce's women. Kirsty, you must go. I will see you soon, I promise."

"If you stay, I stay, Papa." Despite her plea, Douglas shook his head firmly.

"If I may, sir." Liam turned to Lady Kirsten. "We will take you to meet your cousin. It is a long day's ride to the forest from here, but we will take you to shelter with some good loyal folk. And I will bring Lady Tamsin there as well. As for traveling with strangers, we are kin of a sort now, my lady."

"Kin?" Sir Hugh Douglas looked puzzled.

"Lady Tamsin and I were married recently." He smiled, shrugged.

"Married!" Sir Hugh said. "Excellent!"

"Lady Tamsin—a harper's bride?" The girl set a hand over her mouth in surprise.

"In a way. It happened quickly. I will explain later. I know she will be very glad to see you."

"Indeed, that does make you a cousin and kinsman!" Sir

Hugh said in a hearty voice that, although a bit forced, might convince his daughter. "From what I know of you, sir, this guarantees my daughter's safe passage in your care."

"Thank you, sir."

"Now, about that other matter, Sir William. Do you plan to transport the rent that we have been gathering here?"

Liam glanced at his brother and cousin. "Aye, though we have only three horses."

"Lady Kirsten will ride her mare. I will lend you another horse."

"How many sacks are there, sir?" Liam asked.

"Two will do, I think. Mostly silver long-cross pennies, some halved and quartered," he clarified, "and a fair amount of plate that can be melted down as needed." While he spoke, Liam saw Kirsten look from one to the other, eyes wide. Clearly, she was unaware that her father had been assisting Liam the last several months. With Sir Hugh's help, they had collected rents from Bruce's tenants listed on rent-rolls for Lochmaben and other properties. Sir Hugh had continued the work after Liam was taken, then finally released.

Another matter had to be mentioned without speaking too openly. Servants or sentries—one stood near the door—might overhear. One could not be too careful.

"And the rent roster? You have marked the names there?" he asked.

Sir Hugh nodded. "Meticulously kept. A cross for those who support Edward. A cross and star next to—those we can trust," he murmured. "Best keep it on your person."

"Aye then." Liam heard the warning.

BY THE FOLLOWING afternoon, traveling south and then east since morning, they neared the bridge over the River Annan below Moffat, a considerable day's journey from Thornhill. Throughout the day, Lady Kirsten had proved uncomplaining, a lady with an adventurous spirit and a lively wit. Finley seemed taken with her,

Liam noticed, for the lad was increasingly solicitous of her comfort. They stopped twice at an inn for rest and fresh ale, making the journey longer, if less arduous.

"How is Lady Tamsin?" Lady Kirsten had asked almost as soon as they left Thornhill, after she bid her father farewell and wiped away a tear. "I thought she was at Dalrinnie. Papa and I began to worry when we heard more soldiers had gone there."

"She is well, and escaped Dalrinnie of her own accord—a bold thing and a good decision. She is at Holyoak now," he explained. "She will tell you the whole tale as soon as I can bring her to you."

"I want to know everything. Sir Malise came to Dalrinnie, we heard that too. I am concerned about Thornhill and I wish Papa had come with us. He has been ill, you see, and does not travel well. But it could be more dangerous for him to stay."

"They may not take your castle. So far, there are only rumors."

"Did Tamsin leave Dalrinnie because she got the king's orders? She was expecting to hear something soon."

"She did not like the word that Sir Malise brought. We happened upon her and brought her to the abbey, where she has friends."

"Thank you for helping her, Sir William. She must have been as surprised as I was to see you alive and well."

"Oh, she was." He pinched back a smile.

"You showed us great kindness at Lochmaben and now. We are both in your debt. I know Tamsin never forgot you. She was distressed when you were taken that night, and heartbroken when she saw your harp in pieces. She wept so then, convinced you were dead. She had a vision of—but I should not say."

He saw that Finley and Gilchrist were well ahead of them, and spoke more openly, for they did not know the half of Lady Tamsin's worth as yet. "I know the lady has the Sight," he said.

"Aye then. She told me she had seen you on the ground, dead, before we even left the castle. The broken harp confirmed that for her."

"She did not tell me." Liam frowned.

"Nor would she. Her ability—she hesitates to share it, you see. But I can tell you she cared about you. And then somehow your life was saved, and you two found each other, and now you are married! It is a miracle." Kirsty gave a grand sigh. "A tale of love and destiny like in a French *roman*." She gave him an impish, teasing smile. *No wonder*, Liam thought, *Finley was falling for the lass*. "You, sirrah, were saved for a reason."

"To rescue lovely ladies, like every good knight in a tale of chivalry and honor."

"Where is the dragon? Oh! Edward of England," she decided.

Liam laughed outright. *The miracle that had saved him*, he thought, *was the king's impulse to find Lady Thomasina and her wee book*. But in his opinion, finding that book was hardly as important as saving the lady.

Stopping at a third inn to refresh, they sat and spoke of the distance to travel before they reached the outskirts of the forest before darkness. Liam brought the leather bags inside, setting them for safekeeping between Finley and Gilchrist.

Glancing up as another patron entered the inn, Liam saw a tall man, brown-haired with keen blue eyes, in a wide brown hood and leather hauberk. Recognizing him, Liam stood and signaled for the man to meet him outside.

"Jesu, it is a relief to see you, Liam!" James Lindsay said moments later. "Looking heartier than expected, considering what we had heard of you. Well done for finding a way out of it. What happened, and what are you doing out this way?"

"I would ask you the same. It is a long way from the castles of Wildshaw and Aberlady." Liam explained briefly that Edward had seen fit to release him, and that a covert errand for Bruce brought him from Thornhill to Ettrick Forest. His old friend would realize much was left unsaid for now. "How is Cousin Isobel?" Liam finished.

"Content and beautiful, and expecting a child." He grinned at

Liam's quick congratulations. "Aye, another cousin for you, lad. Isobel is with us in the forest, but I want her safe in Wildshaw as she advances. We have been keeping close watch on Edward's soldiers," he added. "They are removing timber from the forest, thinning the fringes and encroaching on places where refugees have been hiding. Not just our few. More people are fleeing into the forest."

"So I understand. By the Rood, it is heaven's own luck to see you, Jamie. We are headed into Ettrick to seek refuge for the girl with us—Lady Kirsten, daughter of Douglas of Thornhill. Bruce wants her safe, along with other Scotswomen."

"With good reason. I am meeting Quentin Fraser to head back that way. We would be glad to accompany you into the woodland. Our center has moved since you were with us last. Come anywhere near the Eldin Linn and we will find you, for good or ill." James gave him a wry smile. "But you will always have safe passage."

"Appreciated, sir. Another matter," Liam murmured. "I have a delivery that must go to a messenger that Bruce will send. That fellow will convey it discreetly to the king. My cousin Finley," he said, indicating the inn, "can bring the lady to the forest for safekeeping, and these bags too, if you agree. Gilchrist and I should return to Holyoak."

"Ah, I understand. We can help. Bruce sent a message recently that he expected something from you and asked for my assistance. He will be glad to know you are well, lad, when we can get word to him."

Liam nodded. "I must meet this messenger when he arrives. Can you help with that? Aye, good. Also, if the others can remain with you in the forest, I want to bring another lady who is in my keeping."

"Also under Bruce's protection?"

"In a way. My bride, as it happens." Seeing Lindsay's lifted brow, Liam half smiled. "I would ask asylum in the forest for her as well, for a little while."

"The great Caledonian Forest provides endless sanctuary to those in need, my friend. Come, introduce me to your cousin and the young lady of Thornhill."

CHAPTER TWENTY

WAITING BESIDE A cart harnessed to two shaggy ponies, Brother Gideon raised a hand as Tamsin approached. He indicated the blue sky and scudding clouds overhead. "A bit cool and windy, but a fine day for an outing. We can leave as soon as you are ready. Ah, and here is Brother Allan."

"Your kinsmen have not yet returned," Tamsin told Gideon, as Brother Allan stepped forward to take the bags she carried and set them inside the cart. "I am concerned. Today is the fourth day since they left."

"Liam said if they were not back by now, he would meet us at a certain place in the forest."

"Good. Then we will not go straight through to Selkirk?"

"Too far in that vasty place, my lady. It will take a day or two by horse and longer on foot to reach Selkirk along the forest paths. Ready?" He held out a hand to assist her into the cart bed to sit on hay covered in a length of wool. She noticed that the cart contained several wooden kegs.

"Are we taking these to market?"

"Should we be stopped along the way, we can say we are out delivering our heather ale. We can give it to the forest folk, come to that." Gideon climbed up to the plank seat to take the reins, while Allan leaped into the cart to sit against a bale opposite Tamsin.

"Did you both promise Sir William that you would keep

watch over me?" she asked. "He feared I might take a cart and set out on my own. I did plan to wait for him. But if we will meet him further on, I am anxious to go."

Gideon tapped the reins and the cart rolled through the gate and over the earthen track to head east and away from Holyoak and its crescent-shaped Loch. As they crossed the moorland toward the forest, dark treetops were just visible in the distance, softened in the mist that had yet to dissolve in the sunlight.

Tamsin shivered in the breeze, grateful to be moving at last. Yet she could not shake the worry that there had been no sign or word from Liam. Had he and his kinsmen found her cousin and come away safely?

Thinking of Liam, his blue eyes so aware, his concern for her sincere, she drew a breath. Though they were handfasted now, she felt wary. He had a keen interest in the book she would fetch in Selkirk, and she was unsure what he would do once she had it. Whether he wanted to obey King Edward's orders or give the writings to Bruce, she would refuse. Kisses, caresses, and promises aside, her sense of caution and determination to protect Thomas's legacy had renewed in Liam's absence.

A strong breeze blew the hood of her cloak back and fluttered through her hair, loosening tendrils along her braid. She felt that instant of freedom like a sip of water for the soul. The confinement of the abbey slipped away behind her with every turn of the wheels.

"Brother Gideon, perhaps you should slow down, we have a lady in the cart," Allan said. "You do seem in a hurry."

"Just keeping a brisk pace should we see anyone we would rather not meet, lad."

"I do not mind a fast pace." Tamsin turned her face to the breeze.

Vast acres of winter-brown grasses streamed past. The trees were turning bare in coppices and woodlands, leaves rustic and golden, some fallen to the ground, while tall pines swathed in dark green thrust into the blue sky. Until now, she had hardly noticed autumn nearing its end as winter approached. The bright, cool, clear morning gave her a sense of promise and hope. She would protect Thomas's writings and find her siblings, and soon they would all be together. For now, it was all she dared hope. As for Liam, she did not yet know, in her heart or her intuition, if their handfasting could endure.

"Apologies, my lady," Gideon called over his shoulder as the cart bounced through another rut. "The drover's track through here is rough after the storms of late."

"Nor are you used to driving, Brother," Allan said. "You prefer to take a horse over the moorlands when we travel and let others guide the cart." He smiled at Tamsin. "Knights disdain riding in carts. Brother Gideon has not lost that."

"I may gain humility, but I will always dislike carts," Gideon admitted.

Tamsin laughed. "Knight? So it is Sir Gideon, then?"

"I was an avowed knight before I came to Holyoak. I would give that up with monastic vows."

"Will you, then?" She saw him shrug; aye or nay, she was not sure.

"The English come too close to the abbey at times," Allan said, "so we are fortunate to have a warrior-knight with us. The abbot has not pressed him to make a decision."

"Because I did not come to Holyoak to find God, but to heal from injuries," Gideon said. "But Heaven dragged me there, so I must consider that message."

Tamsin frowned. The more she learned about Brother Gideon, her friend before she ever met his brother, the more she simply wanted him to be happy. But she sensed he would not be content as a monk.

They rode in easy silence, and soon the abbey enclosure, the blue loch, and the stream flowing through the meadow became specks and gleams behind them. Ahead, the forest loomed dark and dense, larger now. Scudding clouds above, clean wind, and the cart's motion lured Tamsin into a near-doze.

Something changed then in the air, in the peace of the journey. She opened her eyes. Allan seemed asleep, while Gideon drove steadily onward.

She glimpsed something from the corner of her eye. Gray spirals drifted upward to join the high white clouds. "Is that smoke?" she asked. "Near the abbey?"

Allan stirred, Gideon too. "Fire!" Allan called. "Is it Holyoak?"

Behind them, Tamsin watched the spirals of smoke darken, thicken skyward.

"It must be at the abbey," Gideon said. "But there is too much smoke for a bonfire. We had nothing planned that I heard about."

"Look there," Allan said. "Who is that?"

Now Tamsin saw men on horseback coming fast along the drover's track. "Liam and the others?" she asked, but even as she spoke, she realized these riders were burly men in full armor, riding heavy and intently after them. And some wore red and gold.

The riders sank behind the rim of a hillock, reappearing again to come onward, crossing a stretch of open moorland now.

Fire, she remembered then. *Fire in the abbey,* she had told Liam. Her heart sank.

She set a hand to her throat with a deep gasp. Fire at Holyoak, and men attacking—please, it could not be, she prayed. Liam knew, and she had warned Gideon too. But her warning had not stopped it. She gripped the side of the cart and watched the pursuing riders, the smoke curling into the sky, while the wheels bumped roughly over the track.

Gideon urged the ponies faster, and the stodgy pair moved into a clumsy canter. "Hey! Go, you beasts, move! Allan, take the reins," he directed. "Climb over. Take the lady into Ettrick Forest fast as you can go."

"Where are you going?" Tamsin asked as Allan scrambled forward.

"Back to Holyoak." Gideon leaped down from the moving

vehicle, rolling with the fall, rising to his feet. "Brother, hurry!"

As he ran diagonally toward a band of pine trees, Tamsin realized he meant to cut back to the abbey through the grove. The riders came onward, perhaps not seeing the monk, ever relentless in catching the vehicle.

"Allan, who are they? Why would they fire the abbey?" Tamsin asked, frantic.

"English soldiers! I do not know why they would attack Holyoak or chase us." He hurried the ponies onward. "We are a monk and a woman. Perhaps they are hellbent elsewhere and will pass us."

She knew they would not. "They are after me! I brought trouble to all of you."

"We could reach the shelter of the forest if these beasts would hurry. Hi, go!"

Now the riders were closer. Four, Tamsin saw, recognizing none of them. They were not Dalrinnie's men. If they wanted her—and if they had fired the abbey—Sir Malise was behind it. If anyone was harmed, it would be her fault. In leaving Dalrinnie, she had brought disaster to Holyoak. No vision or warning would change that.

The cart rumbled and bucked as Allan urged the ponies over the turf. Holding on desperately, Tamsin saw the pursuers riding fiercely. God be thanked, Gideon had escaped notice. Glancing toward the tree ridge, she glimpsed a dark form moving between the trees.

But he turned back toward the track. Carrying a long tree limb, he tucked it horizontally as he ran, as if it were a jousting pole and he a horseless knight.

Angling across the meadow, he cut behind the riders, running like a fury over the earthen track, pounding after them unseen. Ducking, he thrust the long, thick branch between the rear legs of the last horse. It stumbled, keeping its footing but falling behind. Circling and neighing, it rose on hind legs until the knight in the saddle tipped and fought for control.

Swiftly Gideon whacked the branch upward to unseat the rider and throw him hard to the ground. Tamsin cried out, watching Gideon wield the limb like a club, a single blow sprawling the knight on the grass. Catching up the man's sword, Gideon grabbed the horse's reins and leaped astride, tunic loose, bare legs tight against the animal's sides.

"Allan!" she cried. "Gideon! Look!"

"God's bones!" he burst out just as Gideon rode after the knights still following the racing cart. Allan shouted to the ponies and snapped the reins to coax them to a canter that had the cart careening and bumping. Tamsin clung to the side, jounced hard against the wood. Kegs thunked about; one slammed into her and she shoved it away.

More riders appeared behind Gideon, one in Edward's colors, another with a dark cloak flying out. The monk on horseback would be hemmed in and taken down.

"Gideon!" she screamed. "*Gideon!*"

The first group of men rode nearer, horses thundering, steel flashing as one knight pulled a sword and bellowed for Allan to stop. But the lad urged the ponies onward while Tamsin clung desperately in the cart bed. Men shouted and reached out to grab at the planking, but she reeled away. One knight surged toward the sweating ponies, reaching for a halter but missing it.

Despite shouts for him to stop, Allan was half standing now, calling to the exhausted ponies, whip in hand, cracking it wildly in the air. Another knight stretched an arm toward Tamsin, but she rolled away to slam into a hay bale, pushing it toward him in an awkward but effective move.

Two horses rode tightly against the cart and a third rider edged forward, grabbing at Tamsin. He snatched the edge of her cloak as she frantically scrambled away. He launched nearly out of his saddle to snatch a fistful of her gown and drag her nearer.

Screaming, kicking, she felt his hard grip on her ankle as he pulled her toward him across straw and wooden planking. The thunder of the horses, the shouts, the cart bumping hard and fast over the track sent her careening. Somehow, she held on to the side of the cart despite the man's fierce pull.

Behind him, the muscled bulk of another horse shoved against the assailant's horse, throwing the rider off balance, so that he released his hold on Tamsin and went sliding and yelling to the ground. The cart rolled onward as the remaining knight, dark cloak flapping, reached for her. Tamsin resisted, gasping, sobbing, furious and fighting.

He leaned forward, knocked her hands away, and grabbed her arm. His unrelenting grip pulled her toward him.

CHAPTER TWENTY-ONE

"LADY! TO ME!" He drew her toward him. "Allan! Stop the cart!"

Liam. She threw herself toward him just as the slowing cart threw her against the side. Liam let go of her, pulling up on his horse just as Allan tugged on the reins until the cart rolled at a calmer pace.

Liam rode steadily beside the cart now. In the distance, Tamsin saw knights sprawled in the grass, riderless horses grazing, reins hanging. Farther away, she recognized Gideon riding the charger he had seized, heading back toward the abbey—while a knight in mail and red surcoat hurtled after him.

"Gideon!" she shouted in warning.

"The other one is Gilchrist," Liam said. "He will make sure his brother is fine and then return to guard those men. They are not dead, love," he said. "I saw them moving a bit. Gideon can fetch help to carry them to the abbey hospital."

She nodded, sitting up, breath heaving into a sob. Heart going like thunder, limbs shaking, she reached toward him, just as Allan eased the cart to a stop. Liam dropped back his chain mail hood—she saw he wore only a mail shoulder cape and hood over leather as protection—and took her hand.

"Are you hurt?" Strong gloved fingers worked along her arm, looking for injury.

"Just bruised, I think. Those men attacked us—"

"But I have you now. Allan, you drove like a champion. Well done!"

"I meant to keep the lady safe, sir."

"You did, and I owe you for it."

Tamsin blinked, marveling at such calm in Liam, feeling it infuse into her. Exhaling hard, she felt her heart steady some. He held her hand in a sure grip.

"Sir, what of Holyoak?" Allan asked.

"The monks have the fire under control now. Gilchrist and I arrived shortly before those fellows swept in and tried to fire the abbey. They sent flaming arrows over the walls. But we were ready for them." He looked at Tamsin. "I asked them to fill extra barrels of water and move some haystacks out of reach. I told them I had a feeling."

"Thank you," she murmured.

"Then we followed when they headed this way over the moorland."

"Will they send more men?" Tamsin looked again at the fallen knights, saw one move a leg, the other rolling a bit. Gilchrist had returned, seated on his horse nearby, hand on sword as he watched them.

"Once word reaches Comyn, they well might. We can assume he sent them to attack, thinking you might be there. Allan, stay here with the cart near Gilchrist. They will need your help at Holyoak. I will take Lady Tamsin into the forest. And make sure you give those excellent ponies an extra rubdown and a generous measure of oats later."

"I will. But if I stay here, you and the lady have just one horse."

"There are good horses over there, if the lady will ride a knight's saddle."

"She will." Tamsin rose in the cart as Liam pulled her up and into his lap. She wrapped an arm around his neck as he pressed his cheek to her head in a quick embrace.

"Good?" he murmured. She nodded, leaning against him.

"Good, aye. Oh, my satchels—thank you," she said, as Allan tossed them to Liam, who secured them over his saddle pommel. With a wave, Allan turned the ponies and cart and headed toward Gilchrist. In the distance, Tamsin saw that the smoke had lessened already, straggling skyward in pale streams.

"Was anyone hurt at Holyoak? Is the abbey safe?" she asked.

"No one was hurt, and repairs can be made." Wrapping an arm about her, he took up the reins.

"I am so glad you were there and came after us. I thought you were still away."

"It seems to be my lot in life to go wherever you are going, my lass."

"Gideon was a champion too. He went after them, even took one down with a tree branch and took the man's horse!"

"He knows what he is about, does Sir Gideon."

"He is trained to fight like that, yet he wishes to be a monk?"

"Or thinks he does. My brother feels he must atone for something, but others should atone to him. When the time comes, he will make the right decision."

She nodded. "I am sorry I was not there. We thought we would have to meet you in the forest later. All are safe? The dogs and horses too?"

"The flames caught the thatch on the bake house and the cottage where you stayed. The place will smell of smoke for a while, but all is well. *Providentia*," he murmured, "that you were gone, or you might have been inside the cottage."

"You might have been there with me." She shuddered, pressed against him.

"Tamsin." He frowned. "You warned about fire in the abbey."

"I am grateful that you listened and were not worried by the strangeness of it."

He huffed a little laugh. "Me, I have seen this sort of thing before. I have a cousin who does such things. It is not strange in our family."

"I am glad of it. But why would Malise order an attack on the abbey? That is, if he did this."

"Oh, I do not doubt it. His men must have told him that you could be inside Holyoak. We met one of their patrols when we rode guard around the abbey. But I said the woman inside the enclosure was my wife, and that they should move on."

"Wife! You claimed so in the tavern too. You are the soothsayer here."

"Am I? Though I fear my claim may have raised their curiosity and brought them there rather than away."

Did he feel guilt and regret for it, this strong and reserved man? She pressed closer. "Malise knew I had friends at the abbey. Or perhaps they saw the banns posted on the Holyoak chapel and the village kirk. But it would be lunacy for Sir Malise to order a monastery burned. He could be excommunicated for that."

"He has a touch of madness, that one. I have seen it."

"And I ran from him, which could have stirred his wrath."

"My involvement would infuriate him too. Tamsin," he went on, "does Malise know about your ability?"

"The visions? I do not think so. Unless—" She hesitated. "He met often with my husband—I mean, my late husband..." she amended, glancing at Liam. "I wonder if Sir John boasted to Malise that I had the gift of Sight. Sir John was proud of my ties with Thomas, though he disliked my intuition. It was sinful, he said, and I should beware. He was not pleased if I tried to warn him about a feeling I had, especially if it proved true. So I stopped trying to be helpful."

"He would not appreciate Scottish frankness. Still, I wonder. Edward is sometimes hungry for soothsaying to point the way. Malise may be the same."

"He never mentioned that, but he was certainly intent on the Rhymer's book."

"The king may want it for its predictions."

"There are none in the pages. Just poetry, I assure you."

"Well, we will be diligent. It is all we can do. Now, my lady, which of these horses will you have?" He gestured toward the knight's horses grazing in the meadow.

"The smallest—the dappled one."

Liam helped her slide down to the ground, then dismounted to approach the horse cautiously. Within moments, so effortlessly that she gaped in surprise, he had the horse's rein and was patting its neck and muzzle, talking quietly. Whinnying, the horse tossed its head and stepped forward.

"He will allow it if we make sure he has a good home."

"We will." Liam helped her into the saddle and stood back to let her walk the horse in slow circles, letting him adjust to a different and lighter rider, Liam walked over to Gilchrist to speak with him. Then he came back as Gilchrist and Allan, too, waved.

Soon mounted with her skirts tucked, Tamsin rode beside Liam, stretching to become used to the larger saddle. Her hip felt bruised where the keg had slammed into it, but after a while, eased by the rocking motion, she relaxed into the ride.

"A bit further and we will be in the shelter of the forest," Liam said.

"Gideon said Selkirk is too far to reach today."

"I know it is important for you to get there. I understand it better now. But your wellbeing is more important to me. Selkirk is on the far side of an enormous tract of forestland. The route is not always easy nor safe."

"But when will we be there?"

"I must beg patience from an impatient lady. I promise you will get there soon."

She gave a heavy sigh. "I was foolish to think I could leave Dalrinnie and rush to Selkirk, then Kincraig, and do it quickly."

"You do not travel much on your own, I think."

"I always traveled with an escort. Sometimes I wanted to hurry but it seemed they never did." She looked at Liam, his profile clean in the sunlight, his dark hair waving back in the breeze. "I suppose I do not have a good sense of how to find Selkirk. I am very glad of your help."

"You should not look for your bookseller on your own. Certainly not with Sir Malise searching for you."

She sighed, trying to remind herself of all she could be thankful for that day, from the rescue to Liam's company now, to the placid horse that responded readily to her commands. She glanced at Liam again. "He is determined to find me."

"He wants you, without a doubt."

"You want me too," she blurted.

"Of course I do," he said easily.

"I mean, you want me for the Rhymer's book."

His lips twitched. "Surely you can think of other reasons."

Aware she had spoken too quickly, she shook her head. "You set aside your concerns to take me hither and yon. This book has brought such trouble. I wish I had never—"

"Damn the book," he growled. "I am here for you, Tamsin Keith. You have been under constant threat, and I mean to take you where you cannot be found so easily. Then let us worry about this book."

"What about your orders from King Edward?"

"You need not worry over that."

"I do worry, since you will not tell me all of it."

"I did say Bruce might want the pages. We will find time to discuss the rest."

"Will we? You tell me little enough, so perhaps you are a threat to me after all. Perhaps you think to tuck me away somewhere and take the Rhymer's pages according to your own judgment. So I do worry about the book." She flashed him a sharp glance, impatience and temper flaring.

"True. I do what I think I must. As do you." He guided his horse on in silence.

A little flare of doubt and anger seared through her, freshening her resolve to protect the book. But she needed Liam—not just to guide her to Selkirk. She needed him, wanted him, and hesitated to fully admit it even to herself. But so long as he had orders from Edward and had yet to explain them, she had to be wary.

A wave of loneliness hit her, and with it the sense of isolation and self-protection she had felt at Dalrinnie, trapped in a loveless marriage. For a moment that feeling swamped her. But she was no longer in that situation. This impromptu marriage might last beyond handfasting. Yet Liam Seton kept a barrier around him, just as she did. She desperately wanted to break through that.

As they rode, the silence hung heavily between them. She felt alone in her promise, and in the uneasy sense that Comyn might always be a threat. Liam knew about her ability, but she felt safe in that. Malise suspected it—and could try to ruin her.

Glancing at Liam now, she regretted her bluntness. She felt a wash of gratitude, that he had come into her life when she needed him most. Or was that love she felt? Not so quickly, surely. Affection, thankfulness, tempered with caution. But she did not want to feel this tension. Not now, when he had saved her life earlier. He had proven over and over a caliber of steadfastness that she was not sure she deserved.

"Sir William," she said, breaking the silence. He frowned at her. In the cool sunlight, his black-lashed eyes were like blue glass above purplish shadows, and the tender curve of his mouth was grim. He looked tired. Her heart wrenched.

He lifted his brows as if to invite whatever she had to say.

"I know I am not an easy charge," she said. "I am grateful for what you have done, and I promise you will not have to rescue me again."

His laugh was curt. "I hope it is not necessary, but I will be there if it is."

"Perhaps someday I will come to your aid instead." She wanted to lighten the mood. She had spoken too quickly earlier, and once again he had taken it in stride.

"A lady rescuing a knight? One never knows." He pointed ahead. "Look there, where that wide stream cuts through the moor—that is the Ettrick Water. We will cross that arched stone bridge, see there? Farther on, where the trees grow thick along that ridge, is the hemline of the forest skirt. Where those tall boughs come together like a cathedral arch, over to the left—that is the entrance we will take into the great forest."

"Oh, it is lovely!" The leaves of the tall oaks and birches were turning with the season, gold and rust and purple against canopies of every shade of green and sienna. Against the blue sky, the beauty of it nurtured her soul.

She longed to find rest and peace in that cool sanctuary, though impatience made her wish to take the shortest route to Selkirk to find the bookbinder's shop. She followed Liam over the stone bridge, then drew alongside him again.

"Tamsin," he said then, "perhaps I have held back too much from you."

A sense went through her of truth dawning, feather-light and clear. She waited.

"King Edward gave me the order in September," he said, "when I was a prisoner at Carlisle. He had me brought to him at Lanercost. Said he wanted a book belonging to the Rhymer. Said it was owned by an old woman. Thomasina."

"Ah. The Rhymer's daughter. He was so wrong. He released you because you promised to fetch the book?"

"But I refused."

"He would have killed you if you had refused. A Scotsman, perhaps a spy, already in his custody? You would be dead now."

"She sees truth and speaks it out," he said. "Aye, he would have had me killed, like a cousin of mine, like friends. Wallace. Others. But—" He stopped, rode on until she craned to look at him.

"But what? You agreed, for you went free."

"Because he offered to give me Dalrinnie again. And—Malise was there. He pushed for the king to give him the order. That decided me."

"More than Dalrinnie?"

"I am not so foolish as to trust Edward's word. And I did not want Malise to succeed."

"Or take Dalrinnie."

"Or pester an old lady." He gave her such a wry smile that she laughed.

"Well, he did pester me."

"And still would. We will find a way to stop him. What say you, aye?"

"I think," she said, smiling, "I am very fond of you just now, sirrah."

"Truth will out." He laughed and rode ahead, guiding her up a grassy slope toward the cathedral of trees ahead to enter the forest.

The horses' hooves crunched rhythmically along the forest floor where fallen leaves and pine needles mingled, the path wide enough for them to ride side by side, the trees widely spaced, the terrain flat enough that Tamsin could see through and beyond, to the green and brown density further on. Autumn leaves crushed underfoot, and she realized it was impossible to move silently through this part of the forest. As they rode on, leaves fell around them, spinning down in the breeze. A tapestry of sound wove together the thud of horse hooves, the rustle of the wind, the chatter and trill of birds, and somewhere the constant burble of water.

"It is peaceful here, so golden and quiet," she said, looking up at leafy curtains of gold, copper, green and russet in the oaks and birches and hazelnut trees.

"Aye so," he said, as a fox slipped across the wide flat path between the trees and disappeared. After a while the natural path narrowed and he moved in front of her. The wide, flat ground became more rugged. Now hillsides fell steeply away, where trees grew upright on slopes thick with bracken and fallen branches. Birds flitted through the trees overhead, quick and light. Then she noticed one bird appearing more than once.

"A hawk," she said, pointing. "Up there, do you see? It is here now, and I saw it back there as well. Sitting and watching us, as if it has been following us all along."

"The goshawk? Aye, he may be tracking us." He whistled then, a melodic sequence of a few notes, and repeated it.

As if in response, the hawk flew to a tree closer to them and settled high up.

"It almost seems like he is doing that deliberately," Tamsin said.

"He is. Look closely, do you see?"

She peered, hand shading her brow. "Oh! The jesses. I did not see them before. Where is his master?"

"We might see him soon. They have been watching us for a while."

"They?"

"Come out, you," he said to the trees, "and call your spy down from his perch."

Tamsin looked around, astonished. Then she heard a rustle of leaves and two men emerged. One, the larger of the two, carried a bow and quiver on his back; the other, lean and brown and strikingly handsome, wore a heavy glove. Stepping onto the forest path, the tall, lean fellow lifted the glove and whistled a sequence of notes. The pale goshawk sailed out of the tree to alight on the leather glove.

"Greetings, Sir William," the man said. "Is this the lady you went to fetch?"

"Lady Thomasina Keith, this is Sir James Lindsay of Wildshaw, who prefers these woods to his own castle."

"These woods are my castle. My lady," Lindsay said, and indicated the other fellow. "This is Sir Iain Campbell."

"Campbell!" Tamsin raised her brows. "I have heard of Iain Campbell—are you kin to Sir David Campbell? And Lady Edith?"

"I am," the man said. His voice was deep, distinctive. "I hope they are well."

"They are," she said, and smiled. His return smile was tense. Tall and broad with a wild mop of dark gold curls, he had an angelic face beneath that frown, beneath his scruffy beard.

James Lindsay lifted his hand and flicked his gloved wrist

slightly. In a quick flurry, the bird left his hand and soared upward.

"What a beautiful bird," Tamsin said. "Thank you for the welcome."

"Jamie, my lady. We go by simple names here."

"Tamsin," she offered, and knew suddenly, surely, these were good men, intelligent and worthy, men who had made difficult and dangerous choices out of inner conviction, like Liam had done. Whatever brought them to the forest had not been easy.

Glancing at Liam, she felt shy and a little ashamed, for she had made unforgiving assumptions of him even while she insisted on truth. He smiled, and she felt humbled, hopeful. He had friends here; she sensed his ease, his comfort in these woods. Sensed he wanted her to like them as friends too. Truly she would try.

She glanced up. "That is a beautiful bird."

"Gawain!" James whistled and lifted his glove, and even before he raised it high, the bird sailed back to settle there, bronze eyes gleaming. James shut the bird's curious stare by popping a leather hood over its head.

"That is a very obedient goshawk," she remarked.

"Only when he deigns to be. Your cousin is anxious to see you. This way."

CHAPTER TWENTY-TWO

"L EAVE YOUR HORSES here," James told Liam. "We will see to
them."

Liam dismounted and helped Tamsin down from the dappled
horse. "We cannot take the horses far into the forest here," he
explained. "The slopes are steep and can be treacherous for them.
We must walk the rest of the way." She nodded.

James Lindsay gave a hoot like an owl then, and a lad fairly
dropped out of a tree just overhead. Without a word, he took the
horses and led them into the trees.

"We have a stable through there—a hut in a clearing, well
hidden, where the horses will be content. Our encampment is not
far," James said.

Shouldering Tamsin's satchels, Liam kept a wary eye out of
habit as they followed James along a path just visible through the
thicket. He noted that Iain Campbell had gone ahead, out of sight
now, bow in hand. Liam did not know him, but he remembered
Sir Davey mentioning a nephew in King Edward's service, a
knight and falconer. The man had vanished into the forest,
rumored to have gone over to the rebels and enraging Edward by
taking his favorite hawk. Liam wondered if this was that very
nephew. If Lindsay trusted him, it spoke well for the quiet man
forging ahead on the path.

As they walked, he thought of the events earlier that day—
the fire at Holyoak, where his aging uncle was so vulnerable,

where one of his brothers lived. Did Malise know that? Did Edward?

Tamsin thought the attack was because of her. But perhaps there was more to it. Liam frowned, so lost in thought that he nearly walked into a low branch, lifting it aside as Tamsin passed in front of him. Edward's words, gruff and snarled, came back to him.

You have family in Dumfries and Selkirk. A monk, an abbot, an abbess? Did the attack on Holyoak have something to do with Edward's threat—carried out by Malise?

"Not much farther now," Jamie said, turning. "This new place is well hidden."

"Deliberately," Liam agreed, taking Tamsin's hand to negotiate a steep incline. They walked along the mossy bank of a clear, rapid stream, a slender arm of the Ettrick Water that threaded through this part of the forest, its moist scent fresh, earthy, invigorating.

"Very deliberate. We were forced to move with the English thinning the forest toward the Shaws, where we had roots for a few years. This place, near Eldin Linn, is closer to Selkirk. The Sheriff of Selkirkshire is Aymer de Valence, one of Edward's trusted generals, so we are wary. But we are fortunate in the new sheriff deputy."

"The deputy?" Liam asked.

"A young knight sent here by Edward, but I suspect he is amenable to the cause."

"Can we be certain of his loyalty?" Liam asked. "The delivery we must make depends on that."

"Delivery?" Tamsin asked, looking from one to the other.

"The goods your brother brought here, with the young lady? I believe so. Bruce trusts this deputy. He is young, but smart. Looks the other way when he rides through the forest—and tells Valence he can find no sign of rebels."

"Interesting." Liam pushed another leafy branch out of the way for Tamsin.

"He reported to Valence that the rebels are too elusive and cannot be found easily," James went on quietly, walking beside him. "The deputy showed me the letter when we met at Wildshaw. Edward's general believes him, and Bruce trusts him."

"It is a tricky matter to balance both sides. Many of us have a foot in both camps."

"An art, I vow. You will meet him," James said. "Decide for yourself."

Liam nodded. Sensing Tamsin's curiosity, he knew he had not yet explained his larger mission for Bruce, the matter of rents and the growing list of those loyal to the cause. He owed her that, though it was crucial to the task to remain guarded, and part of his very nature to be reserved. Crucial, too, he thought, to be skeptical about this newcomer in the mix.

As they walked, he kept a guiding hand ready, knowing Tamsin was inexperienced on these paths and had to manage skirts as she went. At least he was not wearing cumbersome armor. At Holyoak, he had changed his chain mail in favor of his ring-studded leather hauberk over tunic and trews, with a hooded capelet of chain mail over the leather. Though not as protective, it would do. He carried a sheathed sword at his back and a dagger on his wide leather belt, and he had a shield—the Seton gold sheaves on a blue field—should threat arise. He had borrowed from Gideon's own gear kept at Holyoak. His brother had not given up the trappings of his old life entirely, still undecided.

The deeper they penetrated the woodland, the less chance there was of threat, he knew. The trees were so thick and densely leafed in places that little could be seen ahead, and steep hillsides formed dangerous angles into crevasses where a man could slide down, hitting branches, bracken, and rock, all the way to rushing streams.

Aware of that, he reached out to help Tamsin. But she did not need his bracing hand as she forged her way through the path with the others.

The tree cover was thick along the way, with ferns and

bracken dense underfoot. The way was surrounded with late blooming buckthorn, cranberry, and rowan, with their red and orange berries. Patches of late straggling heather and gorse grew in clumps, crowding, lush, alive. Here and there, creatures skittered and flitted, and noisy streams sluiced and burbled on their own pathways, while small waterfalls poured from rock to rock. Ahead, light filtered through the treetops in sunset beams. Soon evening would shed cool light over all.

At last he heard the sounds of laughter and a few shouts, and smelled the rich smoke of charring meat. Seeing the glow of a fire, he glimpsed the encampment, seeing the side of a wattled hut.

Walking quickly now, they crossed a narrow burn, stepping stone to stone over the swirling water that formed a natural moat. Here Liam took Tamsin's arm as she kept her balance. Then James Lindsay pushed aside a network of branches to reveal a tiny rustic village in a clearing at the heart of the forest.

The opening James made snapped closed behind them as they entered the space.

Beside him, Tamsin gasped softly as she took it all in, crying out in delight as two young women approached. Liam recognized both—Kirsty, her long dark curls flying out behind her as she rushed forward, and her companion, a black-haired beauty with eyes bright as his own and a sweetly enlarged belly.

"Isobel!" He stepped forward to embrace her.

"I WAS STARTLED at first to see the harper," Kirsty said. "We thought him dead!" She took Tamsin's arm as they circled the clearing, finding time at last to talk.

"I remember. And then he turned up a knight."

"With orders to remove me from Thornhill. Orders from Bruce!"

"Aye," Tamsin murmured. A little thrill of pride went through her at the knowledge that her handfasted husband was wholly dedicated to the Scottish cause. She had needed to hear it, needed to be in his confidence. He had more secrets, she was sure, ones he needed to keep close. And she also knew that King Edward could still find a way to keep Liam under his thumb. That royal threat was a common burden to many Scottish knights. She sighed, then smiled at Kirsty as her cousin talked on.

"—And Sir Gilchrist and Sir Finley were so courteous. Finley, especially, made sure to help me. He is still here, you know. He stayed here so I would not feel I was in a group of strangers. I thought it very kind."

"I have not seen them. Are they here?"

"They go out on patrol day and night. James Lindsay is a strong leader. I like him quite a bit. That bird of his, though, is a rascal. It throws more fits than a child, I vow. Have you met Lady Isobel?"

"Just briefly. She is Liam's cousin. They were keen to talk." She glanced across the clearing to see Liam seated with the lady, a true beauty with ice-blue eyes. They had their heads together, deep in conversation.

"You will like her very much. There is something unique about her, as if she knows all you are thinking with those eyes of hers. But she is gentle and kind."

"Seton eyes. Liam has them too. His eyes absolutely pierce through you."

"I noticed," Kirsty said. "He mentioned that you married him, but you have not said a word of it yet!"

"There is so much to tell you. Did Liam explain it is a hand-fasting, not a true marriage? We had to do that because Sir Malise has become a threat."

"I know Malise demanded that you marry him, so you ran. Finley told me."

"Ran! I leaped from the very tower." Tamsin gave a rueful laugh. "Oh, Kirsty, I had to leave Dalrinnie as fast as possible. I wish you had been with me, I do. I would have agreed to a convent if the king had ordered it. I was prepared for that. But Edward ordered Sir Malise to marry me. Part of some scheme to ensure that Dalrinnie is completely in their control, I think. So I panicked and left."

"You did what you had to do. Had I been there, I would have gone out that window with you. Is Lady Edith still there?"

"Likely so. She had fits over me dropping out the window—all the bed linens and things, you would have laughed so to see it. She did not laugh, but still, she was a help to me. I asked her to make sure Oonagh was safe—Malise did not like the dog. And I hope he is not tormenting Edith over my departure right under her nose."

"If we are lucky, she is tormenting him."

Tamsin laughed. "Sir Davey would not allow his sister to be mistreated. But Sir Malise might expect her to serve ale and chop carrots. He has no respect for women, I think." She shook her head sadly. "I wonder if I will ever see Dalrinnie again, even with Liam being—" She stopped.

"Liam being what?"

Tamsin took her cousin's arm, leaning close. "Did I mention that Sir John never said much about the previous owner of Dalrinnie? He hinted the man was dead and forgotten. But the true owner of Dalrinnie, by Scots law—is Sir William Seton."

"Liam?"

"Aye. Forfeited, outlawed, and determined to gain it back, I can tell you."

"Could that be the reason you he married? It could prevent Malise from trying to do so. But—could Liam regain Dalrinnie through you this way?"

"He says not. There is a jumble of English law and Scots law, while Edward freely grants Scottish lands and titles that he does not oversee except by tyranny. If the English possess Dalrinnie, that settles it, to their way of thinking."

"You could return there if the Scots take it."

"Years from now, perhaps. That is too far ahead to think about." She might no longer be married to Liam then, she thought. "My things are there—my books, and the chests and boxes in storage that came with me from Kincraig. Some of it was part of my tocher, though Sir John spent any dowry that was in actual coin."

"Regaining Dalrinnie would take an attack now," Kirsty said. "They say Bruce has gained back some castles, but lives are lost, property too. Papa says Bruce evacuates people and then burns Scottish castles before he will ever let the English have them."

"Burn now, rebuild later," Tamsin said. "No wonder Bruce is proving a fierce foe. He might burn Dalrinnie rather than let the English keep it."

"Perhaps." Kirsty walked beside her for a moment. "Tamsin, have you heard of the curse of Dalrinnie?"

"The what?"

"My father mentioned it, but you never spoke of it, although you lived there."

"I never heard it. A curse?"

"Curse or prophecy—it came from Thomas the Rhymer. I thought you knew."

Startled, Tamsin stopped and stared at her. "What did Thomas say?"

"Apparently many years ago, he said none who hold Dalrinnie will keep it, until something happens. But Papa could not remember the whole of it. Something about barons losing the castle. And something about a harper. That caught my attention."

"I know nothing of it. But I do not know all that Grandda said or predicted—no one ever will. Sir John never mentioned it, so perhaps only family know about it." She resolved to ask Liam when the chance arose. But she wondered if she had overlooked it among the Rhymer's notes; she would search those old, worn scraps of writing again.

"Every castle in Scotland has its legend or its ghost, I think. And if there is a curse on Dalrinnie, let it fall on Malise and no one else," Kirsty said firmly.

"Just so." Tamsin frowned, thoughts whirling. Was there some connection between Thomas and Dalrinnie?

ISOBEL, ALWAYS GRACEFUL in Liam's regard, had a pinkish and healthy glow as she sat smiling up at him. She was dressed as simply as any crofter wife in a long brown tunic and wrapped boots of soft leather, her sleek dark hair plaited in two long braids. The last he had seen her, she had been a pale, silent, elegant lady with dark shadows under her eyes, haunted by secrets. Inner calm shone through her now, though only natural backbone had helped her survive being used by others to prophesy against her will—and to endure an English siege before James Lindsay had found her.

Well, Liam remembered, initially James had abducted Isobel, believing that one of her so-called prophecies had deliberately ruined him, caused harm to his family, even worse, impacted Wallace's death. James had only the truth, but soon enough, Liam's friend had discovered that Isobel was more a victim than James realized—

That gave him pause. Liam glanced at Tamsin, walking across the clearing with her cousin. He was discovering, as James had, that a woman with the Sight was a complicated and fascinating creature and a treasure of great value.

"Liam?" Isobel asked. "You seem far away."

He smiled. "Just enjoying our reunion, lass." He was learning how well Lady Isobel had taken to life in the forest, and what a help her uncanny ability was in warning her husband of danger or a reassurance of peace. Tamsin and Isobel had more in common than they could know.

"The child is due mid-winter, as I was saying. I will not be here in the woodland much longer if my husband has his way."

"I am not sure he will have his way," Liam chuckled. "But you know he is concerned for your wellbeing and the child's. If it were my wife, I would want her safely tucked away as well."

"I know. And you have a wife now! I did not expect that news of you. She seems lovely. I wonder—an odd question, but does your lady have a touch of the Sight?"

"I think so. How could you tell? Does one seer recognize another?"

"No more than anyone else. But Finley said she is kin to Thomas the Rhymer, so I wondered. And when I met her, I saw a lovely soft light all around her. She has clarity and strength," she said, "and she cares for you."

"Does she?"

"Oh, so much. I saw it in her eyes when she watched you. I am glad you married this one."

"Just a handfasting," he confessed. "Temporary."

She gave him a doubtful look. "Is it? I think it is just what you need. What you both need. Something troubles her, and you have such steadiness. She will benefit from that."

"She does not share that opinion, I think." He shrugged. "She does have the Sight. I have seen it come over her like a storm. It passes quickly but frightens her."

"It can come on that way. Once I found some peace in my heart, it came easier. Now it is natural, something ordinary and reliable. So Lady Tamsin's kinsman was a prophet," she mused, looking toward Tamsin and Kirsty.

"So they say. The gift of the Queen of Faery, if one believes it."

"Life is more than what we see here on the earth, more than heaven above and hell below. I have seen more layers, and God's salvation and peace is there for all. But I do not debate that with priests," she laughed. "Well, Gideon and Uncle Murdoch both understand the world is wider and more magical than we can truly know."

"You," he said, "have grown into a wise woman."

"Always was, but no one asked." She knocked his arm gently, teasing. "Your Tamsin must guard what she can do until she is sure of it. And you—my dear, she is a fortunate lass. You are a rock. You understand and respect her where others might not."

"She does not put much faith in me, my dear. With reason," he added.

"Not yet," she murmured. "But she will."

He cocked a brow in doubt.

"She will." Isobel set a hand on his arm. "It is so good to see you. Now tell me about Gilchrist and Gideon. I miss them so, though Finley told me the twins felt the need to help at Holyoak for now. But oh, those two played such pranks on us as children." She laughed.

"They did. And still look too much alike. But Gideon's tonsure does help to tell them apart," he drawled.

LATE THAT NIGHT, Tamsin rested beside Liam on a thick bed of sheepskins and woolen blankets that cocooned them in warmth. With her head on his shoulder, she listened to his breathing, his heartbeat, even and deep. Untroubled and soothing, his rhythms wove with the random sounds of the forest at rest; wind rustling through leaves, branches creaking, birds and small animals fluttering, chittering, chirping. Never silent, even at night, the woodland sounds surrounded her under soft moonlight. Closing her eyes, she cozied against the man she could call husband.

But she was not ready to do that yet. She had so many questions, including about the hint that he knew more about the Rhymer than he let on.

Yet here, now, he felt so familiar, warm and strong and safe, her head on the firm pillow of his arm, his heartbeat thumping under her cheek, his body blending with hers. They were not strangers in that sense now. And yet he was distant, an enigma still. As she was to him, perhaps. They had much to learn about each other.

They had no home, no celebration. Their marriage had been based on rescue rather than love and affinity. She knew what she deeply wanted: the shield and comfort of family, a peaceful home, a future of hope and happiness, infused with love and passion. A dream, truly.

But she did not know if he shared that dream, or if their agreement, the rescue and favor of this marriage, would last even a year. If she truly had the Rhymer's gift, it did not seem to help her know what to do, what to think.

Word by word and step by step, she would have to make her

own way, she told herself. Page by page and promise by promise, she would do what was necessary, walk through what lay ahead—adventure, danger, challenge... Even love, dared she dream it. She wanted to think it waited for her—just here, in his arms.

She was not ready to open her heart and her hopes entirely though. Her instinct to protect herself was so honed now that drawing in was more familiar ground than acceptance. But now she truly yearned to be free of that wall if she could find a way.

Shifting, she felt his arm snug her close, his breath over her brow as he slept. Sighing, she closed her eyes.

She stood on the slope of a hill. Dalrinnie soared above her and behind her the forest was a spreading filigree of dark branches against a red-gold sunset. She looked about for the knight, the one who had been there when she had left this castle. This time she did not sway precariously but rather stood on solid ground. Waiting.

The knight did not come. She stood alone, her hair long and loose, blowing back in the breeze. She had no shoes, no cloak, and stood shivering in the cold, wrapping her arms about her, waiting—for what? She was not sure.

Then, suddenly, without warning, horses were upon her—giant beasts, their legs strong and rapid, their forms huge, powerful. Then she saw knights on their backs, chain mail sparking like fire in the sunset—

An arm, stout and strong and cased in chain mail, swooped out and down to pluck her up as if she weighed nothing. The man tossed her over the saddle pommel.

The sunlight went out like a candle flame and the world went black.

Then she saw an iron frame, black and cold under her gripping hands. A dungeon door. A cage.

Tamsin, *the knight called from far off.* Tamsin—

But he would not find her in the darkness, would not see her trapped inside the iron bars. She cried out—

Startled awake, she caught back a sob. "Where are you—?"

"Here. Just here," Liam said, his arm braced around her.

CHAPTER TWENTY-THREE

"T HE SHERIFF'S DEPUTY will meet us at Aikwood Tower, a few miles from here," Liam said, riding beside Tamsin. As they left the makeshift forest stable behind, he led the way along another path that skirted the encampment. Well behind them, Finley rode alongside Lindsay's man, Iain Campbell—two guards, one amiable and one dour, securely at their backs.

Tamsin had seen the leather bags they carried on their saddles, covered with blankets so as not to attract attention. Something important was to be delivered to the man they were to meet. She knew it had to do with Bruce, something Liam was part of arranging. She would wait—when the time was right, he would tell her. She felt more sure of him every day. Glancing back, she saw Finley lift a hand, and waved in response.

Brawny and silent, Iain Campbell also gave her a begrudging flicker of the hand. Inordinately pleased, she turned back.

"Is Aikwood held by the English?" she asked Liam.

"No one holds it just now. Fire damaged it beyond use, but it suits for private meetings, as no one goes there now. Though if I feel this fellow is not one I want to deal with, I will entrust the goods to James Lindsay, and we will all leave quick as we can.

"What goods are those?"

"Meant for Bruce," he said simply.

"So you truly need to trust this sheriff's deputy."

"Aye. If all is well, you and I will travel onward."

"On to Selkirk," she affirmed.

"It is another five miles or so from the tower. Then you will be content, hey?" His glance held a twinkle.

She smiled faintly, anticipating the hours ahead. What would she do with the book once it was in her hands? Originally, her plan was to take it to Kincraig, for it should belong to her family. But King Edward still wanted it—and Liam wanted Bruce to have it. But the book was hers to decide, not his. She frowned, determination growing.

In the quiet as they rode, she felt the wind stir her white veil, the simple everyday linen piece that loosely covered the top and sides of her head tied around her brow with a cord, leaving her long braids to hang down. She had crammed the veil in her bag when she had left Dalrinnie—departing a widow, now riding a wife again, at least for now. She smoothed her gray skirts, shabby now but brushed clean, and adjusted her blue-and-green plaid cloak, its generous width draped over the back of the horse.

When she sought better purchase on the iron stirrups with her booted feet, her recent dream came back. Why had she dreamed of standing on a hill, waiting for the knight? The first dream about him had proven true; escaping, she had met Liam again. But this dream felt dangerous, hopeless, for she had been confined behind iron bars as if in a prison. It haunted her.

Where the forest path narrowed, she followed on the dappled horse behind Liam as they passed a pool and waterfall. Finley and Iain came behind at a distance. She slowed, wanting to linger in that pretty place.

"The air is so refreshing here," she said over the sound of the waterfall as Liam turned, questioning. "I wish we could stay."

"Another time." His simple reply brought a spark of hope; his casual certainty about the future made her feel good in the moment. They moved on, leaving the rushing falls and the narrow path behind. Liam rode beside her again.

"We should not stop anywhere we might meet soldiers," he said. "The closer we come to Selkirk, the more chance there is of seeing them. We must keep alert." He glanced back. "Even with an armed escort, we could meet trouble."

"Liam," she said, "are those sacks a source of trouble? Is it gold we carry?"

"Not gold, though revenue," he explained. "I am—a collector of rents."

"A tax collector?" She smothered a surprised laugh.

"Not quite. I keep the rent-rolls for Bruce's properties, aye. Before you and I met at Lochmaben, before I—spent some weeks in King Edward's hospitality, I went about to Bruce's tenants in Carrick and Lochmaben to ask if they could pay rent to help the king. Not all could, nor will Bruce pose a penalty for it, not in this clime. But any money we can gather for him goes to the cause."

"It is good work that you do, then."

"The most important thing we carry, though, is a rent-roll document that is marked to indicate who among Bruce's tenants and neighbors support him and his kingship and could be called upon to help the cause of Scotland. Sir Hugh Douglas," he added, glancing at her, "helped me to complete that work."

"Oh!" she said in quick comprehension. "And you have done this all along?"

"For a while. Between rescuing damsels."

"This man we are meeting will bring the silver and the parchment to Bruce?"

"He promised James, who trusts him. I could go on the strength of that alone. I do not know this deputy, but we shall see what comes of this meeting."

"If he is trustworthy, then he will ensure that no soldiers are near when you meet."

"That is the expectation." She heard something unspoken in his tone.

"Yet he could betray us," she provided. "This could be a trap."

"Aye." He touched his sword hilt.

"I have a dagger," she said, remembering. "I took it when I

left Dalrinnie."

"Best locate it, just in case. Can you use it for other than slicing a bannock?"

She smiled as he laughed. "My brother Henry taught me to use a dagger before I left Kincraig, when we knew I would live in a garrisoned castle."

"The same brother who taught you to climb down a rope? All useful skills."

"He taught my sister Meg to shoot with a bow. She was keen for it, was Meg. My sister Rowena already knew how to wield a knife blade. For treating injuries, you see."

"Or inflicting them."

"She could," Tamsin allowed. "And she rather liked swords— the wooden wasters that Henry and our cousins would practice with in the yard. Later, she studied healing."

"And Lady Tamsin? Arrows and blades for her as well?"

"Books," she said firmly. "Just books, and ink. Very sharp quills, though," she added, as he chuckled.

"How did the Rhymer's work become your responsibility? Your siblings are his great-grandchildren as well."

"He gave each of us gifts. I remember that day so clearly. He gave me a pretty box with ink and pens and parchment pages that were his. My siblings have other things that belonged to him, and he asked us to carry on his legacy. It is not just me alone, you see."

"The Rhymer must have known he was not long for the world."

"I think so. But I was young and did not realize."

"Better that way, lass."

They rode in silence for a while then, leaving the woodland to cross broad, rolling moorland, keeping the wide-flowing Ettrick Water to their right side. Hills rose ahead, thickly fringed with bushes and trees.

Soon she saw a tower on a hilltop, stone walls rising up, a walled keep overlooking a vast rumple of hills, trees, moorland

and glinting water. The tower, though high, was jagged and broken.

"Aikwood," Liam said and led their party over the bridge. Tamsin felt tension in the air and tightened her shoulders. She noticed that Liam sat tall but with wariness in his back and shoulders, his calm gaze keen as any hawk's.

The broken tower had no moat, just the protection of the long hill and the broad view from above, so that anyone approaching could be seen for miles. The gate stood open, a wooden arched door in an iron grid between the fieldstone walls. For a moment, the crisscrossed iron reminded her of the uncomfortable dream.

They rode into the yard and halted outside the ruined keep, dark with char and traces of the fire that had taken in down. Nearby, a low stone building stood whole, its door open on shadows. A lone saddled horse nuzzled at autumn grasses growing around the crooked doorstep.

A man stepped out of the low structure and came toward them. His brawny build and height were made larger by a heavy blue cloak with raised hood, and a green surcoat belted over full chain mail. Lifting a gauntleted hand in a gesture of peace, he paused.

Dismounting, Liam helped Tamsin down and then turned. The man shoved back his cloak hood to reveal a young face with high, rounded cheeks and a swath of thick blond hair. Seeing them, the fellow grinned, dimples flashing. He laughed.

Gasping, Tamsin ran toward him. "Henry!"

"TAMSIN," HENRY SAID later, his arm around his sister, "I thought you were safe at Dalrinnie. But what you say about Sir Malise is alarming. We all know the man, I think." He looked at Liam, who nodded. Standing nearby, Finley and Iain nodded in silent agreement as well.

"So you see, I had to leave," Tamsin said.

While she had reunited with her brother, explaining her

situation briefly, Liam had stood by—thanking heaven's own luck that Sir Henry was the new sheriff deputy of Selkirkshire. He had met the fellow but a few times and had liked him, found him straightforward, intelligent, and discreet. The position he held was an honor, especially for a young knight. Henry Keith of Kincraig must have earned the notice and approval of King Edward, as well as the sheriff of Selkirkshire, Edward's trusted cohort, Aymer de Valence, Earl of Pembroke.

Yet Tamsin's brother gave loyalty to Scotland precedence; even his sister had not realized the extent of his dedication. But Henry Keith was playing with fire if Edward ever learned the truth.

"Sir William," Henry said, leaving his sister's side to come toward Liam. "I recall we met at Carlisle three years back, was it? I doubt you remember it."

"I do. Four years back," Liam said. "Have you been here in Selkirk long?"

"A month or so, sent up to Selkirk Castle with Patrick Siward to work with De Valence."

"Patrick Siward?" Liam frowned. The fellow had been looking for Tamsin not so long ago on Malise Comyn's orders.

"Sir Patrick was at Dalrinnie the last time I was there," Tamsin said. "He came to Dalrinnie sometimes when Sir John was alive, usually with Sir Malise."

"Interesting," Liam said. "We saw him recently leading a patrol for Comyn."

"Comyn and De Valence have been working together to find Bruce," Henry said, "and whoever is working with Bruce."

"Then I hope you are a wary fellow, straddling both sides as you do," Liam said.

"As wary as one can be. Both De Valence and Sir Patrick are gone, one north, one south. I am expected to watch the forest. One could get lost in there for days. Impossible to find rogues. Some days I just give up on the task." Henry shrugged.

Liam liked the lad immensely, even more now than he remembered. "I have something for you," he said, "if you can bring it to its owner. If not, please have the courtesy to admit it, and I will have your sister removed to safety."

"I give you my word on my sister's life, sir. I am here alone, and no one is aware of what I sometimes do. De Valence and Siward regard my position as not very important, so I am not under scrutiny. I have Edward's approval as well, though I had to work hard for that," he added.

Liam studied him. Henry's gaze was direct, his dark blue eyes steady. Liam nodded. "If Bruce asked you to do this, and Lindsay trusts you, that speaks well of you."

"I will guarantee my brother's honor as well," Tamsin said.

"That is good enough for me," Liam murmured.

Henry gave his sister a rueful smile. "Thank you. I would hope Sir William would take the word of a man's sister."

"He would take the word of his wife," Liam replied.

"Wife!" Henry stared, then laughed in delight.

Tamsin went to Liam's side, welcomed under his arm. "We were married recently."

"God's very bones! And you said nothing until now?" Henry grinned. "Had I made the match myself, neither of you could do better. But what of Dalrinnie? It was once yours, Sir William. Will my sister be Lady of Dalrinnie once again?"

"It is currently in Malise Comyn's hands," Liam replied. "But that can change."

"It can, but it will take some doing." Henry leaned to kiss his sister's cheek. "May I take this news to Bruce?"

"If the lady agrees," Liam said. She nodded. He turned back to Henry. "Where is the king now?"

The young lord knew which one he meant. "Heading west. I know where to rendezvous, but if I miss him, James Douglas of Morton, his watchdog, will find me. But I must hurry before they sail for the Isles. I hear that is their plan."

"Do you go alone? It might draw less notice but is the greater risk."

"I have just a few days to ride out and back before De Valence returns from Berwick. Siward rode to Dalrinnie to meet with Comyn." Henry looked toward Finley and Iain, standing nearby. "But should you order your men to guarantee my honesty on the journey, I would not object."

"They are not my men. Confer with them and let them answer."

"I shall. You have brought excellent news, and I am pleased and honored. But we should go our own ways. We have been here a while and could attract notice."

"Aye." Liam and his cousin went to the horses to remove the leather sacks intended for Bruce, and left them with Henry on the stone step. Reaching into one bag, Liam withdrew a leather packet. "This list is as important as the rest, perhaps more so."

"I will guard all of it with my life." Henry tucked the packet inside his surcoat. "Where will you go now?" he asked Tamsin.

"To Selkirk. I left Grandda's pages to be bound into a book—for the family."

Henry nodded. Watching, Liam frowned. More and more, he felt that this book, whatever it was, belonged with the Keiths. "And then?" Henry asked.

"I thought to go to Kincraig to be with Meg and Rowena," she said. "But I do not know what my—husband plans." She glanced at Liam, her cloud-gray gaze hesitant.

"We should stay in the forest for a while," he said, "until we see what Sir Malise does next. Then, sir, I will take Lady Tamsin to Kincraig to see to the safety of your sisters."

"Have you heard if Kincraig is under threat?" Henry asked.

"Not yet that we know, but Bruce wants Scottish noblewomen under additional protection. I will send someone there directly soon, and we will go up there ourselves as soon as we can."

"Send word if you have news."

"We will," Tamsin said. "I am so glad to see you, Henry, and know you are well."

"Where can I find you, Sir William, when this mission is

done?" Henry indicated the bags at his feet.

"Send word to James Lindsay or to Holyoak. Either will know where I am."

"If King Robert has a message for you, I will bring word back."

"I would be obliged."

"Henry." Tamsin hugged her brother. "Can we find you at Selkirk Castle?"

"Or patrolling the forest, so long as I retain this position. Give me a moment for a word with your friends before you go." Henry extended a hand to Liam. "Sir, I am honored to call you kinsman now. Take care of her."

"I will." Liam clapped his shoulder. "Be safe, brother."

AS THEY RODE past a stone-walled kirk and graveyard, Tamsin shivered, crossing herself. Riding beside her, Liam slowed near the small, simple church.

"This path leads past the kirk into the town," he said, pointing ahead. "We follow it to the Water Row and the Back Row—streets bordering the market. You can just see it from here." As he spoke, he looked up at the kirk's bell tower.

"You know this place." Tamsin watched him, understood immediately the connection he seemed to feel. "The town—and this church."

"Kirk o' the Forest, they call it."

"A pretty name for a pretty church on the edge of the forest."

"More than that. An important meeting place, this. A few years ago, Wallace was declared a Guardian of Scotland here. I stood inside that door to witness him swear to defend Scotland."

"You knew him well?"

"I ran with him for two years, a small group of men. James Lindsay was with him too. Wallace was a bold man. A good man, with courage. Too much, sometimes," he added in a bitter tone, then urged his horse onward.

"The Guardians of Scotland," she said, keeping pace. "They

work with Bruce?"

"They were appointed to act as Scotland's guiding council when we lacked a king, and to work with Edward to strive for balance and justice. Not an easy task. The roster changes often. Some step down. Some die in the effort. I have known a few. Admirable men, each one. It is an honor to support them."

"In secret ways," she said. "That is what you do."

"It is." He glanced at her. "And whatever you learn stays secret too, lass."

"It will. I am glad to know you work for Bruce and not Edward."

He tilted his head. "Who said I do not work for Edward?"

That stunned her. "But you did work for Bruce—"

"At times I must work for both. But one king knows the truth."

"Bruce," she surmised, and saw him nod. "Will you take the book to Edward, as ordered, or to your other king?"

"I have not decided."

His words were like a flame to a wick, and her temper flared. "I am thinking this is not your decision," she said. "This book is mine, not yours. It belongs to my family, not either of your kings. I decide what to do with it. If you still think to take it from me— you can just stay here. I will fetch it myself." She pressed the dapple gray's sides and surged ahead, leaving Liam in her wake.

Riding past the old kirk, her heart pounded with a mix of indignation and anger tinged with regret. She did not want to argue with Liam—she wanted his agreement. She did not want to wander into a town alone, not knowing quite where to go. But now hurt and pride kept her from looking back, waiting for him. Yet she hoped he was there—perhaps keeping his distance, for she had not cooled entirely. The book was hers. He did not have the right of it. She desperately wished he would see that.

The kirk path became an earthen street, then turned to a cobbled street lined with buildings, to branch into other streets. Ahead, she saw the bell tower of a larger church and then saw the market area, a three-sided green lined with shops, stalls, carts. A busy place where people walked about, knights on horses rode past.

She slowed, still too proud to look behind her, though she wondered where she was, and where she should go. The market, surely, would be the place to look for the bookseller. One step at a time, she told herself.

Above the town, beyond the tops of buildings leaning unevenly toward their streets, she saw a castle looming over the town. Selkirk Castle, Liam had mentioned along the way. Then, behind her, she heard horses' hooves coming nearer, louder. Hesitating, still fuming—though it began to fade as reason set in—she held her chin high and did not look around.

A moment later, Liam rode up beside her and leaned over to take one of the reins of her horse. She slid him a glare in silence.

"Look daggers at me all you like, my lady," he said, "but the town council does not permit horses on the square. We need to stable our mounts. Come. I know a place."

He released the rein to her control and gestured for her to follow him down one of the branching avenues. "There is an inn down along the Water Row where we can care for the horses. We can also have a meal and find a room for the night."

"A room!" She lifted her chin again, still wanting to be angry. But she needed his guidance here. Needed his calm and assurance. Already she felt the town encroaching on her, the crowds and noise and commotion assailing her, making her suddenly anxious.

"Can we go back?" she asked.

"It is a long way back to the forest, and we would need to ride at night. We must stay. I know an inn. All is well," he added.

"Aye then."

"Keep your hood up. Even with the veil, your hair is bright as new gold. I do not want you noticed."

She tugged at the hood, guiding her horse to walk behind his. When he turned into an alley beside a building, she noticed a painted sign reading "The Grapes Inn," decorated with fat bunches of purple grapes. She stopped when Liam did, in the center of a dusty yard behind the inn, where a stable sat. A lad came running toward them as Liam helped her dismount to take the reins of the horses. Liam took Tamsin's leather satchel from her saddle and led the way through the alley to the inn's door.

A woman looked up from a table, where she was filling jugs from a keg. "Greetings, sir. What do you want?"

"My wife and I would like a room for the night."

Listening, Tamsin felt a sweet shiver go through her at the words, at the quiet confidence. *My wife.* She was still upset with him, yet his murmur softened that.

"We just stabled our horses," Liam continued, "and hope for a room and a meal."

"Extra for the stabling," the woman replied, and walked toward a high table that held papers and a locked box, presumably for coin. "If you want a hot bath that is extra too, and if so, you need to take the room at the back next to the kitchen. We dinna bring buckets up the steps. And we need an hour's notice to fill the tub. Soap is another charge. If you want food brought to the room, it is a half penny more. And no clippin' on the edge of the coins. A full half."

"We will want a hot bath and supper in the room when we return," Liam said.

"Off to market?" The woman picked up a heavy iron key. "This way."

Liam took Tamsin's elbow as they followed the innkeeper. She felt her temper begin to drain away at his touch. No matter how impermanent this marriage, he was her husband. He was Liam, and she felt better when he was with her. Calmer. More certain. More entirely herself.

She stopped in the corridor as they walked to the kitchen.

"My lady?" he asked. "This way."

She nodded, distracted. Just then, she had realized what had not occurred to her before. His words, so casually spoken to a stranger, shed clarity on what had been missing from her life. A sense of belonging. An end to loneliness and uncertainty. A place where she felt at ease.

In so short a time, Liam Seton had become so familiar to her that he was—like home to her. He was there for her, *had* been there for her every time she had needed protection, advice, comfort.

Secrets or not, truthful or not, plans for the Rhymer's book or not—that quality felt so true, so stirring, that it overtook her objections, her doubts. Tears sprang to her eyes. The lonely years at Dalrinnie when she had seen so little of her family, and had lacked the affection of her husband... That loneliness and lack of love had been a burden she had carried, had even taken with her beyond Dalrinnie's walls.

Now, she felt that weight lift, felt a profound change as she stood in an ordinary place, the dim corridor where the innkeeper went on about keys and baths and extra fees. Liam's quiet use of "my wife" moments ago had released something in her that she had not even known was locked. In his voice, she heard caring, recognition of her worth. She dashed tears away with the back of her hand, sniffed—and told herself she was just very tired. Surely, that was it.

"Is there a souter here? A chandler, a woolen merchant per-haps?" Liam asked.

"Look for the signs near the market cross. Selkirk is known for wool and weavings," the woman said with a proud lift of her nose. "You will find more than one."

"Is there a bookseller too?"

"Now what do you want that for? No one asks for the bookseller but the priests. He has a shop near the tanning shop, I suppose because he uses leather for his books. Well, if your lady wants a wee book of prayers you could find one there. But be prepared to pay a pretty penny."

"I am prepared." He gave her some coins. "For the room, stable, food, and bath."

"Generous, sir. Here you are." She led them away from the kitchen that bustled with cook and servants, emanating rich smells of roasting meat and baking bread that made Tamsin quickly hungry. Opening a door at the end of the corridor, the woman stood back, handing Liam a key.

"Should you have goods worth lockin' up. The room is old and plain, but warm beside the kitchen, see. Sir. Madam." She gave Tamsin a shrewd up-and-down look, then returned to the main room.

The chamber was simple indeed, with whitewashed stone walls, a small window looking out on the stable, a crude chair and table, a chamber pot in one corner and a brazier in another, thankfully glowing and warm. A shelf stored candles and cups. A large cupboard with a curtained opening took up most of one stone wall.

Liam dropped his chain coif and pushed fingers through his hair, looking about. "Where is the bed?"

"Here." Tamsin tugged at the curtained cupboard to reveal a mattress covered in a blanket and a sheep's fleece. "A box bed. We have one at Kincraig. Snug and warm."

He peered inside. "Private," he murmured. Her heart fluttered with the word. He turned. "Shall we go to the market?"

"Can I leave my satchel here if we lock the door?" At his nod, she tossed the leather bag inside the enclosed bed.

"I am glad you left your great sack of books at Holyoak and brought just the one with you today. It is less to worry about."

"I thought we would return to the monastery, thought they were safe there."

"They are. Let us find your bookseller."

They walked without conversation toward the market green with its tall stone cross and commotion of merchants and customers. Pausing on the grassy sward, Tamsin turned. "I do not see the shop."

"Is that it?" Liam pointed to a sign on a narrow shop door. "Richard Bisset, Maker and Seller of Books."

"Aye. But the window is closed." Beside the door, the hinged panel that would typically open like a shelf for customers was latched shut.

"Lass." Liam took her arm. "Back there, coming up the main road—knights on horses. Evidently the castle garrison does not heed the council's rules about steeds."

She turned to see three knights riding toward the market. Where she and Liam stood on the triangular market green, the bookseller's shop was just behind them, and the Water Row with its inn was behind that. "What should we do?"

"We must get inside the shop. Quickly."

CHAPTER TWENTY-FOUR

TAMSIN KNOCKED ON the shop door as Liam glanced around. She sensed his tension. When no one answered, he reached past her to try the latch. The door opened easily, and he gave her a push. "Inside, quickly," he murmured.

The tiny front room was empty. The closed shutter leaked a little sunlight but the interior was dark and silent. Looking about, she saw a slanted desk and shelves with locked boxes. A curtain concealed an opening to a back room. All was quiet.

"Halloo the shopkeeper," Liam called out.

After a few moments, a woman came out wiping her hands on a leather apron. "Oh! What do you want, sir?"

"My wife has business with Master Bisset. Is he here?"

"Master Bisset is having his midday meal."

"I am Lady Thomasina Keith. I left pages with him to be bound." Behind her, Tamsin saw Liam go to the shuttered panel to peer between the slats.

"Let me see what he says." The woman pushed through the curtain. A minute later, she poked her head through.

"He wants to know if it is one of the volumes from Holyoak."

"It is," Tamsin said. The woman disappeared.

Liam stood, watching the market square through the crack in the shutter. Again Tamsin sensed an alert tension in him. Pressing his hand to the wall, he rippled his fingers, watchful, on edge.

When he turned, his smile was distracted. Something still

troubled him, she thought. "They seem to be gone for now," he said. "While we are here, is there aught else you need at the market? Shoes made with the souter, or candles from the chandler, we could visit the woolen merchant. We would come back to the town if the things need to be made."

She shook her head. "I need naught, but thank you."

"Sure? I am thinking you do not get to a market very often."

"Another time. For now, I have all I need." She went to the window to peer through another crack, seeing green grass and a portion of the stone cross; shops with shutters lowered for business; people milling about. No knights. No horses. She breathed out in relief.

"Is there nothing I can give you now? I want to." His gentle tone surprised her.

"There is no shop here for what I want most," she said. "A home."

He leaned toward her, his shoulder pressing hers, his voice deep and soft beside her ear, its resonance sinking like heat through her body. "You will have it, I swear. Do not worry that you will never have a home if you stay wed to me. I intend to win back my home. Our home."

She looked up. His eyes, in the light through the shutter, were bright, startling blue. "If I stay wed to you?" she repeated.

His gaze dipped to her mouth, rose to meet her eyes. Something thundered softly through her, passionate, breathless. "I do not want you to worry."

"What worries me," she murmured, "is that my husband will win back his property on pain of his life. What kind of a home would that be? I would rather live in the shade of an oak tree with a rock for a hob, a log for a chair, and a fleece for a bed."

"Would you?" he asked, his voice low.

"We shall see," she murmured, "once I see what you do with my book."

"Tamsin." He reached for her, but she whirled away just as the bookseller pushed through the curtain.

"Lady Thomasina! My goodness. I did not expect you! Pardon me, welcome, my lord," he added, bowing slightly toward Liam.

"This is my husband, Sir William Seton. We came for the book."

"I thought to bring it to Holyoak later with the books I repaired for them. But it is ready now." Bisset set a cloth-wrapped package on the slanted desk.

"Thank you," she said, going to the desk. Bisset untied the cord and folded down the cloth covering, then a second wrapping of parchment. He stepped back to reveal a leather-bound book.

"Oh, it is beautiful." Tamsin caught her breath as she reached out. The book was not large, its cover, a soft leather, was perhaps the span of her hand across. It was tooled with a design—laurel, she noticed, for Keith—at the corners, and the center was simply a tall initial "T," as elaborate as a scrolled initial in a manuscript, that was painted red and blue and engraved in the leather.

"The pages you copied, madam, were excellently done," Bisset explained. "We folded and pressed them into quires and stitched them together. Here—you can see them inside the spine of the book." He tipped the volume to show her. "The boards are wood, covered in leather, with parchment glued inside. The covers will hold for a very, very long time, if not forever. And here, you see," he said, opening the back board, "I have added a wee pocket where you can tuck free pages, if you have them. And a small brass latch, should you store it flat or chained."

She nodded, speechless as she turned the pages. The work she had done for two years was here, the margins straight, the rulings perfectly aligned. The parchment, verso and recto, was good vellum; she felt the soft smoothness of one side and the slightly rough texture of the other. The pages crackled a bit as she turned them carefully.

Each page was so familiar to her that she hardly needed to look closely. Her eyes blurred with tears. No one knew how much work she had put into this over the past few years, copying Thomas's notes and scribbles painstakingly, making his often untidy, blotted writings neat and legible. She had begun copying the pages at Kincraig, before she was married, continuing it through the years she was Dalrinnie, doing some of the work in Holyoak's little scriptorium. She had made more than one copy, adding greatly to the work. Now she noticed, as if she had not seen it before, how neat and beautiful her script was, how meticulous and masterful. Pride ran warm and lovely through her. She had made this. Her great-grandfather would be pleased, if only he knew. Perhaps on some level, in some more beautiful place than this, he did know.

Closing the book reverently, tucking the wrapping around it, she turned to the bookseller. "Master Bisset, it is truly beautiful. I cannot thank you enough."

"A pleasure and a privilege to work on it, my lady," he said. "But do you not want to show your husband before we wrap the parcel again? Sir," he said, stepping back.

With a cautious glance at Tamsin, Liam came forward.

She pulled back the parchment. "See," she said.

Liam reached out to smooth his fingers over the tooled leather cover. He opened the front board and began to turn the pages, reading a little here, there. He nodded, read more, nodded and smiled.

"I see," he murmured, with a knowing glance toward her. "Master Bisset, it is truly a fine volume. My lady's kinfolk will treasure it. Let me pay your fee, sir."

Tamsin gasped softly. "Nay, let me." But Liam held up a hand.

Bisset went to a shelf, then came back with a scrap of parchment with a number scribbled on it and handed it to Liam. "A book like that wee one, if we paid the scribe for the work as well as the binder, could cost a king's ransom, especially with illuminated decoration. But the lady herself did the work. I cannot tell you how much I admire that, sir. Your lady is worth her weight in gold, in that sense. All I did was fold, trim, stitch, make the covers and put it together. So the fee is not nearly as much, you see."

"I understand. And I too appreciate and admire my lady's work. I did not realize until now how capable and talented she is. I would pay a king's ransom for this book."

"But you are glad to not pay that," Bisset said with a laugh.

Liam chuckled. "Three pound Scots, seven shillings. Very reasonable," he murmured, and took a small leather purse from his belt, counting out silver coins. "Four pound Scots, ten shillings, will that do?"

"That is the greater sum, sir."

"The bargain is mine, Master Bisset. My lady is pleased, therefore, so am I."

Tamsin looked at him, wide-eyed, though she said little as Bisset wrapped the book, tied it with a green silk ribbon, and handed it to her.

"My lady, an honor."

"Thank you, sir. If I have more pages for another volume, would you be here to do the work? I believe you are sometimes in Edinburgh."

"I am here most of the year, though I spend winters in Edinburgh. My mother is there, you see. I would be happy to create another book for you, my lady."

She smiled and turned to leave, though Liam stepped outside first, putting out an arm in warning, so that Tamsin stayed in the shadows. "Clear," he said. "Come ahead."

She walked beside him, holding the package close to her heart like a precious thing. "Back to the inn?" she asked.

"I want you to go to the inn." He took her arm, glancing about as they walked. "I need to have a look around. This way— we can cross from this street to the alley beside the inn that leads to the stable. Hurry."

"Are they looking for us?"

"We do not want to be seen, either way. Come." He drew her along, leaving the market street to walk between a few vegetable gardens toward the inn.

"Hurry. Give me the package." He lifted the book from her hands even as he rushed her along. "Run, lass!"

Reaching the alley, she reached for the book, but he kept it, drawing her along with a hand on her arm. When they reached the stable yard, Tamsin could hear horse hooves clattering over cobblestones out on the road.

"Take the back entrance into the inn. Go to the room and lock the door. Do not open it until you hear my voice. Take this." He took the key from his belt pouch. "Go!"

"The book. Give me the book!"

He dropped it into her outstretched hands. "Did you think I would keep it?"

"You own it now. You paid the fee."

"We will talk about this later. Go!" He fair pushed her toward the inn.

"What will you do?" She held the book close.

"Lead them away from you," he said, striding into the stable.

MOUNTED AND SILENT in the shade of the alley, Liam waited as the knights rode slowly past the inn, clearly searching for something or someone. When they reached the far end of the avenue, their backs still turned, he urged his stallion out onto the street and in the opposite direction. Moving casually until he reached the Kirk Wynd, he spurred the horse onward and set out away from the town.

All too soon, he heard the clatter and thud of hooves on cobbles and then earth behind him, as well as the shouts to stop. Bending along his horse's neck, he urged for more speed, and at the old stone kirk, he turned eastward rather than westward. He did not want to lead them back to Aikwood or farther west into the forest where friends might be wandering or watchful.

Eastward lay more forest and hills that were less familiar to him, but safer. Northeast lay Melrose, but he would not go that far. Far ahead, he saw a long, dark swath of tall pine trees, a crescent arm of the Ettrick Forest reaching toward other streams, other hills. He glanced back.

Four men pursued him now, shouting, pounding turf. Chances were, they knew this terrain better than he did, but he had a long view across rolling moorland toward forest to one side, hills farther on, and his horse had a good lead and a powerful gait on solid ground. Liam leaned in, head down.

He had felt uneasy in his very bones over the last few days, not willing to head to Selkirk, but Tamsin had wanted—needed—to go there. He knew that. And he meant to lead these men far from her, from the book, from Comyn's plans.

He rode on, the horse pounding relentlessly, faithfully as it carried him into the wind, then followed Liam's guidance toward the trees. The wind provided more aid than obstacle, and the sun was sinking, clouds gathering overhead. All in his favor.

The first arrow whizzed past him, past his horse's powerful neck. The second missed as well. Liam hunched, riding for the dense tree cover. He slung low over the horse, wishing now he wore chain mail under the hauberk, but glad he had grabbed the blue-painted shield at Holyoak, looped on the saddle now. Grabbing it, he tilted it best he could to cover his back and more of the horse too.

Just in time, for an arrow thunked into the shield. He swerved right, closer to the trees, the rough hem of the woodland soon surrounding him. The track was slower, littered with brush and rock. He pulled the stallion up for safety, though the animal forged onward. Behind him, he heard shouts as the knights veered in their pursuit.

The next arrow struck fast and unexpected. Liam felt the punch and sting just behind his shoulder, catching him where the leather gapped to expose his tunic beneath. Wincing, he stayed flat against the horse, urging his mount onward. The light sank further, daylight falling toward dusk. An advantage for him, but he was not yet clear of the pursuers.

A moment later, the stallion plunged between tall trees and wide sweeps of pine branches, entering a soaring cathedral of evergreens, the smell pungent, the thick layered pine needles underfoot quieting the hoof falls. The trees were tall and well-spaced and the way was clear. Too clear, for the knights came thundering in after him.

But the shadows were heavier here as he cut sideways off the wide natural path and urged the horse to clear a fallen log. He angled the stallion toward a depth of pine boughs ahead, glad when the animal pushed through the screen so that they could vanish into shadows and green.

He could feel the bite of the arrow stuck wavering in him, and tightened his left arm against his side in protection. He rode into the pine forest, lost in its powerful scent and eerie silence. Slowing to let the horse catch its breath, he led his mount down a slope at a long angle. He heard the creak of the wind through pines, heard the loose chuckle of a stream, felt its moisture in the air as he and the horse went further.

He knew how to hide in a forest, knew where to find the deepest shadows and thickets. He knew how to dance away from the fall of light, how to fit the shapes of horse and man to the match trees and boughs, knew to stay still once he found a place.

Where declining light and increasing shadow provided that spot, he eased himself from the saddle, then patted and soothed the sturdy horse. After a moment he let the animal begin to nuzzle grasses and sip from the lapping edge of the stream.

Above, where the slope met the higher ground of the pine forest, Liam heard hoofbeats, voices. The screen along the slope was dense enough to protect him from sight. He had a haven here, and sat to wait.

After a while, he reached back to grasp the arrow, cracking its shaft. Wincing, he left the arrowhead and part of the shaft in place. Removing it would cause too much bleeding; the arrow would plug the wound for now.

Seeing clusters of white-flowered yarrow stalks by the streambank, he moved carefully and pulled a fistful of the feathery leaves. Woundwort, some called it, for it could staunch bleeding and swelling. He pressed the leaves against his shoulder, layering them above the wound, then wet his linen shirt to keep it in place. For now it was all he could do until he could return to Tamsin.

She would be worried by now, he thought, as night fell. But if he left now they would follow him to find his wife—if he survived another pursuit. Resting against a tree trunk, he watched the stallion grazing, then he dozed, exhausted.

After a while, waking to silence, he climbed the slope. The men had gone. Dusk saturated the shadows. Liam moved cautiously outward to see empty moorland. With luck, the men had left the area, having lost him.

He frowned, realizing the knights had chased him deliberately, though Tamsin was not with him. Why? Then he knew. Malise.

The man wanted to capture Liam as much, perhaps more, than he wanted Tamsin. Comyn had a deep resentment of the Setons of Dalrinnie from years back—and Liam in particular. Did that old grudge still burn hot for Comyn, ignited recently by King Edward's orders and then the posting of the marriage banns?

Seven years ago, Malise Comyn's treatment of Agatha Seton had pitted her brothers against him. The fellow was lucky to be alive. Now, standing on the forest slope, he felt certain that Malise meant to strike back at him—and might try to do so through Tamsin. Liam had to get back to her.

Turning, he noticed three conical hills silhouetted against the dusky sky not far from the patch of pine forest. The Eildon Hills, they were called. Suddenly he knew Tamsin needed to see them. Thomas the Rhymer had lived near there, he recalled.

Despite knights and thugs, despite a treasure to be guarded and delivered, and a lady wife who needed no further danger, Liam knew he had to bring her there. It might be vital to her. He felt the urge like a turning in his soul.

Because he loved her. He knew that too, now.

Flexing his shoulder against the pain, he went to find his

horse.

SHE WAS TEMPTED to take the dappled gray and ride out to search for Liam. Listening anxiously for his step, she peered through the little window again, but the stables behind the inn were quiet. With every moment, she grew more anxious.

Earlier she had enjoyed a bath, and thinking he would return soon, ordered food too. Servants brought a tray with a hot meat pie large enough for two, along with cheese, bannocks, apples, ale, even a jug of wine. She nibbled at some of it and covered it. Two servants had carried in a wooden hip bath and toted buckets of steaming water back and forth from the kitchen, and then the innkeeper's wife had appeared to hand Tamsin a sticky ball of soap and some linen toweling. When the woman began to take the supper tray, Tamsin shook her head.

"My husband will return any moment," she said.

Now she sat, still hoping to hear his step, his voice. Unwrapping the book again, she paged through, reading, trying to savor its simple beauty, knowing how much her siblings would enjoy it. Yet the quiet, the worry, were too distracting.

As the room darkened, she was grateful for three bright candles. A glance told her the stable yard was still empty. Her stomach was in knots now. Liam would not leave her alone this long unless something dreadful had happened.

Testing the bath water, finding it still quite warm, she stripped down and slipped into the water, hoping that might ease her nervousness. The pine-scented soap ball was gooey but lathered well as she bathed, washed and rinsed her hair. She stood to towel off. Still the yard was empty. The candles, slender tallow sticks, were burning down.

She was glad to have brought the leather satchel, which held a clean shift, her dark blue gown, and a comb. She was even more glad for something to do as she sat to comb out her hair. Its curl resisted the ivory comb, and its length, nearly to her hips, could be a challenge. But it took up the time.

She prayed softly as she worked through her hair. In the silence, her whispers seemed loud, her heartbeat louder, thumping out the worry she tried to keep at bay. Turning to the brazier to coax her hair dry, she loosely braided its golden gleam.

Then she heard sounds in the yard, but when she went to the window, she saw only shadows. Moments later, she heard a soft rapping on the door.

"Tamsin," he murmured. "Tamsin, love, let me in."

She flew across the room, turned the latch, opened the door. He stood in the dark corridor, face pale, and she grabbed his leather hauberk to pull him into the room. Sobbing, she threw herself into his arms.

CHAPTER TWENTY-FIVE

H IS DEEP WINCE, as she tugged on his hauberk, startled her. "Liam, what is it? What happened?" She touched his face, ran her hands over his shoulders.

"It is naught. I am just glad to be here." He shut the door and bolted it.

"Jesu," she whispered, seeing the broken stump of the shaft jutting out below his shoulder, nearly under his arm. "You were arrowshot!"

"It will be fine. I will need some help to tend it, though. Ah, a bath. Good." His voice was graveled, weary.

"Come here." She took his other arm. "First we will get your things off." She pulled at his wide leather belt as he worked at the fastening, then let it fall to the floor. She pulled at the sleeveless leather hauberk and the tunic sleeve beneath.

"Careful," he said, sounding wooden and exhausted. Reaching up, he pushed back the chain mail hood, wincing.

"Sit, you are so tall. Let me help," she insisted. Piece by piece, his things came away in her hands, though he protested at first. "You do not like being weak, do you? But let me do this."

He allowed her to lift away the chain mail hood and capelet, then the quilted cap beneath, freeing his hair, damp and tousled. The heavy iron-studded leather hauberk came next, nearly tipping her balance as she set that aside with the other things. Then she helped him tug off his brown woolen tunic. When he sat in his long linen shirt and trews, the candlelight illuminated the blood, the torn fabric, the clump of leaves around the base of the ugly broken bolt.

"Is that yarrow? Good, it will help. Who shot at you? Tell me. Please."

"Knights went after me over the moor, eastward. My fault—I stayed too long on open ground. One had a bow, thankfully not a crossbow, or I might not be here. But I made it to a patch of forest and lost them there. I waited until they were gone. I am sorry to have left you so long."

"Hush, I was fine." How simple an untruth could become truth. She had been worried, but she endured, she had been fine. And now he was here. "Awful men! Did Malise send them?"

"Likely so. But they were after me, Tamsin. Not you."

"Why do you think so?"

"An old matter, I believe. Malise still burns over it. We do as well, my kin and I, but we left it behind. No wonder Edward favors him, seeing fury that matches his own."

"Will you tell me what it was?"

"Someday, aye. Ow," he said, as she leaned to examine his wound. She winced as he did, but summoned her courage and wished her sister Rowena was there, calm and knowledgeable, her very spirit soothing. Tamsin did not have that knack. But when she felt sure the bolt could be removed, she stood back.

"Boots," she said. He bent to undo the lacings and the lower legs of his trews, then slid off the boots. His bare feet were long, knobby, strong, beautiful. "Stand," she directed, and he obeyed. "Into the bath with you."

"My wee commander," he murmured. "Will you join me there?"

"Not for this. Besides, I bathed earlier, and that tub is not very big. But it will be easier to tend your wound if you are in there." She pulled at his shirt.

"I can manage," he said, teeth gritted. With one arm, he stripped off the linen shirt, and Tamsin helped ease it off, sucking in a breath when she saw the whole wound. He stood in trews and bare torso, skin gleaming in the yellow light of the tallow candles, the broken shaft an alarming sight. She reached for the waist of his trews.

"I will do it," he said, half turning away as he undid the cord that snugged the waist, shrugged the leggings down to pool on the floor, then stepped free.

She caught her breath, could not help it, seeing the full beauty of his body. His legs were long, lean, back and buttocks powerful, body taut with muscle. His skin gleamed in candlelight. A few scars revealed old wounds well-healed. An arrow puncture, a long, sealed gash, a puckered divot in his side. He had been through much. She frowned. But this wound would heal too, she told herself in relief.

"Into the tub," she ordered briskly. With a soft chuckle, he stepped in.

Though his body, his nudity, the promise and intimacy of it, quickened her breath, the sight of the wound pushed all else from her mind. He sank down, knees up, the barrel-like tub a snug fit for a tall man. His shoulders and arms were burly and well-developed, his chest matted with dark hair, dark as the beard that shadowed his jaw and cheeks, dark as the glossy chestnut sweep of hair that swung over his brow. Sluicing handfuls of water over his hair and face, he looked at her.

"Still warm," he said. "Feels good."

"Aye." She handed him a cup from the supper tray, and he dumped more water over his head. "What should I do now?"

"Take it out." He braced his arms along the tub. "Pull. Carefully," he added.

"It does not look too deep. The arrowhead is not fully under the muscle, I think."

"Good. Use a damp cloth, press against the wound, and pull. Wait! Is there wine or something stronger here?"

She rose and went to the supper tray, which held a jug of ale, and one of wine. "Will a dark wine do?"

"Aye. Pour some over the wound. And give me a bit, do, love."

She filled a cup and handed it to him. Then she took a linen towel and yanked hard to rip through and create strips. Dipping one cloth into the water, she gently bathed his shoulder and peered closely at the wound.

"Bend forward a wee bit. Just there," she murmured. Pressing the wadded cloth to his shoulder, just where muscle wrapped under his arm, she grasped the stub of the shaft in her other hand and pulled hard.

Liam hissed in a breath. The compact point slid out, leaving a small hole that bled freely. She poured a dose of wine over it from the jug, and Liam hissed again. Quickly she pressed the damp cloth against it.

As she held the wad in place, she rested her brow lightly on his arm. He sat with his head forward, silent. Then he lifted a hand out of the water and touched her hair. They sat curled together, Tamsin pressing against the wound.

"Lass," he whispered after a while, "thank you."

"Wine," she whispered, handing him the jug this time. With a rueful laugh, he drank, throat shifting with long swallows, and gave it back.

"Take some yourself." His voice was hoarse. She drank, set the jug aside.

"I must bandage the wound, but it should be dry first."

"Let me bathe, then I will get out." Taking the gooey ball of soap, he rubbed it over his chest, torso, down under the water, washing, rinsing. After he lathered soap in his hair, she took the cup to pour a waterfall over his head as if he were a boy, not a brawny, gleaming, powerful man tucked in a too-small tub.

Clean, dripping, he looked at her, eyes sparkling, the candle-light turning pale blue to jewel-like sapphire. He smiled. "The water is getting cold."

"You should get out."

"I should." He leaned toward her, his voice gruff, honeyed.

"You should," she whispered, leaning too.

His hand came out of the water to delicately tilt her chin up before he kissed her. The touch of his lips was heated, his mouth wet, lips deliciously tender, and the heavy liquid feeling that sank through her so suddenly made her gasp. She curved her fingers around his bristled jaw, her other hand keeping the folded cloth tight against his wound, and she leaned in for another kiss. Raising an arm to pull her closer, he slid his fingers through her hair, kissing her, and she opened her mouth to him, tasting him, letting him taste her, and the tang of the wine shared between them.

"I want to pull you into this water," he growled, "but the tub is too small."

"Then get out, sirrah," she murmured, "and we can find another space to share."

"Mmm," he answered, kissing her again, his tongue sweeping gently over hers.

Breathing quickly, passion rising in her like she had never felt before, she shifted on her knees and suddenly tipped, her arm plunging into the water. Gasping, she straightened.

"By the very saints, if you can fit in here with me, do so now," he growled.

"You are wounded—"

"My wife fixed it for me."

"It needs bandaging."

"I can hardly feel it. There are other feelings now—"

"Come out," she said, laughing. "And to think I worried so about you."

"Did you?" Bracing a hand on the tub's edge, he rose in one swift motion, water dripping, his body rich and hard in the candlelight. Her own desire whirled and pooled deep within her. She threw a folded towel at him that he caught in one hand.

"Over there. Sit." She pointed at the chair.

"A moment and my dignity, madam, if you please," he said as he toweled himself and wrapped it around his waist.

"I like your dignity. But we must bandage that quickly or it will bleed again."

He sat on the wooden chair, his shoulders rising well above the back of it, giving her access to the task at hand. Taking up the cloths, she toweled him off gently, dabbing the bunched cloth over his shoulders, his back, his hair where water dripped down his neck. Liam sat with the toweling scarcely around him, hands folded.

"Dear God, woman," he said.

"I am glad you feel healthy," she murmured, taking up a dry cloth.

"Very healthy," he muttered.

"Did you bring any yarrow back with you?"

"In the pouch on my belt."

She retrieved it, then crushed the leaves and added them to the pad she placed over the clean wound. She wrapped a long strip of cloth over his shoulder and under his arm, then knotted another to run across his chest and back again, tugging it, securing it with knots. Coming around, she stood in front of him to make sure it was taut.

Opening his thighs for her to stand close while she worked, he took her by the hips and drew her toward him. "That feels good, my dear. You did well. Thank you."

"As long as you are comfortable."

"Better than expected, I might say." As he spoke, he slipped his hands up, tracing her hips, snugging in at her waist, his thumbs slipping up her arms to graze the sides of her breasts—up further to her shoulders to draw her forward into another kiss.

Even seated, he was tall, and she was not, and as she bent toward him, her hair, loosely braided, fell in damp golden curtain around them. As Liam kissed her, she sensed his hunger clear and growing, and her own meeting his. She leaned closer, pressing against him, and he lowered his head to kiss the tops of her breasts above the loose bodice, for all she wore was a simple tunic gown, unbelted, over a shift. As his breath soothed, warm and moist, through the cloth, her body spun, melted.

He tugged at the gown, its side lacing already loose, its ties at the back within easy reach. Within moments, he pulled the dark blue woolen fabric upward with one hand in a long sweep and tossed it away to fall with his hauberk, tunic, and torn shirt, leaving her standing there in her shift, breasts suddenly aching for his touch. He seemed to know that as she leaned in to kiss him again. He ran his hands up the gauzy shift, fingers shaping her breasts as they pearled quickly under his fingers. Her body tightened, pulsed, her knees nearly sinking.

He pushed her shift higher, cloth bunching at her hips, his hands spreading warmth, like the heat from the brazier, caressing her skin. "Aye then?"

"Oh aye," she breathed, knowing what he wanted, what she wanted. She would not wait and knew he could not for long. Widening her stance, she sat over his lap, legs spread, and shifted closer. "Oh aye," she whispered against his mouth.

"Ah, there now," he murmured, tilting his body to support her, to meet her, taking her hips in his large, warm hands. As he moved, she went with him, and then found him in the very moment he found her, velvet and hard, warm and honeyed sliding together all at once, so that she caught her breath with a little moan. Kissing her, tugging at her lip, he lowered his head to circle his tongue over her breast making her arch and cry out, then plunge down over him, rocking, rocking as he did. He extended his long legs, knees strong, to brace them both, his hands gliding over her skin.

As he set the motion, she joined him, her breath matching his, her hair draping over both. As she rose and sank, she felt a change within her, within the depth of her heart, as if her very soul was there, within reach, giving, taking, with more to give—

Easing out a long, soft breath, she sank into his arms, laid her head on his shoulder and felt his cheek press against her head. Silently, secretly, she wept a little, realizing somehow that her life was changing. She felt such love, such joy—such trust—that she closed her eyes and just held him, as he held her.

"THIS BOOK," HE said much later, as he sat dressed only in trews, his feet bare. The wooden chair, a bit worse for the use of it, creaked as he leaned to take a bite of the meat pie. "Tell me about it. I noticed," he said, pausing to sip wine, "this is not the book Edward seems to expect."

"I told you it was not."

"You did," he admitted, licking his fingers. "I was hungrier than I thought. These verses are poetic, but there are no prophecies here."

She nibbled an oatcake and took a sip of wine from his cup. "It is an epic poem that he worked on for a long time—the story of Tristan and Iseult—a warrior who fell in love with the young queen of the king he served, his own uncle. And she fell in love with him. It is a tragedy, beautifully told. Thomas put heart and soul into it, I think, for it is deeply told, his version of the story."

"So this is not a collection of his prophecies about Scotland. And nothing to do with our struggle with England."

"It is a beautiful, heartbreaking love story. Edward would have no patience for it."

"He might," he said, surprising her. "He loved his queen, Isabella, very much. He was inconsolable when she died. They say that was when he began to change for the worse."

"Then I feel for him. But he does not need to take out his grief on the Scots."

"True. Tamsin," he murmured. "It is an old, old tale. I have heard it elsewhere. I even thought of it when I stood in King Edward's chamber, wondering if I would survive the day that he decided I should find you and get that book. He reminded me of King Mark in the story—wounded and lashing out. A king to beware."

She tipped her head. "And just like cruel King Mark, who sent out his nephew, the harper Tristan, to fetch the young queen to him—our bitter, cruel King Edward sent out a harper to fetch a lady to him."

He watched for a moment. "Exactly what I was thinking just now. The king pursues the young lovers in a rage. One challenge after another for those two."

"Their story ends tragically," she said quickly. "Our tale will not."

"It will not." He broke an oatcake, nibbled, took another swallow of wine. "May I see the book again?"

"Not with those hands," she laughed. He went to the bath, dipped his hands, rinsed, and dried. Then he turned, splaying clean hands.

Then, as he paged through the book, he returned to the first page and began to read in the voice she so loved, deep and delicious.

"'I was at Ercildoune, and with Thomas spoke I there,'" he read, "'and there I heard read in rhyme who Tristan was, and who was king with crown, and who, there, was as bold a baron as their elders—'"

He looked up. "An epic tale, and naught to do with prophecy." Closing the book, he gave it to Tamsin, who wrapped it and tied it with the ribbon. Setting it aside, she turned back to him and reached out to touch his jaw. He kissed her fingers.

"I would give the book to my family to keep," she said. "I can make another copy, perhaps more, to share with others. It could take years to copy those pages again and again, but I want to do it. But this is not a book to help a king wage war."

"It is a book for kings, my dear—and for knights and ladies, children and households. It is a tale to hear on a winter's night."

"A love story, aye. And I would love to hear you read it aloud—to a family one day, perhaps," she added, feeling shy suddenly.

His smile turned somber. "Tamsin—you know Edward ordered me to fetch the Rhymer's book, and promised me Dalrinnie if I obeyed. What I have not yet told you," he went on, "is that he threatened my family if I did not. The fire at Holyoak may have part of that. Edward may have ordered Malise to come after my kin there. If so, I fear that more may come from that quarter."

"I am so sorry. I did not realize the whole of it."

"I had not told you the whole of it, unpleasant as it is. My dear lass, you see the world as good and kind, as redeemable, even sorts like Malise and Edward. I admire that. And I wanted you to think the best of me."

"I do think the best of you." She came to him, slid her arms around his neck.

He laid his hand over hers. "Would you trust me now?"

"I would. I do. I love you, Liam Seton, more than you know." She tipped her head toward him and kissed him softly.

"Good, because I am whole in love with you, lass, and never saw it coming." He took her hands in his. "And if you trust me, then let me ask this. Do Thomas's prophecies exist as a book somewhere?"

She sighed. "Not quite. He gave me his notes, you see. I have been working on them for some time now, deciphering his scribbles. He wrote on parchment scraps, on cloth, even on oak leaves—wherever he could write something quickly, he did. I have been copying them, making multiple manuscripts, you see. One will not do, for it could be lost or destroyed. A good scribe makes a copy." She smiled. "I also want to include any of his verses that others might know—ballads, predictions, whatever people remember of him. Someday I mean to give all those pages to Master Bisset to make several copies of his work."

"A worthy idea. Where are your pages now?"

"Most are at Dalrinnie," she said. "Malise does not know, and pray God he never discovers them, locked away in a chest."

"Indeed," he said with a quick scowl.

"Some are at Holyoak, locked in a small iron chest in the library where Gideon allowed me to keep some things. Even if the place should burn—I am sorry that happened, Liam—the pages should survive."

"And neither Edward nor Bruce can get them, unless you decide to share."

He sighed. "Before I knew all this, before I knew you"—he lifted her hand to kiss it—"I thought Bruce should see the book, not Edward."

"I would rather finish the work before Bruce saw it. Never Edward. But we could decide together what is best," she added. A little thrill of hope rose in her.

"We could." He was quiet for a moment. "What of your own prophecies? You saw fire at Holyoak. Will you write that and others down?"

"I have. I will put others in words too, aye. There might be some worth to them."

"It seems to be a family trait."

"Like hair and eyes and height?" She laughed. "They say Thomas got his powers from the Queen of Faery. He never admitted it, but he was very wise. I wish you could have known him."

"I hear he visited my grandfather, his friend, more than once. But I was a small boy. If I saw him, I do not recall it. But they say he made a prediction for Dalrinnie."

She straightened, taking his hand, remembering what her cousin had said. "Kirsty mentioned a Dalrinnie curse. Her father knew about it. Do you know the words?"

"Best I recall, it went like this." He began to recite in a low, resonant rumble that vibrated through her.

Dalrinnie, Dalrinnie,
Towers high, walls bold
Knight nor baron can hold
Nor good fortune unfold
When Dalrinnie falls
Three times and more

No king can restore, nor harp sing its lore
And Scotland will burn.

He let the last word fade. "That is what I learned."

Tamsin drew a long breath. A feeling tapped softly at her. "Holyoak and more has burned in Scotland. Dear God. You say this is a curse?"

"My father called it so. When I was a lad, I took up the harp, thinking I could change the luck of Dalrinnie myself if I could play the harp and sing the castle's lore. But it made no difference. My grandfather lost the castle. My father got it back, but I lost it again. Sir John Witton lost it too, by dying," he added, glancing at her.

"He did. Three times and more," she said. "Malise too, as the fourth?"

"With luck," he huffed. "I should have told you. But I thought of it as a curse, not a prophecy. Not something we are proud of, we Dalrinnie Setons."

"So you kept it to yourself. I understand. You have that way about you—that reserve, that need for secrets," she said gently.

"I do. But you are bringing them out of me somehow." He gave her a crooked smile in wry admission.

Her heart filled to hear that. "But Liam, Thomas did not lay curses. He did not claim to be a wizard in that way."

"All I know is the castle has had poor luck, and the verse spoke of ruin for Dalrinnie, and Scotland too."

"Wait—he wrote a curious line once—I wonder." Something forgotten tapped insistently as she found her leather bag and retrieved the narrow wooden box with the quill, stoppered ink bottle, and scraps of parchment wrapped in leather. She had left the larger pages safely boxed at Holyoak, but now, recalling that odd line, she searched.

"Ah! Here." She brought a small, curled scrap of parchment to Liam.

"She carries her books and writing always with her," he said, bemused.

"She does. It is her heart's work. Read this. Is it familiar? It was with Thomas's writings but did not fit with anything else. Some of it has been torn away."

"'Until luck returns,'" he read, "'when the lady of gold—'" He looked up. "'Takes the harp to hold.'"

"I did not understand it until now. His writing is difficult to read, and I never knew—I thought it said harp, but perhaps it is harper. Not a lady playing a harp, but a lady *with* a harper."

He studied the scrap. "It could say 'harper.'" He looked up. "Put it together with the verse. Listen." He recited the Dalrinnie verse again, adding the new line at the end.

And Scotland will burn until luck returns—when the lady of gold takes the harper to hold.

"It does fit the rhyme," she said.

His sky-blue eyes searched hers. "This could refer to us. Do you see it? The lady of gold." He touched her long, loose, thick braid.

"And the harper to hold—my harper-knight. Liam! Our meeting. Our marriage. Did Thomas see it all?"

"And predicted luck would return to Dalrinnie—and Scotland—when we found each other. By the saints!" He stood, wrapping her in his arms. "Pray God it is true. It means so much to Scotland—to Bruce!—if it is the truth foretold."

"Thomas always spoke true." When he kissed her then, the whirling within her felt tender, quieter, a fire banked and eager to grow. She drew back. "Please do not use that arm yet, sirrah. You must rest."

He laughed softly against her hair. "The hour is late, and we have not yet rested, not quite, in that cozy box bed. Come, love." Taking her hand, he drew her to the bed. "In the morning, we will depart. But before we head back to the forest tomorrow," he said as he pulled back the coverlet, "there is a place I want to show you."

She smiled. "Different than you might show me now?"

"You will see tomorrow. Come here."

CHAPTER TWENTY-SIX

"**H**OW DID YOU know I would want to see the place where Grandda Thomas lived?" Tamsin asked, riding beside Liam.

"I had a feeling about it." He guided his horse closer to hers and smiled. She was lovelier in the morning than he could have imagined—and he should stop thinking of how she looked, and felt, in the night. Flexing his shoulder, the wound making the movement stiff, he shrugged. "Have you been there before?"

"As children we visited him with our parents. My mother was his granddaughter. But I scarcely remember."

"See the pine forest there?" He pointed toward the tall pines that had sheltered him. "I waited there after those rascals shot me. When I came out, I recognized the Eildon Hills, and knew the Rhymer lived near here. He is said to have met the Queen of Faery in those hills."

"And from there he followed her into the Otherworld," she said. Ahead rose three conical hills, the middle one slightly higher than its sisters, all of them deep blue in the midday sun, with patches of old heather and scrub along the inclines. "I dreamed of the hills once, after Grandda died, and I felt I should visit them someday."

He sidled his horse closer and reached out a hand. She joined hands with him and they rode in silence, the horses rocking them closer to the hills.

"What else have you dreamed?" he asked.

She hesitated. "I dreamed of you, once."

"Did you! And never said," he teased. "Who is keeping secrets now? Tell me."

"I dreamed I climbed down a rope out of a tower, with arrows flying all around. A knight stood below me. He was there to catch me. I let go and fell into his arms." She glanced at him. "Later I recognized you as the knight in my dream."

"By the very saints," he murmured. "You do have a way about you, my lady."

"I dreamed more recently that I was looking for you—outside Dalrinnie. But I could not find you, and then I was taken. Grabbed by someone. But I woke, and you were there with me. I think it was fear. Just—needing you."

Keeping her hand in his, he rode thoughtfully. "I am always here for you. There is some—kind of destiny here. I have not always believed in such, but this—this between us seems undeniable."

"I used to daydream about a man who could truly love me. I was so lonely at Dalrinnie, in that marriage. I wanted children. A home. I wanted to be free to speak the truth, too. But I had to hold my tongue and be obedient."

He pressed her hand. He only hoped he could give her what she dreamed most of. His own dreams had been in shambles for too long, until he had met her. Now, he dared to hope beyond the next step, the next day, into the future.

"I thought my dreams were all destroyed with Dalrinnie gone," he said. "I wanted a wife, a lady of my castle, a home where we both belonged. Much as you wanted. Now here we are, we two." He smiled slightly. "I wanted a peaceful place with children, with dogs, hawks on perches, horses in the stables, tenants flourishing on the land. A dream that big will take time. But now I think it is possible again."

"When luck returns to Dalrinnie with the lady and her harper?"

"Let us hope our luck extends beyond Dalrinnie to Scotland, love."

"Look there, ahead." She pointed. "Is that a hawthorn tree? And on that low hill before the Eildon sisters... See that stone keep?"

Liam peered ahead, seeing a slight mound where a tree rose, growing as two tall twisted trunks with a great arching, sagging canopy of leaves just turning a rusty color. The small white flowers of spring and summer were gone, the twiggy branches heavy with dark red berries. "Aye, hawthorn. The ballad says Thomas lived nearby and one day sat under a hawthorn tree to play his harp when the Faery Queen rode up. She took him inside the largest hill. Hold up here, lass, and we will walk," he added.

Liam dismounted, and walked over to help Tamsin to the ground. Making sure the horses were tied to low bushes nearby, he patted and murmured to them. He would always be grateful to his great sturdy stallion for keeping him safe, giving all he had, the night they were chased. Taking Tamsin's hand, he walked with her toward the old hawthorn tree.

"I can imagine him here," she said. "Sitting there, under the tree, with a harp."

Hearing a shout, Liam glanced around, on alert. An old man crossed the meadow toward them, walking with a cane, a dog beside him. The man raised a hand. "Who is that?" Liam asked, turning, waiting beside Tamsin as the man walked toward them.

"Good day," the old man called, coming closer. He was tall and bent, a fine gray tunic and shabby green cloak hanging loose on him. His face had a gaunt dignity and his hair was white and tousled beneath a flat cap. "I am Sir Thomas, and that is my tower house. And that is my tree. Who be you?" Stopping, he patted the head of the tall hound beside him.

Liam was pleased to see a sight-hound like the ones he so loved. This handsome beast seemed obedient, friendly, and kindly treated. "I am Sir William Seton, formerly of Dalrinnie. This is my wife, Lady Thomasina Keith of Kincraig. We do not mean to trespass."

Sir Thomas came closer, peering at Tamsin. "Thomasina! Is it you?"

"Sir?" she asked. "Are you—oh! You look so much like him!"

"I am Sir Thomas Learmont. The Rhymer's son." He smiled. "Your great-uncle. I remember you. One of the beautiful Keith girls, the child with the pale gold hair."

"Sir Thomas! I did not realize you lived here! We met when I was a child. How kind of you to remember me, and how good to find you here. You are well, Uncle?" She took his hand for a moment.

"Well enough, my wife and I both. She is home in Learmont Tower, just there, and would be pleased to see you. Will you and your husband visit for a spell? Walk those fine horses this way with me." He beckoned with the cane.

Tamsin nodded and began to walk with the old man, while Liam took the horse's reins and followed.

"When you were a wee bit lass," Thomas said, "I remember visiting Kincraig with my father. I was grieved to hear of your parents' passing. Your sisters and brother are well?"

"They are well. It is kind of you to remember all of us."

"We are kin! Your mother was my niece, my brother's daughter. After she married a Keith and moved to Kincraig, we did not see her much after that. Oh, she was kind and elegant. You have the look of her, you know, her eyes and her hair. A beauty. She wore blond braids to her knees always, I remember. And your father was a handsome and intelligent man, serious in nature, concerned for the fate of Scotland and for the welfare of his family. So much has happened since then—Scotland in turmoil, Edward of England stepping in to take over. We did not need that! Even now he can neither bend Scotland nor break it, much as he tries."

"We are doing our best to prevent it," Liam said. "Sir, may I ask—are you a prophet like your father?"

"Och, nay, that gift went past me. I was a knight and now I

am a farmer. I once played the harp, learned at my father's knee, but I cannot play now." He held up his hands, fingers twisted, joints knobby. "I knew all the songs the Rhymer sang."

"My husband plays the harp," Tamsin said.

"Do you, lad?" Thomas gave him an assessing stare. Liam smiled and shrugged, wondering at the scrutiny. "Do you indeed?"

"And very well, too," Tamsin added. "Sir Thomas, could you tell me more about Grandda, and the legend of those hills too? Did he sit beneath that hawthorn, as they say of him? Did he go into the hillside with her?"

"He did say she found him under that tree playing his harp, and cast a glamourie over him, throwing her magic on him. He followed her into her realm and stayed for seven years. He said it was true. Three years with them was seven years out here. Time is not the same there, see."

"And he came back a truth-teller," she said.

"He did. Later, see you, he went back inside that hill at the end of his life and was not seen again. Some say the Earl of March killed him for predicting something he did not want to hear," old Thomas went on. "But that was not his fate."

"He was quite old," Liam said. "I heard it said he died in his tower. Not so?"

"Nah," said Thomas. "He went back to the faeries. He stood up one day and walked out the house, all the way to the highest hill there, where he met the queen. She was waiting for him, silver bells on her bridle and gold in her hair and all. Oh aye, he was ready to go with her."

Liam listened, bemused, wondering if old Sir Thomas was a little lost in the head himself, eighty if he was a day. "That is a fascinating tale."

"No tale. I saw him go. Come in!" Thomas waved them through the open gate. The keep was a modest stone block enclosed by a fieldstone wall.

He led them up the steps of the keep, where they met his

wife. Dame Learmont was short, plump, dimpled, and merry. She bustled about, offering a hot drink of mint, berries, and honey, and served cheese and oatcakes.

Rather than sit with them at the table in the quiet, simply furnished hall, the dame retreated to a corner to sit at a loom and take up her work, colors and shuttle flying to and fro as she wove a handsome cloth of three or four colors. Liam could tell she was listening, a smile on her face, with fond looks for her aging husband.

"Heaven guided you here, I think," Sir Thomas said. "My father left me his house and lands here at Ercildoune, where he was born. My wife and I have no children to inherit this place. Our daughter died in childbed with her child, and our son, another Thomas, was lost in what I call Edward's war."

"I am so sorry to hear that," Tamsin said.

"Sad, aye. I thought to leave all this to the Keith children as my grandnieces and grandnephew, and I wanted to reach out to you. But Edward's war makes it difficult to do ordinary and important things."

"It does. Oh, Sir Thomas," Tamsin said, "my brother would appreciate this inheritance."

"It is not just for your brother. It is for you and your sisters too. My father would want these lands divided between you. He loved you and often said the four of you are special. He said he gave each of you something of his. Are you the scholar, my dear, or the healer? Or perhaps the bold wee sister?"

"The scholar, I suppose. He gave me his writings. I mean to honor those."

"I am glad."

"So you knew about the Kincraig children all along?" Liam asked.

"I did. But I had no good means nor the health to travel to Kincraig. Sir William, so you are a harper?"

"Aye, and a knight loyal to Bruce, who valued your father's counsel years ago."

"So I understand. Do you know what Thomas said of the harper?"

Liam frowned. "Do you mean the mention of a harper in a verse about Dalrinnie?" They had only discovered it—and here it was, come round again in this meeting. If he never marveled at miracles and magic before, he might have to begin, he thought.

"The very one. I heard the Dalrinnie verse long ago. Did we not, my dear?" He turned to his wife, working at her loom, shuttling and shifting in a rhythm.

"We did," she said. "The lady of gold and her harper to hold. Something like that."

"Aye! And you, lass, you have the truthy tongue?" Thomas asked. "I thought so. And a harper-knight for a husband. Good! Come with me," he said then. He rose and took up his cane, and the tall, leggy gray dog stood with him. "Follow me."

Liam and Tamsin crossed the hall behind old Thomas. The dog trotted along beside its old master. "That is a handsome hound."

"You ought to know. He is a Dalrinnie hound, descended from one called Colla when I was a boy."

"Colla! My grandfather and father had more than one of that name. I am pleased to hear it."

"We have had several of these hounds over the years and bred them ourselves. He is the last of those. When I go, he will go. And my wife—" He stopped.

"You and your wife," Tamsin said, "are always welcome with us. We are family."

"Thank you. Come. I want to show you something." Thomas grabbed a torch from the wall in a shadowy hallway and brought it outside, crossing the bailey in daylight, then inside an arched doorway down a corridor that went past a kitchen on one side and storage rooms on the other.

He led them down a few steps, where the torch became necessary. Liam held the door for the old man, the dog, and Tamsin as they entered the cellars. Barrels and shelves held food stores, grain sacks, farming implements, wooden boxes, even a pile of old muddy boots.

Opening a creaking wooden door, Thomas ushered them into a vaulted stone room. Liam ducked to pass under the lintel. Thomas, hunched with age, held the torch aloft.

"Thomas's things are here," he said.

Liam saw that the room held wooden boxes, a large chest, some chairs, a dismantled bed. Taking in the disarray, he wondered what this Thomas wanted amid the jumble.

"Here." The old man pulled a cloth off a large bulky shape to reveal a wooden chest. Opening its lid, he rummaged about and drew out a leather satchel. He held it out.

"Sir William, this should be yours."

"This?" Liam looked at him, puzzled.

"It is his harp." Thomas opened the satchel to show the uppermost edge of the harp, a smooth and sinuous curve of polished wood inset with moonstones in a spiral pattern.

"By the saints," he murmured, "it is a beautiful thing. I could never take this, sir."

"You can and you will. This is True Thomas's own harp, the one the Queen of Faery gave him, and you must have it."

"I could not, sir, but I am very grateful."

"Take it. You are the harper in the prediction he made for Dalrinnie. You are the harper that the golden lady, our Tamsin, found. You must have this. I have no use for it now, and no children or grandchildren to play it. Tamsin and her kin are my kin now. Take it and live well and make good music with it."

"Sir Thomas, it is an honor, truly," Liam said.

"It is a privilege, and so generous," Tamsin said. "What can we do for you?"

"For me? Keep this harp alive. Here, packed away, it is like a dead thing. My father would want his harp to be played."

"I cannot thank you enough," Liam said, and then reached out to finally take its weight in his hands. The harp strings chimed softly. It felt like his own harp, somehow.

"Thank me by making music with this, and by making your lady happy. And by allowing my father's legacy to thrive. It is what he would want. It is what I want."

"You will always be part of our family," Tamsin said. "We have much to make up for. You must come to Kincraig, you and your wife, to spend time with us."

"We would like that." He beckoned them out of the room and led them back out into the bailey yard. He paused, still in shadows, still holding the torch, the dog standing quiet and tall beside him.

"You know," he said, "the night my father went into the hillside, he was sitting by the fire after supper. Then he stood up. 'My sand is run, my thread is spun, those bells are for me,' he said. And then he walked outside."

"To the hills?" Tamsin asked.

"Aye. We followed, my wife and I, but could not catch him. He began to walk like a young man, long strides and fast. A light appeared in the hillside, like a silver flash, and I saw a door open in the very rock. Then he was gone."

"He disappeared there?" Liam frowned. Was this possible?

"Aye. Ancient legends tell of a portal hidden inside those hills. The queen waited there for him, I am sure. She was his true love, much as he loved my mother. She took him back into her world. Perhaps he still lives in there."

"Forever," Tamsin said in a hushed voice.

"They say one day he could return to save Scotland. Remember that, you two."

"Aye so," Liam said.

"I have lots of stories, you know," old Thomas said.

"And I would love to hear them," Tamsin said.

CHAPTER TWENTY-SEVEN

"WILL THIS ALL be over soon?" Tamsin asked the next morning as she rode beside Liam along the route that would lead over the moorland and back to the great forest.

"What will be over? Not our handfasting agreement, I hope."

"Not that! All the rest. We have the Rhymer's book now, which will not go to Edward. And you promised that after a little stay in the forest we could ride to Kincraig to make sure my sisters are well."

"Soon, aye, we can ride to Kincraig. You seem eager to go."

"I have been away too long, and so much has happened."

"It has. But patience, lass. I want to stay long enough for Henry, Finley, and Iain to return. When they find Robert Bruce, he will want to study the roster of support and also consider the information that Finley and Gilchrist, too, previously gathered about readiness among Scottish castles. I suspect Bruce may want to move on Dalrinnie soon if he has enough support in the area."

"Battle?" she asked.

"A takeover can happen peaceably, but it is less likely."

"And Malise?"

"That lad may not be long for this world." His voice went grim and flat.

"I do not want anyone's death on my account—or on your soul either. I just want peace and truth, and what is right."

"Truth to you is all. Ideals are all to you. To me, truth is a more malleable thing. We do what we must."

She shuddered. "If returning to Dalrinnie means death for some, I would not want to go back."

"Not everyone feels that way, my lass."

She did not reply, feeling dread churn within her as she rode. Lives might be lost at Dalrinnie if an attempt was made to regain it. Liam might be lost. She could not bear to consider it.

As they came closer to the forest fringe, she saw two men on horseback emerge from the tree cover and saw the gleam of light on steel. Two knights rode toward them, one in red, the other in blue.

"Who is that?" she asked.

Liam lifted a hand to shade his eyes. "Gilchrist, surely. And the other... My God," he said, "that is Gideon."

"In armor? Something must have happened!"

"Aye, some sort of trouble. Come ahead." He spurred his stallion to a canter across the long stretch of moor. She followed, but Liam reached his brothers first, talking with them as she rode up.

Seeing the twins in full knight's gear, she was awestruck by the sight—their size and hard beauty, their strong resemblance. But for their surcoats, she could not tell one from the other at first.

"I stayed on at Holyoak to help. Ah, Lady Tamsin," Gilchrist greeted as she drew her horse in beside Liam, greeting them.

"Gilchrist. And Brother Gideon," she said.

"Sir Gideon," he answered with a twist of his lips.

So Gideon had made a decision. What had prompted it? Trouble indeed, as Liam had said. Dread spun again in her center.

Liam explained quickly about meeting Henry Keith and the mission to bring the revenue and rosters to Bruce with Finley Macnab and Lindsay's man, Iain Campbell.

"Let us hope they return soon and safely. We may need their help." Gilchrist frowned. "We came out to find you. There is news."

"I thought so. Trouble?"

"Comyn's men went past Holyoak yesterday," Gideon said. "They wanted to be sure we saw them. An escort of a dozen knights with a cart. Carrying a cage."

"The empty cage we saw at Lochmaben," Gilchrist added to Liam. "But they have put it to use. There was a woman in the cage."

"They have Agatha," Gideon said.

"Jesu!" Liam burst out.

"They went to Lochmaben and then Lincluden, very deliberately," Gilchrist said.

"Where were they headed with the cart?" Liam asked.

"Dalrinnie. Sir Malise means to lure us there. Especially you, Liam."

"He is succeeding." Taking up the reins, Liam cantered over the moor toward the forest. Tamsin and the others followed in his wake.

As Tamsin rode between the twin brothers, no one spoke, their determined gazes straight ahead as they surged onward. Entering the forest, they slowed to a walk on a wide path between oak and hazel, birch and pine. Where the canopy grew heavy and shadowed, they followed narrowing pathways into the forest.

"MALISE IS FURIOUS, I tell you, Liam," Gilchrist said later. A few of them still sat around a fire contained in a circle of stones, deep in a clearing in the forest. After supper, the comforting smell of roasted meat, consumed with oatcakes and ale, lingered in the air. Though that spoke of home and friends, they planned invasion and rescue.

"He is a madman." Liam broke a twig and threw it into the fire, crackle and spark rising. Beside him, Tamsin sat quiet. He sensed her worry, felt it in his bones. He wished he could take it away. "Now he has our sister."

"He saw the banns posted at the village kirk near Holyoak,"

Gideon said. "While you were gone, he came to the monastery while you were gone, frustrated with his men's failure to burn it or to find either of you. He shouted at the gates to be let in, demanding to see Abbot Murdoch."

"And then?" Liam asked.

"Our reverend uncle came out to calm him. We stood in the yard ready to defend like warrior monks." Gideon huffed a flat laugh. "Malise finally left, still in a rage, insisting his betrothed was stolen from him and Liam Seton would pay for it."

"This because of your handfasting?" James Lindsay leaned forward. "It was your decision and naught to do with Malise."

"He will never accept that," Tamsin answered.

"He is furious over Edward giving me an order that Malise asked for," Liam briefly explained. "And he is still furious over what happened between him and Agatha years ago."

"Was Agatha not in a convent then?" Tamsin asked.

"Not then. She entered the convent after she refused Malise's offer of marriage," Gilchrist explained. "He wooed her, but she despised him for a vain and selfish man. Our father refused his suit, and Agatha refused him too. Malise could not tolerate it."

"How can he still be angry about that?" Tamsin asked.

"One day he waited outside the village kirk," Gideon said, "and accosted her, trying to convince her. Liam was there and came to her defense. The fight was fierce, and Malise was injured. Worse, Agatha was hurt terribly," he growled. "We wanted to kill the man. But Father took it to the magistrate, who fined Malise. When King Edward learned, he was furious with us, not with his favorite young knight."

"Bad blood, I see," Lindsay said.

Liam threw another stick into the fire just to watch it pop and burn. "Now he has Agatha, and he wants her brothers to come get her. It is a trap. And I will step straight into it."

Tamsin laid a hand on his arm. "Please do not—"

"I have to. *We* have to." He gestured toward his brothers.

"We must take the bait and turn this in our favor," Gilchrist said.

"When I saw Agatha in that cage," Gideon said, "I knew I had to leave Holyoak. Our uncle gave me his blessing, and I left with Gilchrist."

"We all knew you would do that someday," his twin said.

"But how do we get into Dalrinnie to get the abbess back?" Lindsay asked.

Gilchrist looked up. "Liam could get in as a harper. Wait. Your harp is broken."

"I have another now—but I will not play it for Malise Comyn."

"Liam would be recognized," Tamsin said. "But...tomorrow is Samhain. *Oidhche nan Cleas*, the night of tricks, when the veil between our world and the spirit world dissolves. People disguise themselves as otherworldly beings. If you did that—perhaps you could get inside the castle."

They all stared at her for a moment. "Lass, that is brilliant," Liam said. "All Souls' Eve, of course! A night of madness and revelry."

"Perfect," Gilchrist said. "Bonfires in the village, guisers going about with torches and bells, wearing masks and cloaks, singing and shouting—and threatening pranks."

"Some of those revelers could bring that celebration to the castle," Gideon said.

"I could think of a prank or two," Liam growled.

"But any of you might be grabbed at the gate," Tamsin said. "Perhaps it is not a good idea."

"Masks, my lass," Liam said. "Guisers. We go in as a group calling for cakes and ale. They will not notice the forfeited laird of Dalrinnie."

Gilchrist shrugged. "It could work. And we have no better plan."

"Ready by morning, then," Lindsay suggested. "It is a long ride to Dalrinnie. We will bring as many men as we can, leaving the rest to guard the camp. I can promise ten men or so. But it is not much against a garrison."

"It is a good number for guisers. We only need to get in and get Agatha just now," Liam said. "Though I would like a wee chat with Sir Malise. The rest of the dispute can wait until Bruce's men arrive. Henry brought him the news that Dalrinnie may be ripe for the taking. I intend to weaken Malise's hold—when Bruce is ready, the castle will fall more easily."

"We can gather some disguises—sheepskin blankets, soot, leaves and branches, great cloaks and such will help," Gilchrist said.

"I will go with you," Tamsin said.

"You will not," Liam said. "Stay with Kirsty and the rest. Stay safe."

She stared at him, her gaze silvery gray, somber, worried—verging on anger. He returned her unwavering gaze.

"I will go with you," she said, standing, sweeping away from the firelit circle.

⟫⟪

LATER, LIAM RETIRED to the cocoon of blankets and sheepskins that he and Tamsin had shared in the forest clearing before. She lay there, awake, and when he murmured good night, she gave him a long, cool gaze, then turned her back without a word.

In the morning, he saddled his horse, then turned to saddle hers in silence. She accepted his assistance to mount and settled herself, still quiet. As they rode, he could not endure the silence any longer.

"I know you are furious with me," he murmured. "But I have to do this."

"I am not furious," she said. "I am afraid."

IN THE GLOAMING, the fading light spread long, soft blue beams through the forest surrounding Dalrinnie Castle. Everywhere

Tamsin looked seemed edged with an almost mystical light—bare and lacy trees, steep slopes and deep scrub and bushes, soaring castle walls; a dozen men donning sheepskins and cloaks, rubbing soot on their faces, adding branches and leaves, even tying on antlers in eerie silence; while horses quietly grazed, tied far enough away so as not to be seen or heard from the castle walls.

Standing under the cover of the trees, Tamsin watched Liam and the others prepare. She was glad to see Sir Finley and Sir Iain with them now; they had returned to the forest just that morning, back from riding with Henry, able and willing to join Liam and the others in this mad venture. She had not seen Henry, who had gone on to Selkirk Castle by another route, taking no further risk of being seen consorting with men who frequented the forest.

She overheard Finley and Iain reporting that Bruce was gathering men to advance eastward, with an eye toward Dalrinnie and other castles. Liam replied, just then, that if battle came about he would gladly take part, and that one of them should ride to find Bruce once they were done with Samhain and had Agatha safe. Fear drove through her, hearing that, and she had walked away trembling.

Though she was glad that Liam and the rest had gathered more men, their number was still small. She continued to feel an awful sense of dread for the outcome and the risk to their lives. But she had no vision of this—no clear sense of what might happen. No warning to share beyond deep concern.

Gazing at the castle gates now, standing at the bottom of the forested slope, she thought of the day she had left Dalrinnie. Liam had found her in almost the same spot.

From here, she could see torches beginning to glow like golden stars in the village beyond the castle. Samhain had begun, and men and boys, women and girls too, were preparing for the celebration of All Souls' Eve. Soon they would come out of their houses to bother the demons and spirits and chase them away with fire, bells, shouts and songs, frightening disguises, and merry threats. Householders could demand songs or jests in return for a bannock, an oatcake, or a bit of dried fruit. Harmless enough.

Angling as she looked up at the castle, now she noticed the cage situated high on the parapet. Its iron bars were shaped like a macabre lantern. Inside, she saw a silhouette moving now and then. From her vantage point, it seemed that the cage sat on a corner of the wallwalk. Its top and bars were just visible in the crenel gap between two merlons.

When they had all entered this part of the forest not long ago, Tamsin and the others had cautiously approached to peer up at the castle walls. Seeing the cage that trapped Agatha inside, Gilchrist and Gideon had turned pale and walked away. Liam had uttered a hateful oath, and whacked his sword viciously against a tree.

"At least they did not suspend it outside the walls," he had said, and stomped off.

When he returned with a cooler head, Tamsin helped him don a sheepskin blanket for a cloak over chain mail. A tall, leafy hat over his chain mail coif gave him a giant's stature, for he was no small man to start. Finally, the soot he rubbed on his cheeks made his Nordic-blue eyes eerie as the moonlight rising above.

"Still angry with me, love?" he asked.

"Still afraid," she replied. He caressed her cheek.

"Tamsin," he murmured. "If you ever trust me, the time is now."

"I trust you with my heart and my whole soul. Will that do?"

"Aye then," he said, and kissed her brow. Then he turned away to join the others as they murmured plans in the gathering dusk.

"When the villagers arrive," she heard Liam say, "the guards should let them in by tradition. We will chance it happening tonight. You lads wander in with them through the gate and I will go another way."

"The tunnel you mentioned?" James Lindsay asked.

Listening, Tamsin remembered that he had once asked her why she had not simply taken the tunnel out of the castle on the day she escaped. It seemed so long ago.

"Aye. It starts in the hillside and goes under the postern gate to the back wall of the keep. I can get inside by the servant's staircase tucked in the width of the wall and get up to the parapet. It is narrow though. Only a few of us can go that way."

"Gil and I will go with you. We all learned the way as lads," Gideon said. "The rest can distract the soldiers with some commotion, while we go up to the parapet."

"Good. For now, we will wait on the villagers and more darkness," Liam answered. "Lady Tamsin can wait here with the lads who are tending to the horses."

Listening, Tamsin scowled. Waiting was not her preference, but Liam had been adamant that she could not risk going inside. Yet as she stood with nothing left to do, fear swamped her again. She knew how dangerous this was for all of them. If anything went wrong, Liam and the others could be killed.

"I will go up the hill to see if the castle gate is open," she told Liam.

He nodded. "Be careful. Stay out of sight."

Walking up the hill between the trees, she glanced again at the disturbing sight of the cage on the battlement. In the increasing darkness, a torch flared high up, revealing a girl's silhouette there. Someone moved nearby, presumably a guard. Tamsin moved upward, hidden by thick scrub and overgrown shrubs. She searched for a better vantage point to watch the gate.

Nearing the top of the slope where the massive castle block rose, she could not see the gate that was recessed behind the arched barbican. But she saw that the drawbridge was down. They were expecting someone—perhaps the Samhain revelers. Perhaps the garrison did not mind a little celebration.

Edging her way up the slope, she stood at the top, keeping near some upward-thrusting trees, careful not to be seen. But her cloak billowed outward in the wind, even as she held it down. As she turned to go, she heard horses' hooves thudding toward the drawbridge.

Were the guisers coming now, some on horses? Poised to run, she knew Liam would want notice when the guisers were coming. She could help in that at least. She turned.

Not guisers, but four knights riding for the drawbridge. Tamsin backed away, recognizing the leader—Malise Comyn. She whirled away, but heard one knight shout and heard another canter toward her over the grass.

She ran, cloak flying out, but felt her cloak yanked upward, the brooch and fastening choking her. Stumbling, she fell to a knee only to be dragged up by her cloak. Then strong gloved hands grabbed her arm and lifted her as if she were a straw doll, tossing her over the saddle and into his lap.

He controlled his horse, rounding it, and peered closely at her, ripping away the linen veil that obscured the side of her face. Sir Malise grinned.

"Lady Thomasina! I thought it was you. Welcome home."

CHAPTER TWENTY-EIGHT

C LIMBING THE SLOPE when the plans were in place, Liam heard shouts and laughter from the direction of the village. Torch flames floated toward the castle, carried by men and women in strange costumes with odd beastly and comical shapes. Liam went back down the hill among the trees.

"Get ready," he said, then looked around. "Where is Tamsin?"

His brothers turned. In their disguises, he was not certain which was which; he had not noticed which one donned the green hooded cloak, mask, and antlers, and which dressed like a nun, masked in black robes and white veil.

"She went up the slope," one said. Even their voices were similar. "She probably came down a while ago."

Hearing a shout, Liam turned as one of the grooms tending the horses ran toward him. "They got her! They have her!"

"What is it?" Liam and James Lindsay ran toward him.

"The lady! They took her! A knight on a horse—she went up to look for the open gate just as the men rode through. One came like the very devil and grabbed her."

"I will meet you on the parapet," Liam growled. He did not wait to hear more, but strode through the woodland and up the hill closer to the back of the castle. Behind him came the green man and the brawny nun. He waved them on. He and his brothers knew every inch of Dalrinnie and could get inside faster than the others.

But he shook with fury now, and must collect his ire, let it fuel him. Now, damn the man, Malise had Tamsin as well as Agatha. The worst had happened, with worse to come if he did not get inside to snatch the women from danger—and make short work of the man who had plagued him, one way or another, for years.

Sir Malise Comyn had harbored rancor against the Setons for too long. But Liam knew that his own grudge, now, was far more justified. The time had come for recompense, retribution, and an end to this—Malise, the fate of Dalrinnie, all of it.

He cleared the hill, driven by urgency, fear, anger, his brothers behind him. In the shadows at the back of the castle, he found what he was searching for under heavy undergrowth and arching branches—the old stone that blocked the entrance to the tunnel he and his brothers had used as boys. With a heave and shove, and the help of the nun's strong hands—Gideon?—he pulled the stone aside to reveal the tunnel.

Crouching, he stepped inside, coughing from musty earth and timber. He had not been inside the tunnel for years; he and the twins, their sister, too, had used it in their games, but their father had forbidden it, fearing a collapse. Now it was shored up by old wood and overgrown roots. He tore at roots as he went, crouched and on his knees in places, half-standing in others. His brothers came behind him, doing the same.

"We have passed the postern gate above us," he said. "We are nearly to the walls of the keep. Where the way slopes up, we will step out into the space between the keep's double stone wall. The we can find the steps up to the parapet."

"We remember. Ow, watch those antlers, Green Man," said the nun.

SHE KNEW EVERY bit of Dalrinnie in darkness and daylight, yet she stumbled repeatedly in the stairwell as Sir Malise pulled her up the stone steps. Missing her footing again, she fell, banged her knee, cried out. He hauled her to her feet, her heels teetering on the inner corner of the wedge-shaped step.

"Come up," Malise Comyn said. "I have no time for this!"

"Wait! You are pulling me so fast, I cannot get my balance. Let me climb by myself." She tried to shake him off but he kept a fierce grip on her arm. The stairs, each step narrowing to rotate around the central pillar, were steep and could be treacherous, though a thick rope ran along one side. But she could not grasp it as Malise, strong and sure on the steps, dragged her upward.

Below, he had ordered Sir David and Sir Patrick—who vehemently protested when Malise brought her inside—to go to the gate because revelers were fast approaching the castle. He promised to shut the lady in a room and deal with her later. Then he had pulled her up the steps so roughly that her cloak caught and her brooch tore away. She had lost a shoe as well.

"Where are we going?" She knew this way led to bedchambers on three floors, and to the battlement at the top level. Malise stopped on the stone platform, his grip so tight that she could feel bruises forming on her arm. His breath heaved.

"Here," he growled, and yanked her along as he opened a heavy wood door on the narrow landing. He all but tossed her inside and she fell to her knees with the push. Standing, she recognized one of the bedchambers, a small room kept for guests. Apparently, Malise used it now, for she saw things tossed about— boots, a draped black tunic, documents scattered on a table, a jug and goblets. It was surprisingly untidy, she thought, for such a demanding man. Lady Edith, taking care of the castle in Tamsin's place, must not be pleased, if she or a servant was even allowed inside now.

Where was Lady Edith, she thought suddenly, and a frisson of worry ran through her, a thread of guilt that she had left the woman here, albeit under Sir Davey's protection. Where was Oonagh? She felt sure Sir Davey would watch after both.

Malise kicked the door shut behind him. "You were to be my wife," he said. "We had an agreement."

"I never promised that." She turned to face him, backing away.

"The king ordered it. Yet you married Seton—I saw the banns. This is a legal matter now. The king will want to know that you disobeyed his order. You will have to annul. Our betrothal takes precedence."

"We had no agreement!" A marriage that was fully consummated could not be easily annulled, nor would she reveal that the union was a handfasting. "I have no intention, now or ever, of ending my marriage."

"You have been cajoled. Fooled. He does not want you," he said, taking a step forward. "He wants this Dalrinnie. But I have them by royal orders, and I was to be your husband. I want what was promised me by the king—and you."

"I promised you nothing, and you know it!"

"The book!" he barked. "King Edward expects it. Give it to me. Or did you give that to Seton too, along with your body?" He moved forward again, looking down at her breasts, where her quickened breath rose and fell. "That body belongs to me. I have watched you since you were John Witton's bride, and hardly touched. That body will bear my sons. It will please me. And I you."

He reached out. She stepped back. "Get away from me. A widow has the right to decide who touches her."

"Until betrothal. Then the man has the right."

She angled to avoid his reach, but he grabbed her and pulled her hard to him.

"You seem more wench than widow to me," he said, grabbing her hips, pressing her against him, so that she gasped and pushed and thanked heaven for a good layer of chain mail between them. "I could claim my rights as your betrothed right now, and any magistrate would decide in my favor over the man who abducted you from me."

"Abducted!" She pushed, but could not free herself. "I left of my own accord."

"That is not what Lady Edith said. Not the girl's fault, she said. Must have been taken from us. Where is that damned book? Edward is sending a messenger to fetch it from me."

For a moment she breathed out in relief—Malise had not mentioned finding her copies of Thomas's prophecies at Dalrinnie, which she had locked away in a chest. Thanks all the saints for that. "The book is in a safe place. And it is not what you think it is. Ow," she gasped, as his hand bruised her arm and his chain mail bit into her abdomen.

"What! You lie about that book."

"I never lie." She shoved, breaking away when his grip shifted. "The Rhymer was a poet. He wrote songs, verses, tales."

"He made predictions about Scotland! Edward wants to know all of them."

"He did not write a book of predictions. The king is a fool to think so." Breathing hard, she circled away, edging toward the door, putting the heavy table between them. He rounded on her, came closer. "He was a harper and carper, a bard."

"Harper! I will kill your harper for taking my woman. He had no right."

"I gave him the right," she said fiercely.

"But I have the order. He does not."

Something occurred to her then. Both Liam and Malise had orders. "Show me the document. Is this it?" She grabbed up parchments, crumpling them. "Or this?"

With a snarl, he snatched a page and flapped it. "See for yourself. King's command."

She snapped open the page, held it up, but the room was dim. Three candlesticks were alight on the table. She lifted one.

"Do not!" he shouted, lunging for her, missing.

"I will not burn it! I cannot read it." She held it up to the light, turning away from his grabbing hand. Examining it quickly, she saw, as she had before, that changes had been made. Partial lines had been scraped away. But the original inked words had bled deeply into the vellum. Traces were visible when she held it to the candlelight. Only a practiced eye would see the difference. She caught her breath.

"This says—Sir William Seton is to marry Lady Thomasina Keith, widow of Dalrinnie." She looked up. "This was altered! The original order was for Sir William to marry me—not you!"

Malise set a hand on the hilt of the dagger at his belt. "That was the king's jest on Seton, thinking you were an old woman. It amused him. But I knew better. I promised to deliver the document to Seton and then paid a clerk to make a false copy for Seton and another version for me. Worth the coin," he muttered. "Worth getting you in my bed."

"But you will never." She could hear shouts outside through the window—and far below too, echoing in the stairwell. Someone was coming—she had to get to the door. She moved. He stepped with her, glaring, his handsome face distorted, beauty gone ugly with his vile hatred, his vanity, his cruelty.

She had to delay him, distract him. "So that was why you came after him at Lochmaben! Not because you were hunting an outlaw. Because you could not let him find out about the orders you changed!"

"He is an outlaw and does not deserve the chance Edward gave him. He does not deserve you—or Dalrinnie either. I have wanted you since the first day I met you here," he growled. "Witton's luscious young Scottish bride. He was an old man. He did not deserve the prize he got."

"Neither did you!" As she said it, he moved, grabbed her, yanked her so hard she fell across the table. One of the candles tumbled, catching the edge of a parchment.

"Fire!" she gasped as he dragged her across the tabletop. "Fire!"

"Damn it," he growled, shoving her aside and grabbing a jug of liquid, tossing it over the flame. But it only bloomed higher. He upended a goblet over it. "God's blood!"

Tamsin ran to the door and pulled hard, yanking it open. "Fire!" she screamed.

The shouts she had heard were men on the lower part of the steps. Now they pounded upward. "Fire! Fire! Lady Tamsin, is that you?" She heard Sir Davey.

"Here!" She ran out to the platform step. But Malise had smothered the fire and came after her, grabbing for her. "Sir Davey!" she screamed.

"The fire is out. Go back," Malise snarled as David Campbell came into view.

"No, sir—not here. The bonfire in the bailey! Fire in the yard!"

"What!" Malise would not let her go, even as she twisted against him.

"The guisers from the village—they came in. We saw no harm in it. But they went mad, that lot. Set a bonfire in the bailey, set fire to a hay wagon. It is pandemonium."

"Get rid of them! Kill them if you must. Where are the bowmen—"

"Sir Malise!" Footsteps again, armor chinking, and Patrick Siward came around the stair pillar. "The guisers—among them are men from Ettrick Forest. I recognize some of them."

Malise shook Tamsin. "Did you bring them here? Is Seton coming for you? Good!" He turned for the stairs that led upward, still gripping her arm. "Go deal with them," he yelled to the men over his shoulder, and pulled her fiercely up the steps.

She knew where he was taking her. To the parapet. To Agatha. To the cage.

HIGH ON THE battlement walkway, the wind struck her, blowing back her hair and her gown as Malise pushed open the door and dragged her out to the parapet level. Twilight had gone full dark, the moon floating above, riding in clouds, casting eerie shadows over the stone walls. The wide stone walkway was enclosed by the parapet wall on one side and was open on the other, looking down on the bailey. In the corners, the walkway widened to platforms. The cage sat in the nearest corner, under glowing torches in brackets. Malise pulled her that way.

Fumbling for a key at his belt, he tore open the door and shoved her in like bread pushed into an oven. She fell nearly on top of the woman who cowered inside the narrow space. Slamming the door, he spun and walked away without a word. He did not take the stone steps leading to the bailey—where shouts and commotion reigned—but instead headed for a door leading back into the tower.

Tamsin helped the other woman, knocked over by her entrance, to sit up. "Dame Agatha? I am sorry—are you hurt? I am Thomasina Keith."

The woman looked at her, torchlight glowing along her face, her hair, her body. Without a veil, her hair was dark, tousled, trimmed short; she wore a rumpled, formless black gown over a white shift showing here and there; her feet were bare. She held a tartan blanket in her lap and stared at Tamsin as if stunned to see her.

"Lady Tamsin?" She peered, then smiled. A deep tuck appeared at the corner of her mouth, part of the long ugly scar that ran from her chin upward along the side of her face, pulling at the corner of her eye, disappearing into the tousle of her dark hair.

"You know my name?" Tamsin asked.

Agatha nodded. That beautiful Seton face, Tamsin saw, was delicately expressed in the sister; the prominent scar made no difference after a moment. Her large, long-lidded eyes were dark in torchlight, her brows thick and dark, her smile charming. She was younger than Tamsin had expected.

"I know you. My reverend uncle sent a message to tell me the news—you and Liam." She extended a hand, long and graceful, two fingers short stubs at the knuckles. "I believe we are sisters now."

On impulse, Tamsin opened her arms to embrace Agatha. "We are sisters. I love your family." Hugging her, she felt Agatha's half-sob. "And I love your brother."

"I know." Agatha drew back, pushed her hair back. "It is good news in all this. But why did Malise bring you here?"

"He is. . . unhappy that Liam and I are married. And I have something he wants, and I will not give it to him."

"The book? I heard about that." Agatha huffed. "He is so angry that you refused to marry him. He shouted at me about it. I too refused to marry him years ago, so I laughed. I could not help it, and must confess and do penance, I suppose. Such a man is hurt and angry and deserves compassion."

"I do not have much sympathy for him. So I too must do penance. You laughed at him—he must have hated that."

"I laughed because I will never show him my fear. He did this, years ago." She gestured toward her cheek with her stubbed finger. Tamsin realized suddenly that the facial scar was very like Gideon's; she wondered if Malise gave the brother that wound too, perhaps when the brothers defended their sister. "Malise did not mean to do this, I think, but it happened. An awful day I wish I could forget," she added. "But when he took me here and complained about you, I told him he is a handsome knight many women might want to marry—until they learn what a beast he is."

Tamsin half-laughed. "True."

"Change that and ask God's forgiveness, I said. Give up your beastly temper and hatred and find your better nature in prayer. Then you might find a wife to tolerate you."

"Oh, that did not please him!" Tamsin kept her arm around Agatha, a slight woman, bony shoulders, thin hands clutching the tartan blanket.

"It did not." Agatha shrugged. "He ordered the soldiers to hang this cage from the parapet, but they did not have rope stout enough. I have been here five days, I think. But Lady Edith has been kind, bringing me blankets and food and sitting with me at times."

"Has she? I am glad. And I am glad she is here and safe. I left this place—I am sure Malise told you something about that. I do not know what he plans, but I can tell you," Tamsin continued, "that your brothers are on their way here. You may not recognize them though. It is Samhain night, you see. Listen. Do you hear the guisers in the bailey yard? They set the bonfire down there?"

From the angle of the cage, they could see only part of the bailey, though the light from the fire seemed contained now. Tamsin heard shouts, loud singing, and raucous laughter from the villagers, the forest men too, down in the central yard. Bellows and shouted orders came from guards trying to keep them at bay to no avail.

"I may be an abbess, but I enjoy any pagan ritual that will help just now. Are my brothers with the guisers?"

"They spoke of taking a tunnel rather than the gate."

"The tunnel! It goes to a hidden stair in the wall of the keep where it is hollow inside the double wall. The steps lead up to the battlement. I hope they got in safely and were not seen."

A moment later, a door at the far end of the parapet walk burst open. A giant beast, a horned green man, and a nun emerged, swords at the ready.

"Ah, here they are!" Agatha's face brightened in that serene and beautiful smile.

CHAPTER TWENTY-NINE

L IAM EASED THE door open, peering out at the walkway, which appeared empty in the merged light of torch and moon. The commotion in the bailey was more than he had expected—and while more merriment than threat, he knew it could turn bad at any moment. This must be done quickly. He turned, beckoned to his brothers, set his hand to his sword hilt, and stepped out.

Up here, he was prepared to maim or kill anyone who came between him and the cage that held his sister. But the walkway was clear as he moved forward. He expected to break the lock, free Agatha, give her to the care of the twins—and then find his wife.

But he did not expect to see Tamsin huddled inside the cage with Agatha. Under torchlight, he hurried there, Gilchrist and Gideon following, all three hunched low to avoid notice by the guards in the bailey a good twenty feet below.

"Agatha—Tamsin!" He took hold of the bars. The women stood, arms about each other. The cage was taller than it was narrow, crowned by joined bars just above his height. The girls reached out, fingers gripping the bars, and he cupped a hand over each of theirs for a moment. He was reminded once more that he could not forgive Malise Comyn for damaging his sister's face and hand. Then he tugged at the narrow door and saw the lock dangling there.

"Damned Viking lock," he muttered, pulling at it, knowing

the Nordic designed loop would not budge without a key. Trying to crack the iron might break the blade of dagger or sword. Perhaps there was a blacksmith among the village guisers. "Agatha, who has the key?" he asked.

"Malise," she replied. "On his belt. He went back into the keep."

"Are you hurt, either of you?" Gideon came forward and took Agatha's hand.

"We are not hurt," Tamsin said. "Just get us out of here before he returns."

"What a perfect disguise for you," Agatha said wryly, looking at Gideon's nun's outfit. With a grumble, he stripped off the veil and tossed it away, his blond tonsure gleaming in torchlight. Beside him, Liam tore off his leafy bonnet and cumbersome sheep's fleece, throwing those aside as well.

"Liam," Gilchrist said, looking impossibly tall in the antlered helmet. "Liam! They are coming up here."

Spinning, drawing his sword, Liam saw men running up the open stone steps to the walkway. Though most were still occupied by the madness in the bailey, these few could cause trouble. Then he recognized Sir David Campbell on the steps, waving for men to follow—and breathed in relief, realizing he was an ally. Turning, Liam then saw other soldiers, English from the look of them, running up a second stretch of steps.

By now, his brothers had drawn their swords, stepping wide, ready to fight anyone who threatened the cage. Elsewhere on the walkway, a door opened, and men burst out, three, four, five—James Lindsay, Finley Macnab, Iain Campbell and others, armed with bows. Nocking arrows, they stood in a line, training their arrows on the men in the bailey and the English climbing the far set of steps.

Nearby, Sir David stepped up to the walkway and came toward Liam. "What do you need?" he asked immediately.

"A key, and a way out of here."

Beyond, a door to the keep burst open. Malise Comyn

stepped out, sword drawn, striding fierce and heavy along the walkway. He wore no helmet—few of them did, not expecting battle—and his blond hair winged about his head as he surged forward.

"Seton!" he bellowed. "William Seton!"

"Here," Liam said, motioning his brothers behind him. All stood ready, Liam now closest to the cage, his back to the women there. From the corner of his eye he saw Patrick Siward and others, including villagers, crowding up the steps to the walkway.

Liam turned, sword in his hands, and braced his feet. "Malise Comyn."

The man came closer, sword raised, alert. "We have a grudge, you and I."

"More than one, I would say." Liam moved toward him, away from the cage. He sensed men shifting out of the way, clearing the space between the two men. On another angle of the wall, Lindsay and the others stood, bows nocked and ready, guarding against anyone else who might try to take the battlement.

Malise strode toward Liam, fury in every muscle, in the lines of his face, chain mail gleaming in the torchlight. Close enough then, he stilled. Liam stilled too, wary. As Malise raised his hand to strike, Liam leaped back, eyes flashing forward, sideways, to judge the precipitous edge of the open walkway. Malise raised his sword.

Gripping the broadsword in his right hand, Liam sliced it upward with a twist to meet Malise's blow, the loud ring of steel jarring, the blow shuddering along his sword arm to his shoulder. He angled left, right, keeping an eye on the wall, the men nearby, the cage, the drop. Stepping left, he swept the weapon downward, struck steel, felt the shudder again. He pushed upward to drive Malise and his sword back. The man managed to thrust forward again as Liam turned. The blow met air.

Liam offered another quick thrust of his sword and Malise answered with a glancing strike, the scrape of steel on steel raising sparks. Sidestepping, Liam missed the next blow; that threw him off balance to stumble, shuffle, regain. Ever alert to the edge of the walkway, Liam realized that the narrow space was making his opponent anxious. Good, he thought.

He lunged and struck Malise's forearm, the blade sparking on chain mail. Liam shifted forward, back, forward, back. Malise came at him again, forcing Liam toward the wall, against stone. The next few steps reversed their positions. Now Malise had his back to the cage. Liam either had to back up, risking blind spots, or force Malise closer to the cage.

For an instant, he glimpsed his sister clinging to the bars, face pale, eyes bright with hatred more than forgiveness. Then Malise drew his attention with another move.

Comyn pushed forward, striking, steel ringing. Swords met up, met down, to the side, blades sliding, shrieking. Leaping sideways, Liam neared the cage, keeping his balance and awareness. His wounded shoulder was weak, but he forced it, lifting the blade again, arcing down in a powerful blow that would have been lethal—

But Malise shuffled to the side, beside a tall merlon, his back shielded. He was closer to the cage now. Dipping his sword, he drew a dagger from his belt and turned.

Liam saw then what he meant to do—Comyn raised his arm to bring the blade down between the iron bars within range of one girl or the other.

With a roar, Liam leaped forward, knocking him against the wall with enough force to stun. But his sword struck a cage bar and tilted out of his hand to clatter to the stone walk. He stretched for it just as Malise turned to raise his sword high and strike down toward Liam's back. Noticing, Liam started to roll away.

But suddenly, strangely, Malise tilted, missed his footing, and tipped forward, stumbling. His sword flew from his hand as he fell forward awkwardly, arms outward. With a shriek, he tumbled over the edge of the walkway and down, down to the bailey. The crash and thud of his fall was a sickening sound. Scrambling to his feet, Liam reached the edge just as Malise tipped over. Liam had no way to stop the man's descent—or he might have. That was his immediate instinct.

Sprawled on the bailey floor, Malise lay face down, body contorted and motionless. Men rushed toward him across the bailey and others hurried down the steps. Liam stood, breathing hard, wiping a hand over his mouth, pushing his sweat-damp hair back, stunned, trembling with the aftermath of the fight in his blood. He watched the flurry below. What had happened in those few moments, that blur of turmoil between them? He was not sure.

He turned toward Tamsin and Agatha, standing in the cage, holding the bars, their eyes wide, fearful, their faces white with fear and distress. Then he noticed that Agatha held the hilt of Liam's sword in her hand with its missing fingers. The point thrust between the bars. Meeting his gaze, she set the sword down.

He walked toward her. "Did you stab him?" He was glad of it.

She shook her head. "I only meant to trip him. I did not know he would fall that way." Her eyes were rimmed with liquid. She dashed away a tear.

"Just as well, dear. You saved my life." He was glad to see Tamsin put an arm around his sister and draw her in.

Below, Patrick Siward looked up and called out. "He is alive!"

Liam went back to the edge and held up a hand in acknowledgment. Then he looked toward his brothers. Gideon came to the edge and looked down.

"Make a litter. Bring him to the hospital at Holyoak," he called down. "Ride through the night. I will go with them," he added.

Liam nodded. "Well done."

TAMSIN HELD AGATHA in her arms until the abbess drew a breath and stepped back. "I am fine—thank you, Tamsin," she whispered.

"Thank *you*," Tamsin murmured. "You saved him." For a moment she recalled a snatch of conversation—tell Liam perhaps a damsel would save him one day. She nearly laughed, lifting a shaking hand to her tousled hair, looking around for Liam.

He came toward her then, reaching between the bars for her hand, and she fought back a half-sob, half-laugh as his fingers, hard and cool, closed on hers. Behind him came a phalanx of men, soldiers, forest men, villagers. Sir Davey came too, looked weary, moving slowly. Liam glanced at him, keeping Tamsin's hand in his.

Campbell gave him a nod, clapped him on the shoulder. "What do you need, William of Dalrinnie? Anything. Anything at all."

Tamsin felt the slight startle Liam gave at the address. "Men," he said then. "Loyal men. And a key."

"A key. Sir Malise has it." The man looked toward the bailey, where the bonfire burned low and tame. Men gathered there, some in a cluster around Comyn, lying on the ground, while others watched, waited.

Sir Patrick Siward came up the steps now, and Tamsin saw Lady Edith behind him. She gasped, relieved to see the older lady. But she could not help but wonder how this would go—Siward was loyal to Malise, and to Edward. But he stood by silently.

"Dalrinnie Castle," Sir David called out, "is returned to its rightful owner, Sir William Seton, Lord Dalrinnie. Any who disagree with that can leave now." He waited a moment or two. "Those who agree and stand ready to support Lord Dalrinnie in his natural right as his father's firstborn heir, are welcome to stay as part of his garrison. You know the meaning of this in terms of the crown. I will wait."

He stood watching. Tamsin saw a flurry of activity below, men talking, gesturing. Others gathered Malise and carried him to a cart filled with straw, laying him there. Gideon stood with them. He stopped and looked up. The men with him, Gilchrist included, stopped as well. All listened, watched.

No one moved. Not one man. Tamsin caught back a sob and renewed her grip on Liam's hand. His fingers responded, pressing, while he, too, waited in silence.

Then a rousing cheer rose up. Tears started in her eyes. Beside her, Agatha stepped forward to rest her hand on their joined hands.

Liam turned. "Sir David—I will speak to them. Tamsin should come with me. But sir, we need a key. Or a blacksmith."

Then Lady Edith pushed forward. "Key? I have many keys. Will one of these do?" She jingled the ring of keys at her belt.

"What are you doing with the key to the cage, woman?" Sir David asked.

"You gave me charge of Dame Agatha," she told her brother. "You gave me the second key to the cage so I could take her to the pot! In all this madness, you forgot that." She handed the key to Liam. "You!" She stared hard at him. "Are you the harper?"

He laughed, low and dry. "I am, my lady."

"By the saints! Excellent, sir. Rescue these ladies now, please."

Tamsin waited as her husband inserted the key in the lock and twisted it, then yanked open the door and stretched out his arms. She stepped back to let Agatha go first, waiting as brother and sister hugged for a long, long moment.

Liam whispered something to his sister and kissed her scarred cheek. She spoke low, fervently, as he listened. Then he handed her into the arms of Lady Edith—who, Tamsin realized, may have known these Setons for years, for the Campbells had been at Dalrinnie for years.

Then Liam reached for her, and Tamsin stepped out of the iron cage and into his embrace, pressed close in his arms. He cupped her head, smoothed her hair, tilted her face to his and kissed her brow, her cheek, her lips.

Then he took her hand and kissed her knuckles. "Baronness Dalrinnie," he said, "come to the edge with me, and we will talk to these fine people."

She would always go to the edge with him. She would go anywhere with him. As she stood beside him, he set an arm around her and another loud cheer went up—from those who had held Dalrinnie when she was lady there before, those who had come with Sir Malise and disliked his actions, and the villagers who had come for a bit of revelry and found something far more important. They cheered, hoorahed, rang bells, clapped.

Then Sir William leaned toward Lady Tamsin and kissed her for one and all to see. Hearing the cheers, feeling a warm blush rise in her cheeks, Tamsin laughed, looking out at those gathered below.

"Lass, do you trust me now?" Liam murmured. "This place, our home—this is the truest and best thing I can offer you. That, and my heart always."

"I always trusted you, my love," she said, smiling, waving. "I just did not know it."

EPILOGUE

Dalrinnie Castle
February 1307

T AMSIN ADDED A delicate pen-stroke in red to the tall rubric initial and sat back, pleased. The parchment page, spread flat on the table and weighted with stones, was almost done. Liam would surely be surprised by the latest addition in the growing collection of the Rhymer's verses. For months, she had been carefully copying and preparing the pages to give Master Bisset as soon as they could travel to Selkirk.

Setting down the quill, she flexed her arms and rolled her neck a bit. She had been hunched over parchments all afternoon, and her shoulders and neck were stiff. Near her, Oonagh looked up from a nap, ruffed low, and settled again by the hearth fire, a content hound guarding her mistress on a cold winter afternoon.

The light was fading. She would put away her writing things soon, for she was sure Liam would return today; she woke that morning with a strong sense that he would be heading home. Glancing toward the arched windows where the tops of pine trees showed dark through thick leaded glass, she prayed he would be back by nightfall.

She had counted eighteen days since he had ridden west to bring another roster of support to Robert Bruce, along with news gleaned from compatriots in Ettrick Forest and elsewhere. She longed to see him, feel his arms around her, know his strength and warmth beside her at night. The bed was cold without him. And she had news to share now, for she had been counting the days for another reason.

Setting to work again, she was determined to finish the page. But Oonagh made a gruff sound, jumping to her feet. Startled, Tamsin made an awkward stroke in the last word, and set her pen down as a knock sounded on the door.

"My lady?" Liam stepped into the room, Roc loping in behind him. Tamsin flew to him, arms wide, and Liam wrapped her in the embrace she so loved and craved. He crooked a finger under her chin to kiss her tenderly. Feeling herself beginning to melt inside, she laughed, then stepped back and took his hand.

"Liam, my love—I am so relieved that you are home safe. Was your errand to good purpose? Is the king well?"

"Aye, and in good spirits, for his support grows strong. Scottish winters keep the English away, which gives us some respite. Bruce means to take advantage of the lull and travel south to reclaim Scottish territory and a castle or two."

"Will you go with him?" She felt a flutter of disappointment, knowing his reply.

He nodded. "Since Bruce sent men here to help guard the place last November, Dalrinnie has been even more firmly in my hands. He may go to the Isles for the winter, and if he does, I will stay here. But I am indebted to him and fully in this effort. You know that, love."

"I do." She pressed his hands in hers, his fingers still cold from the long ride. Brushing away snowflakes on the shoulders of his gray cloak, she stroked his ring-studded leather hauberk. "You will want to change out of these."

"I came up quickly, anxious to see you. Dearling, you look beautiful," he murmured. "Glowing."

"Just glad you are here. And it is warm by the fire. Did Gilchrist and Finley come with you? Are they downstairs in the hall? I so want them to meet Thomas Learmont and his wife Marion."

"I saw Thomas and his wife in the hall—a nice surprise—and told them we would be down soon to share supper with them. But Gilchrist and Finley went on to Holyoak to ask Gideon to come with them into the forest to work for the cause."

"He is still at Holyoak?" She went to a cupboard, took out a jug and a goblet. "Will you have wine?"

"I will, thank you." She poured, and he accepted it. "And you?"

"Not just now. I thought Gideon decided to leave the order?"

"He did. But our uncle is not strong, and Gideon wants to be nearby. Oh, and I hear Sir Malise will leave Holyoak soon to return to his own castle. They say he may not walk again. Agatha feels torn with guilt for tripping him up."

"She saved your life! And to think what he did to her earlier...and then put her in that cage." She shook her head.

"She may decide to leave Lincluden and give up that life altogether. Gideon has been talking with her about the decision they each have. They were always close, those two, and are a help to each other now."

"Hey, Roc," Tamsin said as the hound bumped against her for a rub and a pat. Oonagh surged to her feet to nudge Roc away from her mistress. Laughing, Tamsin and Liam gave them some affection and sent them to sit by the hearth.

"Oonagh seems very protective of you," Liam said.

"She is," Tamsin said, smiling a bit. "Here, I want to show you something." Taking his hand, she drew him toward the table. "I have been working on the pages for the next book of the Rhymer's work—his ballads and verses."

"Master Bisset will be pleased. You have done a good deal of work, I see, since I left. My lass, I am sorry I had to go away again. It is just necessary at times."

"You are back safe now, and that is all that matters. With winter here, I hope you will stay for a while. We have peace here now, and much to be thankful for. No matter what happens beyond Dalrinnie, we have what we wanted. Our home. Our haven."

"I will stay as long as I can." He drew her close and she sighed. "What did you want to show me?"

"Old Thomas has been reciting some of his father's verses for me. He knows ballads and a few prophecies, too, that were not in the notes Grandda gave me. I have been copying them to new parchments. Come look."

"Beautiful work. Very neat." He glanced over her shoulder. "Is that an error, Lady Tamsin?" He chuckled.

"I jumped up when you came in. I will scrape it away and redo it, like the changes Malise made to the document that had your name originally," she murmured. "Edward ordered you to marry me, and wanted you to take command of Dalrinnie—trusting he would have the book he wanted, of course. Malise has much to atone for now. I wonder if he recognizes that."

"He might someday. Edward is unhappy with him, I would guess. But the king is ill again, with less strength for revenge. He will let Dalrinnie go back to the Scots. The luck of Dalrinnie returned with you, love." He kissed her hand. "It was meant to be."

"Something else was meant to be. Read this page." She tapped it with a finger.

"Oh?" Looking puzzled, he glanced down and began to read aloud.

Three lasses, three ladies, three brides all
Born and flowering in Kincraig's hall
One shall loose an arrow in the heart of greenside
One shall heal a king and woe betide
And one shall be the harper's bride . . .

"By the saints," he whispered. "Harper's bride! What is this? One of the Rhymer's predictions?"

"Uncle Thomas remembered it. It was made before we were born, he says. He heard it as a lad but did not know what it meant. When he found it scribbled on the margin of a page in one of Thomas's own books, he brought it to me here."

"Before any of you were born," Liam breathed. "What of Henry?"

"Thomas thinks it was a longer verse. He will keep searching."

"We were meant to be." He slipped an arm around her.

"Thomas recited Granda's ballad about meeting the Queen of Faery—the ballad you heard when you were young. I want to add it to these new pages. He wants you to play it on the Rhymer's harp."

"I want to learn anything your great-uncle wants to teach me. 'And one shall be the harper's bride,'" he repeated softly. "You are no longer the Scottish bride, hey."

"All that is past." She smiled. "I am thrilled to be just a harper's bride."

He brushed a hand over her hair. "We have much to look forward to, Tamsin. Once Bruce accomplishes all that he wants for Scotland, our future will be bright."

She felt tears starting in her eyes. "Our future is already bright." She took his hand, cupped it low over her belly.

He paused, breathed out low and long. "Is it so?"

She nodded. "High summer, I think."

"My love." He pulled her close again. "With all my heart, I promise to be here with you." As he kissed her, she knew he had her whole heart, always.

"Liam—promise what you can, aye. But we can never truly know the future."

"Even you say that?" He cocked a brow.

"Even I. Whatever happens, we have all we need here and now. Our home, our safety. Each other, and what will come of that joy. It is all I need."

"All the truth anyone could ask for." He kissed her again. "But I must change, for they are waiting supper on us. Then I am for bed, my lady, with you."

"Ah." She laughed softly. "Tomorrow I want to send a messenger to Kincraig. I need to see my sisters. And it is time you met them."

"Aye so." Whistling for the hounds, he escorted his wife to the door.

Author's Note

Thomas the Rhymer is one of those intriguing legendary figures from history who truly lived. His presence as an off-stage character in *The Scottish Bride* mingles fact, legend, and a fictional spin. Medieval Scottish documents record him as "Thomas Rymour de Ercildoune" (Earlston today) in the Scottish Borders. Thomas Learmont was a laird, a harper and singer ("harper and carper" describes him in the ballads), a poet, and a prophet who died in 1298 and was born in 1220 or earlier. Several local sites near Earlston and the Eildon Hills retain his name—a tower ruin, a cave, a meadow, and more. Little is known of his family, though documents indicate at least one son and heir, another Thomas Learmont.

Called True Thomas and Thomas the Rhymer, he was renowned in his time and over the centuries not just for his foretelling ability, but for his encounter with the faeries. As a young man, he sat under a hawthorn tree one day playing his harp when the Queen of Faery rode by, bells on her saddle (in some versions, she is the Queen of Elfland). She lured him through a portal in the Eildon Hills, where for seven earthly years he was her captive lover. When he emerged, he had the gifts of prophecy, truth-telling, even a magic harp. The tale exists in many versions, from an original ballad said to be composed by Thomas, through literary studies and novels in our own time. As a poet, Thomas authored a long epic poem in Middle English, *Sir Tristem*, based on the old Arthurian tale of Tristan and Iseult.

Thomas worked with kings, nobles, and common people alike, and his reputation for foretelling the future in verse was legendary in his lifetime. Many of his prophecies proved true, or true enough; some foretold events occurred centuries later. As a contemporary of Robert Bruce, William Wallace, and King Edward I, he witnessed the turmoil surrounding King Edward's invasive demands on Scotland in the beginning years of the Wars of Independence. Another facet of his legend—perhaps with a grain of truth—holds that Thomas acted as a spy for Robert the Bruce in the years before Bruce was king.

The history of Scotland and the Scottish Wars of Independence, too, fascinate me as both an art historian and a fiction writer. Years ago, I left academia and the land of painstaking research and meticulous footnotes on fascinating subjects to write Scottish-set historical fiction across a range of centuries. My medieval-set novels feature forest outlaws, forfeited lairds, falconers, warrior-knights, and Highlanders matched with strong-willed ladies who are themselves prophets, healers, archers, weavers, harpers, swordfighters, and more. I will always strive for accurate research, and I hope my books conjure for the reader an authentic sense of what it was like to live in Scotland in earlier times.

The Scottish Bride is the first book in a trilogy about three sisters who inherit the gifts of their kinsman, Thomas the Rhymer, and do whatever they must to preserve his legend and legacy—while finding love and purpose along the way. What a privilege, and what fun, to put my own spin on True Thomas's tale.

I hope you enjoyed Tamsin and Liam's story, and I hope you'll look for the rest of the trilogy (and my other books). All of them mix deep research and heartfelt romance. Thank you for reading what I've been busy writing!

Susan

About the Author

Susan King is the bestselling, award-winning author of (so far) 28 historical novels and novellas, a hefty nonfiction history, and dozens of magazine and web articles on education and the craft of writing. Her books, including mainstream historicals Lady Macbeth: A Novel and Queen Hereafter: A Novel of Margaret of Scotland, have been published by Penguin, Random House, HarperCollins, Kensington, ePublishingWorks, and Dragonblade. Praised for historical accuracy, lyrical writing, and storytelling quality, she is a USA Today bestselling author with numerous awards, nominations, and career achievement awards as well as starred reviews from Publisher's Weekly, Booklist, and Library Journal. Most of her books are set in Scotland ranging from the 11th to the 19th centuries.

Susan is a former university lecturer in art history, a private school teacher, and a founding member of one of the longest-running author blogs, "Word Wenches" (wordwenches.com). She holds a Bachelor's in studio art and English literature, a Master's in art history, and completed most of her Ph.D. / ABD in medieval art history. Raised in Upstate New York, she lives in Maryland with her husband and three sons in an ever-growing family.

Website – www.susanfraserking.com